Sacrifice

George Brown has spent much of his life in South East Asia, initially fighting terrorists in the jungles of Malaysia before retiring to run a plantation. He has kept close links with counter-terrorist colleagues throughout the world, and his books are consequently filled with the most accurate and up-to-date information on a hidden war unseen by the public.

His second novel, *The Double Tenth*, was shortlisted for WH Smith's Thumping Good Read award. This is his fourth novel. His previous titles are all available in Arrow paperback.

SACRIFICE

George Brown

ARROW

First published by Arrow in 1995

1 3 5 7 9 10 8 6 4 2

Copyright © George Brown 1994

The right of George Brown to be identified as the author of this work
has been asserted by him in accordance with the Copyright, Designs
and Patents Act, 1988

This book is sold subject to the condition that it shall not, by way of
trade or otherwise, be lent, resold, hired out, or otherwise circulated
without the publisher's prior consent in any form of binding or cover
other than that in which it is published and without a similar
condition including this condition being imposed on the
subsequent purchaser

First published in the United Kingdom in 1994
by Century, Random House UK Limited

This edition published by Arrow in 1995,
Random House UK, 20 Vauxhall Bridge Road, London SW1V 2SA

Random House Australia (Pty) Limited
20 Alfred Street, Milsons Point, Sydney,
New South Wales 2061, Australia

Random House New Zealand Limited
18 Poland Road, Glenfield
Auckland 10, New Zealand

Random House South Africa (Pty) Limited
PO Box 337, Bergvlei, South Africa

Random House UK Limited Reg. No. 954009

ISBN 0 09 933751 7

A CIP catalogue record for this book is
available from the British Library

Typeset by SX Composing Ltd, Rayleigh, Essex
Printed and bound in Great Britain by
Cox & Wyman Ltd, Reading, Berkshire

for Pauline Oliver – *Glook*

ACKNOWLEDGEMENTS

I am indebted to:

United Kingdom

Lt/Col Fred L. – still on the inside looking out.

Dr John H. Cole, healer and musician, of the Wellington Medical Centre who showed me how to keep 'S' out of the endgame.

Captain Nick Corden-Lloyd, adjutant 2nd Battalion the Royal Green Jackets, County Tyrone, and his lovely wife, Sarah, who lightened for me the darkness of Northern Ireland.

Roy Follows, author, ex-Malayan Police Special Operations Force, who activated the 'System' in . . .

Australia

Major Noel Dudgeon, formerly the Royal Marines, the Royal Australian Regiment and Australian SAS.

And Lt/Col Mike Casey, formerly the East Yorkshire Regiment (The Duke of York's Own), and the Royal Australian Regiment.

Russell Kilbey, musician, for enlightening me on Canberra's 'Social Architects'.

Christine Ryan, Melbourne, who led me by the hand . . .

Detlef Thinius, Kerrie, and Helga Kaiser – the 'Sydney Connection' – who proved that it was all possible.

Malaysia

Terence Daley, for nautical advice freely given and the sacrilegious use of his yacht the *Lady Charlotte*.

And, of course, Paula, the 'Ozziephile' whose labours never cease . . .

SACRIFICE

sac+ri+fice n. 1. a surrender of something of value as a means of gaining something more desirable or of preventing some evil.
Collins English Dictionary

sac+ri+fice n. 2. The forfeiture of something highly valued, as an idea, object, or friendship, for the sake of someone or something considered to have a greater value or claim.
Reader's Digest Great Illustrated Dictionary

10 Expendable agents are those of our own spies who are deliberately given fabricated information.

Tu Yu: We leak information which is actually false and allow our own agents to learn it. When these agents operating in enemy territory are taken by him they are certain to report this false information. The enemy will put the spies to death.

Chang Yu: ... In our dynasty Chief of Staff Ts'ao once pardoned a condemned man whom he then disguised as a monk, and caused him to swallow a ball of wax and enter Tangut. When the false monk arrived he was imprisoned. The monk told his captors about the ball of wax and soon discharged it in a stool. When the ball was opened, the Tanguts read a letter transmitted by Chief of Staff Ts'ao to their Director of Strategic Planning. The chieftain of the barbarians was enraged, put his minister to death, and executed the spy monk. This is the idea. But expendable agents are not confined to only one use. Sometimes I send agents to the enemy to make a covenant of peace and then I attack.

Sun Tzu, *The Art of War* (c. 500BC)

The universe is so vast and so ageless that the life of one man can only be justified by the measure of his sacrifice.

F/O V.A. Rosewarne (1940)

PART ONE

1

The tramp shuffled along the path bordering the rose beds and stopped to peer into the rubbish bin. He wore a long, dirty brown raincoat, torn under the arms and frayed where it flapped around his ankles. In one hand, enclosed in a grey woollen fingerless glove, he carried a bulging plastic carrier bag with the logo of a Dublin supermarket blazoned across it. The other hand went into the bin and rummaged around among the empty crisp packets and sticky toffee papers. He seemed oblivious of anyone else in the park.

Only one of the three men sitting on one of the wooden slatted benches a few yards further along the path in St Anne's Park gave him a second glance. Just one of Dublin's down-and-outs; the place was full of them. Nothing unusual. The man on the bench turned back to his two companions, his jaw still set, listening to what appeared to be unpleasant news. The other two men, olive-skinned, with pinched, Middle Eastern features, were well wrapped up against the crisp late-autumn weather. Only one of them was doing the talking; the other, like his Irish companion, listened, but without the same intensity. Whatever the news, it was familiar to him. When the man stopped for a second the Irishman leaned forward and peered into the expressionless Arab face.

'You could be wrong,' he growled. 'You've got to be wrong.' His voice carried no further than the man addressed.

'There is no possibility of that. It's defi . . .' The Arab's voice tailed off as his eyes left the Irishman's face and stared over his shoulder. The shocked look lasted only a second.

The tramp had discarded his shopping bag and drawn level with the three men. He'd straightened himself up; he was tall, well built, and moved athletically on his toes as he aimed the stubby MP-9 assault pistol at the Irishman. Then the shooting started. The big Irishman had registered the look but had no time to turn before the bullets began thudding into his back. The gunman then brought round the MP-9 to cover the two Arabs. The scruffy raincoat, open and flapping with his brisk movements, showed where he'd concealed the weapon. His face showed no emotion as again he tightened his finger on the trigger. One of the Arabs managed to throw himself over the back of the bench as the short burst took his companion in the chest. He screamed something incoherent and tried to turn himself to face the gunman, but in his panic his knees gave way and as he tried to scramble back up, the man with the machine pistol moved quickly to one side, flicked the selector switch to single action, and fired four shots into the back of his neck. The man collapsed on to his face, still on his knees, as if at prayer.

The Irishman, his back torn by half a magazine of 9mm, was still trying to get away. Covered in blood and on his hands and knees, he dragged himself across the grass towards the sheltering trees. But he was hardly aware of what he was doing. The gunman watched him out of the corner of his eye as he fired a single shot into the first Arab's forehead; then, without releasing the safety grip, he gave a quick half-jerk on the cocking handle and checked the breech. He snapped it shut and caught up with the crawling Irishman.

'Mr O'Dwyer?' he asked conversationally.

4

The dying man's knees and arms gave way and he fell forward into the damp grass. He managed to turn his face and with a supreme effort focused on the man standing above him.

'Who . . . ?'

But it didn't matter who. The gunman leaned over and, with the MP-9 held pistol-fashion in one hand, lowered the gun to within an inch of O'Dwyer's eye. He squeezed the trigger. There was only one round left. It was more than enough. The big Irishman's head burst open like a rotten orange.

Without discarding the weapon, the man slipped unhurriedly into the wood O'Dwyer had been trying for and joined the footpath he'd reconnoitred earlier. Folding the stocky assault pistol under his raincoat he continued through the woods, briskly, but with no sign of panic, until he emerged on a shallow grassy bank on the east side of the park, He listened for a second to the urgent howling of a police siren and screams coming from the other side of the wood. He joined the quiet, deserted road and branched off into an even quieter, narrow, tree-lined drive and stopped beside a dark blue Sierra with Republic number-plates parked under one of the young chestnut trees. He opened the boot and wrapped the MP-9 into an old, well-worn Barbour jacket, then jammed it into the spare-wheel compartment. He climbed into the car, threw the raincoat on to the back seat and lit a cigarette. The flame of the match was rock steady.

He stayed on the B-road and joined the main Dublin– Belfast trunk road at Swords. He kept a steady pace, and the traffic was thin enough for him to be able to isolate any possible follower. He needn't have worried; nobody was pushing him. At Balbriggan he left the main road and took the small turn-off into town. When he reached the coast road he turned right and went back a few miles towards Skerries, then pulled off. He sat smoking another cigarette and staring at the sea below him. After a moment he looked up, glanced in the rear mirror, then turned in his seat and studied the road behind him. He was alone. The coast was deserted. When he'd finished his cigarette he got out of the car, looked up and down the road in both directions again, and listened. There was no traffic; the only noise was the breaking of the waves below on to the hard, shiny rocks. He opened the boot and, waiting a few seconds, unwrapped the MP-9. Lifting it out, he grasped it by its short six-inch barrel, then swung with all his strength.

He watched it splash into the deeper water beyond the rocks before returning to his car. He was back on the T1 in ten minutes.

At Dundalk he drove into the railway station, parked the Sierra and removed the Barbour from the boot. He slipped the key into the exhaust pipe and strolled to the far end of the car park. On his way he peeled the flesh-coloured, skin-thin surgeon's gloves from his hands, rolled them up into a small ball and dropped them into the waste bin. He waited by the public lavatories and smoked another cigarette. Nobody paid him any attention.

After a few minutes a brown Cavalier with Ulster numberplates cruised into the car park and slotted between two parked cars. A man got out, walked briskly across the courtyard, and without looking left or right, disappeared into the station. The man waiting by the lavatories dropped his cigarette, crushed it with the toe of his boot and walked across to the Cavalier. The key was in the ignition, the engine was nice and warm, and when he switched it on the heating fan wafted a gentle breeze of warm air on to his face. He smiled and caught a glimpse of himself in the rear mirror. The look was out of place, and vanished. It was a face that didn't often smile.

He sailed through the Republic customs post like a fairy.

There was a little extra activity at the Carrickcarnon frontier post. 'Something to do with a shooting in Dublin,' a chatty, pink-faced youth in Garda uniform told him as he waited in the queue, 'but only routine ...' They weren't interested in the Cavalier. They waved him through and he sat stoically at the Killeen post while one unsmiling RUC man, puffed up in his navy-blue flak jacket, asked him the usual questions. A second officer, equally grim and unfriendly and standing back from the car, cradled a well-worn SA-80 rifle across his body with a seriousness that brooked no doubt that he knew exactly what he would do with it if the situation demanded. A short distance down the road he was put through it again, this time by two tired-looking, grim-faced, beardless youths with Staffordshire accents, dressed like soldiers. They ordered him out so that one of them could look into the boot. When he got back into the car another face appeared at the window. A civilian, older than the boys, a few more lines on his face and dark rings under his eyes — a man who worried. He wasn't relaxed.

'Can you give me a lift, please?'

The soliders didn't seem curious.

'Sure. Hop in.'

He hadn't even said where he wanted his lift to.

'Where d'you want this?' The newcomer showed a heavy, worn .45 Colt self-loading pistol to the driver. They'd only gone half a mile.

'Cock it, stick the safety on and hang on to it until we get to Lisburn. I'll grab it if I need to.' The driver didn't take his eyes off the road. 'Light me a fag, will you.'

'I don't smoke. Where d'you keep yours?'

'Jesus! You must be the only fuckin' idiot in this bloody country who doesn't smoke. What's the matter with you? Aren't you frightened shitless like the rest of us?'

The passenger gave a slightly nervous giggle, lit one of the driver's cigarettes, passed it to him, and said, 'How'd you get on in Dublin?'

'Don't ask.'

He didn't. They didn't speak again until the Cavalier pulled up in Lisburn's High street. The passenger handed the Colt to the driver, who slipped it into the compartment in his door. He didn't say thank you. 'Don't forget it's cocked.'

'Up your arse!'

'Nice to be appreciated.'

'Fuck off!'

'Ciao!'

'Yeh.'

He'd been born in Belfast. But not this Belfast. This was a battleground; it stank of blood and smoke and suspicion and everybody had that shifty, worried look about them: 'Are you one of them, or one of us?' It didn't matter who was them or who was us. You had to be on one side or the other, and it was what you did with your hand when you went into church decided who you liked and who you didn't. There were no neutrals in Belfast this year; you got yourself killed just by dipping two fingers into the holy water. What a fucking country. What a place to be born in. What a fucking place to die.

He had a special place in Belfast where he hid the Cavalier, and a special hole where he hid himself. But you couldn't relax. You'd have felt safer in a shell hole on the Somme in 1916. He changed his scruffy working clothes for a pair of pale jeans, a clean shirt and a round-necked sweater. He didn't bother with shoes or socks; he didn't even bother with a bath – that could wait. He poured himself a large Jameson's and dropped a couple of ice cubes on top of it. It tasted like nectar. He lit a cigarette to go with it and looked at the time. Five to six. He switched on the television and stretched himself out on the worn sofa. One of the springs twanged as he worked himself into a comfortable position and then she was there, in the room, the pretty, doe-eyed, innocent-looking girl staring straight at him and telling him all about the dreadful happenings at St Anne's Park, Dublin.

He waited until she'd finished, then turned down the sound, reached over his head and brought the telephone on to his chest.

It rang three times. He recognized the voice. 'Have you seen the news?' he asked.

'I heard it earlier on the wireless. What about the other two?'

'Just a minute. Can we talk a bit more about today's Mickey Mice?'

'No. It's finished . . .'

'Not quite. Did you know one of them was a friend of ours?'

'How did you know?'

'I recognized him. He must have been working both sides. I heard him mention a name he shouldn't have known.'

'And?'

'None of my business, Clive. He won't mention it again and I've forgotten it.'

The silence didn't last very long. Just long enough for the Jameson's and ice to be smoothly swallowed. Then the voice silked down the line: 'Try not to let it go to your stomach. About these other two –'

'What have you told them?'

9

'To do as they're told. They're arriving in Belfast tonight, separately. They'll contact you; you'll arrange a meeting place.'

'Names?'

'Paper ones. George Fortnum and Fred Mason.'

'Very original. That should confuse all our enemies . . . And talking about enemies, where do these two fit in?'

'Don't think about it, David.'

'I'll ring you tomorrow.'

'No, don't do that. When you've collected your winnings catch the night flight and I'll meet you at the General's place in Chelsea. We can drink some of his gin while he consults his Ouija board. Then I'll buy you breakfast.'

'Sounds almost civilized, Clive.'

'It's these funny times we live in, Murray, old son. See you later.'

They must have been waiting for him to finish his London call.

The phone had barely settled on to its lugs when it rang. It was Mason. Three minutes later Fortnum had his turn. He was in a bad mood. He didn't like being shunted from Dublin to this shithole, and weren't there any other buggers in Ireland who knew how to twiddle the dial on an antenna?

Murray let him have his head and when he'd finished told him what he'd told Mason – nothing. He arranged, as he had with Fortnum, to wait at the Europa at half-past eight on the dot, in the bar. 'Don't approach Mason or me, just follow us out into the car park. Everything's been explained to Mason.'

'What about our stuff?'

'All arranged. It can be picked up at Ballykinnough. They're expecting you.'

'Transport?'

'Fixed up.'

Murray put down the phone, poured himself another Jameson's and took it with him into the bedroom. It was as sparse a room as the other – a bed, a small table and a wardrobe, no extras. The wardrobe had nothing in it except one change of clothing, a couple of shirts and some underwear, and a small holdall, already packed. He put on his shoes and socks and shrugged into a thick, slightly scruffy hacking jacket. It covered the heavy Colt tucked into a small leather toggle threaded on to his belt. The whiskey went down in one gulp as he picked up the bag, switched off the light and let the front door swing shut behind him.

He ran an automatic check over the car. The engine was still warm. But you never knew. He threw his bag into the boot, then, with the usual bladder-squeezing chill, turned the key and started the engine. No bang. No blinding flash. His muscles relaxed and his bladder went back to normal as he crossed Queen Elizabeth Bridge and joined the Sydenham bypass. Not so much traffic here, but he wasn't worried about that. He didn't stay long. He turned off and took the overpass into Strandtown.

It was an ordinary-looking house on the edge of Catholic Ballymacarrett, a little bit of no-man's-land in no-man's-country; a corner house with a slightly more than head-high wooden fence and a rickety back gate. Murray parked on the opposite side of the road and, without looking round, crossed over and went through the gate. He rang the bell at the back door, which he absently tested with his finger. It felt heavy and solid, although it looked like any ordinary housing-estate door. The man who opened it looked as if he'd just woken up.

'Hello, Charlie. Everything OK?' asked Murray. The man shrugged his shoulders; it wasn't tiredness that gave

11

him his expression. The door closed behind them with a solid, almost metallic clunk as he led Murray into what should have been the kitchen. It was fitted out like a well-designed workshop.

'This is Major Murray,' the man who'd opened the door said soothingly to a hard-looking youngster sitting in a scruffy armchair next to a solid, six-foot-high steel cupboard. He wore a loose black pullover, dirty, un-pressed dark trousers and heavy black boots. His hair was grimy and neck-length and he carried two days' gritty, unshaven growth on a jutting chin. Resting on his knee, pointing at Murray, was the barrel of a shortened H&K33 machine pistol. It was cocked and the safety was off. He raised one grimy finger at Murray; at the end of it was a black-engrained, chewed fingernail. Otherwise he didn't move an inch. 'Captain Lord Millcombe,' introduced Charlie.

'Don't get up,' said Murray, cheerfully. He turned back to Charlie. 'The tone in this shithouse, Charlie, is rising all the time. Let me know when the Prince of Wales turns up for a watch . . .' Nobody smiled. Fear had solidified the muscles for smiling; it'd be ages, a thousand cigarettes, a dozen bottles of Grouse and five hundred miles from East Belfast, before they unfroze again. His Lordship laid the H&K, still cocked, safety still off, on the floor beside him and stretched back, his legs out in front of him and his hands cupped round the back of his head. He closed his eyes. He'd already lost interest in Major Murray.

Murray eased his bottom on to the edge of the re-inforced kitchen table and juggled a packet of cigarettes in his hand. He didn't open it. It was too close an atmosphere for smoking. 'Charlie,' he said, 'have you got any of that surplus C4 left that we nicked off the O'Leary people?'

Charlie dragged his eyes away from the television monitor by the draining board; nothing exciting, just a no-frills static picture of Murray's car viewed from somewhere above them. 'Sure, but it's gone green. It's trademarked – Libyan stock, Provisional IRA for the use of . . . What d'you want it for?'

Murray didn't reply. He stared unblinkingly into Charlie's eyes. Charlie got the message.

'Official or unofficial?'

Murray gave him the same look.

Charlie shrugged. 'OK, how much d'you want?'

'A car job,' said Murray.

'A pound and a half.' Charlie stood up and rubbed his hands together. 'Detonator?'

Murray stared at the packet of cigarettes in his hand. He didn't look into Charlie's face. 'Make it ten pounds, Charlie – and an Irish starter set.'

Charlie stopped rubbing his hands. There was no surprise on his face; he'd lost that particular emotion an age ago. But one of Lord Millcombe's eyelids raised fractionally, allowing him to stare blankly at Murray, then closed again. 'That'll turn your car into confetti, David. You sure that's what you want?'

Murray nodded. 'And a rocker detonator – for angle, not vibration. Say, one in ten . . .'

Charlie shook his head. 'I wouldn't recommend it, not with an Irish set, they're bloody unreliable at the best of times. Can't you do a time job?'

Murray thought about it. It didn't take long. 'Have you got an Irish timer or haven't you?'

'Yes, but as I said, there'll be nothing bigger than a pinhead left to look at.'

'That'll be enough to show where it came from. OK, a sixty-minute fuse on a depression-action timer. We'll have the gunge in the spare-wheel compartment and the starter where it can be easily got at in the boot.'

13

'Give me five minutes.'

'Take as long as you like, Charlie. I'll just sit here and chat with his Lordship about military discipline.'

Charlie didn't laugh. Neither did his Lordship.

At a quarter-past eight Murray depressed the Semtex timer switch.

At half-past eight, in the car park of the Europa Hotel, he handed the keys of the Cavalier to Mason.

'Which of you two's driving?'

'He is.'

'OK. You're expected at Ballykinnough at half-past nine. Don't be late. Pick up everything you need for short and medium-range surveillance, including your speciality. I suggest you stay the night there and ring me when you get back. I'll brief you in the morning.' He glanced down at his wrist. Twenty to nine. 'D'you know the way to Ballykinnough?'

'Tell me,' said Fortnum.

Murray pointed over his shoulder. 'M1, A4. I suggest you leave now. There are some funny buggers out there, you don't want to keep them waiting.'

'OK. See you in the morning.'

'Cheers.'

Dublin's second great cathedral, Christchurch, withstood the cold afternoon's onslaught of American and Japanese tourists with its usual dignity. There were the elderly, those with a more pressing urgency to close with their spiritual destiny, and the well-to-do, the well dressed, off-season sightseers, mingling with a group of West African clerics who gazed about them with intense religious expressions.

In a side confessional box, a tall black priest was kneeling, waiting for someone. He sensed rather than heard the presence on the other side of the booth. And as he did so he began an incantation in a tone of hushed reverence: '*In the name of the Father, the Son and the Holy . . .*' Even whispering his voice was deep, resonant and cultured. English cultured. He felt the hot breath of the other occupant against the side of his face as the man cut in, his thick Irish accent almost obliterated by the cane latticework between them.

'You can shut the bloody profanity, Reason. Listen . . .' The Irishman didn't wait for Reason's acknowledgement. There was an undercurrent of urgency, a rasping, breathless suggestion of fear – definitely fear – in his whispered voice. 'Peadar O'Dwyer going down in St Anne's has turned everything on its bloody head. By God, your man Murray does a proper job of work when he puts his mind to it! They're running around like chickens at the moment, trying to make up their minds who did it – and why. Killing the Arabs was a good move. They can't work that one out either. They can't make up their minds whether it's drug people moving into the game or a Brit trick. Brit's always favourite when they're not sure.'

'They know we don't work South,' interrupted Reason, 'same as PIRA. Are you back on solid ground now? Has the leak been stopped?'

'Only time will tell,' whispered the other voice philosophically. 'You going to find out how it happened in the first place?'

'I don't think it matters now. We slipped. The Libs are not bloody silly. They got in somehow and marked you, probably a double. But he won't be doubling any more. We've just got to make bloody sure they don't do it again . . . Anyway, I've closed the book on you. It's just you and me.'

'Sure! That's a good one, Clive! But just remember whose bloody arse it is. OK, as things go we might have

15

done ourselves a bit of good. When the boys stop running round the farmyard they'll have to reorganize themselves. They're short on the Executive. O'Dwyer's place is up for nomination – any one of three. I'm not one of them – not at the moment. But anything could happen now.'

'Hang on.' Reason took his face away from the grille and through a gap in the curtain watched another group of whispering Americans pass down the aisle. It gave him time to think. He leaned forward and put his mouth to the grille again. The outline of the head on the other side hadn't moved. 'D'you want to have a chat with Murray? He could take some of the others out if you want.'

There was a suppressed hiss. 'Jesus! I said he does a good job, but by Christ he frightens the life out of me. Keep the bloodthirsty bastard under lock and key. I don't want to see him over here. We can't afford any more "funny" killings. We've gotta have some normal wastage or they'll smell Whitehall. Think about it, Clive. Go for the Executive rather than the reserves. Know what I mean?'

'Top man?'

'Yeh. Fitzpatrick. Could be vulnerable to a subtle whisper campaign. Subtle, though – it's got to be subtle. He's got English connections – ex-British Army, a plodder in the Irish Guards years ago. Same sort of pedigree as Sean MacStiofain, ex-RAF who became PIRA Chief of Staff in the seventies. Throw a bit of shit around – it might stick. It did with MacStiofain.'

'Who've we got to convince?' whispered Reason.

'Eoin McNeela. Everybody trusts him. He gives the nod and everything happens. Can't be bought, can't be turned, but he's the one you've got to get to do the dirty bit for you . . . OK. That's it,' the voice said abruptly. 'I'm going with the next bunch that walks past the door. You all right?'

'Just a sec. Play everything straight from now on. Whatever happens, don't interfere. If I start something, you're not going to know about it. Do your job – forget us. OK?'

'Bye, Clive.' There was a rustle of movement on the other side of the grille, a wafted smell of damp cloth and mothballs, and Reason was alone in the confessional. He waited a few moments, then slipped out and into the pew he'd occupied earlier, and carried on with his prayers.

Ten hours later, with his raincoat collar turned up tight around his neck against the cold English rain, he walked briskly down Oakley Street, Chelsea, mounted the three concrete steps leading up to the large Georgian town house at the far end of the road, and tugged the big brass bellpull set into the wall beside the anonymous black door.

2

London, November

General Sir Richard Sanderson cupped his chin in his hands and stared across the width of the long mahogany table into the eyes of the man sitting opposite. It took a lot to surprise Sanderson. What he'd just heard had done exactly that. And the surprise showed. 'Clive, the bloody thing's too complicated. It'll blow up in your face, and I'm buggered if I'm going to stand to attention in the Cabinet Room and take a bollocking from that jumped-up little bastard with the coiffured hair and horn-rimmed glasses when it does.'

Reason grinned. 'What jumped-up little bastard is that, Richard?'

'You know bloody well who I mean.' He sighed. 'OK, tell me again. Slowly this time.'

There was an affinity between these two; an affinity of two hard men, two soldiers who knew which end of the bayonet did the job. Richard Sanderson had had a full war – the real one – and a DSO and MC to vouch for his professionalism and bravery, and for the last ten years had been head of the special intelligence group formed by Mrs Thatcher in the early eighties to offset the petty face-slapping and the 'share-no-evil – share-nothing' rivalry of the two DI branches, MI5 and MI6. It had been a success-ful enterprise. Sanderson answered to only one executive; the one she'd passed it on to, the top one: the incumbent prime minister.

Clive Reason was a different kettle of trouble, still in his thirties, black, with clean-cut features and steady dark eyes that, try as he would, never lost the slightly mocking and humorous glint with which they viewed his job and the world in general. A six-foot-three, fifteen-and-a-half-stone graduate of the 2nd Parachute Regiment school of hard steel, Reason was Sanderson's number two. Combining intelligence with guts, he was where he was because he knew what intelligence matters were all about and because his favourite place was where it all happened – at the front. Holding up a packet of cigarettes for Sanderson to see, he raised his eyebrows. Sanderson nodded and sat back in his chair while Reason lit a cigarette.

'As we know, the Irish are deciding whether they're going to give up domestic terrorism,' said Reason. 'They've found something that brings in more money and doesn't get their legs shot off.'

'Such as?'

'They're laying down the groundwork for a monopoly in this part of the world in hard narcotics.'

'Clive, I know all this – '

'OK, but did you know that they're planning a major pipeline into Europe and the UK with Ireland as the distribution centre and Libya as the central depot?'

'Yes, that too. What's their next move?'

'Well, first they've got to get us off their backs. A large amount of their present cocaine holding, currently in Libya, has been earmarked as collateral for the purchase of arms, ammunition and some fairly sophisticated hardware for one final, all-out assault on the mainland UK if the current "negotiations" don't work out.'

Sanderson's eyebrows raised slightly. Reason carried on.

'They're getting the stuff not only from the Libs, but other, more interesting market places. One of these is the ex-Soviet Union. They've developed a thriving black market in "special" explosives – loud ones, big ones, and the ultimate, nuclear. There's a flat in an apartment block in Ulyanovsk where you can negotiate, for cash, the makings of a bomb that would turn the entire London metropolitan area into the biggest football ground in the world. Better, you can buy, and walk away with, a triggering mechanism for a nuclear device that would fit into a rep's samples case and could be carried through any of the City's new anti-bomb roadblocks. The currency for buying these things? Hard cash in US dollars if you've got it, or even better, cocaine. Richard, for a fraction of the Irish cocaine being held by the people at Qaddafi's Villa Pietra, the Irish could stop pissing around with little bangs like the Baltic Exchange and Bishopsgate and really let something off. Think what that inoffensive-looking triggering device would do, even on its own, if it went off outside the Mansion House. The City would vanish in a puff of smoke.'

'That trigger mechanism,' interrupted Sanderson, 'when did you hear about it?'

Reason gave him a funny look. 'It's common knowledge in the marketplace. I've got someone looking into it, finding out how many have been sold, and to whom. Funny you should mention it. I've been giving it quite a lot of thought.'

'That's very satisfying,' retorted Sanderson. 'Did you know the Irish claim to have one in position in London, with its timer set for sometime early in March next year?' Sanderson smiled bleakly. 'And that unless the British Government adopts a very serious approach to the current negotiations – in other words agree to an unconditional withdrawal of British interests – the thing'll go up with a bloody great bang . . .?'

Reason's funny look became a very serious one. 'It's a joke?'

'Not at all,' said Sanderson dryly. 'It's not a joke and what I've told you, and am going to tell you, must not leave this room. You're not on the list of "need-to-know", so this is for your ears only. OK, this is what we've got. Notwithstanding everything he says in the papers about not giving way to terrorism, Major's been given six months to come up with a definite negotiating position with Sinn Fein and the PIRA. They don't want to rush him! No publicity, no *public* threats, and to show how serious his position is and that they reckon they've at last got a winner, they're allowing him six months to effect a compromise that won't leave him too red-faced. They'll stop the clock on the bomb when the six months are up and a positive British stance towards negotiation has been established.' He paused for a moment.

'I think the forced-negotiation ploy is this new Dublin Executive's influence on the gunmen. It's managed to persuade Adams and McGuinness that you can't bomb the British into surrender, but you can do it by other means. It's psychological. John Major can't afford to have the City of London held to ransom. He dare not take the risk of thinking it might be a bluff, so he's got to go along with it. Hence these "first" steps towards dialogue with Gerry Adams, though as we, and all the world know, it's hypocritical. Secret talks have been taking place between senior members of Sinn Fein and John Major's representatives from the Northern Ireland Office for months.'

Reason spoke at last. 'They're bluffing, Richard.'

'Are they?' countered Sanderson. 'You know these trigger mechanisms exist and are available to anybody with the right money. You've proved the new Executive has money, but you can't tell me whether they've been to the market or not. What we do know is that it is possible for them to have a device – they could even have two if they've got the wherewithal to pay for them. Nobody in

21

his right mind would attempt to call a bluff of this magnitude. Would you?'

Reason thought deeply for several long moments, then met Sanderson's grey-blue eyes. 'Let me go back to what I was saying before you brought this thing up – the thing that Harry Barlow and I have been working on. When I've finished, I'll talk to you about calling bluffs.'

'Keep it short and uncomplicated, Clive.'

'OK. The thing Harry Barlow and I set into motion was to get inside the New Executive. It's running everything now, but I'll come to that. The endgame of these people is shooting narcotics into Europe. What you've just said about getting our people to back off by threatening to pulverize the financial heart of the country is the opening gambit, which has already been made. The goods are in position. Richard, the organization in Dublin has taken a good look at itself and stopped bashing its head against the wall. The Officials have come out of hibernation, they've joined up with the Provisionals. It's the worst possible scenario for us: the brawn and the brains, the left and the right, sitting round the same table and looking across the water at us.' Reason stubbed his barely touched cigarette out, crossed his legs and sat back in the chair.

'What we have to penetrate is the committee that's in control of this new combined task force of Officials and Provisionals. As you know, this New Executive is made up of the three top men from the army councils of both the IRA and the PIRA: the Chief of Staff, the Adjutant-General and the Quartermaster-General. But the seventh man, the chairman of this Executive, is Michael Fitzpatrick, an original "Stickie" – Official,' he explained to Sanderson's raised eyebrow. 'I mention him specifically because he's our target. We've found a gap, we think he's vulnerable . . .'

'To what?'

'In a minute. Going by what you've said, these seven will initially play us out of the game by making it financially impossible for the war to continue, and with the crew we've got guiding the country at the moment, they've got a fairly easy job. In five months' time we surrender. When we lower the flag in Northern Ireland they'll turn their attention, and their resources, to the business of making themselves rich through domination of the European drug market.' Reason stopped and studied Sanderson's sceptical expression.

'There are some very hard cases already running the markets on the Continent,' Sanderson reminded him. 'Established ones – Dutch, German, Spanish, the Mafia! They've got their lines and their resources. There'll be a fair amount of blood in the gutter before they relinquish control. What makes you think the Irish can shift them?'

Reason didn't slow down. 'Well, first of all the drug problem as we know it will seem like a piss in the ocean in a few years' time. It hasn't even got going yet. But as for your question. Hadn't you noticed, Richard? A couple of hundred hard nuts, the best-trained and most experienced terrorists in the world, have held off the British Army, the most technically skilled anti-terrorist police force in the world – the RUC – and one of the best intelligence systems going – ours – for nearly a quarter of a century. They'll eat any European drug organization that doesn't toe their line, and they'd swallow whole, national, so-called antidrug agencies without a hiccup once they put their full resources to it.'

'You think the Irish Government's going to sit around twiddling its thumbs while all this is going on?'

Reason almost raised a smile. 'The drug people'll pay their way. Ireland's always been an easy touch, otherwise the IRA in its various forms couldn't have survived to this day. The only thing that arouses passion in Dublin is talk of French letters and abortion. They've no anti-anything organizations, and the Dáil is packed with guys who for little more than a free boat trip round Clonakilty Bay'd turn a blind eye to the Pope being mugged on the steps of the Knock basilica. Think what some of them'd do for an annual cut of several billion dollars!'

Sanderson shook his head. 'I'm not sure I can go along with that hypothesis, Clive, I think you're going over the top. We're all in this together now – we're a European Union, all working for the good of the Union. We're not individual countries in this thing: it's a universal problem that everybody wants to get under control. But go back to the Dublin Executive. Who's this target you were talking about?'

Reason shrugged aside Sanderson's reservations. This was 1993, not 1941. Everybody's motives were suspect. No government was doing anything for nothing and it didn't matter a fuck whether civilization went up the spout. Nowadays politicians were out for what they could get. Personal wealth and ambition came first, national interest second, and the European Union and the rest of the world nowhere. But Reason wasn't a politician; he could say what he thought.

'The Executive, as I said, is in place and working. There are three reserves, all of similar status but without active allegiance to either of the two wings. This maintains an equal strength on the board – they're still feeling their way with this new-found brotherhood. Any accident, any fallout, and a reserve moves into place and the continuity is maintained.' Reason leaned forward and placed his elbows on the table. 'The system is about to be tested. One of the seats on the Executive is about to be filled, leaving one of the reserve places vacant.'

'So?'

'We've got an agent ready to move into it. He's been a senior background figure in the Republican organization for some time. Kept his nose clean, played a very professional game, he's highly thought of and just the man to sit on the Executive. All we need now are another couple of empty chairs.'

'Why don't you turn David Murray loose on them?'

Reason almost smiled. 'Suggested and rejected. It's too obvious. They won't buy top people, reserves or otherwise, getting themselves knocked off like street fighters or having funny accidents while walking down to the pub. This has to be different. We have to get the Executive to do the knocking-off for us. It's not as silly as it sounds. With a little bit of imagination this is exactly what could happen. I have in mind a little game that's been tried and tested – and accepted.' Reason stopped talking and lit another cigarette. Sanderson watched. Then ran out of patience.

'You want me to guess the name of this game?'

Reason trickled smoke down his large nostrils. 'We do a Peter Wright – Australia, *Spycatcher*, the lot.'

Sanderson's face remained blank.

'We'll instil into one of our shortly-to-retire executives the urge to go to Australia and write his memoirs. He'll do the whole Wright performance: stories of his early life, boring things about how he kept the Russians at bay, and his behind-the-scenes involvement in the modern saga – the Irish game, North and South. When it's finished he'll put it out for auction among the Aussie publishers and we'll pounce as we did before and spend millions trying to prevent its publication. We've good experience at trying to get injunctions in Australia on undesirable revelations! We'll bring thingy Armstrong out of retirement to fight our corner – that'll guarantee we go up the spout – and the Aussie judiciary, sticking close to form, will make laughing stocks of us and refuse our injunction.'

'What if they grant it?'

'We can worry about that if it happens. You know what the Chinese say?'

'I'm not sure I want to.'

Reason smiled. 'The Chinese say, "Don't trust anything that ain't pinched," or words to that effect. The harder you have to fight, the more blood that trickles into the gutter, the higher the importance of the loot.'

'Get back to the point, Clive. How does this help our man achieve his, and your, ambition, and what's it got to do with people wanting to blow up the City of London?'

Reason was ready for him. Almost. 'You'll see in a minute. The authenticity of the book's contents will be established by our struggle to prevent its publication. That's the major talking point. Next comes its contents – or a particular section of its contents. Somewhere around page two hundred and eighty there'll be a chapter on the new developments in and around Dublin. This will include a hint – something like a fifteen-pound hammer between the eyes – that a British agent has infiltrated the New Executive at a very high level. Without going into his birthmarks and war wounds, we'll plant enough incidental detail to give them solid leads. The Executive will go into a cold sweat. They'll dig and they'll dig, they'll find what they're looking for, our target will go into the hole, hopefully taking a couple more with him, and our man'll be nominated for one of the vacant chairs. Once he's sitting down he becomes privy to state secrets. Among other things he can talk and ask questions about nuclear trigger mechanisms planted in the City ...'

Reason reached forward and pulled another cigarette from the packet on the table in front of him. He took his time lighting it. He could sense Sanderson's impatience but refused to hurry. 'Or nuclear trigger mechanisms *not* planted in the City!'

'Ahhh!'

'Which brings me back to your question about calling bluffs . . .'

'I've got the message. Make the bloody thing work. Who is our man?'

Reason's eyes never left Sanderson's face. 'Sorry, Richard, you're going to have to trust me on this one. I don't think I want to say a name yet. I've still got to work out the nuts and bolts with Harry Barlow. It's going to take a fair bit of fine-tuning to get it absolutely right . . .' Reason continued to hold Sanderson's quizzical expression, then inclined his head with a wry grin. 'In fact, I'm not altogether sure I understand it all myself. Harry seems to, though. He thinks up all sorts of funny ideas in his bath. I keep telling him he should play with empty shampoo bottles like the rest of us.'

Sanderson didn't see anything to smile at. 'I'll curb my impatience until he has another bath,' he said dryly. 'Who've you got in mind for this Australian literary effort?'

'A middle to senior professional executive on the MI6/5 coordinating committee who's just about run out of time. Name's Greville Sixsmith. Joined MI6 in 1957 when he came down from Cambridge and did nothing for thirty-six years except keep his nose clean. Did a few years with Five – desk work and interviews mainly – but made no real mark, just increased his status along with his wages by toeing the line, wearing the right suit and tie and always sucking the nob of the bloke in charge. And then he became in charge himself. That's where we come in.'

'I wonder what your epitaph of me will be,' Sanderson growled. But Reason kept his silence, smiling slyly. Sanderson sighed, leant forward and rested his chin lightly on

27

his fingertips. 'All right, what makes you think this gentleman is going to play games with you and Harry Barlow?'

Reason dragged on his cigarette before replying. If he didn't know his General as well as he did he might have presumed he'd already gone too far. But Sanderson was a modern general, dirty thoughts and dirty tricks had become part of the norm; they came every morning just after the first spoonful of cornflakes. He wouldn't wince at the thought of a colleague being compromised if national security required it. 'Greville Sixsmith has made a lot of money over the years. Clever stuff on the market. It appears honest – at the moment – but one never knows. Anyway, we won't let that stand in our way. We'll have another look at that in the cold light of a very early dawn. You never know what frightened people will reveal when confronted with "evidence" of wrongdoing.'

'I'm not sure I like the sound of that, Clive.'

'National security, Richard, takes priority over personal feelings.' Reason grinned humourlessly. 'With due respect to the rank of that person's feelings, of course.'

Sanderson shrugged his feelings aside. 'You were saying?'

Reason continued. 'He became a high-risk Name at Lloyd's, just in time to join all the other Names on the bungy jump. My information is that regardless of what's coming in, he's going to have to spend the next few years bailing out some smart syndicate's wide-boys inefficiency. Our research bears out an obvious fact – to us in the know – that Greville Sixsmith's just the bloke who would like a supplementary pension to replace the one he's going to lose. His retirement date is almost two months to the day. It fits in perfectly.'

'And that's all you've got to go on, that he's a loser at Lloyd's?'

28

Reason's expression didn't change. 'At the moment. But we can improve on it. We'll make him a very attractive proposition. The average British sixty-year-old in great financial difficulties would find it hard to resist the chance to earn a bit of tax-free cash and take an all-expenses-paid, post-retirement holiday in the sun.'

'And if he does manage to resist it?'

'We'll offer other inducements.'

Sanderson knew what 'other inducements' meant. 'Nothing illegal, Clive.'

'Of course not, Richard.'

'You'll let him know exactly what the game is? What he's letting himself in for?'

'I very much doubt it. I think I'll play that bit by ear.'

'Be delicate, Clive.'

'As always, Richard.'

Clive Reason lit a cigarette with the car's cigar lighter, wound the window down a fraction to allow an escape route for the smoke, and glanced keenly at the man sitting beside him.

Greville Sixsmith's fifty-nine and three-quarter years showed, but only in places. Ten of the years that showed had descended on his previously unlined forehead over the last two years with his crushing losses at Lloyd's – two years when the Lutine bell had rung for itself. Greville was a short man with a tendency towards overweight who carried his fetish for fine clothes to an extreme. They were the last things he was going to give up. His suits by Henry Poole cost a fortune and his Harvie and Hudson shirts a bus driver's weekly wage. Greville looked after his sartorial appearance as if it were a lifeline to better things. His receding hairline he dealt with by plastering wisps of the ginger hair that still encircled his crown across the top of his head, Bobby Charlton style.

The disguise against baldness fooled only him. His eyebrows were a feature. Heavy, bushy, salt-and-pepper tinted, they projected outwards over a freckled, hooked Roman nose below which was a carefully cultivated thin grey moustache. The military effect that he strove for was ruined by an effeminate mouth, a protruding lower lip that inclined to droop as if in a sulk, and a chin that started receding too soon. He somehow typified his type. He'd never heard a shot fired in anger; he was a senior civil servant with Department of Intelligence credentials, a desk man through and through, and it showed. 'OK, Reason,' he said without turning his head. 'You've brought me out into the cold. What d'you want to tell me that couldn't be said in a warm office over a cup of coffee?'

'You'll understand that when I've finished,' said Reason.

'Make it snappy, then. And close that bloody window.'

'The smoke – '

'Then don't smoke.'

Reason ignored him and carried on smoking. 'The Primitives, Greville, are becoming more sophisticated. Their shopping lists are showing intelligence. They've got bigger and better bombs, and real mortars that are hitting their targets now. They've even managed to lob a couple into the Prime Minister's back garden. They've given up knocking off Protestant taxi drivers, lay preachers, and petrol pump attendants. The long knife's out for the police, the RIR and our own pongos. Give 'em a year or so and it'll be like 1941 again. The people won't like it. They'll want somebody's balls, and you know whose.'

'Go back to the beginning.'

'The Primitives – '

'Don't be smart.' With a look of distaste but no further objection, Greville lowered his window with a muted electronic hum to allow more of the cigarette smoke to escape from the car. It was an L-registration Jaguar, a perk of high office – Government high office – and was parked cosily in the underground car park below Cavendish Square. The cars on either side of it were empty. The window wound itself up about three inches again, until Sixsmith took his finger off the button, half-inclined his head and stared from under the bushy eyebrows at his passenger.

'You make it sound like the plot of a spy story,' he said. 'But why tell me? I'm no longer interested in the bloody Irish – or anybody else, come to that.'

'Friendship, Greville,' Reason said with a smile. 'Old times' sake. Call it what you like. And I owe you one.'

'Bollocks. You owe me fuck all! You've never had cause to call me friend, and anyway, I'm retiring in six months. Why don't you go to Buller-Shadcock, he's coming over from G9. He's a bit more gullible than me – I think!'

'It's a rare quality is loyalty, Greville, and you've got it. One can be frank with you. You're loyal, and honest – '

'Bollocks again! You're spitting pearls at the wrong girl, Reason. Whatever it is you're after, I haven't got any. Whatever comes at the end of this bullshit, I'm not interested.' Greville pressed the button on the console and wound the window fully up. He didn't look at Reason. 'I'm not listening to any more of this, it's boring. Was that it?'

Reason kept a sympathetic expression on his face. 'You're misreading my motives, Greville. I don't want anything except the benefit of your vast experience. It's because you're leaving the Club that I'm talking to you.' Reason turned in his seat and faced the man behind the wheel. 'You going to write your memoirs, Greville?' he asked casually. He managed to keep his tongue away from his cheek.

'You're joking of course!'

'You're looking at a grimace, Greville, not a grin. You must have a few thoughts to put on paper after all these years. People like reading about spies.'

'Christ, Reason – they'd have my balls on a dinner plate and my pension used as a dartboard! We don't even think about things like that, let alone talk about them.' Greville stopped and thought about what he'd said. He didn't take very long over it; there was money in memoirs. He peered at his passenger through narrowed eyes. 'They would, wouldn't they?'

'Not necessarily,' said Reason carefully. 'Peter Wright got away with it. Made a fortune.'

'He was in Australia.'

Reason stared pointedly through the windscreen at the damp, concrete wall in front of him.

'We're letting it be known that we're offering recipro-cal arrangements to Australian intelligence operatives who want to come to England and get things off their chest and on to the hardback shelves. It could develop, could be the done thing: our people telling all in Disney-land, Aussies baring their souls in the UK; the CIA publishing in Tehran, the Russians in Singapore, there could be no end to it. Nobody'd know who the bloody hell was telling what after a bit!'

Greville wasn't amused. 'Let's get this thing straight, just in case I'm not following your script. By your open-ing remarks you want to pull a fast one over some poor unsuspecting bastards – Irishmen, by the sound of it – and somehow this is related to your hint about my writ-ing a few memoirs. Tell me if I've got the drift – and then I'll tell you to get stuffed!' Pompous he was, but obtuse Sixsmith certainly wasn't.

Reason smiled gently. Sixsmith, watching him closely, frowned before turning his head away. 'There could be a lot of money in it – our money,' said Reason, softly. 'There'd also be a nice break in the sunshine of the southern hemisphere while you recover from all those years in Whitehall.'

Greville didn't meet Reason's eyes. But he was thinking about what he'd heard. By the sound of it, it wasn't something to be tossed aside lightly. But with buggers like Reason you took your time, you studied the lie of the land, and you showed no enthusiasm. Very carefully, he said, 'If you're suggesting I go and spend part of my retirement in some godforsaken part of the world and put down a few words on nearly forty years of telling funny buggers like you how to get from one side of the road to the other, you're very, very much mistaken. No way! You're pushing your luck here, Reason.'

'We'll see.' Clive Reason slowly eased smoke out of his pursed lips and watched it plaster itself against the windscreen. He'd got the hook hovering just below Greville's pouting lips. A little touch, and who knew? 'We're suggesting an extension of your contract. You wouldn't forfeit your pension.' He dispersed the smoke with a wave of his hand. 'In fact, you'd increase it by benefiting from a generous consultancy fee. Think what that would do if you'd had a bit of bad luck and run up a few debts.'

'What d'you mean by that?' snapped Sixsmith suspiciously, glaring hard at Reason's innocent expression.

Reason stared at the wall in front of him. He knew what was going on in the driving seat; he didn't have to look. 'I'm thinking of those poor buggers who've gone up the spout with Lloyd's. Life savings some of 'em, poor sods. Greville, can you imagine it, their savings, everything, even their homes and furniture, vanished overnight? I bet they wish they had something to sell to get themselves off the hook – '

'Listen, you bastard!' Greville was almost jumping up

and down in his seat. 'Have you been sticking your bloody nose in my – '

'One can't help hearing things over the cashews and peanuts, Greville. You know how people gossip, specially in our trade. Still, it's only hearsay. Of course, as you know, there are those among us who would go to all lengths to clear their debts. You're not the only one, just the first one I've spoken to . . . But all this is neither here nor there – at the moment,' Reason added ominously.

'Going back to your memoirs.' Reason turned to face Sixsmith with a reassuring nod. 'They could be a life-saver. We'd all buy a copy of the book and you'd get the royalties. And who knows, they might make a movie out of it! You'd get a free holiday in good old Australia – but you wouldn't have to mix with the natives; you'd find some of your own sort out there – and, of course, in addition to what I've suggested your index-linked would attract a fifty per cent hardship and rough-living clause. You'd have a bigger income than Jeffrey Archer.'

Some of Sixsmith's truculence had vanished. He could see the figure on his latest syndicate demand. 'Whose authority are you quoting?'

'I'm not allowed to say.'

Greville stared blankly at the damp wall. He looked distinctly unhappy, but Reason's little picture was impressing itself on top of the one of a wet, bone-chilling, penny-pinching retirement in the Guildford hinterland with the man in the bowler hat knocking on the door asking for ever-increasing payments to jack up his Lloyd's guarantee. 'I don't know. Give me a cigarette. I think I'd better have a think about this.'

A cigarette was passed over and Reason held his lighter underneath it. Before he flicked it into life, he said, 'No thinking allowed, Greville. It's yes or nothing. Decision now.' He lit Greville's cigarette. 'Time's running out; we can't afford the luxury of a good long think. Have a go at this one. Doing this little job for us could send you out of the Business on a high, make a difference between an O and a C.'

'An "O" and a "C"? What the bloody hell are you talking about?'

Reason puffed out a thin jet of smoke and tried to look serious. 'An OBE, Greville. Yours by right, but it could be upped to a CBE, and who knows, I have heard talk of a possible K in the offing if the book has a happy ending.'

Greville liked the sound of this. But he didn't show it. 'I'll ring you from home tomorrow.'

'No, don't do that, you might be being looked at.'

'D'you know something I don't?'

Reason's grin reappeared easily and he gave a slight shake of the head as if the question didn't deserve a proper answer.

'It's the times we live in, Greville. Nobody's immune from the big eye nowadays.' He stopped smiling and scribbled a number on a piece of paper. 'Ring me from your club, about half-past eight tomorrow night. I'll be at that number. All you have to say is yes or no and I'll pass the word to God.'

Greville turned and looked Reason in the face. He didn't like what he'd just heard, but slotted it away for later. 'I don't trust you, Reason. I don't bloody trust you at all.'

Reason smiled condescendingly.

Sixsmith's drooping lips tightened and clamped together, but the thought of the lifeline Reason had offered him prised them apart again. 'Let's assume,' he said, his lips parting like those of a ventriloquist's dummy, 'let's assume I've heard what you're saying. No commitment, no obligation, but if – and a very tentative if it is – I agree to consider this crazy idea, I'll want a lot more assurance than you're programmed to give. I'm not going down the lane with my fly buttons open, not for you or anybody else, without knowing everything's covered – double cover. I'd want assurance, foolproof cover – say a letter in the PM's safe showing whose side I'm on – and in addition to the pension and those other clauses you mentioned, an irreversible yearly bonus structure for life that goes up fifty per cent every time the Chancellor takes a crap.'

'It'll all be taken care of.' Reason touched Greville's knee by way of reassurance and stepped out of the car. 'Half-past eight,' he repeated. 'I'll be waiting. Be good!' The door closed with a solid clunk.

Reason didn't hang about. He strolled casually up the ramp towards the narrow door marked *Exit To Cavendish Square North*, and pushed it open.

When he reached the surface he strolled across the square and sat down beside Harry Barlow on one of the seats overlooking the car exit channel. Barlow acknowledged him with a quick glance but said nothing until Sixsmith's Jaguar had crawled up the ramp and joined the rest of the traffic moving round the square. He watched it disappear, then stood up.

At half an inch under six feet, Harry Barlow was not a tall man but he had broad, straight shoulders and a springiness about him that indicated a man who, despite his forty-four years, hadn't yet let go. He looked what he was: hard and fit, the legacy of more than half a life spent as a soldier. A fighting soldier, Barlow had tired of regimental soldiering as quickly as the regiment had of his restlessness, and his selection into 22 SAS had been a formality. Two tours with the regiment had failed to dampen his enthusiasm. Action at Jebel, Mirbat and Northern Ireland had added to his character.

But Harry Barlow was essentially a loner. He didn't enjoy the company of other people, preferring to work things out for himself, and so it wasn't a surprise to the Hereford hierarchy when he took up a vacancy in the ultrasecret 14th Intelligence and Security Group. Lonely and solitary, his new life suited him. With nobody's back to watch but his own, undercover work in the no-man's-land of the Irish Republic's border areas brought him most satisfaction. It was here that he had met up with the man standing beside him and formed the only real friendship of his life. It was with Reason that he had earned an unpublicized Military Medal during a clandestine operation on mainland Argentina during the Falklands conflict, and it was Reason who, four years later in the tap room of a Hereford pub, had persuaded him to leave the army and accept General Sanderson's invitation to join the Chelsea team. It had come at the right moment. Still suffering from a marriage that had fallen apart, he was drinking too much. And it was being noticed; he was becoming a risk. Reason had put it into perspective.

'Fuck all women,' Barlow had said.

'I agree,' replied Reason.

'And the army.'

'I agree,' said Reason. 'D'you want a job?'

'Guarding rich Arabs' wives and kids!'

'You should be so lucky, Harry.'

'Carrying diamonds in a bag strapped to my balls! More money than I can spend! I've heard it all, Clive.'

'You wouldn't have any difficulty spending what I'm offering.'

'Have another Guinness?'

'Cheers.'

It had been a move he'd never regretted and a friendship that had never faltered. Now he lit a cigarette, held the match to Reason's and said, 'Let's cut across there. Did he bite?' The deep brown eyes that met Reason's matched his hair, which was thick and slightly unruly;

there wasn't a comb stuck in any of his pockets, and the nearest his hair would get to a grooming after its initial morning brushing would be an unconscious flattening with his hand. The eyes were the dominant feature of his face. They were not smiling eyes, nor were they cold; they didn't believe an awful lot of what they saw, and neither did they betray what was going on behind them.

Without moving the cigarette from his mouth, Reason shook his head. 'No. He's thinking about it. He'll play a cagey game. I reckon he'll say no for openers, then reluctantly cave in when the ante goes up.'

Barlow picked up the step as they walked through the square towards Oxford Street. He didn't look at Reason. 'I think we'd better lay down a little bit of insurance, just in case he does get skittish. I think he's got to be our man. He's tailor-made for the job. Let's promise him the earth – but first get the bugger out to Oz.'

'This insurance?' queried Reason.

'Leave it up to me, Clive. When I've finished with him our offer'll be irrefusable.'

'Is there such a word?'

At twenty to nine the next evening Reason's phone rang. It was Greville Sixsmith. There were no preliminaries.

Sixsmith said: 'I've thought about it. Nothing doing,' and put the phone down. Reason kept the receiver in his hand, stuck his finger on the lugs, waited for the dialling tone and then punched out seven digits.

'It seems he wants to see our hand, Harry.'

'OK,' replied Barlow. 'If that's what he wants, I'm game. We'll do it the hard way.'

In the dark, curtained room the telephone sounded like a full West Indian metal band, but the man squatting on the floor, surrounded by record sleeves, paid no attention.

It stopped after four rings.

Unhurriedly, he gathered some LPs together and stacked them neatly on the shelf alongside another enormous pile. It was obvious that Sixsmith had not caught up with the CD craze. There must have been a couple of hundred records altogether, mostly classical, but otherwise a disorganized, catholic collection. However, it wasn't the contents of the sleeves that interested the man in the dark room. He ran his fingers along the edges, straightening into line the odd protruding cover, then stepped back and shone his torch, its beam diffused by his hand, up and down the shelf until he was satisfied he'd returned the records he'd displaced to their original order. The phone rang again. This time he picked up the receiver and listened.

'He's on his way,' said a voice. 'You've got about two minutes.'

Without replying, the man in the room replaced the receiver, moved silently into the hall and, still guided by the diffused beam of his torch, made his way down the corridor and into the kitchen. The back door was closed but not locked. He stepped outside, pulled the door on to its Yale and locked it. He was just in time.

A lamp came on in the hall and corridor, then in the kitchen. The ice-white fluorescent light scythed through the window and flooded the patio and the small back garden, making the tall cypresses that lined the wall separating the house from its neighbour cast long, unmoving shadows. Concealed in these shadows, the man who'd just left the house stood and watched Sixsmith pour himself a small jug of water from the tap beneath the kitchen window and then disappear into the house. He left the light on but it didn't disturb the watcher.

The watcher waited a few seconds longer in case Sixsmith decided he wanted ice with it, then pulled himself over the wall, cut across the neighbour's lawn, and clambered over another wall that let him into a small cul-de-sac.

He brushed himself down, opened his jacket and straightened his tie before he strolled casually back to the main road. He beat a drum roll with his fingers on the roof of the Cavalier parked by the telephone box, opened the passenger door and slid in beside the driver.

'I think I can manage a pint,' he said, 'but let's get away from here in case chummy sounds the alarm.' He sounded as casual as a union man with his eye on the clock.

So did his companion.

'He won't find it, will he?'

'Not unless he fancies a Matabele war dance this time of the night! Let's get that beer.'

'I'll ring Mr Barlow while you're getting 'em in.'

'Or the other way round. Drive!'

Harry Barlow put the phone down and poured himself another whisky before returning to his armchair. No water, no ice, whisky halfway up the sides regardless of the size of the glass. Harry Barlow was a creature of habit where drink was concerned. He turned up the sound of the ten o'clock news and relaxed back in his chair, sipping from his glass as he watched and listened to Carol tell him about the country's problems. They didn't seem half so bad coming from her.

He waited until she'd finished, then went back to the telephone. He checked the extra wire that led into a small recorder beside the phone, then unscrewed the mouthpiece and inserted a thin metal baffle wafer. He was in no hurry. He moved the baffle slightly with his finger, screwed back the mouthpiece, listened to the dialling tone for a few seconds and started the recorder. He sipped more whisky from his glass as he pressed out a number.

'Greville?' he said when it answered. He could imagine his voice at Sixsmith's end of the line, muffled, but still audible.

'Who wants him?' asked Sixsmith.

'Don't ask questions,' said Barlow abruptly, 'just listen.' He didn't give Greville a chance to interrupt.

'Your name's come up on the lottery board. A team's coming to see you in the morning – half-past five. Get out while you've still got a pair of legs that work.'

'What the bloody – '

'I can't cover you any longer, Greville. You've been blown.' He listened to the shocked silence for a second and managed another gentle sip of his whisky. 'If you've got anything at home,' he continued, 'clean it and run. And Greville, I think you've got a wire too.' Without waiting for Greville's reply, Barlow replaced the receiver and went back to his place in front of the television.

Greville Sixsmith hung the receiver back on its hook on the kitchen wall and stared hard at the calendar to make sure it wasn't April the first, then shrugged his shoulders and carried his supper tray into the front room where he switched on the old but highly effective Sony record player. He removed an LP from the array on the shelf. He knew exactly where to look and after a few seconds the room was filled with the voice of Kiri Te Kanawa singing Berlioz's *Les nuits d'été*. He picked up his tray and, balancing it on his knees, began to eat. The phone call had worried him briefly, but it had done nothing to diminish his appetite. He ate greedily and untidily, as a man living alone usually does.

It was a puzzle, nothing more than that, a simple practical joke. He'd call somebody from A on Monday morning to see what they thought about it. Meanwhile, his meal was going down nicely. He had absolutely no idea what the idiot had been talking about.

41

By the time he'd finished his microwave dinner and half a bottle of Saint Emilion, Kiri was winding herself up for the finish and the phone call had vanished from Greville's mind.

Sunday morning was like any other Sunday morning, except this time it wasn't raining. It was bitterly cold, though, with an early frost still glistening on the branches of the plane tree that had been planted right outside Greville's gate by a considerate property developer in the years when property developers had needed to be considerate.

Greville had seen the car from his bedroom window. It was parked on the opposite side of the road, its windows steamed up and a gentle puff of exhaust powdery white against the chilled outside air to show that inside the vehicle the heater was doing its stuff. He was only mildly curious.

He opened his front door and reached down for the bundle of Sunday papers. As he straightened up he saw the passenger door of the car open.

Harry Barlow walked across the road and up Greville Sixsmith's short drive. Sixsmith watched him come. His face was expressionless. Nine o'clock on a Sunday morning was a funny time to come visiting. But there was something familiar about the man approaching him; familiar but vague, like a slightly out-of-focus face in a group photograph.

'Morning,' said Harry Barlow. 'I hope I'm not disturbing your Sabbath.'

Sixsmith shook his head slowly; he was still half asleep. He tucked the papers under his arm without taking his eyes off Barlow. He said nothing.

'I'm from Whitehall Court,' Barlow told him.

He didn't need to go any further. Sixsmith knew what

he meant. Whitehall Court – Ministry of Defence – MOD police. Just like the bloody Gestapo. It was a wonder he hadn't come barging in at three o'clock in the morning. He remembered the telephone call of the night before. Somebody mislaid a box of bloody paperclips? He held out his free hand, rubbing his finger and thumb together.

Barlow gave him the card he was holding and said, 'May I come in, please?'

Sixsmith barely looked at the card; instead he glanced over Barlow's shoulder at the car. The steam had been wiped from the windows and he could see three faces staring at him. He stood to one side. 'I'm just making some coffee. Would you like one?'

'Thank you.' Barlow walked into the hall and waited for Sixsmith to point him towards the kitchen. He was very much at ease. Sixsmith met his eyes briefly. He found them disconcerting. They seemed to probe, leaving him with the impression that if he wasn't guilty of something, then he jolly well ought to be. Just before he looked away, Barlow smiled. This was better; he looked human, even apologetic. Sixsmith shook off his misgivings. He'd slotted him. The MOD was full of them, career soldiers, usually ex-Parachute Regiment with an SAS attachment before graduation, now hard front men. A bit more intelligent than the average street bobby, but nothing more than glorified coppers.

More relaxed, he squeezed past his guest and nodded towards the kitchen.

'We'll go in there, it's warmer. What can I do for you,' he glanced down at the card in his hand again, 'Mr Barlow?'

Barlow followed him into the kitchen and waited while Sixsmith poured half a bottle of milk into a saucepan, and stood it on the stove with the coffee-maker. Barlow wasn't given the chance to answer Sixsmith's query. Sixsmith turned to face him.

'Seems a strange thing to do, send you out on a Sunday morning. Couldn't it have waited until Monday?'

Barlow put his hands in his overcoat pockets and smiled faintly again.

'We've lost something at home,' he said casually and glanced at the hob to make sure the milk wasn't boiling over. 'This morning seemed as good a time as any to start looking for it.'

Sixsmith followed his glance. 'And you think I might be able to point you in the right direction?'

'Better than that,' said Barlow. 'I think I'm already in the right direction. I was thinking of starting right here – in your house.' He jerked his chin at the stove. 'Your milk's about to boil over.'

Sixsmith hurriedly reached behind him and removed the saucepan from the ring. He didn't take his eyes from Barlow's face.

'I hope you're not suggesting what I think you're suggesting?' He stared coldly at Barlow.

Barlow again allowed a slight movement of his lips. But this time it didn't reach the smile stage. He made no reply.

Sixsmith continued to stare. The only sound in the kitchen was the lid of the coffeepot jumping up and down with agitation. After a few seconds he gave in.

'Hmmm!' His pursed lips tightened into a thin straight line as he moved around the kitchen table to the telephone on the wall. 'I think I'd better have a word with Sir Hugh Collier. MOD police, you said you were?'

Barlow shook his head. 'No, I didn't actually, but as you ask, it's C.'

'C? Our C? MI5 C?'

'That's right,' lied Barlow.

A brief flash of uncertainty clouded Sixsmith's eyes; uncertainty mixed with wariness. 'I've never heard your name mentioned in connection with C Branch. Barlow, you say?'

Barlow nodded. 'I'm at Oakley Street. Sir Hugh'll confirm that when you phone him.' He reached into an inside pocket and brought out a folded sheet of paper. 'He told me to tell you that when he issued this authorization to commence surveillance on you.' He dropped the paper on the kitchen table and slid it across so that Sixsmith could reach it, then put his hands back in his pockets and raised his eyebrows.

'Surveillance?' Sixsmith dropped his hand away from the phone as if it were live. 'What the bloody hell d'you mean, surveillance?' He picked up Barlow's sheet of paper and studied it, his backside resting against the aluminium sink. As he absorbed the details his pale face went a shade paler and he suddenly looked very much his age – and very ready for retirement. 'I can't for one minute imagine what it is you're looking for.' He spoke gruffly to the sheet of paper, as if his advice on its contents were being sought. 'Or why on earth you've chosen me. Look at my record,' he said harshly. 'Thirty-six years and I've never been known to take even a dried-out biro from the building, let alone something that would interest you.' He looked up from the paper and met Barlow's eyes. 'You didn't say what it was you'd lost.'

Barlow made no reply.

'There's no need to play bloody games with me, Barlow, we're in the same business. What is it you're looking for?'

Barlow studied Sixsmith's face for a moment as if mentally debating whether to let him into the secret, then softened his expression. 'Anything that will substantiate Mr Hamed al Jaburi's allegations that you have done business with Iraq's Al Mukhabarat and are on the list as having supplied them with information, for money, about British Air Force dispositions in and around the Gulf, and that you are controlled from Baghdad by General Khalil al Azzawi himself – '

'What utter rubbish!'

'Our masters don't think so.' Barlow looked almost apologetic.

'I didn't mean that,' said Sixsmith quickly, then frowned his bushy eyebrows together and jerked his head aggressively towards Barlow's. 'Who's this al Jaburi and what's he got in his pocket to bring you sniffing around?'

'I'm surprised you're not up to date with events, Mr Sixsmith,' said Barlow politely. 'Mr Hamed al Jaburi was Iraqi Ambassador to Tunis before he defected to London. He was also concerned with Western intelligence generally and British intelligence in particular. He and an associate arrived seeking political asylum last August. He brought with him a list of people in British administrative circles, some more prominent than others' – Barlow raised his eyebrows slightly to indicate that Sixsmith came into the second category – 'who have been, and some of whom still are, sympathetically inclined towards Iraq's Gulf aspirations. In other words, a list of people in places that matter who are receiving payment for information of a military nature, who are easing access to supply channels for prohibited weaponry, and who are diverting goods and falsifying documents to obtain access to these channels. I think that's enough to be going on with, except to add, of course, that your name was on that list as one in a more sensitive area. But you're not the only one getting a visit this morning.'

Sixsmith was stunned into silence. His mind raced. There was something very wrong about all this. His voice dried up. 'It's just not possible,' he began, then stopped in mid-speech. The enormity of the possibility that he was being lowered on to the rack suddenly hit him.

'Then you won't mind my people coming in and moving the odd stick of furniture around?' Barlow was saying.

'I beg your pardon?' Sixsmith was still in shock.

'We'd like to look your place over,' repeated Barlow patiently. 'I've brought a couple of fellows with me: they're sitting outside in the car. But don't worry,' he added considerately, 'they're house-trained. They won't break anything!' He didn't wait for Sixsmith's response. He left the kitchen, walked along the narrow corridor, opened the front door and waggled his fingers at the once again steamed-up windows of the car.

Three men got out and came across the road. Two of them stepped past Barlow and waited in the hall. They looked about them like an engaged couple inspecting the house for purchase, only they didn't seem shy. Sixsmith came to the kitchen door and watched. He'd forgotten about the coffee and tried a nonchalant lean against the doorframe. It didn't impress the men in the hall. They could smell fear a mile away.

Barlow told the two to wait and took the third man into the kitchen with him. Sixsmith followed and took up his place by the sink.

'This is Mr Royle.' Barlow introduced the tall, sombre-looking man standing beside him. 'He's come to see that things are done properly; to make sure we civil servants don't overstep the mark.'

Sixsmith didn't offer to shake hands. Royle nodded, leaving all the talking to Barlow. But Sixsmith had a question.

'What department's he from?' he demanded. He was almost entering into the spirit of things.

Special Branch,' replied Barlow, with a sideways glance at Royle. 'A detective sergeant with powers of arrest and all that sort of thing. D'you want to see any warrants?'

Sixsmith pulled a face. 'You've got a search warrant?' he asked Royle. He looked almost incredulous. The strange telephone call was coming home to roost. Barlow he understood, but Special Branch was another animal. Barlow must feel on solid ground, bringing a Special Branch sergeant along. Jesus Christ! Barlow was going to have him arrested! Royle was nodding. The bastard probably had an arrest warrant as well. Sixsmith found his voice. 'Where d'you want to start?'

'You don't want to say anything before we do?' asked Barlow.

'You're making a mistake.'

Barlow almost smiled again. Royle kept a straight face. That's how he'd got to detective sergeant, by not laughing at senior civil servants' silly remarks.

'Can we go into your drawing room?'

'I'd rather stay here. I haven't had my breakfast yet.'

Barlow didn't agree. 'Bring your coffee with you, toast as well if you like. But I'm afraid you've got to be with us. You might accuse us of doing all sorts of strange things behind your back.'

'Like what?'

'Planting.'

'Huh!' snorted Sixsmith. Even he knew that if there was to be any planting, it had already been done. He knew the form; he'd been doing more than sucking boiled sweets for the past thirty-six years. 'Righto! Let's go and see what's been hidden in my drawing room, then.'

Barlow and Royle followed him down the corridor. The two men waiting in the hall joined the procession, but once inside the room they separated, one taking the bookcase while the other went to work on the reproduction Georgian mahogany bureau in the corner. Neither man gave the record library a glance.

They worked silently and efficiently. All books were removed, opened, the leaves riffled through, and then tidily replaced. The bureau was literally taken apart, even down to its secret drawer. The man searching it raised his eyebrows at Barlow, who shrugged. Sixsmith caught Barlow's eye and pulled a face again.

'I didn't know it had one,' he told the man searching it. 'Anything exciting in it?'

The man didn't answer. He looked at Barlow, shook his head and clicked the drawer back into place. He glanced through all Sixsmith's papers but read none of them. He gave the impression that he knew exactly what he was looking for. When he'd finished with the desk he peered behind Sixsmith's Impressionist prints and checked the backing nails on their expensive frames. He smiled gently to himself as he realigned the last one, admiring it for a few seconds, then turned away and stared around the room again. His eyes focused on the elderly record player.

He walked across the room towards it, looked closely but didn't touch. Then his eyes moved fractionally to his right and he studied the serried ranks of LPs.

'I'm afraid I'm going to have to go through all these,' he said to no one in particular. Nobody answered him. 'I'll try not to finger them.' He sounded as if he had teenage children. He picked them out one by one, weighed them, felt them and every so often slid the record out and peered into the sleeve. He was a quarter of the way along the shelf when he pulled out one with a picture of a long row of Africans in tribal dress disappearing into the distance into a huge, red, setting sun. it read: 'Tribal Drums and Dancing Music of the Matabele'.

He frowned at the picture, weighed the cover in one hand, then pursed his lips. Making sure everybody in the room was watching, he pressed both ends of the opening together and peered inside. He didn't put his hand in. Raising his eyebrows, he looked up at Barlow and after a brief nod handed him the record.

Barlow did the same thing and handed it to Royle. It

looked like a relay race where all the participants were standing still. All except Greville Sixsmith. He was changing feet and expressions. At the moment when Royle spoke he had reached incredulity.

'You are not obliged to say anything,' began Royle.

'Don't come that bloody crap with me!' spat Sixsmith. 'Whatever it is you've got in there is bugger all to do with me. Ask him.' He stared at Barlow. 'It's a put-up. It's some sort of bloody joke! Go on, tell him.' His conversation with Clive Reason in the car park hit him between the eyes. The bastards were spreading him on the bed and prising his legs apart without even giving him a chance to bargain.

'But anything you say,' continued Royle, unabashed, 'will be taken down and may be used in – '

'OK!' Sixsmith's throat had dried up again, leaving him slightly hoarse; his face had gone pale as well, paler than usual. 'OK,' he repeated, 'leave all that for the moment. Let me have a word with this bastard – in private.'

Royle stared at him for a second, then glanced sideways at Barlow. Barlow nodded almost imperceptibly, including the searchers in the gesture.

'There's some coffee on the hob, Tim. I'm sure Mr Sixsmith won't mind, will you, Mr Sixsmith?' He looked quite serious. Sixsmith didn't reply. He had other things on his mind.

When they were alone, Sixsmith said, 'Do you know a big black bastard named Reason?'

Barlow didn't answer. He didn't look up. He was examining the wad of paper he'd removed from the record sleeve.

'How did you get hold of this?' he asked innocently. 'There should only be seven copies. This one makes eight. Your DG gets one. That's the nearest you should get to it.'

'Can we drop the play-acting, Barlow? What is it you want?'

Barlow wasn't finished. 'You know what the policeman said – you've a right to remain silent, et cetera.'

'Piss off!'

Barlow didn't react. He smiled sadly and stared for a moment at Sixsmith's record player. 'Does that thing have a gadget for playing cassettes?'

'What's that got to do with it?'

'Be patient.' Barlow put his hand in his overcoat pocket and brought out a C60 cassette. 'Play it.' He tossed the tape on to the settee.

'What is it?' asked Sixsmith suspiciously, although he had a good idea.

'Play it,' repeated Barlow. He lowered his backside on to the arm of the settee and put his hands in his pockets, looking as if he was about to enjoy thirty minutes of good music.

The tape didn't last that long. Sixsmith listened with mounting agitation to the strange conversation he'd had with the unknown voice on the telephone the night before. 'I know nothing about any of this,' he said. The slightly higher pitch of his voice betrayed the outward calm he was trying to project. 'I'm denying everything. I don't know who was on the phone, and those bloody papers were planted – '

'There is another matter,' said Barlow casually. He sounded to Sixsmith like a dentist who, having attended to two nasty cavities, had found one more on the other side.

'What's that?' Greville knew he shouldn't have asked. But it was too late now.

'Tracy Martin.'

Sixsmith's eyes narrowed.

'Karen Dobson. D'you want any more?'

'I don't know what you're talking about. Who are these people?'

'Girls, Mr Sixsmith,' replied Barlow. 'Little girls. Underage. One is twelve, the other fourteen. We have pictures and all sorts of things. In the eyes of a serious family judge, paedophilia is a far greater crime than pinching the family jewels . . . Puts espionage in the shade, too. Shall I go on?'

Greville's bottom lip dropped. He seemed to be having problems with his breathing and he stared with difficulty into Barlow's bland expression. 'I asked you if you knew a man called Reason . . .'

Barlow stared back for a few seconds, then nodded.

'Get hold of him,' barked Sixsmith. 'Quickly, before this bloody nonsense goes any further. He knows what the bloody hell this is all about.'

Barlow nodded again, contentedly.

'You can discuss it with him yourself. We're going to meet him shortly. In the meantime, I think I'd better call Sergeant Royle back in so that he can arrest you properly. I think at this stage you'd better consider all the angles and start working on some form of explanation. You don't need me to tell you of the seriousness of espionage. Blake got thirty years. I forget how much Vassel got, but neither of them was half as high up the sticky pole as you are. I'd work on about thirty for that one if I were you, and then add on the little-girl business. You know, of course, how your fellow prisoners react to child molesters and their like?'

Sixsmith didn't waste time thinking about it.

'What d'you want from me, Barlow?'

Barlow smiled genuinely. 'I want to see you receive that nice big fat pension you so richly deserve, and to come and pay little visits to you in your nice house by the billabong in happy, sunny Australia.'

'Are you Reason's bum-boy?'

'We sometimes have a drink together. Why don't we make it a threesome and try and sort out this little peccadillo of yours? We could probably hush up some of it . . .'

'Come off it! You two bastards have set me up on this Iraq nonsense – and this bloody kid thing. I'm not saying anything about that until I see something, so you can get stuffed on that one!'

'We could produce those two little girls themselves, if you like – in front of a magistrate tomorrow morning. How would that suit you?'

'Bugger you! OK. Get rid of that copper in there and send your men home. We can sort this out between us. But tell me who's in charge of this.'

Barlow made no reply.

'Sanderson?' hazarded Sixsmith after a suitable pause. Then, 'If it's not him it must be Hughie Collier – the underhand bastard!'

Barlow smiled sympathetically. 'I wouldn't bother speculating if I were you. Just read your lines and convince yourself it's all in a good cause! Can I have your passport, please?'

'What!'

'Your passport.'

'Is this a joke?'

'D'you want it done officially? Royle could come and ask you, if you prefer.'

'This is becoming ridiculous!' Sixsmith walked across to the bureau, found his passport and slapped it in Barlow's outstretched hand. Barlow put it in his pocket without inspecting it.

'We'll be in touch,' he said. 'Either Reason or I. Go to work as usual. We'll do all the organizing and arranging. Don't worry if you smell a watcher – it's all part of the script. He's there to look after you. We don't want you falling under a bus, do we?' Barlow smiled. This time it was genuine. It changed his face entirely. Thanks for your cooperation, Mr Sixsmith.'

'Piss off!'

PART TWO

3

Greville Sixsmith looked up from the keyboard of his word processor, took a heavy pull from the chunky glass of whisky and water standing in a little puddle of condensation on the table beside him, and stared out of the window.

Below him – three storeys below – Melbourne's Yarra River flowed upside down towards the bay, But Greville wasn't interested in the Yarra, or where it was going; he was interested in Greville Sixsmith and where Greville Sixsmith was going. A whole month – it seemed like nine – he'd been looking out of this bloody window at the view, and the scenery, the sky full of puffy clouds of unpredictable Melbourne weather, and above all the bloody ever-moving khaki-coloured river, had lost their appeal.

Not for the first time the thought crossed his mind that he might have been better off taking his chance in London, calling Barlow's, and that cunning bastard Reason's, bluff and screaming, 'I've been bloody set up! The fuckers have framed me!' But the thought brought no relief; just a tightening of the scrotum at what might have happened if he'd done just that. Sanderson's people didn't play at playing the bastard. They'd cooked him both sides – beautifully done. Sanderson had had it all worked out, and so had his bloody scavengers Barlow and Reason; they both knew how English judges enjoy a treason trial, not to mention the other bloody thing they'd thrown on the table. He wouldn't have stood a chance; he'd have gone sliding down the chute and the next poor bastard in line would have been pegged out for the same treatment. But the money helped.

Greville refilled his glass. He knew he was drinking too much, but so what! He drank half the glass in one go to prove he didn't care and gazed at the rubbish he'd just typed. What a bloody life! 'Write a book,' Barlow had said. Just like that. 'You might have a hidden talent, you could enjoy it.' Some bloody chance! 'Learn to type, it could help you in a new career when this one's finished . . .' A joke? Or being kind? You couldn't tell with Barlow. Well, this bloody rubbish would tell whether or not he had a sense of humour. One thing was sure: he had no latent talent for writing. And he wasn't enjoying it either! Greville replaced his empty glass in its puddle and dragged his eyes away from the window. Spreading his fingers across the keyboard, he wondered whether bursting into tears would do any good.

From the window of his office in the plain, featureless building on the corner of Russell and Kelliher Drives in Canberra that housed the Australian intelligence organization ASIO, Heros Dubrovnik could, if he wanted, gaze out on one of the best views in the Territory. But it was wasted. Heros Dubrovnik wasn't interested in views; he wasn't interested in gazing out of windows. From his drab, functional office, Dubrovnik was interested only in the security and wellbeing of Australia.

Heros Dubrovnik – jet-black hair, bushy eyebrows that threatened to drop over his eyes like an Old English sheepdog's, and a firm, granite-like chin with a five o'clock shadow that appeared five minutes after his first shave of the day – had been an Australian since 1947.

Before that he'd been a Yugoslav named Izetzelbegovič; his father had changed it to Dubrovnik as being shorter, easier for the Australian tongue to wrap around, and it reminded him where he'd come from. Heros Dubrovnik was Director of Room 24, Australian Security and Intelligence Organization.

Room 24 was a small but select branch of the department that included in its mandate responsibility for special cases of immigration. Dubrovnik's particular paid fetish was foreign intelligence personnel infiltrated into Australia under the guise of immigrants, and, worse, people from Western Europe in general, and England in particular, with money to settle and permission to lead the life of Riley without obligation. Dubrovnik very often gave of his own time, he was that keen on his job. He was doing that now.

He played a drum roll with his stubby fingers on the buff-coloured file he'd just finished reading and looked up at the man sitting, one leg crossed over the other, in the only comfortable chair in the office. Dubrovnik's bushy eyebrows made him appear to be frowning angrily. His companion knew better.

'Who told you about this guy?' asked Dubrovnik.

'The name rang a bell.' Toby Grant was the complete opposite of the Yugoslav. Young, tall, short-cut blond hair, very fit, a typical Australian. He could have been a lifeguard at Bondi. 'Three years ago I did a sundowner with MI6 in London. When they got to know me they sent me with one of their operatives to Singapore on a slightly damp job.'

Dubrovnik raised one of his eyebrows. 'You mean wet, don't you? *Dela Mokri?*' He savoured the Russian vowels like a man reviving the forgotten taste of a childhood delicacy. It was only a murmur, but it travelled across the table.

'Pardon?'

'Means a "wet job". Russian. *Dela Mokri* means kill. What d'you mean by "damp"?'

'No kill. We dropped the subject in the shit with Malaysian SB. They found a plastic bag with half a kilo of heroin in his luggage. In KL that's like having an iron bar shoved up your arse until it comes out of your ear – it's one way, you can't go back.'

'Brits arranged that, did they?'

'Yeh. I don't think I'm capable of thinking along those lines.'

'OK.' Dubrovnik yawned. He didn't put his hand over his mouth. He just opened it and let go. 'What were you going to say about this guy Sixsmith?'

'It was the name. The exec officer who steered us on the Singapore run was named Sixsmith. The name seemed to go with the job, so it stuck.'

'Why?'

'MI6.' Grant allowed a smile to curl his lips. 'Six times Smith running a "Six" operation!'

Dubrovnik didn't smile. 'So, a guy named Sixsmith rents a pad in Melbourne and you open a file?'

'Not quite. I rang up a friend.'

Dubrovnik opened the file again and lowered his eyebrows over it. 'A friend in British intelligence?'

Grant ignored the question. 'He said Greville Sixsmith went full term with MI6, latterly chairing the joint MI5/MI6 coordination committee, and retired on full pension with a sackful of gold nuggets for honest service and a CBE for keeping his nose clean when all about him were losing theirs, etcetera! He was a Philby boy but didn't get splashed,' he explained to Dubrovnik's frown. 'All a long time ago. More recently, he got bored digging flowerbeds in his back garden and applied for residential status here.'

'Anybody help him?'

'What d'you mean?'

'Anybody from Pommy intelligence pull strings?'

'No, he did it all on his own. Strolled down the Strand, chatted to the girl at the desk, got all the forms and brochures, checked the rainfall and sunshine graphs – and opted for Melbourne, silly bugger!'

'What's the name of this friend of yours?'

'Which one?'

'You've got more than one friend?'

It was Toby Grant's turn to raise his eyebrows. He meant well. 'I didn't think people of your race had a sense of humour!'

Dubrovnik's eyes flashed. 'Watch it, Grant. That sounds like Pommy talk! What's the name of this friend of yours?'

Toby Grant let his face go blank. 'Why d'you want to know?'

Dubrovnik's moment of Balkan passion had passed. He was an Australian again. 'I want to know because I don't like the sound of British intelligence people shooting their mouths off. So, tell me again, what's your Pommy friend's name?'

'Reason,' replied Grant. 'He's the fellow I went to Kuala Lumpur with. He's middling to high in the Business, neither Five nor Six, but known to run the ball for both. He's a hard bastard, but straight.'

'Doesn't sound like your average Pom.'

Toby Grant pulled a face. He wasn't quite so biased. 'He doesn't look like one either.'

'What's different about this guy?'

'He's black.'

'Jesus Christ! A black Pommy spy! Whatever next?' Dubrovnik had his moment of amusement, although it didn't show. He became serious again as he ran through the papers in Greville Sixsmith's file. 'Application for residence – approved. References, copy of birth certificate, marriage certificate . . . His wife's not with him?'

Grant jerked his chin at the file. 'Divorce papers further down. He was the innocent one. She ran off with the milkman.'

Dubrovnik's eyebrows shot up in surprise.

Grant smiled. 'Not quite the milkman. Someone a bit lower down the British social scale, a politician of some sort.'

'Any children?'

'A daughter, aged about thirty-two, thirty-three. He hasn't seen her for years. That's what it says in the Australia House comment . . . ' He pointed his chin again at the file. 'At the back, attached to the divorce report.'

'It says here,' said Dubrovnik, without raising his head from the open file, 'that he's an ex-civil servant.'

'That's right. They don't call them spies or spycatchers any more. Peter Wright put paid to that as a job description.'

But Dubrovnik seemed to have lost interest in that subject. He closed the file and looked up at Toby Grant, 'We're talking here about a British nobody who can pay his way and is taking up room that an Australian can't afford. I don't even know him and already I don't like the bastard.' Dubrovnik wasn't being facetious, nor had he forgotten his own origins; he just had a pathological dislike of the English. Still, he was an Australian now and you had to be fair. 'But all you've got here is a guy who you think – only think, mind you – used to work in a swivel chair in London in some sort of intelligence capacity and is now living in Melbourne. So what? Is there some new and just legislation that's slipped through Canberra without my hearing about it?'

'What d'you mean?' asked Toby Grant. He was quite

used to Dubrovnik's anti-English outbursts; they went straight over his head. He had no hang-ups. You either liked the Poms or you didn't. Dubrovnik didn't; he did. So what?

Dubrovnik bared his teeth. 'That we're now kicking the Brit's arse out of the country just because he's a Brit.' His mouth closed on the suggestion of a smile. It was a pity the world wasn't a perfect one! 'Because that's what you're implying here. There's bugger all else to justify a file, and nothing to warrant a better look at the guy.'

'Didn't I mention that there's a word processor on the go in his front room?'

'I won't ask you how you came by that bit of useless information, but so what? He's writing a book.'

'So did Peter Wright, and look at the kerfuffle that caused.'

Dubrovnik's glee shone briefly through his antagonism. He didn't say anything. He merely nodded his head.

'My MI5 contact,' continued Grant, 'tells me that there was a full JIC meeting in London recently and it was attended by our own dear and beloved Director-General. Amongst other things they discussed were British ex-intelligence officers publishing embarrassing memoirs during overseas retirement. Our D-G agreed this wasn't on. That's why I opened a file on this Sixsmith character.'

Dubrovnik's moment of happiness passed from his face like a rain-cloud over the parched outback. His eyebrows almost joined up over his nose like an overlarge, elongated caterpillar as he stared unblinkingly into Toby Grant's eyes.

'I hope I'm not hearing what I think I'm hearing,' he rasped ominously.

'What's that?'

Dubrovnik waited a few seconds. 'It sounds suspiciously to me like you're acting under the instructions of British intelligence. Tell me I'm wrong.'

'You're wrong,' responded Grant. 'My instructions came from Arthur Gunne – the Director-General himself. I happened to be standing next to him at a little booze-up the other evening and we talked. This came up in the conversation and he seemed interested. He asked me to have a look at Sixsmith and take my findings, and conclusions, to the head of Two-Four. He said "findings and conclusions" – not recommendations. They were to be left to you.' Grant kept his expression neutral. He knew all about Slavs who reckoned people were going over the top of them. 'And before you karate-chop your desk to death and kick the wall in, what the D-G suggested was within my mandate – it didn't need divisional clearance. But this does and it's all yours. If you want, I can pursue the matter further myself, or I can wait until you've made your assessment to the D-G. D'you mind if I smoke?'

Grant's casual request took Dubrovnik by surprise. He almost shook his head out of habit. A nonsmoker for two weeks, he was struggling, but, like a newly anointed Roman Catholic, he'd embraced his new status with fanaticism, and nobody with any sense lit a fag within a hundred yards of him. But his mind wasn't on it. He was still working out the political ramifications of the Director-General's involvement. It didn't take long. Arthur Gunne was a smooth bastard, but he was no bloody Pommophile; if he wanted a closer look at Sixsmith, then it wasn't going to be Heros Dubrovnik who frustrated that desire. But what about Grant here? Maybe he was on the side of the Brits – maybe they'd bought him! He'd let the thing run while he thought about it ... The rasp of Grant's match brought him out of his reverie.

'Leave this with me,' he said and flipped the file shut. 'Who've we got in Melbourne at the moment?'

'Sophie Ward.'

'How well d'you know her?'

Grant shrugged. Sophie Ward was not one of the boys. She wasn't one of the girls either; she was Business woman and good at her job. Attractive – very attractive – but it didn't mean a thing, and he should know. Nobody had tried harder to get Sophie Ward into bed. Either she'd got something very serious going on, or she didn't do it at all. Her job was to run Dubrovnik's Melbourne Station, and that she did better than anyone else. She wouldn't be there otherwise. That was his assessment.

'Does it matter?'

Dubrovnik lowered his eyebrows and stared hard at Grant. 'It does to you. Go to Melbourne and work something out with her. Apart from what this Sixsmith's writing about, I want to know who his friends are, who he meets, where he meets – you know the sort of thing. Above all, I want the names and business of any Poms who come to see him.' He picked up a blue Biro and tested its strength with his teeth; it helped the thought process. It didn't bend or snap. He held it at eye level and studied it. 'Particularly any of those shifty buggers you met in Curzon Street.' He dropped the pen on the desk. 'Know what I mean?'

'Yes, but what do *you* think he's up to?'

Dubrovnik thought about it. Nothing came. But there had to be something very fishy, and one thing he could do without was a Pommy intelligence-gathering in Melbourne, for whatever reason. 'I don't think anything – at the moment.'

Grant shrugged again. Dubrovnik hadn't finished.

'You can start now by passing Sophie Ward the word to keep her ears and eyes open for any activity around this guy's flat, but not to go mad about it.'

'A watcher?'

'Not even. Just ask the local police to report anything that happens with the name Sixsmith attached to it.'

Dubrovnik leant back in his chair. It was the end of the interview. 'Personally, I reckon it'll die a death. I think you're overreacting. But we won't throw it in the basket just yet. OK?'

Toby Grant stood up. 'What do I tell the D-G if he asks for a progress report?'

'He'll ask me, not you, and I'll tell him what I've just told you – no immediate action necessary, the file's on the hook, it's available if anybody wants to make anything out of it.'

'And if anything comes up?'

'Clear it with me.'

4

'I've managed to get Greville Sixsmith's name bubbling gently in the right places in Canberra,' said General Sanderson to Clive Reason, 'but Arthur Gunne wants to know what ASIO has to gain from this thing you've started.'

'Nothing,' replied Reason, then, after a pause: 'What did you tell him?'

Sanderson didn't turn his head. He seemed to be concentrating on a difficult job at hand. 'How much tonic d'you want in this?'

'Right to the top, please.'

Sanderson finished pouring Reason's gin and tonic, gave himself a weak whisky and water and placed both glasses on the marble-topped coffee table between them. 'I told him that Australia – Melbourne in particular – was riddled with dormant PIRA cells and that when they've finished with us in Ireland they were going to turn their attentions to a bit of political argy-bargy in the Lucky Country. I quoted captured PIRA documents. I didn't realize there are almost as many Irishmen in Australia as in both Irelands – Australian nationals as well as runaways and shell-shocked Republicans. Did you?'

Reason didn't consider the question. 'Did he believe you?'

Sanderson shrugged. 'I doubt it. Arthur's no bloody fool, but he did agree a tacit cooperation, and I did get a little sparkle of interest when I mentioned that there was strong evidence linking the IRA with some of the major drug people. He positively shivered when I suggested that they had the guns, the organization and the lack of scruples to become the major force in the worldwide drug organization and distribution business, and nowadays Australia wasn't all that far away.'

Reason grinned humourlessly. 'Me too. But I'm not sure it's the same sort of shiver that set Arthur's belly wobbling. Imagine it, an army of middle-aged Colombian gentlemen, Pakistani middlemen, Mafia godfathers and Burmese generals all stumbling around on shattered knee-caps because they'd upset the Mickies!'

Sanderson didn't find it funny. He sipped his drink reflectively. 'By the way, I've had a few unofficial feelers put out. Our friends at Langley, quoting a DEA report about IRA stock in Libya, assess that this New Executive now has enough narcotic collateral to bid for half-a-dozen Russian nuclear trigger mechanisms. It's worse than I thought. They've even got the wherewithal for an unsophisticated nuclear device, should one come on to the market.' He returned the glass to the table. 'Not nice, is it?' He stared into Reason's dark eyes for a moment. 'Why don't you look worried?'

Reason shook his head. 'There aren't half a dozen on the market. The hole's been closed. Yeltsin's people suddenly woke up and moved in before the market became blatant. The latest Russian security-police assessment is that four devices got out and of those four, we think we know where one went, don't we? The other three they're still working on. Apparently the guy running the market got himself killed in the roundup. It could have been an accident or deliberate, but he was the only one in the ring who met the buyers. Other than our friends in Dublin, we have a choice of Iraq, China, Pakistan, South Africa, and anybody else who's dabbling in big bangs. But that's a universal problem, not ours. No, the thing worrying me is the thought that one of the four could be sitting in a cupboard in a house at the end of the road with its timer set for sometime in March. But that, Richard, is too far away for the worry to show. Try me again on St Patrick's Day!'

Sanderson stared at him for a moment, then washed his mouth out with a large swig from his glass. He swirled it around, swallowed and said, with a grimace, 'It looks to me as if we're on a hiding to nothing. Even if this thing of yours works and your man moves on to the Executive, there's no certainty that he'll be part of the committee dealing with the British mainland, and there's no certainty that they'll swallow this spycatcher thing. The only bloody certainty is that we're running out of time – and you're not worried!.

There was still no reaction from Reason; he'd heard it all before. At gutter level things were never quite so passionate. He stared into his gin and tonic, studying the bubbles on the segment of lemon. Without looking up he said: 'Did you tell Arthur Gunne any of that?'

'Of course not. But I did suggest that as PIRA had all the help they could use from America, Australia could start making life a little more difficult for the sizable contingent of supporters they've got there. I suggested there might be a welcome for a few dozen highly trained ex-PIRA gangsters in his highly liberal society when they run out of opportunity in Northern Ireland . . .'

'Not a whisper about infiltration and New Executives?'

'Don't take me for a bloody idiot, Clive.'

Reason took the rebuke in his stride. He lit a cigarette and blew out smoke with a whoosh. He wondered what sort of picture Arthur Gunne would treasure after his recent conducted tour of the backstreets of West Belfast, which had ended with an over-the-wall glance at the shiny black headstones in Milltown cemetery. Melbourne would never look the same to him again. But serve the buggers right! 'And you got around to Sixsmith?'

Sanderson smiled coldly. 'Oh yes. I hit him while he was still groggy. I told him that the Sixsmith agenda was as much in his interest as ours.'

'But you didn't go beyond that?' insisted Reason.

'No. He suggested that things be allowed to unfold naturally, and that when things got going he would tell his side to cooperate with us.'

'Looks like I've beaten him to it,' interrupted Reason. 'I've already done a bit of whispering myself. There's a fellow named Grant – ASIO – who's going to take up baby-sitting duties outside Sixsmith's flat in Melbourne. He's pure. He thinks Sixy's a man from our lot who might want to do another *Spycatcher*. I suggested that Sixy was at one time on MI6's Far East desk and was specifically involved in tracking ASIS's Burma involvement, and that his memoirs might compromise their work in this area.'

'So what's happening about these memoirs?'

'They've already been written. Harry Barlow's taking them out to him in computer-disk form. Once everything's in place we'll find him an agent, get him to drop the typescript on a publisher's desk and hope he's sufficiently patriotic to call in the ASIO gendarmerie to do a bit of censoring before taking it any further. We'll hear about all this and demand that we have a look as well – and off we go! There are plenty of sympathetic Irish ears in and around Melbourne – that's why we chose the place – and it won't take long for word to get back to Dublin that there's interesting stuff on offer in a new set of memoirs from a frustrated British MI executive. Harry and I are convinced that the Irish dimension in the memoirs will leak out once the legal people, Australian intelligence, and, of course, the publishers get their teeth into them.'

'Put that way, the more the merrier,' agreed Sanderson. 'You can't have too many cooks . . . ' He drained his glass and placed it carefully on the table; the meeting was over. In his hurry to join the General, Reason swallowed an ice cube and pulled a face as it worked its way down to his stomach. A second lump that found its way past his front teeth was ground into powder. 'Will you be going to Melbourne yourself?' Sanderson asked as he stood up.

Reason shook his head. 'I thought I'd let Harry face the first few overs. I'll go and join him when the ball's lost a bit of its shine.'

'Does Harry know who our IRA friend is, Clive?'

'No. He may have his suspicions, but that's all they are.'

'Good, keep it that way.' Sanderson continued to study Reason's face for several moments. 'I mean that, Clive.'

'I heard you, Richard.'

5

The immigration officer at Melbourne's Tullamarine Airport had completed the advance course at the government charm school. Ice-cold eyes, thin lips, no civility, he'd have done well at Auschwitz. He took his time over Harry Barlow's passport photograph. Barlow's papers were genuine. They'd decided in London that Keating's Australia was nominally, if only marginally, friendly, and that real names and numbers and scruffy, well-used navy-blue passports with the correct visas and stamps could only reassure the Australians.

The officer let him through and Barlow collected his bag and cleared customs. Strolling out of the main building, he stared up at the grey cloud swollen with warm rain that was moving in ponderously from the east.

'Mr Barlow?'

It was a softly spoken Australian voice, without menace, and its owner was a short, stockily built, grey-haired man in his early fifties wearing light cotton trousers, polished brown casuals and a blue striped shirt. He had a folded newspaper under his arm – the London *Daily Telegraph* – and he waited for Barlow's reaction with an easy expression.

'Thompson?' responded Barlow.

The man nodded. 'Here's a paper to read on the way into Melbourne.'

Barlow accepted it and glanced at the date. 'D'you know where I'm staying?'

'Yes.'

'Who told you?'

'Clive Reason.'

Barlow shook his head but didn't smile. Were they really necessary, these little charades? Who knew? It was all part of the game. Mistrust, deceit, lying and dirty habits – it was like schoolboy tricks. But the dirty habits wouldn't go away.

'Where's your car?'

The Australian jerked his head and moved off. He didn't offer to carry Barlow's bag, but instead walked briskly on with a stiff-legged gait, the metal tips of his heels going click-thump, click-thump, click-thump on the paving stones as he led Barlow out of the airport to the car park. He stopped by a dark blue taxi and lifted the boot, holding it up while Barlow threw in his soft leather holdall. He started the meter running when Barlow climbed into the passenger seat beside him and grinned sideways, 'It's my day job. Official. Sometimes I make more money driving this thing than I get from my UK "investment fund dividends". I'm thinking about asking for a rise!'

Barlow wasn't interested in MI6's rates and methods of payment. But he was interested in the Reason–Melbourne set-up.

'How many are you – Mike, isn't it? How many people has Reason got to call on here?'

Thompson glanced sideways. Questions always put a dampener on conversation – and familiarity. He gave it a second's thought, then turned his eyes back quickly to the road. 'Just me . . . ' *As far as you're concerned*, he nearly added, but held that one back. 'But if you –'

Barlow got the message. He didn't know why he'd asked in the first place. 'It's OK,' he said lightly. 'Can I call on you at any time?'

73

'Sure. That's what I'm here for. I've got a flat with spare rooms as well, but Reason thought it better you cut your own furrow than join in with me.'

Barlow smiled lightly. 'Is that Reason's phraseology?'

Thompson smiled as well. 'I believe you're here on the level. I'm permanent. He doesn't want you showing ASIO that you've got friends here. And, by the way, I don't know what sort of people you're going to be mixing with, but if you look in that little bag under your seat you'll find a Smith & Wesson and a box of .38s. It's a short barrel, no marks, no numbers, no history. Drop it in the drink if you look like running into anything official . . . Here we are, your hotel.'

He pulled into the courtyard and got out to open the boot. 'You know how to get hold of me?' he asked.

'Yes. You always available?'

'For you? Yes, but this doesn't make for long-distance running.' He tapped his leg and gave a wry smile. 'Or speed.'

Their eyes met. They both knew what it meant: Thompson's 'availability' was restricted to driving him around Melbourne.

Thompson didn't make a big deal out of it. 'A couple of .50mms. 'Nam, Phuoc Tuy sixty-eight,' he said softly. 'Two SAS, "Mike Force". Sorry, mate.' Barlow gave a perfunctory nod. There was nothing more to say about it; it was one of the hazards of the job.

'Thanks,' he said finally. 'I'll call you at that number if I want a shove.'

'No probs,' said Thompson and held out his hand. 'That'll be twenty-five dollars.'

'You joking?'

'No.'

The motel was small and discreet and the room was clean

and quiet, overlooking a green park scattered liberally with huge leafy trees. But Harry Barlow was a city boy; to him open spaces were just open spaces. He pulled the lace curtains together, showered, and stretched out on the bed. It was half-past two. He set the buzzer on his wristwatch to go off at 6pm and closed his eyes.

The gentle nagging of the alarm felt like a Chinese girl's fingers massaging the delicate skin behind his ears. But it was enough to wake him from a deep sleep. Sleeping had never been one of Harry Barlow's problems. Several generous Qantas whiskies on the aircraft and one economy-class dinner washed down with the best part of a bottle of Penfolds Bin 389 and he'd slept until the 747 thumped and squealed into Tullamarine Airport. Barlow put it all down to a clear conscience and a pure mind.

He resisted the temptation to order a pot of tea, instead poured himself a liberal dose of duty-free Teacher's, threw in a handful of iced marbles from the miniature fridge, and sipped reflectively as they melted out of sight. At half-past six he swung his legs on to the floor and, sitting on the edge of the bed, picked up the phone. It was answered immediately, as if the girl at the desk had been waiting for him. He asked her for a Canberra number and replaced the receiver. He had time to finish his drink, smoke a cigarette and pour another glassful of whisky and water before the phone sprang into life.

Toby Grant waited until Merv Hughes had sorted out his run-up before switching down the sound on the TV and reaching over his head for the telephone.

Barlow said: 'My name's Barlow. Clive Reason told me to ring you if I needed an introduction in Melbourne.'

'Are we talking about six times Smith?' asked Toby.

'Yes. Have you got anyone watching him?'

'Not seriously. One of our local people glances over his

garden wall occasionally, but there's no check on ins and outs. A computer keyboard's clicking away night and day, though.'

'How d'you know?'

'The lady who looks after our interests down there has developed a nodding acquaintance with an old boy who lives in the same block. She makes a point of having a cup of tea and a bit of toast with him every so often – that means every week on a Wednesday. Dare I ask whether you intend paying him a visit?'

Barlow made no reply. Toby Grant formed his own conclusions. 'Perhaps we could have lunch tomorrow?'

'Where?'

'I'll fly down in the morning. Go to South Yarra, the Fawkner. I'll meet you in the bar, about twelve. And Barlow . . .' Barlow raised his eyebrows. ' . . . Don't go anywhere near Sixy's place until you and I have had a look at the menu. I don't want to have to come and bail you out of Coberg prison.'

'No chance of that,' replied Barlow.

'Fawkner Club, then,' said Grant. 'See you tomorrow.'

Harry Barlow finished his second whisky, washed his face in cold water and dressed casually in a pale blue shirt, tie, and fawn cotton slacks. He picked up a plain plastic shopping bag and, with his jacket slung over his shoulder, made his way to the hotel entrance. The girl at reception looked up and smiled as he walked past. She was very pretty, very Australian; young, healthy, nice body and well groomed. But the smile was only friendly. It made him feel old.

The evening weather was developing quite nicely, although the soot-coloured cloud he'd noticed at the airport had moved six inches or so and now hovered with uncertainty over the centre of Melbourne, threatening unpleasantness. But it didn't worry Barlow; where he'd just come from it was like that all the time. Even so, the temperature was pleasant, warm with a touch of the sultry as the sun moved downwards, taking with it the threatened humidity from the overhanging blanket. He waved at a passing taxi. He was in luck. The driver was Greek and he didn't want to talk either.

Barlow paid him off on the corner of Flinders and King's Streets, and then strolled back along Flinders as far as the underpass, where he admired the buckets of flowers outside the flower shop at the entrance before walking briskly through to the river. He turned right, crossed the wooden footbridge to Southbank Promenade, past the diners and drinkers savouring the gentle evening sun, then, just before the steps to Princes Bridge, stopped and gazed over the low parapet into the Yarra's muddy depths.

Glancing out of the corner of his eye he studied the tree-lined promenade he'd just negotiated. Everything looked normal. The diners dined, the drinkers drank, and nobody stopped talking; nobody dived for cover, nobody stopped suddenly to study the light-festooned gumtrees. He felt like the unwashed swagman – all alone. Nobody was interested in him, or, by all accounts, in Sixsmith either. He straightened up and went down the circular stairway to Southgate Street, staying on the shady side of the road, then walked to the junction of St Kilda and City Roads, where he stopped suddenly, turned on his heels as if he'd forgotten something, crossed over and came back down Southgate Street to Prince Philip Mansions. He was still alone. The area was deserted except for a line of cars parked on meters on the opposite side of the street.

If Greville Sixsmith was delighted to see him he managed to conceal it.

'About bloody time!' He was into the evening session –

whisky with ginger ale and a mood of despair. He showed Barlow into the front room, where, without offering him a drink or a handshake, he lowered himself into the room's solitary comfortable armchair and stuck his feet on the window-ledge. He hunched his neck into his shoulders, sipped his drink and stared moodily through the gap in the lace curtains. 'Anything happening?' he asked, without taking his gaze from the window.

Barlow pulled up a chair, manoeuvred it with his foot until it was in line with Greville's, then lowered himself into it and, like Greville, stared at the lace curtains. He lit a cigarette, drew deeply on it, exhaled and watched the smoke disappear into the curtain. He did it again, then glanced out of the corner of his eye. 'I think so, Greville. The story is the Australians want to know what you're up to. They've looked up your dossier, didn't much fancy what they saw and marked you down as a dodgy customer. They're going to come and have a look around, probably tomorrow.'

Greville, in the middle of a large swallow from the thick glass in his hand, turned his head slowly towards Barlow. His pop-eyes blinked lugubriously as he swallowed what he had in his mouth. 'And what, precisely, do they expect to find?'

Barlow reached down into the plastic bag and brought out an HD computer diskette. 'I think they're expecting to find some closely guarded secrets.' Barlow smiled thinly. Sixsmith didn't respond. He had no sense of humour; everything to him was serious business. 'But all they're going to find is this – your memoirs,' said Barlow. 'And when they've got over the shock that SIS employ people who can write, the ball will start rolling down the hill and I can go home and enjoy the winter. As far as you're concerned, the game's just starting. You go along with events and play the thing straight.'

'I thought my part was finished when the Aussies took over. That's what you and Reason led me to understand.'

'Then you misunderstood. Read Turnbull's book on how it all happened with Peter Wright and you'll see how far you've got to go.yet. Don't worry, we'll have you out of it in a week or two.'

Sixsmith stared into Harry Barlow's even features. There was no animosity about Barlow; he was cool, calm and almost friendly. It gave Greville a nasty little chill at the base of his spine. Perhaps it would have been easier if Barlow had sniffed and snarled, but then, as he'd already found out, Barlow didn't sniff and snarl. His cool manner was worse; he made it sound as if he felt sorry for you. He shrugged. 'I could be here for years.'

'I don't think so, Greville. All you've got to think about is that you've written a book. You've nothing to hide. Your only motive is to get it published and earn some money. That's your story. Just play it out.'

Leaving him to his thoughts, Barlow walked over to the table by the other window and studied the gibberish on the computer's blue screen. He trolled down another page and shook his head sadly. Greville was never going to earn a living writing. He sat down and checked that Greville's rubbish was easily accessible. He slipped the new disk into the computer's drive and downloaded its contents into the machine's memory. That done he sat back in the chair and stared at the desk. It looked what it was – a writer's workbench. Nothing hidden, nothing to hide; just a retired Englishman trying his hand at the writing game. Everyone was doing it now, it was money for old rope. It all looked very normal. All that was needed now was to make life more interesting for Toby Grant . . .

'Come over here, Greville.'

Sixsmith didn't move.

'Greville – '

But Sixsmith had been brooding. It had built up inside him like a dark storm cloud, and then it burst. 'I've just about had enough of this!' he snarled, his weak jaw quivering. 'I've had this fucking place right up to my bloody eyeballs. I'd rather go and live in bloody Brixton!'

Barlow looked up slowly from the desk. He wasn't really surprised. 'Too late, Greville, old son,' he said amiably. 'We're not issuing any more visas for Brixton. Calm down, have another drink, and let's get this bloody thing off your back. When we've done that you can start making plans to pack your bags. You've got a contract'

'Like fuck I have!' snapped Sixsmith. It was probably a mixture of strong whisky and claustrophobia, but the outburst was genuine. 'Contract? Contract be fucked! I'm doing this because I have no fucking choice. Blackmail, Barlow, that's what it bloody is, so don't let's hear any more fucking talk of contracts. OK?'

'Whatever you say, Greville. Now do as I say and come over here!'

Greville's face was flushed, but he did as he was told.

Barlow pointed at the directory on the screen and indicated the new entry he'd made. 'In there, Greville, are your memoirs. Convince yourself that you wrote them and any money coming out of them is yours – that shouldn't give you any trouble. One thing, though, read through the stuff and make sure you know what the story's all about, just in case you're invited to chat about it on the telly.' Greville's jaw dropped. 'But don't worry,' added Barlow, quickly, 'that's not likely to happen. They've been there, done that, with your mate Peter Wright. The Australian public'll be bored to bloody tears by now with Brit spy memoirs.' He picked up the diskette, pulled the drawer right out of the desk, stood it on its handle on the table and with the help of a roll of Sello-tape attached the packet to the other end. Greville watched as he manoeuvred the drawer back into place.

'What did you do that for?' he asked.

Barlow studied the drawer. 'Insurance, Greville. It's for some other people.' He avoided Sixsmith's eyes. 'Once the Australians have had a look and taken what they want, everything goes undercover.'

'Why?'

'There's sure to be some smartarse in Canberra who's got a granny in the Republic who he reckons ought to know what the crafty Brits are up to down here. You know how it works, don't you?'

Greville knew how it worked, and he didn't like it. 'Some ugly bastard's going to come all the way from Dublin to have a look for himself. I'm not sitting here as a bloody Irish target, Barlow. There was no mention of anything like – '

'It won't come to that. Let me finish. When the Aussies have lost interest in this stuff, we'll take it away. We'll move you out – we'll cover you, you'll have nothing to do with it any more. If the Irish take it up and come in for a look, they won't want to see everything lying around just waiting for them to collect. They'll want to find it hidden. They'll tear the bloody place apart. That's what they want – to do it the hard way.'

'I know all that. But it's me I'm worried about, not that bloody disk stuck to the back of the drawer.'

'You're going to have to trust me on this one, Greville. I promise, you're not going to get hurt.'

'Bollocks! I don't want your promise, I want out. I'll take my chance in court in London. Getting my bloody head shot off was not part of the deal.'

'OK. I understand, Greville.'

Sixsmith swallowed, took a deep breath and stared suspiciously at Harry Barlow. 'You do?'

'Sure. I said I understand. Give me a week and I'll get it all fixed up. One week. Hang around and play the game

81

for another seven or eight days and I'll see you're played out of it.'

'I'm not sure I trust you, Barlow.'

'Try.'

'I've no fucking option. But I'll tell you one thing, the first Irish voice I hear anywhere near my front door and it's the phone, the bloody police and the story from A to Z. I'm not kidding!'

'You've nothing to worry about, Greville. Just take it easy.'

'Just bugger off, will you!'

'As soon as I find out when your visitors are likely to call, I'll let you know so that you can go to the pictures or go shopping. We don't want to make things too difficult for them. If the phone rings, make sure it's me before you start chattering.'

'Nobody rings anyway.'

'Exactly. Which goes to show that anything can happen from now on. Don't let anyone in until you know who's on the other side.'

Barlow turned towards the door. No hands were outstretched; there was no friendly smile of farewell. They were strangers with nothing in common, like two people sitting opposite each other on the London underground. Greville didn't look up; he was already refilling his glass. Barlow stood by the door for a second and watched him, then, with a final glance around the room, he slipped out into the corridor, closing the door gently behind him.

6

Toby Grant walked through the door of the Fawkner Club, hesitated briefly to adjust his vision to the gloomy interior, and made his way to the bar. It wasn't his first visit. He ordered a pot of Foster's and while he waited for it stared at the rows of drinks behind the bar. He didn't bother looking around at the other customers; he'd already seen what he'd come for.

He sucked the inch of froth from his glass and walked down to the far end. Barlow watched him come without raising his head from the sports page of the *Herald*. 'Barlow? My name's Grant,' said Toby.

Barlow looked up slowly. 'How did you know?'

Toby grinned. 'Let's go outside.'

He led them to a shaded corner of the grassy garden. They were far enough away from the nearest people to be able to talk freely, but near enough for Barlow to be able to study in detail the woman sitting on her own at a small round metal table a few yards away. Dressed in an elegant but casual dark grey skirt and top, she could have been a doctor or maybe a lawyer meeting a client. Her dark brown hair hung neatly just above her shoulders. Barlow noted a slightly turned-up nose and full, well-shaped lips. An attractive woman, with clear wide eyes, she oozed self-reliance, and a firm, determined chin warned that anything beyond an unknown male's appraisal would be wishful thinking. Her legs, crossed to reveal smooth, rounded knees, were long and elegant. In her late twenties, early thirties, she appealed to Harry Barlow. He would rather have been sitting with her than Toby Grant. She didn't blush or flutter her eyelids at Barlow's inspection; in fact she didn't even notice him as she concentrated on reading a glossy magazine and sipped from a small, condensation-covered glass of chilled white wine. When Barlow brought his eyes back to Grant, the Australian was busy reducing the level of Foster's in his glass. He wiped the froth from his lip and said, 'Did you know Sixsmith in London?'

Barlow nodded fractionally. It could have meant anything.

Grant took it in his stride. 'Good. You give him a ring and get him out of the flat, and I'll nip in and make some sort of assessment of what he's up to. If it's of no interest to us you take over and do what you like with him. Is that OK with you?'

Barlow played hard to get. 'I thought I was going to do the popping in while you hung around in the background making it all legal and above board?'

Toby smiled gently. 'This is Australia, mate, not Knightsbridge. If you get picked up breaking and entering they'll have your balls hanging off the battlements on Norfolk Island before you even have time to plead insanity. You'll be out of the bloody country with a "Never darken our doorstep again" blot on your passport.'

Barlow didn't smile.

'All I'd get,' continued Toby, 'would be a rap across the knuckles for getting caught.'

Barlow conceded reluctantly. 'When d'you want to do it?'

Grant didn't hesitate. 'No time like the present. Go and ring now and see how quickly you can move him. Suggest an early dinner, say about half-past seven.'

Toby bought another round of drinks while Barlow made his way through the now fug-laden bar to the phone. He dialled Sixsmith's number.

'You and I are going to have dinner together, Greville,' he said when Sixsmith answered the phone, 'and while you're out somebody's going to come and look over your place.'

'Just a minute – '

'Don't interrupt, Greville, just listen. Don't make things too easy for them. Lock a few things away, things like disks and paperclips, stick hairs or something across the drawers – you know the sort of thing, you've seen James Bond at work. Behave like somebody who's doing something he doesn't think he ought to be doing, somebody who's got a conscience and stuff to hide . . . Have you read the memoirs yet?'

Sixsmith managed to complete a sentence. 'No.'

'What the bloody hell have you been doing with yourself then?'

'Don't talk to me like that, Barlow – you've no bloody right.'

'OK.' Barlow grinned to himself in the smoky confines of the telephone box. The mouse was snarling. 'Calm down, Greville. Don't bother reading it, it's too late now. Just make sure it's not sitting on the screen. Switch everything off. Just make it look as if you care. OK?'

'OK. Where shall I meet you?'

Barlow scowled to himself in the mirror. He hadn't a clue. 'Name your favourite caff, Greville.'

'It seems he's lonely for the mother tongue,' said Barlow when he rejoined Grant in the garden. 'I told him I was passing through and heard he'd taken up residence here. I reminded him of the good old end-of-term Christmas Eve booze-ups we used to have in the Pig and Eye Club.' Barlow pulled a face. 'He suggested I popped round now for a drink and a sandwich. I put him off.'

Grant wasn't all that interested. 'Quite right. I need time, Barlow, a couple of hours at least to do a proper job.'

'You've got it. He's booking a table somewhere for dinner but I'm meeting him at a quarter to seven for a whisky and a bowl of peanuts in the Hyatt, so you've got about six hours to play with.'

The attractive woman Barlow had admired in the pub's garden met Toby Grant at the entrance to Greville Sixsmith's block of flats. She had changed into her working clothes: dark-coloured jeans, a cream rollneck sweater, soft leather moccasins, and a lightweight, rust-coloured suede blouson. Her demeanour, as earlier, was serious.

'Thanks for the call,' said Toby and glanced down at the watch on his wrist. 'You sure he's out for the night?'

'Best bib and tucker,' responded Sophie Ward, 'and an eager, boyish look in his eye for the fleshpots of naughty Melbourne. About your friend – '

'Harry Barlow?'

'I like the look of him.'

'Forget it. You're not paid to like the look of him; you're paid to watch him and mistrust his motives.' Toby grinned at her to show he wasn't serious. 'But apart from that, what were you going to say about him?'

'After he left you at the Fawkner he went straight back to his hotel, made two calls – both to London – then stayed there until he called a taxi to take him to the Hyatt.' Sophie forestalled Grant's query: 'The girl at reception was very cooperative . . . He had one large whisky in the atrium before he was joined by Sixsmith.'

'Good girl. Have you got a key?'

'Not necessary.' Sophie brought her hand out of her jacket pocket and with a few deft twirls of a thin wire instrument the lock slipped its catch with a barely audible click.

'Lock it,' ordered Grant after they'd entered the flat, 'and then go through his wardrobe. I'll take the desk and cupboards.'

'What am I looking for?'

'Anything that doesn't fit in with the general picture of a retired English gent. Anything out of the ordinary.'

'Like what?'

'Use your imagination. You've seen a bloke's pad before.' He went straight to the computer and turned it on, then flicked through to the directory and studied the list of files.

Sophie joined him. 'Nothing out of the ordinary in there,' she said. 'He likes good clothes. All London stuff. They must pay their spooks bloody well – there's a fortune in suits and shirts.' She glanced at the screen. 'What have you got there?'

'You tell me.'

She sat down at the desk. Toby peered over her shoulder. She retrieved part of Sixsmith's ramblings and flicked down a page. Then another, then shook her head and turned and met Toby's eyes. 'It's rubbish.'

'Try one of the other files.'

It was the same. One after another she flicked them through the computer, then shook her head again. 'Looks like you've been wasting your time, Toby, unless this is all in some sort of funny code.'

'Try something else,' he said.

'Bloody hell!'

They'd found Sixsmith's memoirs.

'He's no bloody fool, is Sixsmith. That rubbish was a bloody smokescreen. Let's have a look at this.' Grant swapped places with her and trolled through the text. Much of it was pure retired old intelligence-organization desk man's ramblings of the Peter Wright genre. Until page 134 flashed past his eye. He stopped flipping and worked his way back. He hadn't been mistaken: ASIS – Australian Secret Intelligence Service – jumped out of the screen. He concentrated on this section. It was about past ASIS operations in New Zealand – enough to get the Kiwis doing a Haka in Parkes Place! Also in Jakarta – good for Australian/Indonesian relations – and a nice one for Lee Kuan Yew in Singapore. The smile on Grant's face broadened. Good on yer, Sixy! he thought as he flipped through the pages. But the smile vanished abruptly at page 162.

This wasn't funny or 'Good on yer, Sixy.' This was bloody dangerous – a killer. It was the breakdown of ASIS's highly efficient undercover anti-opium operation in the Burma Triangle, with unveiled suggestions of its infiltration of the joint KGB/Burmese military-junta apparatus for laundering the proceeds, and an outline of the revamped KGB management of the Eastern European area of opium production. Dynamite.

Grant pursed his lips. And very interesting – if true. He knew nothing about ASIS activities. He hadn't heard even a whisper about operations in the Rangoon district. He was domestic, ASIO, but he'd read enough of Sixsmith's explosive revelations to know that the British had got their nose into it somehow and couldn't keep it to themselves. Or, more to the point, Sixsmith couldn't. At least Wright had had the discretion – or ignorance – to keep Aussie intelligence affairs, the secret ones anyway, out of the covers of his book. If this thing took the same route as *Spycatcher*, quite a few heads would end up in Rangoon's muck-strewn gutters. And there'd be a few Australian ones among them.

Grant thought quickly. At the moment it seemed that in Australia only Sixsmith and he knew about Rangoon. Not even Dubrovnik with his flapping ears pressed against the drainpipes would be in on this one. But Arthur Gunne would know ... Should he go straight to him or through the channels? Better show it to Dubrovnik in case it splattered against the fan. Let him carry it up the ladder. But what about Harry Barlow? Grant pulled a face. He'd worry about Harry Barlow when he'd stopped worrying about this little lot.

'Get a copy of this made,' he said to Sophie. 'Can you manage that?'

'No probs.' She selected an unused disk from the box by the computer. There were still enough for Sixsmith not to miss it. 'What shall I do with the stuff in the memory?'

'Scrub it.'

'Won't that make it obvious we've been here?'

'That's the idea. This stuff's a potential security risk. I want to scare him off writing before he goes any further. Now that we've got the only copy, he's going to have to remember it again.'

Toby Grant and Sophie had a fish-and-chips supper and a bottle of De Bortoli Chardonnay in her flat near the airport. The next morning he was on the first flight back to Canberra.

7

Dubrovnik read through the typescript made from the disk with irritation rather than interest.

Until he got to Chapter 16.

After the closure of their Embassy in London in 1984, the Libyans moved the intelligence organization they'd built up in Britain to the Irish Republic and made themselves at home in their Dublin Embassy. The British infiltration of Irish Special Branch brought the bonus home to the front porch and in no time at all they were able to activate long-time listening devices built into the wall of the Libyan Embassy cypher room and into the unscrambled system of their telephone network. The yield was at times spectacular and, to say the least, surprising in its revelations . . .

Sixsmith, Dubrovnik decided, felt he owed his people a real and honest kick in the crotch. For the second time in living memory a disgruntled British intelligence executive was behaving like the woman scorned. He hoped Sixsmith had got his pension tied up in pink ribbon and his gold-nuggets handshake buried in concrete. His ex-masters weren't going to like this any more than they'd liked the other one . . .

Switching on the light, he made himself comfortable and, with his mind geared to Sixsmith's 'revelations', absently reached into his drawer for a cigarette. He stuck it between his lips but made no attempt to light it as he continued reading:

· . . . Over a period of two months a series of guarded calls established a rapport between Abdul Fitri, the commercial attaché at the Libyan Embassy, and one Nial Byrne. Abdul Fitri was identified as Major Mohammad al Hashim, a senior official in the Foreign Liaison Office and former London chief of Al Mukhabarat, the Libyan intelligence service. Nial Byrne took a little longer to identify. His calls were traced to Rathfarnham, a working-class suburb to the south of Dublin, and Byrne himself turned out to be Peadar O'Dwyer, a former quartermaster general of the Provisional IRA and now a selected member of the new IRA/PIRA Executive in Dublin. For MI5 this high-level fraternization between the New Executive and Al Mukhabarat constituted the worst possible scenario. It was like rubbing red-topped matches together . . .

A full-time surveillance operation was mounted, Sixsmith's writings revealed to a fascinated Dubrovnik, and when the affair moved from whisperings down the phone to holding hands in pubs and parks, O'Dwyer, complacent in his suburban anonymity, moved the meetings to his red-bricked terrace house. His frequent outings had permitted his British watchers, with the help of the 'British Section' of the Irish Special Branch, to install a 'special facility' apparatus on O'Dwyer's telephone. A two-man team of Dublin specialists – MI6 recruited radio technicians under direct control of London – were insinuated into the district on a twenty-four-hour watch to 'sit in' on the new friends' more intimate discussions.

A pattern was very quickly established. It appeared that Peadar O'Dwyer had been chosen by the Dublin

Executive to test, through Abdul Fitri, first of all Qadaffi's willingness to act as paymaster against collateral (unspecified) held by the Executive for the purchase of heavy offensive weapons (unspecified) for a major, and final, assault on the British mainland, and secondly, when they'd forced a withdrawal of British interests in Northern Ireland, to persuade him to offer close co-operation and storage facilities in Libya for in the mass European distribution through the Executive in Ireland, of a substantial portion of the world's production of cocaine, crack, heroin and other opium derivatives. O'Dwyer, it seemed, along with the rest of the New Executive, had no doubts about the first option; Qadaffi was already enjoying watching the fruits of his dislike for the British being adequately and competently offered by the PIRA to the British wherever and whenever they chose.

Abdul Fitri, continued Sixsmith, was more than interested in increasing arms shipments. There was now some very good ex-Soviet Army hardware on offer, hardware extending even to devices of Hiroshima proportions. O'Dwyer cast his first fly with confidence . . .

It was good stuff, and well written. Dubrovnik had imagination; he could almost have been there. Sixsmith helped him with excerpts from the highly secret and confidential tapes recorded by the two experts from the tap on O'Dwyer's phone. Whilst he didn't reveal how he managed to get a verbatim transcript of the tapes, or offer regret for the consequences of his revelations, as explained by Sixsmith, when they became known, the closing moments of the meeting would have disastrous significance for the men of the Dublin Executive:

O'Dwyer When d'you want me to arrange this meeting with the Executive?
Fitri Very soon, of course. But not all of them.

O'Dwyer	What d'you mean, not all of them?
Fitri	The British have a man on your Executive. (Long pause . . .)
O'Dwyer	How d'you know?
Fitri	You don't ask.
O'Dwyer	Who then?
Fitri	At the moment I can only tell you who he is not.
O'Dwyer	Jesus Christ! This doesn't make fuckin' sense!
Fitri	You and three of the other, erm, senior officers are totally cleared by my source. It was not possible to establish foreign credentials on the other three members of your Executive, but one of them, and you may take my sacred word on it, is a British double agent – a very long-term sleeper. But he's there, very high, waiting, and a threat to any global-scale ambitions you and your colleagues may have for the future. Certainly any future with my country. (Long pause . . .)
O'Dwyer	Christ! The fuckin' shithead! When I report this the whole fuckin' structure'll collapse round our ears. It'll take months – years – to investigate each of these men. Jesus! (Long pause) Can't you help me any more than that?
Fitri	I think so . . . (pause) Say nothing yet to your colleagues for fear of bolting the traitor. The day after tomorrow, meet me in St Anne's Park, half-past eleven – in the rose garden. I shall bring someone with me who will describe the man who is going to betray you. In the meantime, please arrange, without discussing – (Tape ends without explanation . . .)

Dubrovnik spat out the damp, mauled, unlit cigarette, let his feet drop off the edge of the desk, and opened the top drawer again. His movements were slow and deliberate. He took out the packet of cigarettes, selected one with care and this time lit it. He broke his New Year's resolution without pleasure, but the cigarette tasted sweet and he inhaled the smoke like a dying man dragging life-giving oxygen into his lungs. He contemplated the burning tip for a second or two, then rocked his chair on to its back legs, stared at the blank ceiling and allowed his imagination to run riot.

Heros Dubrovnik was a complicated man. He wasn't interested in Europe or its problems; professionally, the IRA and their activities held no interest for him. But as far as England was concerned, if he'd been asked to take sides, his savage Slavic soul would have opted for the IRA. It was part of the culture of oppressed people subdued by bigger, more ambitious neighbours. But Dubrovnik didn't have to make the choice – not yet. It was the drug element that sat like a lump of suet pudding on his digestive system.

From one side of the fence it was known as 'freedom fighting'; from the other, 'terrorism'. From a distance you never learnt the difference; the choice was a gut decision, and you had to live with it. But drugs? That was different; that took all the romance out of being oppressed.

He shook away his impending depression and concentrated on the immediate.

It looked as though the British had got themselves a man on the other people's planning committee. Nice work! Or it was until some superannuated bastard looking for a boost to his pension decided to blow him into the wind. And he'd done that all right. Sixsmith had given them everything but the poor bastard's name; Christ, even he could have pointed the poor bugger out in a crowded street . . . It looked like it was goodnight, mate! Dubrovnik looked up and offered to the ceiling a short *requiescat* for a British spy in Ireland. But it was very short. This was nothing to do with him, Heros Dubrovnik. Let the bloody British work out their own problems . . .

Only it wasn't that easy. Dubrovnik had a kinship for that other man, the one forever waiting for the touch on the shoulder, the whisper, the black bag over the head, the cold kiss of the pistol barrel behind the ear – the oblivion. It was the game. There was enough running against the poor bastard without Sixsmith doing it to him as well. So what had Heros Dubrovnik got now? A fucking mess! the Brits would go bloody berserk trying to stop this one going any further, and all the bright Australian boys with their navy-blue suits and law-school diplomas would be defending the miserable bugger's right to tell everybody anything he liked. Dubrovnik choked on an overenthusiastic drag from the cigarette and stood up to clear his throat. He stared at the three-quarters of cigarette left and dropped it into the dregs in his coffee cup.

And what was he going to do about this poor bastard in Ireland who was going to get his skin pinned to the shithouse wall because Sixsmith owed somebody a grudge? He found himself with a sudden interest in Irish matters.

Dubrovnik flicked the switch on his intercom and said: 'Mary, who's the expert on Irish affairs at ASIS?'

'Can I ring you back?'

'Of course. No – just a minute.' Dubrovnik stared for a moment at the stack of typewritten sheets in front of him, then made up his mind. 'Find out who it is, then ask him if he could give me half an hour of his time.'

'D'you want him over here?'

'No, I'll go and see him.'

While he waited for Mary to ring back, Dubrovnik

sorted out the sheets of Sixsmith's manuscript dealing with O'Dwyer's meeting with the Libyans and slipped them into an unmarked file. He'd barely done that when Mary knocked on his door.

'Your Irish expert hangs out in King's Avenue and is a fella named O'Donnell.'

'Sounds appropriate. What's his Christian name?'

'Barbara.'

'Pardon?'

'Barbara. It's a female fella.'

Dubrovnik didn't laugh. Nor did Mary.

'She'll see you in her office at half-past two.'

'When she comes back from her two and a half hours at the hairdresser's?'

'No. When she comes back from machine-gunning an invasion of Mongolian spies.'

'I'm getting worried about you, Mary. Shut the door behind you.'

Barbara O'Donnell was an attractive brunette in her mid-forties. She'd been an even more attractive brunette in her mid-twenties, pretty as well, but she'd grown out of the prettiness. She'd kept her figure, though. She looked hard and firm in the right places. And she didn't waste time on chitchat.

It suited Dubrovnik.

'I'm interested in an Irishman named O'Dwyer. He was something to do with the IRA.'

'Here?'

'No, in Ireland.'

'What's your interest?'

'We've got another Englishman who's about to bare his soul on his career in British intelligence. He's chosen to do it in Melbourne. I've got a copy of his ramblings and one chapter mentions this guy O'Dwyer in connection with Libya, arms and other things. I'd like to know a bit more about him.'

'How does it concern us?'

'Only peripherally. The British had a listening watch on him. We were mentioned in a conversation.'

Barbara O'Donnell stared for a moment into Dubrovnik's dark eyes. There was nothing devious there. He'd been perfectly honest. She accepted that. 'Was your O'Dwyer's Christian name Peadar?'

Dubrovnik opened his folder and riffled through Sixsmith's manuscript. Then he looked up and nodded. 'That's right. Funny name . . .'

'No funnier than Heros.' She didn't give Dubrovnik time to respond. 'Peadar O'Dwyer was murdered in . . . ' It was her turn to look into folders. 'In Dublin on the third of November 1993.' She continued looking into the folder. It was thick and heavy, and where she'd pulled it from were a lot more of the same colour, just as thick and just as heavy, all stamped either 'IRELAND – Republic' or 'IRELAND – Northern (ULSTER)'.

'It caused a hell of a stink in the Republic because O'Dwyer was identified as a senior member of the PIRA, which, as you know . . . ' Raising her eyes, she looked into Dubrovnik's and saw, as she'd guessed, that he didn't. '. . . is an illegal organization in the Republic of Ireland as well as in the North. He was arranging some business in Dublin with, as you've just mentioned, the Libyans.'

Dubrovnik's eyes went back to the sheets of manuscript on his knees. According to Sixsmith, early November was when the British had had the bug on O'Dwyer's meeting with the Libyan intelligence officer, Major Mohammad al Hashim, otherwise Abdul Fitri. He turned the sheets. And they'd arranged a meeting. Fitri was going to bring someone to finger the British infiltrator. Interesting . . . But not for her. Not yet. He looked up. Barbara O'Donnell was watching him. She was waiting for the next question. She wasn't disappointed with it.

'How was he killed?'

'Shot. Sitting on a park bench in the middle of Dublin. He was hit by about fourteen rounds of nine millimetre. But the one that killed him was a close-range shot into his face. The two Libyans he was chatting with went down too, all finished off with close-range head shots. Very professional job. One of the Libyans was identified as Major Mohammad al-Hashim, a senior official at the Libyan Liaison Office, at the time on attached duties in Libya's Dublin Embassy. The other one has never been identified, but, as I said, it made a hell of a stink.'

'Anybody charged with the murders?'

'No.'

'Anybody suspected?'

'Unofficially – British intelligence.'

'Based on what?'

'Nothing. They couldn't think of anybody else. The Republic gets quite agitated when the squabble in the North spills over and sheds a bit of blood on Dublin's spotless pavements. The people in the know automatically blame the people up North. In this case they were probably right. On that day there were a total of five killings involving the Republic.'

'Five?' Dubrovnik sat up in his chair too abruptly and the Sixsmith manuscript showered on to the floor. He left it where it lay for the moment and leaned with his elbows on Barbara's desk, staring into her face. Turning in her swivel chair, she pulled out another file from the shelf. Dubrovnik read the cover as she opened it beside the other one: 'IRELAND – Northern (ULSTER) July '93/ Dec '93.'

'Cross-reference,' she explained. 'Northern Ireland killings with Republic connections. Two men blown up in their car on a small country road in County Down on the night of November third. Smithereens is the description. The biggest thing they found was a shirt button.' She didn't smile. 'That's not strictly true. British forensics decided, according to this' – she tapped the thick wedge of paper in the new file – 'that it was PIRA material of probably Libyan origin that caused the explosion. At first they thought a Provisional IRA bombing team had got their wires crossed, but then, with a bit of back-tracking, they discovered the victims were two Irishmen who'd travelled up separately from the Republic earlier that day.'

'They discovered all that from a shirt button?'

She smiled. 'There was a whisper, and don't ask from whom, that they were a couple of MI5 or MI6 operatives stationed in Dublin and called up North for a special operation that went wrong. The odd thing was that when things go right for them, the Provisionals usually claim the responsibility – in other words the credit – for a good kill. But in this instance, and although the makings of the explosion were ostensibly PIRA, they didn't own up to it. Neither did anybody else.'

'D'you read anything into that?'

'No,' said Barbara, curtly. 'But here,' she removed the sheet of paper from the file and passed it over the table, 'you can if you like.'

Dubrovnik glanced down at the report but he wasn't reading it; he was thinking of Sixsmith's Chapter Sixteen. Two men being listened to by two men made four. Abdul Fitri was going to introduce a fifth to blow the comfortable cover of a planted British agent – or a turned Irishman? Five men killed on the day the blowing of covers was going to take place. Coincidence? Like bloody hell! The British were unprincipled bastards at the best of times, but would they go that far? Would they kill two of their own men? Of course the bastards would — they wouldn't think twice about it. But what were they protecting — their high-riding implant job in the IRA Military Command, or the fact that they'd broken into the IRA's cocaine-mountain conspiracy? The first was understandable, but why hadn't they told the world that the people who want to rule Northern Ireland were also going to be the world's new drug barons? What had it got to do with Heros Dubrovnik? Fuck all! Except some bloody Pom holed up in Melbourne was intent on making it his business. Dubrovnik curled his lip. Then he frowned.

So what happened to the guy who directed the O'Dwyer surveillance operation?

'Well?'

Barbara's voice dragged Dubrovnik's eyes upwards from the sheet of paper.

'Have you managed to read anything into it?'

Dubrovnik managed a half-smile as he shook his head. He wasn't concentrating on Barbara; there was something else bubbling away on the edge of his mind. She was looking at him curiously but managed to change her expression when their eyes met. She held out her hand and he handed her back the sheet from her file. It wasn't what she wanted.

'Perhaps I could glance at that stuff you've thrown all over my floor?' When she smiled, it highlighted traces of that earlier prettiness; smiling suited her, but it was fairly obvious she didn't do enough of it.

And then it hit him.

Christ! It must have been Sixsmith! Sixsmith was the bloody control for that Irish job!

Barbara was still talking, ' . . . because O'Dwyer's death has left a lot of unasked questions, particularly — '

Christ Almighty! Sixsmith!

'Can I use your phone?' Dubrovnik didn't wait for permission. He snatched the phone off its cradle and waited impatiently for the operator. He avoided looking at Barbara. 'Six-nine-two-seven-four,' he snapped. 'Extension two-four, please.'

'It's engaged.'

'Break in on it!'

'I'm sorry – '

'Do as you're told. It's urgent.'

'Mary,' he barked when he was put through. 'Get hold of Toby Grant and make sure someone's keeping an eye on Greville Sixsmith's apartment. Ring me the minute he gets this message. Is that clear? Good. Get on with it. No, I'm coming straight back.'

Barbara gave him another of her unaccustomed smiles when he replaced the receiver. 'Another funny name,' she said lightly. 'Sixsmith! Is that the name of the man whose memoirs are strewn on the floor there?' She didn't wait for Dubrovnik's reply. He was already out of his chair and on his knees gathering in the manuscript. 'Shall I send them over to your office after I've had a look at them?'

'I'll send you a copy,' he said. There was no conviction in his voice. Dubrovnik reckoned he had a load of gunpowder in his little folder; he had no intention of sharing it, even with this close a cousin. Sixsmith had put a snake in the bag, and Sixsmith was going to be made to put his bloody hand in and bring it out. And Heros Dubrovnik was going to be standing right next to him when he did it. The Poms were going to have haemorrhages when one of their intelligence people had a look at this manuscript. Jesus! If they knocked off two of their own men to keep this under wraps, what the bloody hell were they going to do to Sixsmith . . . 'Thanks for your help, Miss O'Donnell.'

'Ms O'Donnell.'

'Of course. I'll keep you in the picture if anything nudges into your field. Perhaps we could have a drink some time?' But he was being polite. Dubrovnik wasn't interested in drinking with the Ms brigade. He liked his women simple and unliberated.

8

The waters of Canberra's Lake Burley Griffin looked placid and docile, with the early reflections of the lakeside illuminations beginning to sparkle as evening closed in. But Barbara O'Donnell had other things on her mind as she turned into Kaye Place and the Hyatt car park.

She ordered a gin and tonic and in between sips chewed absently from a delicate palmful of cashew nuts. She was very thoughtful. Half-way down the glass she suddenly made up her mind, left the cocktail lounge, and walked briskly towards the telephone room just off the foyer. She dialled the Irish Embassy. She didn't need to look up the number. When it answered, she asked for the Third Secretary. Then: 'Tom, how would you like to eat Sydney rock oysters and drink Montrachet with a jaded working girl?'

'In other words, Tom,' answered a soft Wicklow accent, 'I want to pick your brains, unofficially, on behalf of the Australian Secret Intelligence Service and I'm bribing you with an offer you can't refuse! Where're you going to buy me these oysters, Babs?'

She told him.

'You going to tell me what this is about before or after these?' Tom Collins sent the waiter away and poured the wine himself. The oysters looked cool and comfortable on their bed of crushed ice and seemed in no hurry to leave it.

'How do you know it's not just a yearning for your company?' Barbara tasted her wine and wrinkled her nose in approval but didn't wait for his reply. They both knew it was more than that. Keeping her glass close to her lips, she studied the man sitting opposite. Theirs was a friendship that went back a long time. Nothing romantic, purely sexual. It had started off in Dublin with good intentions but had developed into friendship – a long, uncomplicated and undemanding physical friendship that Collins's recent attachment to Canberra had rekindled. They were both happy with the situation. 'Do you know anything about an Englishman named Sixsmith?' she asked softly.

Collins shook his head.

'Greville Sixsmith . . .'

'He could only be English with a name like that!' There was an easy camaraderie between the Irish intelligence officer and his Australian counterpart. They were, after all, first cousins once removed by virtue of ancestral transportation, with an inherited dislike of the bastards who had done the transporting in the first place. 'What makes Mr Sixsmith worth a dozen of Sydney's finest rock oysters?'

'Do you know Heros Dubrovnik?'

'ASIO?'

'There's only one! He came to see me today. He wanted information about a man named O'Dwyer.'

Collins's expression didn't change as he lowered his eyes and carefully slid his fork into a loaded shell and expertly detached its contents. But he didn't raise it. He left his fork with its burden hovering and looked into her face.

'Peadar O'Dwyer?'

She nodded.

'How do these three end up in the same puddle?'

Barbara touched her lips with the edge of her napkin. 'Sixsmith is a former British intelligence officer who's written down his thoughts on matters general. He's chosen Melbourne to spring this lot on a suspecting, I would imagine, British intelligence community. For some reason Dubrovnik has been given, or has acquired, a review copy in which there appears to be a chapter, or more, concerning the late Peadar O'Dwyer. Dubrovnik wanted to know all about him.'

Collins stopped fiddling with his oyster and ate it. He followed it with a thin slice of brown bread and butter and washed it down with half a glass of the Montrachet.

'Surely,' he said, 'if O'Dwyer was mentioned in any capacity at all your friend Sixsmith would have covered his activities, and his death. O'Dwyer was, after all, a senior official of the PIRA. He was more than senior – he was Quartermaster, one of the top half-dozen in that lot. But more than that, at the time of his killing he was deeply involved in a totally new organization in the South. Didn't Dubrovnik elaborate? Surely he didn't roll into your office and say "Babs, I've fallen in love with Peadar O'Dwyer, tell me about his life and last minutes . . ."?' Collins had finished his Sydney rocks and set about doing the same with the bread and butter. He didn't waste time. He folded the triangles in half, then half again, and shoved the little parcels into his mouth one at a time. Then he reached for his glass to wash his mouth out, nodding as he did so. 'The O'Dwyer episode has been very well documented – even the most junior member of MI5 would know the details of his murder. I can't imagine what your man Sixsmith could add to make his book any less boring than all the others by disgruntled Brits.'

'According to Dubrovnik,' responded Barbara, 'in his capacity as literary critic, the British were watching

O'Dwyer. They had him wired for sound, they listened to him playing footsie with a Libyan arms delegation – '

'I just told you, Babs, the bloody man was PIRA Quartermaster General. He'd be involved in any large-scale arms negotiations.'

'Dubrovnik didn't seem too interested in that aspect.' Barbara sent her empty glass across the table and watched Collins refill it. She didn't stop talking. 'It was something else that agitated him. Those Slavonic eyes of his almost vanished behind his cheekbones when I mentioned the total casualty list – North and South – for the day of O'Dwyer's death.'

Collins completed filling his own glass and looked up into her eyes. 'Mention them to me.'

Barbara looked surprised, but only for a second. 'I've got copies of the reports here in my bag.' She reached down beside her, but he stopped her.

'Not here, Babs – later. Tell me what you told Dubrovnik.'

'There was O'Dwyer and the two Libyans, Major Mohammad – '

'Don't bother with names.'

'OK. The three in Dublin plus two in Northern Ireland. It was the mention of the two up North that sent his eyebrows into the ceiling.'

Collins frowned. 'That's very interesting. I didn't make a connection, and I saw all the reports.'

Barbara shrugged the interruption aside. 'These two were identified as Irish. I told Dubrovnik about them. They'd arrived in Northern Ireland from Dublin that day. It was broadly suspected that they were MI5 or MI6-recruited people called in for a special job that went wrong. Nobody claimed the credit.' She pulled a face. 'And I thought it was only our lads who sometimes tweaked the wrong button . . .'

But Collins wasn't interested in claiming responsibility or tweaking wrong buttons. He was thinking along another track – and he was thinking fast. It was the bit about the British listening in to IRA/Libyan negotiations that started the process. OK, so O'Dwyer's Libyan connection was well documented. A British ex-MI executive wouldn't cause any clouds to fall by including that and other similar arrangements in his book of bedtime stories ... So what had got Australian MI crossing and uncrossing their legs? Collins picked up his glass and drank another mouthful; it was a reflex action, he could have been sipping concentrated lemon juice. He stared at Barbara over the rim of the heavy Waterford crystal, but there was no expression in his eyes. 'I don't suppose,' he murmured, 'that your chum Dubrovnik offered any job description on the two Northern Ireland deaths?'

Barbara shrugged again. 'Something flicked through his mind, Tom, as it's doing through yours! He didn't tell me what it was – and neither, I suppose, will you?'

Tom Collins smiled. But it was a superficial smile. He said nothing. So she continued:

'But after we'd chewed over the County Down explosion his little lips suddenly tightened and he was reaching for the phone to his secretary. He told her to get in touch with Toby Grant in Melbourne and tell him to set up camp on Sixsmith's front-door step. "Nobody in or out," he ordered. "Particularly British." His very words.'

'Is there any chance of getting a little preview of the offending chapters?' asked Collins hopefully.

It was Barbara's turn for the superficial smile. 'Not through Dubrovnik,' she said. 'He suddenly became very possessive about his little stack of papers. I think he must have realized he'd got something very sensitive, something like a time bomb ticking away under his arm, and I have an awful feeling it was something I might have said.'

'What d'you think it was?'

'I've no idea.'

'Think.'

'I can't, Tom. I've gone over it and I can't for the life of me think of anything that was said, or that happened, that sent him running back across the bridge. And what's more, I don't think he came by it honestly in the first place and if you ask me, he's going to have to play his next move very carefully, otherwise the Brits are going to come down on him like a ton of wet sand.'

'At what stage d'you think things are now, then?'

'You mean publishing-wise?'

Collins nodded.

'No idea.' She thought for a moment, then frowned and said, 'I wonder how Dubrovnik managed to focus on Sixsmith in Melbourne all the way from his concrete shed over at Russell?'

'That shouldn't be too difficult to find out for a girl with your charm and resources,' suggested Collins light-heartedly. 'Who's this Toby Grant? Is he a Melbourne boy?'

'No, he's ASIO. One of Dubrovnik's senior operatives, a troubleshooter for the department. It shows Dubrovnik's serious about what's going on in his bailiwick. Grant is good by all accounts – he could run a shop on his own. He's more unorthodox than his Yugoslav boss, but a little bit suspect in my reckoning ... ' She studied Collins's raised eyebrows for a second, then, with a crooked little smile, shook her head. 'No, Tommy, don't get me wrong. I'm thinking he may have friends in Curzon Street. He's been on a couple of exchanges with the Brits.'

But Tommy wasn't getting her wrong; he was thinking along other lines. 'What's he look like, this wonder boy? Have I seen him around?'

'Probably.' Barbara sipped from her glass and allowed a mischievous twinkle into her eyes. 'He stands out. If I was into the toy-boy phase, he's the boy I'd like to toy with. Tall, blond, good-looking, nice shape, and impeccable manners!'

Tom Collins wasn't jealous. 'And his full-time occupation at the moment's the study of Mr Sixsmith?'

'Looks like it.'

'Where exactly does Mr Sixsmith do his writing in Melbourne?'

Barbara gently put her glass down on the table but kept her fingers wrapped round its stem. The twinkle had returned to its hiding place. 'I don't recommend you go poking around there,' she said firmly. 'I think you should leave it to me. I'll get you a copy of the manuscript somehow.' She smiled broadly for the first time. 'I think it's going to be a smasher. Sir Bobby Armstrong'll be sorry to be out of this one!'

Collins didn't see the funny side of it.

Back in the Arkana Street Embassy, Collins spent about an hour and a half in the basement coding room. First he brought himself up to date on the official Irish reaction to the murders of O'Dwyer and the two Arabs and tried to make Dubrovnik's connection between those and the County Down explosion. Nothing fitted. There was no obvious connection. He'd missed something. Dubrovnik hadn't. But Dubrovnik had help – Sixsmith's help. Collins put his thoughts to one side and set to work on the coding pads. He asked for Greville Sixsmith's name to be fed into the system and for any information on his probable involvement in Dublin and the Counties and any Australian overflow that could have caused Dubrovnik's heightened blood pressure. When he'd finished he watched the message disappear into the Embassy direct transmitter and then sat, his feet on the table and his eyes focused on the featureless ceiling, and worked out a strategy for broadening the audience of Greville Six-smith's literary adventure.

On his way home he pulled into the Canberra International at Dickson. Leaving his half-finished Jack Daniels on the bar, he found a pay phone near the reception and rang a number in Melbourne. It was an Irish accent that answered – pure dog Irish, straight from the gutters of Belfast's New Lodge Road and unadulterated by any exposure to the Australian twang.

'Ring Stephen Slattery in Belfast,' Collins told the voice, 'and tell him to get Fergal Flynn out here. I want to see him in Melbourne by Monday at the latest. I'll contact you Monday morning to arrange a meeting place. OK?'

'If he can't make it?'

'He will. Monday morning. No argument.'

Collins's coded thoughts were intercepted by the British MI group in Dublin and decoded almost as quickly by the Irish experts in Upper Merrion Street. The message arrived in London before the lunch-time exodus.

'It looks as though they've bought it . . . ' General Sir Richard Sanderson slid the piece of flimsy across the table to Reason. 'You'd better go out there, Clive, and stir it up a bit more. Make sure they stay on the right track and don't get themselves tied into knots.' Sanderson shook his head sadly. 'The Australians, if nothing else, are bloody efficient at getting classified information into unclassified hands. I wonder if they do it deliberately?' He didn't dwell on it. 'Better get Greville out of his armchair and hidden somewhere over here, just in case . . .'

Reason skidded the sheet of paper back across the

desk. 'Harry's got his eye on him. They've become almost inseparable. I can't see any harm coming to him, and it might be a good thing to dangle him there for a bit longer. Bait. His walking away might raise an eyebrow or two.'

Sanderson considered it. 'OK. Do it your way.'

9

Barlow looked mildly pleased when he examined the hidden computer disk in Sixsmith's desk drawer.

'You can slip into your purple satin shorts and put on your running spikes, Greville. We've moved on to the fast track,' he told Sixsmith. But Sixsmith wasn't interested. He swallowed a mouthful from the large glass of whisky he'd poured himself and, kicking off his shoes, settled back in his chair.

Barlow ignored him and began riffling through the computer's memory. He smiled when he saw that the new version of Greville's memoirs had disappeared. Glancing across the room, he looked at Greville, now fast asleep, the three-quarters full glass of whisky precariously balanced on his stomach. Barlow didn't disturb him. He switched off the light, slipped out of the room and closed the door quietly behind him.

There were no messages for him when he got back to the hotel. His new friend Toby Grant seemed to have forgotten him already. But he wasn't upset. Like Sixsmith, but for different reasons, he went to bed and slept like a baby.

Toby Grant phoned in at half-past eleven. Barlow wasn't interested in social chitchat. He went straight to the point. 'How did you get on in Sixy's place?'

He wasn't disappointed.

'I had a good look round,' Grant told him. 'Nothing. I think you're chasing water. My little sister's diary would pose a bigger threat to national security – yours or ours ... ' He left space for a chuckle, or a sigh of relief that didn't come, and added, half apologetically, 'But let me fill you in properly. What are you doing for lunch?'

'Nothing.'

'Meet me in the News Bar at the Regent Hotel, Collins Street. About one o'clock?'

It was a whisky-and-water or gin-and-tonic bar. The beer was not recommended, and the clientele looked like a bunch of extras from *Citizen Kane*.

Toby Grant was talking earnestly to an Orson Welles lookalike, but detached himself in mid-sentence when he spotted Barlow. He brought with him a nearly empty glass of gin and tonic and touched it down on a dry patch of the bar.

'Whatcha drinking, Harry?'

'Whisky and water – no ice.' Barlow didn't open the conversation and the two of them stood awkwardly and uncommunicatively, pressed shoulder to shoulder by the *Citizen Kane* mob, as Grant waited patiently to catch the eye of the waiter with the fancy waistcoat.

Grant picked up the two drinks once they arrived and pointed his chin across the room. 'Let's go over there.' He headed for an empty table in one of the small, discreet alcoves against the far wall, sat down and put on his sincere expression. 'No problem getting in,' he said after he'd lit his cigarette and tested the strength of his gin. 'But I reckon he was up to something shifty – everything was neatly tucked away in a locked drawer. Far too tidy. Writers don't behave like that,' he explained, with a serious expression. 'They like to work in a shithouse atmosphere with everything left lying around in untidy heaps all over the place.'

113

Barlow stared. His expression remained one of gullible interest. 'So he was definitely writing something, then?'

Toby Grant stared back; it was one of his strong points, his honest expression. 'Didn't I say, Harry? I thought I'd told you. Oh yes, he was writing all right. He'd got a whole bloody book there. I had a good look at the stuff he'd put in the computer and, as I told you on the phone, there was nothing in it to set Canberra's arse twitching. I made a note or two of an oblique reference to ASIS, but apart from that ... ' Toby shrugged his shoulders. 'Nothing.'

Barlow waited a second and allowed the young Australian to take a long pull from his glass. 'I'm glad Canberra's arse is comfortable, Toby,' he said, then smiled – no warmth, just an elongation of the lips. 'You don't mind me calling you Toby?'

Toby's smile was genuine. 'No, I wish you would – Harry.'

Barlow's smile remained in place. 'But it's London's arse I'm more interested in. It's the general content of Sixy's memoirs that we're curious about. You said you had a good look at what he'd been writing, but did you manage to get into it at all?'

Toby Grant grinned happily. He reckoned he could afford a happy grin.

'I've done better than that, Harry. I whipped it out and made a copy for you.' Barlow wasn't to know that all reference to ASIS's adventures in the Triangle had been eliminated from the text.

Barlow gave him a proper smile. 'Good work, Toby. You haven't shown this to anybody else, have you?'

'What do you think I am, Harry? I made a disk copy then erased everything from Sixsmith's computer. I got it printed up and read it, cover to cover, last night.'

'Well?' asked Barlow.

'I think you're going to have to read it yourself, Harry. There's a bit of Irish stuff that could be embarrassing for you. Trust me on that one. I'll pretend I didn't read it.'

Barlow picked up his glass and drained the whisky from it slowly. 'Thanks, Toby. I'll have a look at it right away.' He placed his empty glass back on the table and stood up. Then, as if it was an afterthought, he looked Toby in the eye and said, 'It was only the one copy you made?'

Toby didn't blink or blush. 'That's right.'

'And nobody else has been through it except you?'

'Take my word for it, Harry.'

Toby Grant watched Harry Barlow's taxi until it was out of sight, then walked briskly into Flinders Street and across Princes Bridge. He found Sophie Ward sitting in a car tucked between a sporty BMW 3i8 and a black Ford saloon under the trees in the parking bays opposite Six-smith's flat.

He slid in beside her. 'Have you had your lunch, Soph?'

'It's my diet day,' she said without smiling. 'Which is just as well. Is this the best we can do, two chiefs and no Indians?'

'Why, what's happening?'

'Nothing. Why are we doing this?'

'Dubrovnik thinks the Brits might move in and whistle Sixsmith away to a place where everyone wears white coats – or worse.'

'The silly bugger's gone over the top! Since I've been here nobody's gone in and nobody's come out. It's a waste of time, Toby, and boring.'

'That sounds like the whole philosophy of life, Sophie. D'you want to go and get something to eat now?'

'No thanks. Oh, something that might interest you if this little time-waster is going on for more than another hour or two.' She jerked her chin across the road at Six-smith's flat. 'The flat on the floor below our friend's place is empty. The owners would be amenable to a short-term let.' She pulled a face. 'With a little bit of official elbow I reckon we could be sitting in comfortable armchairs staring through a crack in the door at anybody going in or out of the place upstairs.'

Toby stared across the road for half a minute. It couldn't be better. 'Does it have a nice, soft, king-size bed?'

Her eyes hardened. 'I thought you Canberra-based people never drank on duty?'

Grant touched her jean-clad thigh. It was firm and un-yielding. She didn't move.

'You can't see the landing from the bedroom,' she added after a while.

'How d'you know?'

She wrinkled her eyes but didn't reply.

'You've done this place before,' he said accusingly. He felt a pang of envy. 'Is that what's known as an in-depth recce?'

'You could be right.'

'Well, you're going to be doing it on your own this time.'

'Why's that, Toby? Have I hurt your feelings?'

Toby Grant smiled crookedly. 'You've done that all right! But that's not the reason. I've been taken off this little caper. Arthur Gunne has demanded the pleasure of my company in Washington.'

'You lucky sod! How long for?'

'Three weeks. I think this Sixsmith is a dead dog any-way. I'm going to miss your company, Sophie.'

'I'll miss yours too, Toby, but I'll learn to live with it. I'll bring in Frank Robertson. He can do the in-depth part of it. Shall we see you when you come back?'

'Count on it, Soph!'

10

Two days later, another flight from Canberra brought Tom Collins to Melbourne's main airport at Tullamarine. With no baggage to delay him, he cut through the airport to the Travelodge Motel and booked a room. He needed it for the telephone. He sat on the edge of the bed and dialled the number he'd rung on Thursday from Canberra. It was answered by the same coarse Belfast accent, but there was no conversation, just a short exchange of instructions and directions. He replaced the phone and returned to the main foyer and reception area, where he found a soft-backed chair facing the plate-glass doors. It was a short wait. He'd barely reached the fourth page of the *Age* when the navy-blue Toyota drove into the entrance porch, stopped for a moment while the driver wound down his window and showed his face, then drove off again.

Collins folded his newspaper, dropped it into a waste basket, then got to his feet and casually strolled through the door and out into the sun.

The Toyota was waiting in the car park, its engine still running. Collins opened the door and ducked into the front passenger seat.

'Hello, Flynn.'

The driver just looked at him and brought a slight hawking grunt from somewhere at the back of his throat. It could have been 'Hello', it could have been the makings of a Bombay oyster. It didn't bother Collins. He didn't turn round; he'd already seen the two men sitting in the back. They weren't talking either. There were no introductions; they all sat in silence until Flynn drove the car into a deserted picnic area in the Organ Pipes National Park and switched off the engine. At a nod from Flynn, the two men stepped out of the back, lit cigarettes and strolled across the grass to a nearby wooden picnic table and sat down. They didn't talk to each other, they just sat, smoked, and looked around as if it was the first time either of them had seen grass growing wild.

Collins watched them for a second, then brought a sheet of paper from his inside pocket and turned to face Fergal Flynn. Flynn wound down the window on his side and, like his two friends, lit a cigarette, blowing smoke out of the open window and staring straight ahead. He didn't offer the packet to Collins. It wasn't bad manners, it was just something he never did.

Collins studied the Northern Irishman with interest. His reputation as a wet-work expert had been built over twenty years of killing security forces in Northern Ireland and cold-bloodedly executing those of his own side who had dared to stray. He had other qualities; tenacity and determination. Flynn would die before he gave up on a job. But for all his dubious talent, he looked nothing special. Clean-shaven, with jet-black hair, he wore a crisp white shirt open at the neck, exposing an overlarge Adam's apple. If he had a weakness, it was his eyes. They betrayed what he was. Dark blue, with heavy, almost black, rings beneath, they stared coldly, almost unblinkingly, as if they had lost the propensity for compassion or emotion. They were the eyes of a killer. Flynn sensed Collin's examination, but just sat and smoked. He didn't speak.

Collins broke the silence with a preliminary cough,

then said, reading from the sheet of paper on his knee: 'Tall, very fair, blond hair, looks like one of the muscle-men in an Australian soap. Name: Grant, Toby. You've been here before. Does that mean anything to you?'

Flynn shook his head.

Collins didn't expect anything else. 'He's an Australian Security and Intelligence Organization operative and he's watching a guy named Sixsmith. Sixsmith's an English-man, ex-MI, living somewhere here in Melbourne. We want the Englishman, so find one, find the other.'

'Big place, Melbourne.' Flynn hadn't been holding his breath, but the smoke left his pursed lips as if through a fractured exhaust valve. 'You'd need more than the description of an Aussie beach bum to find someone who doesn't want to be found. What's he doing, this Brit?' He pumped out another burst of used smoke. He didn't bother with the open window, but directed it against the windscreen and allowed it to find its own way out. 'And why's he being looked at by the G-men?'

Collins didn't laugh. He wasn't expected to. He ex-plained to the taciturn Irishman what it was all about, and, without mentioning her name, Barbara O'Donnell's thoughts on the subject. He concluded by saying, 'I want this Sixsmith's manuscript and I want him to authenticate its contents. What you do with him afterwards is your own business, but he must put his mark on whatever it is that has got the Aussies sniffing the air like gun dogs.' He folded up the sheet of paper and shoved it back in his in-side pocket. 'As far as is known, the British aren't in the field yet, so I want this done before they hear about this guy Sixsmith's venture into the literary world.'

But Flynn's thoughts had gone off on a tangent.

'Does this stuff say that he killed Peddy O'Dwyer?'

Collins shrugged. 'I don't know what it says, but I understand he was involved. You knew O'Dwyer?'

'Didn't we all? I'd like to meet the fuckers who topped him.'

'Well, here's your chance. Find Sixsmith and you'll probably be in the company of someone who might at least know something about O'Dwyer.' Collins was an intelligent man. Like most of his countrymen, he was dedicated to a united Ireland and the cause of Republicanism, but he wasn't a PIRA boot boy; not one of the bombs, bullets, blood and 'peace through superior firepower' brigade.

Flynn spat out of the open window and stuck the cigarette back between his lips. He allowed a few seconds' requiem for Peadar O'Dwyer, then twisted his head and by pursing his lips round the cigarette, pointed it at the two men in silent communion at the picnic table. 'They'll find him,' he rasped, 'and his writing, then we'll coffin the bastard. No sweat there. What d'you want done with the Aussie?'

Collins jerked his head round abruptly. 'Steady on, Flynn,' he snapped. 'We're not, as you quaintly put it, coffining anybody this season – not Sixsmith, not Grant, not anybody else. We're all right here, thank you, and I want to keep it that way. We've no arguments with the Australians, quite the opposite, and there's nothing to be gained in upsetting them. Let's concentrate on the bloody British. Leave the Aussies out of it – and that'll be an order right from the top of the tree. Don't forget it, Flynn. It'll be your head bouncing in the gutter if you start the Australians on the warpath. Am I making myself clear?'

Flynn's eyes remained blank. If Collins's words had gone in, there was no indication. He flicked the ash off his dwindling cigarette and turned to look out of the open window. 'OK. But you haven't said what you want done with blondie. What happens if he gets in the way?'

'See that he goes for an early bath. Hurt him. Break his

legs so he can't chase you – you know what to do. Christ, Flynn, you don't need me to spell it out, just be careful you don't drop him over the edge . . . ' Collins hesitated for a second, then relaxed the tight line of his lips. 'Unless you can guarantee no sound or vision – if you get my meaning.'

Flynn nodded. He got the message.

But Collins wasn't finished. He leaned forward slightly and studied the two men sitting at the picnic table. The one sitting on the right-hand side looked like a third-year theology student having a break from an early lecture. He had ruffled, light brown hair and glasses with thick double-pebble lenses; he'd be totally blind without them. His protruding teeth, resting wetly on his bottom lip, gave him a somewhat slack-jawed expression. His companion couldn't have been anything but Australian; long-limbed, tanned features, determined, hazel-coloured eyes, and a straightforward, honest expression. He looked as though butter wouldn't melt in his mouth. 'Are those two all right? What are their mouths like?'

Flynn didn't follow his gaze. 'Don't worry about them,' he grunted. 'They come from good families. Vinnie Doyle, the one with glasses, has been with me before. We know each other. He's all right. He walked out of the Kesh in 'eighty-five. He was on a fifteen for doing a Provo tout. Not bad, considering the tout was sitting with his feet up in Castlereagh surrounded by his new Proddy police chums. Vinnie did him all right – and got away with it. He was shopped by another tout after they'd picked him up for speeding along Ormeau Road. Speeding, would you fuckin' believe!'

'I asked about his mouth, Flynn, not his bloody life story. What about the other one?'

Flynn shrugged the rebuke aside. 'He's Australian. Jack Sullivan. His family's Irish. He's been helping out. He's been a front-liner in London but at the moment he's over here clearing the wax from his ears after the Windsor Castle bombing. He likes the work, and he's keen to get back to the front line. He'll be very pleased when I tell him the front line's come to him.' Flynn glanced at Collins out of the corner of his eye and studied him for a few seconds. His face didn't show what his findings were, but his thin lips tightened into an even thinner line. It didn't worry him that the only name he had for the man giving the orders was 'Galloglass'. The fact that it was the code-name for the head of the Joint Official and Provisional Intelligence Network Far East was sufficient for Fergal Flynn.

Flynn flicked his cigarette out of the window and without turning his head said, 'You well covered here?'

'Don't worry about me,' Collins replied. 'Just find this bloody Sixsmith, squeeze the bugger's balls and get him to spew up a complete set of his memoirs – which you'll deposit at a drop in Canberra. I'll let you have its location in a minute.'

'How do I get in touch with you?'

'You don't. You don't even try. After today I don't want any personal contact with you, or any of your friends. You're on your own, Flynn.'

'If I run into a problem?'

'Get yourself out of it.' Collins stopped for a moment, considered the possibilities, then relented. 'I'll ring your Melbourne contact number at nine minutes past nine three days from now. That'll be Wednesday. If you don't answer, I'll do it again three days after that. If there's no reply the second time, I'll send someone to come and see what the bloody hell's gone wrong. Does that suit you?'

'Why don't I ring you when I've got something to say?'

'I've just told you, it's out of the question – end of argument. And here's the other thing. There's to be no trouble for the Australian authorities – no bodies, not even British ones, photographed lying in Melbourne's gutters, and no blood splashed up and down Flinders Street. Have you got that?'

Flynn ignored him.

It wasn't good enough for Collins. 'The ups and downs of this one, Flynn, are on your bloody head. If it goes wrong, you'll be the one with your trousers rolled up to your knees telling the Army Council enquiry team all about it.' He glanced sideways and waited a second. 'Do you understand?'

Flynn nodded his head. 'Let's go back to the Sixsmith guy,' he said. 'You want his acknowledgement that everything he's written is kosher. OK, he'll do that, or say it's a load of bloody eyewash he made up on the plane over. Whatever it is, he'll have something to say. But what I want with him is some talk about Peadar O'Dwyer's murder, which you reckon he might know a lot about – you did reckon that, didn't you?'

Collins said nothing.

'Well, whether you did or not – what happens if, when we've finished with him he trips up and breaks his neck on his way to the bank?'

Collins appeared not to have heard. He straightened up in his seat and stared at the heavy gold watch on his wrist. He didn't look at Flynn. 'Get me back to the airport, Flynn, I want to make the half-past two airbus.'

Flynn didn't move. 'I said, what about this guy Sixsmith?'

Collins considered the question, then, raising his eyes from his watch, made his decision. 'OK, he can go. No noise though.'

Flynn sniffed wetly. It was an expression of satisfaction.

11

Flynn and Vinnie Doyle moved around the right places, spoke to the right people and listened for anything that sounded like Greville Sixsmith. Jack Sullivan took the other direction. He went for Toby Grant. It got him nowhere; every other third-generation Australian answered his description.

'I know a girl who works in Australia House in London,' said Sullivan.

'A lot of fuckin' good that is!' snarled Flynn. 'You're in friggin' Melbourne, not friggin' London, in case you haven't noticed. If you've got fuck all constructive to say, just sit there and say fuck all while me and Vinnie rack our friggin' brains.' Flynn's hold on his temper, fragile at the best of times, was edging towards the homicidal. Vinnie Doyle, who knew all about Flynn's temper, kept his mouth shut and his eyes averted. He concentrated on studying the tin of VB in his hand. But Sullivan was different. Sullivan was an Australian; he didn't subscribe to homeland Irish respect for homicidal maniacs.

'I could ring her up.' he continued unabashed, 'ask her to find out when this Pom left England, where he was heading, and the address of his Aussie sponsor. We could get at him that way. At least it'll be better than buggering around here with our heads in paper bags.'

'I just said fu . . . ' Flynn's bared teeth froze in midsentence as his mind caught up with Sullivan's suggestion.

His face relaxed as his anger subsided, only to be replaced by a mixture of surprise and cunning. Doyle was way ahead of him. He allowed the silence in the room to develop while he finished studying the words on the tin of Victoria Beer, then looked up slowly.

'There might be something in that, Fergal,' he said casually.

It had no effect on Flynn. He kept his eyes on Sullivan's face as his brain worked over the possibilities – and then he saw the light. 'This girl in London,' he said. 'How sure can you be that she'll do the right thing?'

Sullivan raised his head and crossed the second finger over the first. 'We're like that, me and Charly,' he said with a grin. 'She'll do what she's bloody well told to do. I've got her trained.'

'When did you last see her, Jacko?' asked Doyle, and prayed that the silly bugger wouldn't say five years ago.

He needn't have worried.

'Six weeks ago,' replied Sullivan. 'She went back to London to get some sleep and learn how to walk again.' He grinned broadly. A lethal mixture of Ireland and Australia, he looked like one of the Kellys on a wanted poster. 'She'll play any sort of game I put in front of her.'

Flynn had already made up his mind.

'OK.' He looked at his watch. 'It's a bloody long way round,' he said, 'but let's give it a go.'

Just before lunch Charlene called in at Immigration in Australia House, London, and sat chatting about nothing with Annie Ross. Annie Ross was senior secretary in Records; like Charlene she was from Bendigo in Victoria. It was the small-town connection, a long way from home. Just as Annie started showing signs of impatience for her daily lunch-time salad sandwich and spritzer Charlene said, 'D'you remember Jacko Sullivan?'

'Who doesn't!' Annie glanced pointedly at the clock.

'Don't be like that,' pouted Charlene. 'I had a call from him this morning. He's got a little problem that he thinks we could help him with.' She ignored Annie's arched eyebrows. 'It seems a cousin of Jacko's mother emigrated to Oz quite recently and has been swallowed up somewhere in Vicky, they think – probably Melbourne. Anyway, they can't find him and he didn't leave a forwarding address.'

Annie wasn't all that interested. 'I don't see how – '

Charlene explained: 'On his application form he'd have to put his home address, right?'

'Right.'

'Jacko could start there. But you know what funny buggers these English relations are.'

'Don't I just.'

'And wouldn't the application form also show where he intended settling in Australia? He'd have to give an address, wouldn't he?'

'Yes, but it's all confidential.'

'Of course it is,' agreed Charlene quickly, 'but you're not betraying any confidences, you're telling me, and I work here too. I'm the one committing a sin – that's if either of us is.'

Annie tapped the table with an agitated finger while she worked out the implications. After a moment she gave Charlene a tight smile and said, 'I'll give it a thought after lunch. You buying?'

'Jacko?' Charlene beat a tattoo with her ball pen on the edge of her computer keyboard as she spoke down the phone to Sullivan. 'Your mother's cousin gave his UK address as Surbiton on his application form. That's a suburb just – '

'Never mind that,' cut in Sullivan. 'What about Oz?'

Charlene ended the drum roll with a flourish and allowed herself a little smile of satisfaction. 'Melbourne,' she said. 'He's living in Melbourne.'

'Where in bloody Melbourne?'

Charlene's smile disintegrated and the pen started another frenetic tattoo. 'That's all the form asks for,' she replied nervously. 'State and town. Like I said, Melbourne, that's in Victoria.'

'Oh shit, Charly! That's fuck all good to me.' Sullivan let his temper have full rein. He closed his eyes. Fuckin' marvellous! He could just see it: *'I've got it, Fergal. That guy Sixsmith is living in Melbourne, and in case you don't know it, Melbourne is in Victoria!'*

'Jacko? You still there? What's the matter?' Charlene's anxious voice brought him out of his trance.

'I'm thinking, Charly.' His eyes narrowed. 'Can you get through to Canberra on the fax?'

'Not if it's anything to do with immigration. That's confidential, and it's not my department.'

'How did you get this info, then?'

'From a friend who looks after applications.'

'For Christ's sake, Charly! Tell her to do it then. Get through to Canberra.'

'What if she won't?'

'Fuckin' make her!' The blood was pounding behind Jacko's eyes again. Charlene was lucky she was on the end of a telephone. If she'd been anywhere within reach she'd have had Sullivan's horny hands tightening around her throat by now. As it was, the atmosphere had no difficulty travelling down the line. She felt it and shivered. She'd been on the receiving end of one of Jacko Sullivan's frustrations before. It wasn't nice.

'Listen,' he hissed. 'Tell your bloody friend to call her mates, unofficially, in Canberra. She can tell 'em she needs a signature that she forgot to take when she was

127

dealing with Mr Sixsmith and that she's going to be up shit creek if she doesn't get it. She can say she hasn't time to go through the channels because the boss is screaming blue murder. They'll do it. These bloody people are as thick as shit when one of them's about to get her fingers chopped off. Tell her to tell them she must have this bugger's address — nothing written, just off the cuff.' It all sounded perfectly reasonable to Jacko Sullivan.

'Jacko, I can't — '

'Ring me back with the address.' Sullivan's voice had a note of finality in it. Charlene was suddenly on her own. The phone had gone dead in her ear.

But she needn't have worried. Annie played the game through for her and rang her opposite Brownie in Central Records (Immigration) ACT. The old-girl network slipped into gear and, within the time it took for her to run her fingers across the keyboard, Greville Sixsmith's security was blown.

'Your mother's cousin's address, Jacko,' said a relieved Charlene into the phone, 'is — have you got a piece of paper? OK? Apartment 5B, Prince Philip Mansions, Southgate Street, South Melbourne. His phone number is — ' she went on, to show how efficient she'd been.

But Jacko wasn't interested. He cut her off roughly. 'You sure that's it? You sure he's still at that address?'

'Canberra Registry says he is — at least he was about fifteen minutes ago. You can tell your mum, and she can pop round for a cup of tea. Be a nice surprise for him, won't it?'

'It'll be that all right!' said Jacko in a rare burst of humour. 'I owe you one, Charly.'

'Make sure you don't forget it.'

12

Flynn and Doyle spent the next twenty-four hours watching Greville Sixsmith's flat. They marked the watcher in the flat below, but missed Sophie Ward.

'That guy'll have to be taken out,' said Flynn.

'Permanently?' asked Doyle. There was nothing in his voice, this was normal conversation for boys who'd first seen the light of day in Belfast's 'Little India'. He could have been querying the price of potatoes. But it caused Flynn to react.

'No, not a bloody hope. He's to be shoved to one side with a bump on his head and a blinding headache that stops him seeing what's going on around him. But he's gotta be able to walk about after we've been in and lifted this Sixsmith bozo and his bundle of papers.' Flynn stared unblinkingly into Vinnie Doyle's blank face. 'Have you got that, Vinnie? D'you understand? We're not knocking off Australian spooks, that's if you still want to be able to enjoy next St Paddy's Day.'

'So how're we going to do this one?' Vinnie Doyle wasn't particularly worried about next St Patrick's Day — next week was about as far as his horizon extended. Neither was he cowed by Flynn's stare; he'd been stared at by bigger and tougher bastards than this one.

'By the look of it,' said Flynn, turning his head to study for the thousandth time the entrance to Prince Philip Mansions, 'the Aussie's on a minder job. We don't know whether Sixsmith knows he's got a minder, but I'd be bloody surprised if he did. Our info is that he's no better loved by the Australian security people than he is by us, so Christ knows what they're doing hanging around.'

'You sound as if you've got a personal interest in the Brit, Fergie,' said Doyle as he wound down his window about four inches and lit a cigarette. He didn't offer one to Flynn. He flicked the spent match through the gap and sent a mouthful of smoke to follow it before turning back to study Flynn's profile. 'Is he for burning?'

Flynn's jaw stiffened. 'My information is that he could have been involved in the murder of Peadar O'Dwyer. That's what we're going to find out – among other things.'

'And if he wasn't involved?'

'He goes up the same pipe. He's a Brit, ain't he? He'll do for a start. Let's hope old Peddy appreciates all I'm doing to find the bastard who put him in his coffin, God rest the poor old sod's soul.'

Flynn didn't cross himself; neither did Doyle. Doyle hadn't time for the niceties of killing. He was one of the bullet-in-the-back-of-the-head school, or between the shoulder blades, anywhere that reduced the risk of getting one back, and anyone who offended the rules was eligible. Killing was killing for Vinnie. Vendettas and high ideals belonged to the others.

'I think you're going to have a ball, Fergie.' Doyle drew deeply on his cigarette, then changed the subject. 'What do we make of the skirt that's been going in and out of that building?'

'Nothing. The Australians don't use skirt for outdoor work. They're not like the Brits. Forget her.'

'Suits me. When do we go in?'

Flynn studied his watch. 'Tonight, say, ten o'clock. It's

130

a good time, getting on for night, but with plenty of traffic about to cover our movements in case we need to bolt for it. But I'm not planning for a panic.'

'What about transport?'

'I'll leave it up to you and Sullivan.' His eyes continued to cover the area outside the flat. 'It can wait over there.' He pointed to a no-waiting zone on Sixsmith's side of Southgate Street. 'It won't be there long enough to attract interest.'

'Three-quarters of an hour?' Doyle was doing his own sums.

'Christ, no!' rasped Flynn. 'We're not dealing with a bloody British Army brick holed up in Clonard. This is one frightened old man. Bang the bugger on the head, drop him down the stairs ... ' Flynn held up his hand, palm forward, and touched each finger as he showed Doyle how he'd worked it all out: 'Five up, five to fix the watcher, five to do the Brit, five to find the paper and five back down to the car.' He turned the hand into a fist and slammed it into his other hand. 'Twenty-five minutes for the job and the rest of the night to make the bastard hum. You happy about that?'

Doyle flicked his cigarette end through the gap in the window and wound it up. 'You're the boss, Fergie. If you say it's OK, then for me it's OK. You want me to do the Aussie?'

'Yeh. I don't think Jacko's got the arm for that sort of thing.'

'Or the balls, I wouldn't wonder. Keep him with you. I might trip over him.' Doyle looked down at his watch. 'How about a drink and a pie? I'm bloody famished.'

'Go on then.'

'You coming?'

'No, I want to watch some more. Don't bring me anything back. I'll eat when we start talking to the Brit.'

131

13

Somewhere in the centre of the city a clock struck ten. Flynn, Doyle and Sullivan got out of a dark blue car, gathered on the pavement and walked naturally towards Prince Philip Mansions. There was a brief confusion at the entrance while they sorted out who went first, but at Flynn's hissed command they entered the building and allowed the door to close on its spring behind them.

Frank Robertson, Sophie's agent, came out of the bathroom, pulling at the zip of his trousers as he glanced at the open front door. It was the scheduled time for reporting to Sophie, who should be on station outside the apartment in half an hour or so. He moved his head fractionally so that he could see the stairs leading to Sixsmith's upper flat. Satisfied, he turned his back on the door and reached out for the phone.

He hadn't seen the three men standing in the blind spot at the top of the stairs, waiting. Robertson began to dial. This was the moment Vinnie Doyle had been waiting for. He raised his finger to quieten the others and moved. The clicking of the phone buttons muffled the silent sound he made as he sidled through the gap in the door. Instinct made Robertson turn. But he was too late. He caught a vague movement of shadow behind him before it was blotted out by an enormous, explosive thump as a rubber-covered steel bar thwacked just behind his right ear.

Distorted by the flashing, searing white streaks at the back of his eyes, he had a vague impression of three white holes in a black, woolly face as momentum kept him turning, and then nothing. He heard the swishing sound as the steel bar cut through the air again, but was already on his way down and didn't feel the sickening smash across the bridge of his nose.

Doyle waited until Robertson stopped twitching, then stripped the mask off his face and shoved it into a pocket. Leaning down, he turned Robertson on to his back and studied his face. Something had disturbed him – a flicker of an eyelid? A miniscule twitch? Whatever it was, Doyle wasn't going to let it pass. The steel bar reappeared in one hand, and with the other he grasped a handful of hair, lifted Robertson's head six inches off the carpet and with a crisp wrist-whip cracked the bar viciously just above the ear again. His timing was perfect, but it wasn't going to please Flynn. Frank Robertson was dead. Except for a faint flush from exertion, Vinnie Doyle's face was devoid of expression.

He closed the door quietly behind him, moved into a shadow on the landing cast by the overhanging stairway, and waited.

It was a short wait.

Flynn was a little more delicate with Greville Sixsmith's head, but no less emphatic.

He touched the unconscious Sixsmith with the toe of his boot, then ground his heel into Greville's hand and studied his face. Greville didn't feel a thing. Flynn looked almost happy. 'Stick that in his arm,' he told Jacko, and handed him a loaded syringe. 'No! Not through his shirt, you bloody idiot! Roll his sleeve up – that's it – jab the bloody thing in his vein. There. That's it. Good. Give 'im the lot, and then watch for the whites of his eyes.'

He turned his back on Jacko and inspected the flat.

The room was unchanged from when Harry Barlow had last visited it. The remains of a bottle of whisky lay on its side, and a glass, into which Greville had been pouring his supper when Flynn arrived, lay on the carpet in a disappearing puddle below the desk. Flynn stood the bottle upright and, without expectation, grasped the handle of the drawer and tugged. It was unlocked. Flynn regarded it suspiciously, then, with another sidelong glance at the half-empty bottle, tightened his lips and pulled the drawer to its full extent.

It was empty except for Sixsmith's passport. Flynn compared the photograph with the face of the man lying on the floor. This was the man.

Flynn pulled the drawer out of its housing and turned it upside down. He studied the packet taped to its outside before ripping it off and inspecting the disk. He knew exactly what he was dealing with. He knew time was short, but he had to know what was on the disk. He switched the computer on and loaded it. He scrolled through the text rapidly, stopping every so often until, with a sudden flash, the name O'Dwyer seemed to fill the screen. This was it. He needed a hard copy to study at his leisure, but he knew computers were another world to Doyle and Sullivan. He was going to get no help there. He'd have to print on Sixsmith's machine.

'Go and tell Vinnie I'm going to be a while,' he hissed at Sullivan. 'I want enough time to print this thing here. Tell him to watch the entrance.'

Sullivan's eyes boggled. 'Jesus!'

'Just do as I bloody say!'

Sophie Ward finished manoeuvring her car into a vacant slot and looked at her watch. Robertson should have called in half an hour ago. She frowned for a second, then sat up stiffly in her seat and poked the aerial of a Motorola out of the car window and depressed the key.

'Robbo,' she said under her breath. 'Answer the bloody thing . . .'

There was no response.

She jabbed the buttons again and raised her voice another octave. 'Answer the bloody phone, Robbo!'

Still nothing

She stared for a second at the entrance and then bent her head to look higher, at the fourth and fifth floors of the building. It told her nothing. 'Oh, Jesus!' She shook the handset violently, then swore again and threw it on to the seat beside her.

Flynn watched as the last page slipped out of the printer, then leant across and collected the sheets together. He didn't bother reading any more but stuffed the bundle into a plastic shopping bag. He half-turned when the door opened and an ashen-faced Sullivan peered round the corner. It had been a long half-hour for Sullivan.

'Shouldn't we be going now, F-Fergie?' he said in a hoarse whisper. There was a definite quiver in his voice that he made no attempt to control. Jacko Sullivan was made of different stuff to the others. Different environment, different character. Blowing up Brits at long range in London was one thing; coming face to face with the result was not quite the game he'd joined to play. He wasn't happy with this lot and it showed. He was breathing heavily and his face was flushed with an underlying fear. Averting his eyes from Greville's body, he darted a nervous glance around the room, then back to Flynn's impassive face.

Flynn was not to be rushed; this was his speciality. 'Put a coat on him,' he said in his normal voice. He could have been in a Saturday street market selecting a bag of apples. He stared hard at the Australian.

Jacko gave a nervous twitch of his head in acknowledgement, closed the door behind him, then turned on his knees and scrabbled across the carpet to Greville's coat, thrown casually on to the back of a chair. He tried to thread Greville's limp and useless arms into the coat but his hands weren't up to it. He turned him on his side. Greville's head bounced uncomplainingly with a sickening thump. It was too much for Sullivan. 'I need help.' He gritted his teeth to stop them bouncing against each other. 'I need f-fuckin' help with this f-fu – '

'Shut up, you stupid, useless bastard!' hissed Flynn. 'You'll have the whole fuckin' building awake. Just fuckin' get on with it!'

'I can't get the bugger dressed all on my own. Let me get Vinnie up here.'

'You'll get no one. Get that raincoat off the back of the door, lay it out flat, then roll the bugger into it. You're like a fuckin' old woman!'

'Look at the time!'

'Sod the bloody time!' Flynn walked across the room to the telephone. Beside it was a notepad and a cheap Biro. He stared at the pad. It had one word written on it: BAR-LOW. This was surrounded by the squiggled doodles of a very tortured mind. Flynn put the pad in his pocket, walked back to the still struggling Australian and knelt down beside him. Between them they manoeuvred Greville Sixsmith's passive body into the dark-coloured raincoat.

'Will he be able to breathe?' Jacko rocked himself back on his knees and stared at the body. His voice sounded like that of a man who'd just run halfway up the Eiffel Tower.

'Better than you, I should imagine! Here, I'll give you a lift up. Stick him over your shoulder and collect Vinnie on the way down. The two of you can walk him along the road to the car. I'll follow you down.'

*

Sophie got out of her car, walked quickly along her side of the pavement, then cut across the road and came up behind the illegally parked dark blue car. She glanced casually, saw it was empty, then came back and checked the inside. Nothing unusual. An old banger. A twelve-year-old Holden. She noted its registration, then moved quickly to the entrance of Prince Philip Mansions, and waited at the foot of the stairs, listening. She heard a vague murmuring above her, then definite heavy movement down the stairs. As the sounds grew closer, the murmurings became distinct, although hushed, voices. She waited another second, then moved quickly out of the building. She dashed across the road and threw herself into her car, lowering her head so that only her eyes appeared above the dashboard.

She'd left it tight.

She'd barely recovered her breath when Doyle's head appeared round the doorway. Cautiously, it swivelled to the right, then to the left, then gave a long, searching glance across the road. His head vanished and Sophie watched the rest of him reappear a few seconds later, followed by Sullivan. There was no hesitation this time. Doyle waited at the entrance while Sullivan trotted down the road to the car and swung open the rear nearside door. He rejoined Doyle and, one on either side of the unconscious but well-wrapped-up Sixsmith, they staggered down the road like three happy drunks. They bundled Sixsmith on to the back seat with all the finesse of coal men, and with Doyle clambering in beside him and Sullivan taking the wheel, they slammed the doors. The engine started with an indiscreet roar.

As he darted out of the doorway and strode with concealed haste towards the car, Sophie couldn't see the third man's face, but by the way he waved his free hand at the driver he wasn't very happy. She waited for him to turn as he slid into the passenger seat, but his face remained shielded. Neither had she had a clear look at the faces of the other two. But what about Robertson? She shrugged to herself as she straightened up in her seat and prepared to follow the blue car. Robbo would have to nurse his own headache. Sophie had never entered a house after a PIRA active-service unit had paid a visit.

Sophie ducked again as, under Flynn's management, the blue car moved carefully out of its parking place and at a funereal pace went down the road, through the car park underpass and out into City Road and then St Kilda Road. The Holden paused at the major road, then, turning sharply left, gathered speed over Princes Bridge and into the city. Sophie followed at a distance and settled comfortably and unobtrusively behind Flynn and his crew as they made their way out of the city centre and headed north, past the cemetery, until they joined the Hume Highway and settled down to a steady 110 km/h.

Sophie, some distance behind, had no difficulty keeping in touch. She even had enough time to consider what it was all about, but after several miles she gave up thinking. Nothing slotted into position. Nothing made sense as they headed out of the built-up area of Melbourne and into the country. Had she glanced over her shoulder she'd have seen something else that wouldn't have made sense. A Melbourne taxi, its dome light extinguished, its interior in total darkness, had joined the procession and was plodding doggedly in her wake.

14

A few minutes earlier Mike Thompson had swung his cab sharply into Southgate Street from St Kilda Road, then braked hard and slowed to a crawl. Under the generous glow of the overhead lighting he watched as Sullivan and Doyle staggered the last few yards with their drunken load and then made heavy going of humping him into the rear of the car. He turned his head sharply to check whether Barlow had seen it too.

Barlow had.

'Looks like someone's had a few jars too many,' drawled Thompson. 'Must be a party going on in your flat. That drunk wouldn't be your mate, would it?'

'Wait here a second.' Barlow didn't like what he was seeing. The warning signals were buzzing in his inner ear. 'Pull in here.' There was a row of cars along the kerb, but ample gaps.

Thompson slipped into one of them, switched off his engine and half-turned his head. He didn't take his eyes off the activity further along Southgate Street.

'Anything wrong?'

'I'm not sure,' said Barlow thoughtfully 'Give 'em a couple of minutes. Let's see if anybody else comes out in that condition.'

The two men watched in silence as Flynn hurried along the pavement and ducked into the car. 'OK,' said Barlow, preparing to get out of the car as the Holden moved away. 'Let's go.'

Thompson didn't move.

'Mr Barlow?' he said after a moment.

'Yes?'

'Somebody was watching that performance. They're following the car.'

'You sure?'

'Take my word for it.'

Barlow did.

'I'm getting out. There's somebody in one of these flats I'm covering. I want to make sure he's all right, so I'll leave you to sort that lot out. Find out where the three with the drunk go to ground and then come back here for me.'

'What's the number of your mate's flat?'

Barlow told him, then slipped out of the front seat and walked with a casual air towards Prince Philip Mansions. It was an illusion. There was nothing casual about what was going on inside him. He could almost touch the feeling of impending disaster.

Now Barlow was running. Sixsmith's door was firmly closed. He stood in front of it for several seconds, listening, sensoring, but nothing happened. He knocked urgently. He didn't expect the door to open. It didn't. He stepped back a pace and glared up and down the stairs again. Now he was certain it was Sixsmith who'd been bundled into the car. The whole building had the heavy, cloying silence of a chapel of rest. Barlow's expression didn't change. He touched the brass plate of the simple lock with his finger and gave a little pressure. There was a miniscule movement of the door. It was credit-card friendly.

It took Barlow all of fifteen seconds to slip the latch on the lock, open the door and glide into the tiny hall.

The lights were on. He flattened himself against the wall and peered into the sitting room. There was no upheaval; the tables and chairs were all where they should be. There was no Greville Sixsmith either. He looked into the bedroom and the bathroom: no one.

He returned to the main room and stood in front of the bureau. He pulled the drawer fully out and looked underneath. The disk had gone – where? The same place as bloody Greville – with the three in the car. And what was the betting on Irish accents? Was that good or bad? Good for his side – a short cut to Dublin – but not so good for Sixsmith!

But why take Greville as well?

That was the worrying bit. Barlow kicked himself for negligence. He'd been too bloody complacent. After he'd set up the Australians with a floppy disk he should have whisked poor old Greville out of the firing line . . . Without moving from the door, he glanced round the room again. That was hindsight for you – the decisions came easy that way. He thought about that little gem for a few seconds, then went into the kitchen and found a clean glass. He filled an empty milk bottle with tap water and returned to Greville's sitting room. He poured himself a large measure of whisky and doubled it with water, but before raising it to his mouth glanced down at his watch. The taxi had been gone for ten minutes. He had to hope that they – whoever 'they' were – hadn't taken Greville to Darwin! Until Thompson came back there was nothing he could do. He turned Greville's favourite chair round so that it faced the door, brought up another chair to rest his feet on, and made himself comfortable.

It was time for soul-searching. Things had gone badly wrong. Where did he go from here? Greville Sixsmith had gone, and it didn't take too long a stretch of the imagination to guess who'd taken him. The Irish were quick movers. It had to be them, this was their style; one sniff and they'd stuck Greville in the bag. And the only one to blame was himself. He should have shifted him the minute Grant had lifted the stuff from the computer. That was when the game proper had started.

He kicked himself mentally. If the Irish had snatched Sixsmith, it was bad news. Now they'd do it their way. They'd want Greville to authenticate every bloody page and that's just what Greville wouldn't do. The first weal raised on his ample backside and the whole bloody story was up the spout.

'Fuck it!'

Barlow swore out loud.

And then the doorbell rang.

He didn't jump. But there was a definite movement at the base of his stomach as he placed his glass carefully on the floor, uncurled himself from the armchair and moved on tiptoes to the door. Listening carefully, he could hear someone whistling lightly through his teeth; it was a nervous sound, coming and going, as if the whistler was looking over his shoulder. Barlow recognized it and opened the door.

'Help yourself to a drink,' he told Mike Thompson.

'Thanks.' Thompson poured a couple of inches of whisky in a glass and rested one buttock on the desk. He sipped. 'The blue car pulled into the closed garage of an old farmhouse at the end of a badly made-up track on the other side of Craigieburn — that's north of here, a small place, of interest only to the people who live there. Beyond it is nothing, just scrubland for miles on either side of the main road. The place they went to must be some sort of safe house. Nobody in their right senses would want to live there. But there you go! It's a biggish place, a spread-out bungalow type, verandah — that sort of thing. Not in good nick — know what I mean?'

Barlow nodded.

'I didn't hang about. I could see what it was from the

road that cut above it. I didn't even slow down, just carried on across the top of the road and backtracked on to a quicker way here.'

'What about the car you said was following?'

'A white Ford Falcon. It tucked itself into a broken-down barn some distance along the track, a short walk from the house.'

'What did you make of the driver?'

'Nothing, except he was on his own.'

'OK, let's go then.'

'Erm . . .'

'It's a one-man job,' said Barlow, kindly. 'A quick in, and a quicker out! Just put me there and then bugger off.'

'You sure?'

'Let's get on with it.'

Thompson edged the taxi as close into the wood side of the road as he could get it, then switched off the engine.

'About a hundred and fifty metres,' he said huskily, and pointed straight ahead. 'The track's on the left. There's nothing else around for miles except fields and scrub – and more scrub. They're welcome to it.'

'Where's that other car you mentioned?'

'Straight ahead. When you turn into the track you'll see the yard of the old barn further down on your right. He's parked in there. You'll have to watch your step. Have you got the piece I gave you?'

Barlow patted the small bulge where the .38 was accommodated snugly in his waistband and nodded.

Thompson seemed to have repented of his earlier eagerness to get away. 'Why don't I wait? Just in case?'

Barlow shook his head. Greville out on his feet, and a one-legged veteran – the place was already overcrowded with liabilities. If he wanted transport later, there was, according to Thompson, a car waiting to be nicked just down the road. He didn't need any more complication than that. 'I'll ring you if I need anything when I get back to Melbourne. Push off, now.' He slipped out of the car, closing the door silently. Moving quietly, he melted into the dark and headed towards the track.

15

While Flynn closed the rickety doors of the garage, Doyle and Sullivan dragged Greville Sixsmith from the back seat of the car and dumped him on the dirt floor. A forced groan came from within the sack as the wind was knocked out of his body. Nobody took any notice.

'Get him into the kitchen,' said Flynn. 'And you, Vinnie, slap some life into him.' He touched Sixsmith's unmoving body with his foot. It looked as though he was testing the air in the back tyre of his car. Greville didn't feel a thing. 'I wanna talk to the bastard in about fifteen minutes.' He stopped at the door and glowered at Sullivan. 'OK, you can fuck off now.'

'What d'ya mean?'

'Get that car away from here in case anybody saw us. Don't come back here. Go home and Vinnie'll ring you some time tomorrow if we've got anything else for you. Have you got money?'

Sullivan shrugged. He looked longingly at the body on the floor. He'd recovered his nerve and liked the rules of this new game. 'I'd rather stay for the fun. What're you going to do with him, break his fuckin' legs? I'd like to watch . . .'

'Jesus Christ!' Flynn spat at the floor. It missed and spread itself out on his dirty black boot. He studied it for a moment, without revulsion, then glowered back at Sullivan. 'Just do as I fuckin' say, will you? Get that pissin' car out of the way, and get bloody lost yourself! I asked if you had any money?'

Sullivan kicked the raincoated bundle bad-temperedly, then said sulkily, 'How about a couple of hundred?'

Flynn was already counting it out. 'I don't want any fuckin' talk about tonight's happenings,' he warned as he screwed up the notes and stuck them into Sullivan's hand. 'Just keep your mouth shut. Not a fuckin' word, got it?'

Sullivan didn't reply.

'I said, have you fuckin' got it?'

'I thought you said I was to keep me mouth shut!'

Flynn spat again. This time he managed to hit the floor. 'Forget it! Help Vinnie with that and then fuck off.'

Greville felt Doyle's hand slapping his face long before he managed to raise his eyelids. The shock of waking came first, then the realization, then the recall, and then, with bladder-bursting horror, the fear.

But that was only the beginning.

It was the accent of the man slapping his face.

'Open your fuckin' eyes, Brit, and look at me.' It was Belfast – west – with all its ugly undertones.

But this is Australia . . .

Sixsmith opened his eyes and blinked into the bright light. He was pulled to his feet and stood swaying groggily, remaining upright only because of Doyle's hand grasping his shirt. 'Who the bloody hell . . .?'

CRUNCH!

Doyle's fist exploded against his cheekbone, sending him crashing backwards. Like a novice ice-skater, his feet scampered to keep up with his body until his back thumped against the wall. For a moment he hovered there, semi-upright, and then slithered to the floor. Doyle moved in, following up like a middleweight boxer closing for the kill, but he wasn't boxing; there was no fist this

146

time as he reverted to the Clonard gutter method and with vicious force brought his boot into Greville's side. Greville tried a scream but a second boot caught him in the throat and knocked the scream back to where it had started.

Flynn sat down at the kitchen table, his chin cupped in his hands as he studied the cassette recorder before him. He wasn't watching the action, his mind was on other things. He'd worked off the excitement of watching helpless men being thrashed into insensibility by the time he'd reached the age of seventeen. He lowered his eyes to the manuscript on the table in front of him and began riffling through the pages, not knowing what he was looking for. He'd barely got started when the kicks and groans from behind him suddenly stopped. He turned round in his chair.

Doyle hadn't even worked up a sweat.

'He's out again.'

Flynn flipped open the flap of the cassette recorder, checked that the tape was in position and clicked it shut again. He pushed down the key and allowed it to run for a few seconds, then switched it off.

'OK,' he said.

'What d'ya mean, OK?' drawled Vinnie Doyle. 'He's still asleep.'

'Fuck it!' Flynn walked across the room and stood above Sixsmith's huddled form. He studied him for a second, then said, 'Wake the bastard up again and stick him in a chair. I'll talk to him in a couple of minutes. Don't let him go again.'

Flynn gave another, expert, glance at Sixsmith's condition and shook his head. It wasn't sympathy, it was contempt. Greville was a dreadful sight. The punch in the face had turned his normal unhealthy pallor into a red sunset and closed his puffy eye to a narrow slit. He sat hunched on a wooden kitchen chair, his arms, crossed and wrapped round his waist, protecting the lower part of his stomach. He came perilously close to falling off the chair as he rocked from side to side and little cooing noises, wrapped in globules of blood, came from between his lips, collecting in the corner of his mouth like the frothy bubbles on the head of a mug of cocoa. Expressionless, Flynn turned away, switched on the recorder, picked up a wedge of the manuscript and began limbering up.

'Did you write this stuff, Sixsmith?' Flynn lowered his voice to a conspiratorial whisper. With both hands he held the pack of typewritten sheets at one end and flapped it up and down. It sent a wave of cool air into Sixsmith's face.

Greville didn't answer. He couldn't. The inside of his mouth was lacerated and swollen, as if the dentist had been at work in it for the last hour.

'Pull his head up.'

Doyle reached out, grabbed a handful of Greville's wispy hair and jerked upwards. Greville stared uncomprehendingly at the tall, skinny Irishman who'd moved away and rested his bottom on the corner of the table. Not a sight to bring anything but cold fear to Sixsmith.

Fergal Flynn stared back, gaunt-featured, his mouth tight and as thin as a thread of cotton, his eyes flat and brooding. There was not a trace of compassion as he studied Sixsmith and read the fear in his eyes. After a moment he glanced down at the pack of paper in his hand. He riffled through the sheets until Peadar O'Dwyer's name caught his eye. He read the page, then, before continuing, placed the earlier chapters behind him on the table.

The silence was oppressive. Greville tried to get his mind sorted out and his thoughts in some sort of order.

Doyle was still hanging on to his hair, but Greville had recovered sufficiently to help him with the task of keeping his face pointed towards the man sitting on the table.

Flynn looked up before finishing the description of O'Dwyer's killing and stared at Greville's screwed-up features. It was hard to believe. This scrawny old bugger arranged the killing at St Anne's and then packed his bags and came out here to write all about it? How did the Brits allow him to do that? He glanced down again at the remaining sheets in his hand. But he didn't read; he'd already taken in what he needed to know. But there was still the other thing – how the bloody hell had the Aussies got on to this little fucker, and how had the head of the Official and Provisional Intelligence Network Far East jumped on to the bus? Why, in the first place, were the Australians watching Sixsmith? Because they were hand-in-bloody-glove with the people who knew exactly what the little bastard was up to – who else but the bloody Brits? Very smelly. So the Aussie intelligence people had raided Sixsmith's place, made themselves a copy of this and passed on the Irish passages to 'Galloglass'. But why would they do that? Nudged by the bloody Brits again? It was a put-up – the whole bloody thing was a put-up and Galloglass had swallowed it. But how the bloody hell could he? He hadn't seen this yet – he'd only had a whisper? Or had he? Flynn pulled a face. The change of expression did nothing for the watching Sixsmith's state of mind, but Doyle locked on to it.

'OK, Fergal?' Reflecting the overhead lights, his bottle-thick lenses looked like two spotlights. They also did nothing for Sixsmith. Neither did Flynn's reply.

'Yeh. Set him up.' His voice was quiet, unexcited, matter-of-fact. 'If he's got any false teeth, drag 'em out of his mouth. I don't want him choking to death on 'em.' He moved across the room and stood close to Greville. 'Hold his head and bang it hard against the wall when I tell you.'

His eyes bored into Greville's and Greville's bladder almost burst – and it hadn't even started. The build-up. The fear. It wasn't a show, something put on for Greville; it wasn't an act, it was the way it was done, it had always been like this. It was called obtaining authentication. And Flynn was a past master at it. He spat on his hands. He was about to go to work.

'OK, Sixsmith . . .'

16

Barlow stayed in the shadows until the taxi's rear light had disappeared round the corner. It didn't really matter. The countryside to the north of Craigieburn had suspended all animation; the whole area was in shadow, nothing moved, no lights, no sound. The place could have been under curfew as the good people of Victoria slept with their windows firmly shut and the curtains fully drawn. He waited a few minutes, drinking in the lack of atmosphere, then moved slowly towards the derelict barn and the car parked around its side in the otherwise empty yard.

When he was close enough he bent his knees and tried to pick up a silhouette against the star-clustered night sky. Nothing showed. The car offered only a darker shadow against the sombre wall of the derelict barn. He stared until it took shape. It appeared to be empty. But he took no chances. He waited a few minutes more and listened for a creak of springs. Nothing. Hugging the untended hedge, he moved closer, then, without breaking out of the shadows, he went on tiptoes and peered as best he could into the rear of the car. There was no mist on any of the windows – the car had to be empty. He ran his hand lightly over the boot. It even felt empty. He moved round to the front and tried the driver's door. It was unlocked. He opened it a fraction, just sufficient for a quick glance into the interior, but not enough for the interior light to go on. He didn't know what he'd expected to see. At the back of his mind had been the vague hope that Greville, wrapped up in his nice raincoat, would be snoring gently on the back seat. But that was a nonstarter, and he knew it. He didn't bother looking, and closed the door as silently as he'd opened it. Initially he'd suspected, even hoped, that Grant might be in on this new act. But nothing doing. One glance was enough to see that Toby Grant hadn't been driving this car. The driver's seat was pushed as far forward as it would go; not only would Grant have had to crouch to drive, but with the seat at this angle the knees of his long legs would have been scraping against his ears.

Barlow stood for a moment longer, frowning at the car. Then he straightened up and stared down the track towards the farmhouse as the far end of the lane suddenly came to life. A car with only its side lights on edged gingerly out of the garage and made its way along the track, giving a short burst of acceleration as it neared the slope to the road. Barlow ducked behind the parked car and watched it pass and turn in the direction Thompson's taxi had taken earlier.

Barlow waited until the sound of the car had disappeared and the farmhouse returned to its tomb-like air of dereliction before moving, still in the shadows, towards the end of the lane.

For Sophie Ward everything, so far, had been too easy. But very boring. Sophie was an action girl. Sitting in a darkened car, hanging around the confines of a semiderelict farmhouse for an hour and a half with no idea what she expected to happen, did not suit her temperament. She needed to be doing something – but what? The radio was still out, so bringing in backup was out of the question, and there was no way of discovering what had happened to Robertson. She was stuck with it, and she was on her own. She moved irritably and after a long glance over her shoulder at the road above and at the dark, deserted countryside on either side of the farmhouse, she decided to give it another quarter of an hour and see if something happened. The quarter of an hour was up just before Barlow stepped out of his taxi. By the time he reached her parked car, she'd made her way down the track and found a path leading to the back garden of the old farmhouse.

Staying in the shadows, Barlow worked his way towards the house and studied it by the light of a barely visible sliver of moon.

It was larger than he'd guessed, and had all the hallmarks of a romantic Australian architect's idea of a prewar Assam tea planter's bungalow, with a verandah back and front overlooking a scruffy lawn of untended grass dotted with wild-looking bushes. It also had privacy. And that privacy made it easy for a burglar, or a former member of the SAS, to ply his trade. Barlow had no difficulty working his way through the hedge and with the grass muffling his footsteps, he followed the boundary until he reached the back confines of the bungalow.

No lights were visible from any of the front windows. He followed the brickwork round to the back until he came level with the rear verandah. He widened his eyes and peered along it. Nothing showed in the thin moonlight. He began to edge his way round, then stopped and melted against the side of the house. Something had moved, something small, something with a little more substance than its dark grey surroundings. A surreptitious movement by something, or somebody, who didn't want to be seen.

He pinpointed the shadow and waited for its next move.

*

Sophie took a deep breath, pulled her thin anorak tighter round her body, and for the umpteenth time nervously loosened the solid Glock automatic in its leather holster jammed into the back of her jeans. She was concentrating entirely on the darkened bungalow, her attention focused on the pencil-thin chink of light coming through the join in the curtains of the window just in front of her. She allowed herself a quick glance at her surroundings. It was quiet. She turned back to the open ground between her and the house. There was no more cover between her and the window, but she'd been there long enough to have read the script. There was no guard in the grounds; whoever was on the other side of the window had no security worries. They were happy and relaxed behind their curtains. She flexed her legs, brought herself on to her toes and took the first step forward.

She didn't hear Barlow.

He timed it perfectly. Waiting until she straightened up, he brought the flat of his hand across the side of her neck with a sharp chopping movement. A muffled sound like the gentle stroke of the bat on a spin bowler's loose delivery and she doubled over, giving a throaty cough on the way down. Before she hit the ground, Barlow grabbed a handful of anorak, held her steady for a second, and hit her again, this time across the back of her neck. Lowering her gently, he dragged her by the arms into the cover of the bushes she'd just vacated and pulled the anorak hood from her head. He stared hard at the dim pale shape of her face and the cascade of hair released from the confines of the hood. He hadn't expected a woman, but it wouldn't have made all that much difference. He went down closer on his knee for a better look and shook his head. He didn't recognize her. What she was doing here, having followed the carload of drunks from Prince Philip Mansions, was a question he was going to have to reserve for the next time they met – if that was ever likely. He laid his fingers on the side of her neck and touched the jugular. It was pumping healthily. He pursed his lips and straightened up. She was lucky, she was still alive, but he had no feeling of remorse. Barlow was a great believer in equal rights.

Dragging her further into the group of bushes, he replaced the hood over her head and pulled the cord so that most of her face was covered. Unless someone ran into the bushes for cover, she'd be as safe as a baby doll in its pram until she woke up. He ran his hand over the grass. It was damp with a heavy dew. He shook his head again. By the time she started digging in her pockets for the aspirins for her headache, she'd probably have flu to go with it.

Carrying on where he'd left off, he crouched double and picked his way silently to the window with the sliver of light.

He could hear Greville's whining voice before he put his eye to the crack.

He could just see him. Greville was a pitiful sight. Not a brave man at the best of times, he had been to the gates of hell, looked at them and, compared with his present situation, found them very welcoming.

His face was a mass of blood, and both eyes were closed. And he hadn't yet been asked the question. This was the softening-up section of the interview, the ritual blood-letting by the Irish gutter brigade whenever they had a helpless Englishman at their mercy. Anything went, as long as the victim lived long enough to croak a few words. Greville Sixsmith was now adjudged ripe. The first question came as Barlow established his view of the drawing room through the crack in the curtain.

The interrogator's voice came from somewhere on the right, out of sight. Barlow looked around as far as the crack would allow, but saw no one else. Sixsmith seemed to be sitting in solitary splendour. Except for the voice. There was no mistaking the accent.

'OK, so we've established who and what you are . . . ' Just the one voice, dry, cool, unemotional. Greville gave no sign that he'd heard. But he wasn't going to get away with it.

'Lift your bloody head when I'm talking to you,' came the voice again, and then, 'Never mind. Vinnie, go back and stick his head against the wall.'

Into Barlow's field of vision came one of the men who'd been supporting Greville along the pavement in Southgate Street, the short one wearing glasses. Now he grabbed a handful of Greville's thinning hair and jerked his chin off his chest. To make it worth his time, he gave him a solid double backhander to bring him back to his problems. Greville managed a bubbly groan and another spurt of blood came from his broken lips and dribbled via his chin on to his once white shirt. His two puffed-up eyes searched for the speaker. Barlow's lips tightened. He'd seen enough.

He felt his way round the house, pulled himself up on to the verandah and moved silently, testing each board before putting his weight on it, until he came to a door. It was half-glazed, a second-hand door that had once graced a lavatory, and little effort had been made to hang it correctly. There was no light behind the frosted glass. It had to be the back door to the kitchen. It was locked but it took Barlow no longer than twenty seconds to slip the catch and squeeze his body into a small scullery. Another door, this one easier, had a strip of light gleaming through a gap at the bottom. Barlow eased the .38 from his waistband and, holding the cylinder with his other hand, helped it round noiselessly as he cocked the hammer. He put one hand on the doorknob and his ear to the woodwork, and listened. Two voices, Sixsmith's, hoarse, laboured, liquid and hard to follow, and a louder, insistent Irish one, came indistinctly through the thin panelling.

No more slapping; they'd got Greville nicely loosened up. He began answering the questions as carefully and as lucidly as his swollen mouth would permit. He was holding nothing back.

As he listened, Barlow tested the doorknob. Very slowly it turned in his hand. He gave it a little pressure – not enough to open it, just enough to show that it wasn't locked. Still with his ear pressed to the panelling, he tried to pick up other sounds, but Greville was monopolizing the conversation. Barlow frowned. Three men had left Melbourne city centre; someone had left in the car. He'd heard one man and seen another – how many more? How many lived in the house, or was it just a handy torture chamber, a safe house for the Melbourne Brigade of the Australian PIRA?

Barlow stopped trying to work things out. He stared blankly at the strip of light coming under the door. There could be the whole of the bloody Tyrone Brigade squatting around the room enjoying the spectacle ... And Greville's droning voice was getting on his nerves. Not the sound, he'd got used to that; it was what he was saying. Whoever was doing the prompting was having a very easy time. He was only going through the motions, and was getting more than he'd bargained for. Greville was giving him chapter and verse, he was even giving him the benefit of his own opinion. Barlow wished he could see the interrogator. He was probably perched on a high stool, his eyes glazed over with boredom and his head dropping on to his chest. Anything was likely. Maybe he didn't believe a word Greville was telling him; maybe Greville was spouting too much and it was coming too easily. Nobody gave in this quickly, not the Brits and

Proddies the IRA were used to interviewing ... Barlow gave up speculating and decided to do something about it.

He opened the door a fraction wider and put his eye to the gap. He had a good view of the kitchen, which was not a large one by any standards, but sufficient. The open-plan system allowed only an arch supported by two ledges to separate it from the room where the interrogation was taking place. He opened the door just wide enough to squeeze through and, shielded by the wall, inched himself towards the arch. From here he could peer into the other room; it was an enlargement of the view he'd had from the crack in the curtains at the window.

Only the man with glasses was visible, and he was leaning against the wall looking down at Greville's head. There was a smouldering cigarette hanging out of the corner of his mouth, but he didn't seem to be smoking it; it hung there like a sleeping baby's dummy. He looked bored.

Barlow moved from the security of the wall. Slowly bringing the revolver up, he pointed it at Vinnie Doyle's head, his eyes darting to the side, searching urgently for the owner of the voice.

'Put your hands on your head and move away from the wall.'

It took a fraction of a second for Doyle to register. He frowned down at the top of Greville Sixsmith's balding head as if suspecting him of ventriloquism, and then, in a flash, the cigarette shot from between his lips like an arrow and his head turned. But he didn't wait. With a shout he ducked and moved sideways.

'What the fuck – ?'

'Stay where you are!' snapped Barlow. But Doyle wasn't listening, he was halfway across the room and ducking for the door when Barlow fired. The bullet caught him in the neck and threw him against the wall. Barlow fired again, a better shot that thumped into the side of Doyle's face and carried him halfway through the door, where he crashed on to his front. It had taken less than five seconds.

Greville hadn't moved. But Flynn had.

Seated round the corner, out of Barlow's view, he moved like a snake. One second he was sitting listening to Sixsmith telling him and Doyle how the British were trying to take them for a ride, and the next he'd grabbed the cassette and was on his knees scrabbling through the other door into the hall. Barlow saw only the back of him as he hurtled through the door. He threw himself across the room, hit the wall, and followed Flynn out into the corridor.

As he rounded the door, he met Flynn coming from another room on the other side of the hall.

Flynn hadn't been expecting this sort of trouble. But after a lifetime of ducking and weaving he had the right reflexes. He knew what he wanted, and grabbed it. It was a solid, heavy Remington, twelve-bore, pump-action, single-barrel. He didn't hesitate. Holding it away from his body, his finger on the trigger and his left hand wrapped around the ribbed pump, he began firing.

The first round splattered the wall by the door. The fallout from the half-dozen or so heavy ball bearings almost blew it to smithereens. Barlow knew all about semi-automatic shotguns. You don't argue with a man holding one, not unless you're cowering behind a good four or five inches of solid cover. Even as Flynn's finger tightened on the trigger again, Barlow fired a single wild shot, hoping to spoil his opponent's aim, and threw himself backwards and over the top of the three-seater settee pushed across the corner of the room. The barrel followed him and the next shot ripped the back of the settee apart, but Barlow hadn't stayed still. His knees gripping the carpet, he was already scrabbling to the other corner as Flynn, pumping, firing, pumping, firing, advanced into the room behind the lethal wall of lead balls.

It was the wrong moment for Greville to come to life and panic.

The noise was too much for him. With his eyes bulging, he took his arms from over his head and looked up at the cold-eyed Irishman standing in the middle of the room pumping steel shot in every direction.

'Don't shoot!' he screamed and dragged himself on to his knees, waving his arms at Flynn. But even if he'd been that way inclined, Flynn was unstoppable. He never gave it a thought. His finger kept working, the barrel moved fractionally in Greville's direction, and he got the full force of the Remington's final round.

At a distance of ten feet the effect was horrendous.

Greville's face, the scream and bulging eyes still etched on it, disintegrated into a bloody mess as it was smashed into the back of his head. He was almost decapitated by the force of the explosion. What was left of the top half of his body was picked up by the impact and thrown to the far side of the kitchen, where it came to rest, a mass of flailing arms and bloodied bone, amongst the kitchen cabinets.

Flynn pumped the empty Remington again and again, and then, with a bellow of rage, threw the now useless shotgun against the wall where he'd last seen Barlow. Hurling himself at the door, he burst through the little entrance hall and out into the cool black night.

Barlow clambered over the wrecked settee and went after him.

He moved through the door just as quickly as Flynn, but less clumsily. Ducking out of the light, he paused for a second or two on the verandah to replace the spent rounds in the .38. He widened his eyes, stared into the night, and listened. There was no sound, nothing moved.

But Flynn was out there somewhere, picking his way through the night with a caution bred of years of ducking ambushes. Flynn knew how to move. His moment of blind panic was over; now it was ice-cold survival.

Barlow waited another few seconds, then silently dropped off the verandah on to the soft, damp grass, and remained crouching where he'd landed. A shaft of light from the open scullery door sliced through the night like a searchlight, but its range was limited, offering beyond the shaft little or no illumination of the garden surroundings, leaving only a suggestion of charcoal grey, enough to see movement, not enough to identify. He strained his ears and his eyes. Nothing. Remaining at a crouch, he scuttled across the lawn and dived into the bushes. Still nothing. On his feet again and moving faster, he weaved in and out of the carefully planted shrubs. Then, two hundred yards to his left, he spotted it: a brief glimpse of a moving outline against the starlit sky, something more substantial than the all-embracing shadows. Brief, but enough. Head down and bent double, he changed course.

That was as far as he got.

One second he was galloping across the grass, the next he was flat on his face with a pair of arms wrapped tightly round his legs just below the knees. Unexpected as it was, Barlow recovered quickly. He threw his body to one side and, dragging himself on to one knee, balanced himself with both hands outspread in front of him, like a sprinter on his block. But there was no starting pistol, instead something harder and more substantial thudded into the side of his jaw. He shook his head. Another blow, this time below the ear, and his arms gave way at the elbows and once again his face ground into the dew-wet grass. Another thump across the face, this one wilder, without

161

precision, without aiming – anywhere on the head or face would do. There was no sound, no grunt of triumph, just a silence broken by heavy breathing. Whoever was doing it had won.

Through the ringing in his head and the red mist behind his eyes Barlow felt a body crash on to his, knocking every remaining ounce of wind from his lungs, and then the hard thing that had been bouncing off his head ground into the soft, fleshy spot just below his right ear and a woman's voice, breathless, gasped: 'Right, you bastard, don't move a bloody inch . . . ' A hand reached over his shoulder and removed the .38 from his unresisting fingers. 'And don't try anything smart or I'll put a bullet in your ear.'

A pause. Barlow blinked the mist away and waited. He could have been dead. He even stopped breathing as he waited. The body on his back moved fractionally, but the gun didn't. It remained, glued to the spongy area and grating against the bone under his ear.

The voice came again, hissing, menacingly close, into the same ear. 'Was that you making all that noise in there?'

Barlow made no reply.

The release of the safety catch close to his ear sounded like an explosion and he heard her intake of breath, but he knew even before she did that there was going to be no gunplay in this little charade. Whoever she was, she'd asked a question; she wanted a reply, not a hole in a stranger's head. He remained still, and silent.

'OK, you bastard, you want this thing wrapped round your head again? That's fine with me. Try playing the dumb fucker with me and that's exactly what you're going to get!'

Sophie was still suffering from the treatment she'd received earlier. Her neck ached, her head ached and she was bloody angry. 'Now do exactly as I say. I'm dying for an excuse ... OK. When I move, stay where you are. When I say stand up, you do that slowly and then stand still.' Sophie ground her knee into the small of Barlow's back, held it there for a moment's maximum pain, and when he groaned, she was off him, on her feet and out of range.

'Right. Stand up,' she hissed. 'Put your hands in front of you – you're going sleep-walking. That's it ... Move into the light and walk, one slow step at a time, towards that door. When you get there, wait until I tell you what to do next.' She remained in the grey undertones on one side of the shaft of light, her feet apart, the pistol held firmly in both hands and pointing at the thickest part of his body. Moving cautiously in his wake, she urged him forward through the door, and almost threw up when she saw Greville's body lying huddled in the corner. She quickly averted her gaze and ordered Barlow to the far side of the living room.

'Put your hands against the wall and stay like that until I tell you to move,' she snapped, and quickly surveyed the wreckage caused by Flynn's artillery onslaught. It didn't take long. 'OK.' She stepped back so that her shoulders were resting against the opposite wall. 'Put your hands on your head and turn round.'

Barlow did as he was told.

He probably wouldn't have recognized Sophie even if she had looked exactly like she had in the garden of the Fawkner Club drinking dry white wine. As he viewed her now in her present state, she meant less than nothing to him. Her face was covered in dry mud. The rest of her, including her head, was covered in a dark, nondescript anorak. She looked like a slightly larger version of the picture on the 'Action Man Undercover Kit' box. But that's where the fun ended. The gun in her hand was rock-steady, and by the look in her eyes she was willing him to do something that would allow her to fire it at him.

For her, recognition was instantaneous. He was the last person she'd expected, though she didn't know why she'd excluded him from the equation. But she kept the surprise to herself and stored away the knowledge as a small bargaining chip. There was no doubt in her mind that bargaining was a definite option, and it wasn't too far away.

They stared at each other for a few seconds, then she gave the squat automatic a very tiny waggle and said, 'Turn that sofa upright and sit on it. While you're doing that, you can think over the answers to some of the obvious questions lying around here. Be careful how you move. Don't try to be clever.'

She waited until he'd sat down, then, without taking her back from the wall, she moved to the corner of the room and with an impatient brush of her hand pulled the anorak hood loose and shook it off her head.

'OK. Cross your legs and clasp your hands round your knee. Right.' She jerked her chin at Doyle's body curled up against the wall. 'Who did that?' She waited a second for a reply, but when nothing came, without moving her head or eyes, she shifted the automatic fractionally in the direction of the kitchen. 'And who killed him?'

'Are you going to tell me who you are?' Barlow played a tentative stroke before getting down to the heavy stuff. But it wasn't going to work with Sophie Ward. The real surprise for Barlow, an ominous one at that, was that she didn't seem the least bit surprised to find an Englishman in this Victoria backwoods shack with two corpses and a third man galloping over the horizon in the middle of a moonlit night. She must have seen Flynn legging it through the undergrowth before she nobbled him. But she wasn't speaking Irish; hers was a clean, Australian accent and had an unmistakable tone of authority. She also seemed to know exactly what fisticuffs and rough-house were all about. She looked a very serious problem.

She ignored his question and stuck her own on hold. She pointed to Vinnie Doyle. 'Who's that?'

Barlow turned his head and stared long and hard at the crumpled figure. After a moment he returned to her eyes and said, 'I don't know. Why don't we ask him?'

Sophie frowned. 'I told you not to be clever. That meant verbally as well ... ' But there was something in the way he'd said it. She glanced again at Doyle's body. 'What d'you mean?'

'There's still something pumping inside.' He took his hands off his knee and held them out in a friendly gesture, smiling as he did so. It sometimes worked with a woman.

But not with this one. 'Put your bloody hands back where they were!' she snapped, then had second thoughts. This was getting them nowhere. 'OK, Barlow,' she said, ignoring his narrow-eyed reaction to his name. 'I'll take it you know about these things. See if you can kick-start that one and ask him who he is.'

Barlow had been right. There was something left in Doyle, though not much, nothing more than a flicker. Barlow dragged him up to a sitting position against the wall and kept him there with his hand on his chest.

'Are you awake, son?' he asked solicitously.

Nothing.

He tried the gentle touch twice more before grabbing a handful of Doyle's hair and shaking his head from side to side; then he brought it forward and banged it hard against the wall. It did the trick.

Doyle opened his eyes. Even if he'd got his glasses on he wouldn't have been able to see anything, and he wasn't going to be there very long. Barlow lowered his head and looked into his eyes. 'What's the name of your friend?'

'Ask him about Frank Robertson.'

'Who?' Barlow didn't take his eyes off Doyle.

'A guy I placed in one of the flats in Southgate Street. He didn't make an appearance when he was needed,' she continued, staring hard at Doyle. 'Look, he's almost gone!' She tightened her lips, glanced down at the pistol in her hand, flicked the safety catch back on, and slipped it into its holster. She'd known it was going to be useless as soon as she recognized Barlow, but she wasn't stepping down and kept well out of range of his long arms. She leaned forward and listened.

'What's the name of your friend?' repeated Barlow.

This time it hit something.

'Who're you?' responded Doyle. It was almost incoherent and came out with a spoonful of frothy bubbles. Barlow had to concentrate to separate the words from the bubbles. But the accent was unmistakable.

So was Barlow's. He swallowed a mouthful of spit and worked his mouth to one side. 'Shanahan,' he said in a fair imitation of an Irish accent, and then softly, confidentially, in little more than a whisper: 'Tyrone Brigade. Hang on, lad, help's on its way. Your friend?' he repeated.

Doyle almost smiled. He believed it. 'Doyle,' he gurgled.

'What's *your* name then?'

'Doyle,' he repeated.

'Bloody hell!' hissed Barlow. Time was running out. 'So who's your friend? I need to contact him – urgently.'

Vinnie got the message. It didn't really matter where his body was dying, his brain was in Strabane, the High Street, with the boys waiting for the Brit soft top to crawl into the ambush, any bloody second now . . . 'Give it 'em, Fergie! Kill the bastards! Watch the fuckers burn!'

'Is Fergie your friend?' insisted Barlow.

'Sure he is. Fergie Flynn. We killed the Brit bastards, didn't we?'

'All of 'em, Doyley, you did well. Where can I find Fergie?'

Doyle dribbled some more bubbles and blood down his chin while he sorted out the question. His dying brain must have changed track. He'd left Strabane. He was on holiday in the Friendly Country. 'The fuckin' Australian . . .' he murmured. 'We killed that bastard too, didn't we, Fergie?'

'What's he saying?' asked Sophie impatiently, and moved closer. Barlow felt her nearness but didn't look away from Doyle's face. 'Hang on,' he grunted, 'don't crowd him.'

She didn't move, but crouched down and leaned forward to listen. 'What Australian?' she whispered to the back of Barlow's head. 'Tell him to talk about the Australian.'

But Barlow wasn't taking instructions.

'No, Doyle,' he said firmly. 'Forget the Australian. Talk about Flynn. Where can I find him?'

'We killed the fucker!'

'Who, Flynn?'

'No, the Australian . . . ' Doyle stopped abruptly, as if in some deep recess of his dying mind a warning flickered that he was saying too much. Barlow didn't give him time to develop the warning. Still grasping a handful of Doyle's hair, he tapped his head gently against the wall to start him off again, but before he could continue, Sophie butted in again.

'Australian? What Australian?' She knew what Australian, but couldn't sit squatting, saying and doing nothing; that wasn't her way. 'Kick the bastard,' she hissed. 'Make him say what Australian. Frank Robertson was in that flat when they collected Sixsmith. If this bastard killed him . . . ' She tailed off.

Barlow finally conceded. He shook Doyle's head again. 'This Australian, Doyley? Was he the one who was with the Brits? Did you top him? Is he dead?'

Doyle's eyes opened briefly. Everything was coated in a red mist, but there was something you never admitted – not unless it was to your brother. 'I don't remember. Who did you say you were again?'

'Shanahan, Tyrone Brigade,' grunted Barlow.

Almost a brother. But share the blame. 'Flynn coffined him. He got in the way . . . ' That was enough for Barlow. He shrugged it aside and let Sophie consider her man Frank Robertson's requiem.

'That's OK, Doyley, you did your job. Now, talk about Flynn. I've got to get to him – I need him. Where is he, Doyle, where will he go?'

'Jacko'll cover him . . .'

'Jacko who?'

'Sullivan.'

'Where can I find Jacko?'

Doyle didn't even think about it. He pushed out another mouthful of blood and froth, but there were no words amongst it – he'd gone. There weren't going to be any more words. Doyle was dead.

Barlow let go of his hair and allowed his head to drop on to his chest. The shifting of weight set up a juddering motion that sent his lifeless body into a slow gentle slide from the waist so that he ended up with his legs outstretched and his head resting neatly between them. Sophie's eyes bulged as she watched the spectacle. She wasn't programmed for violent death; she knew what it was all about, but this was her first.

Barlow heard the retching sounds and discreetly leaned forward to search Doyle's pockets. He ignored the scampering of feet, the banging of the kitchen and back doors, and then closed his ears to the sound of Sophie's stomach emptying itself on to the grass outside. By the time she'd finished he'd placed Doyle's possessions on a small table and had also inspected Greville's pockets. That had been a fruitless exercise; there was nothing in them that shouldn't have been there. The contents of Doyle's pockets didn't help either.

Barlow, sitting relaxed on the settee, tried a half-smile when Sophie, pale, but in full control of herself, came into the room. It had no effect. Sophie wasn't in a smiling mood. She ignored Doyle's body, as she had Sixsmith's, and took charge again.

'Don't make yourself too comfortable, Barlow. Sit there quietly, don't make a nuisance of yourself and re-sign yourself to coming back to Melbourne with me.'

'What are you going to do while I'm doing all that?'

'None of your business. Just sit there and cogitate while I use the phone.'

Dubrovnik sounded almost happy at being disturbed from his sleep at half-past one in the morning. Maybe he was an insomniac. Sophie raised her eyes at the thought and then dismissed it as she began to recount the night's events.

He listened without interrupting until she had finished and then, after a short pause, said: 'OK, Sophie, do this. First of all, take this guy Barlow's passport off him and then have him taken in custody by the Melbourne police – suspicion of murder.'

'But – '

'Don't interrupt, Sophie, just do as I say, OK?'

She tightened her lips after a brief glance at Barlow. He seemed comfortable and at ease, but then he couldn't hear Dubrovnik at the other end of the line.

'You deal with the police in Melbourne. As for this guy Barlow, keep him close by your side until they can bury him in a wet dungeon. Right! Next. They and Special Branch had better start an immediate operation to run down this Flynn character. By first light I expect a ring of iron around the city to stop him breaking out of Melbourne and into the bush. I want that bastard, Sophie! I want him to tell me what Frank Robertson ever did to get himself frozen by those bloody people, and what the fuckin' hell they mean by bringing their Northern Ireland disease over here. It's the fuckin' Brits behind it – I know it – and I want some fuckin' answers . . . I'll be sending a team of our own people to coordinate the show and they can start by pulling the hairs out of this Barlow character's nose.'

'What do you want me to do when I've unloaded Barlow?' asked Sophie with another sidelong glance. 'Do I move your team about or just join it as a pair of legs?'

'Neither. You've done enough. You can run a coordination project between us and the Melbourne police. If there's going to be any more bloodshed, I don't want you within a thousand kilometres of it, have you got that?' Dubrovnik assumed she had. He didn't pause but went straight on as if he were reading a script for a new play. 'You say you got a good visual of this Flynn, and the other one – what was his name?' This time he did stop for a response, even if it was only to make sure she was still there and he wasn't talking to an empty phone.

'No, I didn't get a bloody visual, and I didn't say I did. Neither did I get the other one, but Sullivan was the name mentioned. But Heros,' Sophie went on quickly, 'I want more than a ladies' knitting role in this. I was involved with Toby Grant from the beginning. This thing has implications – '

'And they don't concern you,' snapped Dubrovnik. 'Any implications beyond a straightforward killing are my business, not yours. Do as I've said, get Barlow off your hands, and then go and get some sleep. When you've done that you can catch a flight and come up here and tell me in person how a simple watching job on a harmless Pom turns into three killings involving British MI people and, by the sounds of it, elements of the Provisional Irish Republican Army. You can remind me over a cup of coffee and a bacon sandwich that I'm in Australia and not some godforsaken banana republic where people get knocked off for a packet of fags!'

Sophie's adrenaline was running down, the tiredness was taking over. 'If that's it, Heros, can we wrap this conversation up?'

Dubrovnik caught sight of himself in his dressing-table mirror and stopped what he was about to say. He'd spotted what he'd spent a lifetime trying to eradicate: he was behaving like a Slav. He was getting excited, the hereditary fires were still smouldering and were about to burst into flames. He broke eye contact with himself and became Australian again. 'Go and get some sleep,' he said gruffly and went back to bed.

Sophie replaced the receiver and turned slowly to face Barlow. 'Come on, let's get out of here. I want to go back to Sixsmith's flat before the police start tearing it apart, and I want you with me. You can tell me all about the beginning of this bloody business on the way over, but first I want you to get on your hands and knees and pick up all those sheets of paper strewn around the kitchen. You can start now.'

Barlow stared back at her. He didn't move. 'You know, I've got a feeling I've seen you somewhere before . . .'

It was her turn not to answer. 'Pick 'em up,' she ordered. 'But just a minute.' She took a couple of paces towards him and stared down at him quizzically. 'Are you the one who jumped me outside?'

He held her eyes and tried a brief smile.

'Who neck-chopped me and left me lying in the mud?'

'I'm sorry, it's part of the game. I didn't see your skirt in the dark.'

CRACK!

Her open hand exploded on the side of his face, jerking his head back against the wall. His fists tightened instinctively but he did nothing; his eyes remained locked on hers.

'And if you ever come up behind me again, you bastard . . . ' She left the warning unfinished, but it was there in her eyes – and she meant it.

Barlow reminded himself to be very careful about coming up behind Sophie Ward in the future.

17

By the time Sophie drew up at Sixsmith's flat she and Barlow had cleared the air. Neither had told the other anything new. But Barlow now remembered where he'd seen her before. He didn't tell her. It was the game, always the game: poker, five-card stud with nothing showing. It made for perfect understanding between consenting agents of friendly powers.

Sophie led the way up the stairs and stopped outside the door of the apartment she'd arranged for Frank Robertson. There was a suggestion of hesitation as she studied the closed door; not quite trepidation, but something very close. She had a good idea what they were going to find and she didn't fancy it. She could still taste the bile from her earlier dose of sudden death, but there was something stronger than that preventing her from inviting Barlow to go first. She'd already shown weakness – and regretted it. She tightened her lips and gently eased the shaped wire into the lock. It gave a well-oiled click and she eased the door open an inch.

'Would you like me to go first?' Barlow's voice breathed into her ear.

She didn't turn, but gave a small shake of her head and opened the door wide enough to slide her slim body into the miniscule hall. Barlow followed and quietly closed the door behind him. They both knew what they were going to find and it wasn't going to solve any problems. But

Barlow understood her motives. She was fuelling a hatred for a man named Flynn. That couldn't be a bad thing.

While she stared down in silence at Frank Robertson's stiffening body, Barlow gazed around the flat. It was a replica of Sixsmith's – same furniture, same pictures, same window, same view. He glanced at Sophie. She was still staring at the body. He wondered how close the association had been. His impatience got the better of him. There was an exercise to be carried out. Damage limitation equalled Flynn with his tongue ripped out and the back of his head staved in.

She must have heard his thoughts.

'Let's go to Sixsmith's place.' She looked up from the body. Her face was set, pale and taut, but there was nothing wrong with the determination in her eyes.

'What for?'

She didn't answer. 'Come on, close the door behind you. Wipe the door handle. We might as well go the whole hog while we're at it.'

She performed the same bent-wire operation on Greville's front door but this time didn't hesitate. She stood in the middle of the room and gazed about her. There was nothing exciting about it; she'd seen it all downstairs.

'What are you looking for?' Barlow was bored, he'd already done this scene. Where the bloody hell was Flynn by now? Who'd he be talking to? Was there anything left to salvage?

Sophie had a different set of priorities. 'I'm trying to make myself happy,' she said grimly. 'I'm looking for something that gives you a reason to be here. So far all you've given me is a load of cowshit about your office in London not being totally relaxed about this Sixsmith guy and his memoirs. It doesn't ring little bells, Barlow, so either you tell me exactly what the game is and where it stands at the moment, including how you managed to con Toby Grant into doing the dirty part of your work, and through him, me, and through me Frank Robertson . . .' She paused for a moment and stared coldly into his eyes. She was never going to forgive him for Frank Robertson, but that was going to be the least of his worries.

He stared back as she continued. 'Or we pour ourselves a drink from that bottle and sit around waiting for the Melbourne Police Department to kick the door in, break your arms and take you off to some quiet padded cell for treatment. Then I'll come and testify that I saw you kill one of those men out at Craigieburn.' Her expression didn't change. 'And here's the gun he did it with, Officer!' She put her hand under her anorak and withdrew Barlow's .38 revolver, holding it up for him to see.

He shook his head slowly. 'What did you say your name was?'

'I didn't, but it's Ward.'

'Ward what?'

'Sophie.'

'Nice name.'

She bridled. 'And I don't need any of that chauvinistic crap! You can start by thinking about some of the questions I've just asked, and then let me have the answers. No bull, just matter-of-fact, straightforward answers. Start now.'

But Barlow had had enough. He wasn't used to working relationships with women, certainly not of the Australian variety, and Sophie Ward was far too pushy for her own good – and his. Barlow wasn't a woman's man, and it showed. 'I think I'd prefer to take my chances with the police. They can't be half as irritating as you, Sophie Ward.' It stopped her dead in her tracks, but before she'd formed a retort he added, 'Pass that bottle of whisky over here and let's make ourselves comfortable.

Are you going to ring the police, or are you going to leave it up to your friend Dubrovnik?'

She didn't move.

The seconds ticked away, and as they did so he knew she wasn't going to ask again to see his hand. She'd overplayed hers; it was time to settle.

Sophie glanced down at her watch. 'We'll continue this at my place. Here . . .' She flicked open the cylinder of the revolver, emptied the chambers and tossed the weapon on to the chair beside him. There was no softening of her expression as she crossed the room and held her closed fist over his hand. When he held it out, she opened her fingers and allowed the six rounds to spill into it. It was as good as a handshake.

Sophie studied, without appetite, the breakfast Barlow had cooked for her while she showered. She had changed into an overlarge, man's pink shirt, which she wore outside a pair of loose, casual white trousers. She wore nothing on her feet and her wet hair was wrapped turban-style in a fluffy white towel, but it didn't detract from the exquisite beauty of her features Barlow had admired so much outside the Fawkner Club. She wasn't trying to make an impression on Barlow. She wore no make-up, but this, if anything, enhanced her attractiveness to Barlow. She looked tired, but it wasn't going to interfere with the business. She shrugged the tiredness aside and ate a tentative mouthful of toast.

'I didn't think you Poms went in for cooking and the like. I thought the little woman did all that sort of thing for you.'

It was unexpected. Barlow stared at her. She even smiled.

'Don't tell me you haven't got one?'

'A little woman?' He shook his head. 'Not any more.'

'She run out on you?'

'D'you mind if we talk about something else?'

'Still hurts, huh? I'm sorry, Barlow. It's none of my business.' The smile and the forced lightness vanished before they had really got going. She lowered her head over the plate and attempted to eat. But it wasn't working. After three or four mouthfuls she went back to being Head of Station. 'You were going to tell me about your arrangement with Toby Grant and the depth of your interest in Sixsmith,' she said.

He told her what he'd told Grant, that his help was a favour repaying a favour, strictly friendly, no file, no exchange beyond a couple of glasses of Foster's. There was no mention of Reason or the London connection. His brief was a watching one, with the spectre of another Peter Wright débâcle dictating the terms of his actions. Whether she bought it or not didn't show. Arranging her knife and fork carefully on the plate, she sat back in her chair and studied him critically. She didn't say anything. She seemed to be digesting her breakfast rather than the words coming across the table. Barlow reckoned he'd said enough to establish a more workable relationship. Sophie Ward, in anybody's language, would be better as an ally. He pushed his unfinished breakfast away and rested his elbows on the table.

'How far are you going to be allowed to run with this thing, Sophie?' he asked. Her name ran quite easily off his tongue.

This time she didn't bridle at the familiarity, but seemed almost to like it. She smiled bleakly. 'My boss wants me to stay out of it.'

'Your boss?'

'Heros Dubrovnik.'

'What does he know about me?'

Sophie frowned in recollection, then said, 'Funny that.

He seemed not to have heard of you. The only thing he knew was what I told him over the phone. Toby appears to have kept his side of your bargain as far as Dubrovnik is concerned.' She reached forward and stirred milk into her coffee. She continued looking him straight in the eyes while she did so. 'You sure there's nothing more you want to tell me about yourself? Is Toby, for instance, playing honest, or had you worked him into your team? It all sounds too pat to me, a bit on the shifty side.'

'Why don't you ask him?'

'I can't, he's in Washington.'

Barlow shrugged. 'So what are you going to do about Flynn?'

She didn't hesitate; she'd already made up her mind. 'I'm going after Flynn myself.'

'Officially?'

'I think this one'll be out of Dubrovnik's hands. It's not his thing. This is murder, straight up and down. The police'll want it all the way.'

'Even though most of the cast were foreigners?'

'That won't make any difference. Dead bodies are dead bodies over here. Spooky goings on are for the KGB, CIA, and some of your bloody silly desks. Dubrovnik'll foam at the mouth for a bit over one of his operators getting killed and he'll probably slip in a team to look for specifications, but the police'll run the show, and that brings me back to you.' She sipped her coffee and pulled a face. 'You can't make coffee, by the way.'

He gazed back blandly.

'Dubrovnik wants you handed over to the police. He doesn't like the sound of you. I'll bet that even at this moment he's drawing up extradition papers in case the police can't find enough to hold you down and you bolt back to England.'

'So what are you going to do about it?'

She continued looking at him as if sizing him up for the cattle market, then gave a tiny shake of the head. 'You want to find Flynn?'

Barlow gave a reluctant smile but remained noncommittal. 'I'm not particularly keen to get involved in your business, Sophie, but putting it that way, I wouldn't mind the opportunity of having a chat with him. I'd like to know why he killed Sixsmith – and I don't like the way he killed your man in the flat.' She was still studying him. She'd got used to the taste of the coffee and absently kept the cup at her lips, waiting. Surprisingly he found it disconcerting. It wasn't enough, she wanted more. 'OK,' he said, still reluctant, 'yes, I'd like to find Flynn.'

'Good.' Sophie took another sip from the cup, put it back in its saucer and wiped her lips with a napkin. 'We'll find him together.'

We? This wasn't quite what Barlow had had in mind. 'I don't think . . .'

She smiled genuinely. There were little fragments of toast still clinging to the corners of her mouth. He found it strangely provoking – sexual. He shook the thought from his mind; this was neither the time nor the place. Her eyes narrowed. She was a mind-reader.

'You have no choice, Barlow.' She paused. 'Well, that's not strictly true . . .' The smile vanished and so did the toast crumbs, helped on their way by the tiny pink tip of her tongue. 'You have two choices. You can either spend the next few days in Flinders Street Police Station while they sort you out, or you can help me find Flynn. You've got as long as it takes me to get changed to decide.' With that she stood up and pushed her chair back. 'Pour yourself some of your coffee while you're making up your mind.'

She didn't want it in writing. She didn't even want it in

words, she just took it for granted that he'd made the right choice.

'He could be anywhere by now,' said Barlow when she came back into the breakfast room. She'd dried her hair, put on make-up and was in her working clothes. The make-up made all the difference; she looked wide awake and as fresh as a dew-spattered buttercup, and she was eager to get on with it.

'No, he couldn't.' She barely gave him a glance, but instead pulled the curtain half back and held it open. Half-past five. It was pitch-black outside, but there was a feeling of dawn somewhere out there. 'He's not going to get very far until dawn. No trains, no buses, and he won't find many cars to pinch where we left him. Wherever he wants to go, he's going to have to walk. I'm not worried about that.'

'Telephones?' Barlow voiced his greatest fear.

Sophie wasn't on the same wavelength. 'You worried he might ring for a taxi? Forget it. Melbourne taxi drivers won't go into the sticks until the sun's belting through the tree tops. No, he'll be on his feet and he'll be walking in the dark. He won't get far.' She'd convinced herself, but Barlow was still sceptical. He'd been around people like Flynn for the past twenty years. They didn't curl up on the side of the road and wait to be picked up; they put their head down and went for it. But he didn't disillusion her.

'He could always double back to the farm,' he said meditatively.

'I doubt that one as well. He'll expect it to be swarming with police by now.'

'And will it be?'

She shook her head. 'Dubrovnik won't have been in touch with the police yet. He's expecting me to do that locally. And that's what I'm going to do in a minute. Go

180

down and wake the idle sods up and get them out on the road. They're going to love me for that!'

'Why not phone them?'

'Time-wasting. Anything other than the personal touch and they'll send somebody out to see whether their leg's being pulled. When everything clicks into place then they'll all start screaming at the top of their voices and start doing something about road-blocks and things. I'll give them a personal briefing and they can get on with it right away – saves hours.'

But she'd forgotten something.

Barlow hadn't. 'Doyle mentioned someone named Sullivan.'

'Oh, Christ!'

'You've got the number of that car you followed?'

She wrinkled her nose. 'It's sure to have been pinched.'

'Not necessarily. You want my advice?' Barlow tried to sound humble. It didn't work. Taking advice from whatever source was not one of Sophie's strong points, but she let it go. 'My invitation for you to come along with me on this trip was not for your manly body and good looks, Barlow. Among other things it was for suggestions, but I'll include advice in that. Let's have it.'

Barlow grinned. It took fifteen years off his age, but it didn't last long. He'd have to watch it; abrasive and attractive, he was beginning to like this woman. It hadn't happened for a long time. But he didn't allow it to show. 'Let the car run,' he said. 'Don't have it brought in, even if it has been reported nicked. One of those guys, Sullivan I presume, left before the ball started. He wouldn't know what happened, and he certainly wouldn't have known he'd been followed. Put out a call for the car, have a tight watch on it and see what happens. There's always the chance that Flynn will put in a cry for help and Sullivan will take off in the car after him. We'll go too.'

'That's a bit of a long shot, isn't it? What if Flynn warns him over the phone?'

'It's the only shot you've got, Sophie.'

She held his eyes for several seconds while she thought about it, then tightened her lips and nodded. 'You might have something there, Barlow,' she conceded reluctantly, and then stood up. 'Make yourself comfortable, have a bath.' She stared pointedly at his chin. 'There's a packet of plastic razors in there. I can't stand that pansy designer stubble on men.'

'You think we're going to get close enough to each other for it to matter?'

'Forget it, Barlow, you're not my type.' There was nothing that wasn't forthright about Sophie Ward. She knew what sort of men she liked and how they should look. 'I'm going down to my office and then I'm going to put things on to the conveyor belt. I'll call in at your hotel on the way back and collect your things. I don't think you're going to be sleeping there again.'

Barlow wasn't put off by Sophie's abrupt manner; he was getting used to it. He leaned back in his chair and stared at the door as it closed behind her. So much for the tight security. She'd even known where he was staying, which brought into question who was running rings around whom in this little venture. Reason reckoned he'd set up Grant to do one for their side, but it looked like the Australian wasn't as simple as he appeared. And how much had he known about the big game before handing it over to Sophie Ward? And how much had he told her? And who else was reading from the same script? Dubrovnik for one. Just him and Sophie? Or half the Australian Security and Intelligence Organization? And why suddenly shoot Toby Grant off to foreign parts? And who shot him off, Arthur Gunne? Toby had got the memoirs fluttering around exactly the way Reason had wanted and then buggered off, probably because he knew too much about the endgame? Very convenient. But convenient for who? And who was *he* working for, ASIO or Reason? Bugger it! It was getting out of hand.

Barlow got up from the table and moved across the room to the window. He stood there and watched through a chink in the curtain until the lights of Sophie's Ford Falcon disappeared down the road, then began a systematic check of the apartment. He was thorough. Room by room he gave it the works, corner by corner, crevice by crevice. Leaving it till last, he took the phone apart, opened the main connection with a potato peeler and inspected the wiring. Only then, satisfied, did he dial the 44 code and drag Clive Reason from his pre-dinner drink.

18

Flynn did exactly what Barlow had expected him to do – he put his head down and kept going.

The countryside was pitch-black. He turned his head briefly and thought he could see the lights of the bungalow in the distance, but it didn't help, and it didn't matter. He wasn't going back.

He had one object in mind: to contact Collins via the 'Galloglass' drop and get this bloody tape on to a machine so he could hear for himself how they'd walked right up to the edge of the cliff. But that was the easy part – thinking about it. He had no idea of the time, though had he known it was still only half-past one it wouldn't have made any difference. Thoughts of Sixsmith kept his mind occupied as he loped through the night.

So the bastard was a bloody fraud, his story was a put-up, the whole bloody thing was a Brit trick to push somebody from the top end of the stick right into the bloody bin. And the bastards could probably have done just that but for one lousy Brit who couldn't stand being hurt. Thank God for all the bloody Sixsmiths of this world! But the buggers had lost it. The fuckin' Brits had lost their game to Fergal Flynn! But they hadn't lost it yet.

'Phone, bloody, fuckin' phone . . .' Flynn began talking aloud to himself as he stumbled across seemingly endless scrubland. There were no hedges, no fields, no roads, just an interminable black nothing with a scrubby bush every so often reaching out to hook its barbed thorns into his fending arm. He didn't know whether he was going north, south, east or west. It didn't matter as long as he was away from the hard-looking bastard who'd dropped out of nowhere and blown old Doyley away. A pity he hadn't been able to give him the same treatment he'd given Sixsmith. A momentary picture of the Brit hurtling across the room with no face brought a little shiver of satisfaction, but he didn't dwell on it. 'Where the fuckin' hell d'you find a phone in this fuckin' wilderness?'

He stopped for a moment to regain his wind and peered once again into the blackness behind him. There was nothing to be seen. The bungalow lights had disappeared into the distance. He gave an involuntary sob as his lungs, released from the pressure of haste, began to settle to a less frenetic pumping. He crouched down and allowed the thumping of his heart to have its way. There was no one else in the chase; he could afford to take it easy for a time. Flynn relaxed and wished he'd had the chance to pick up his cigarettes.

He remained crouching, his back resting against the base of a solid bush, dozing fitfully and shivering as the night crawled on its way to morning. Something jolted him wide awake. He opened his eyes warily for the umpteenth time and stared straight ahead. He had no way of knowing how long he'd been there. He narrowed his eyes, then opened them wide. The denser shadows a few yards in front of him gave the illusion of shape. Gradually the illusion became real and a thick outline of another bush became apparent. Without moving his body, he quartered the area; another bush, and nearby the outline of another. Dawn was threatening, not yet definite, but there was a distinct breaking of the deep grey night.

It arrived very quickly, like a curtain being lifted on a

room already partially lightened by the outside light. Suddenly, he was squatting in broad daylight surrounded, not, as he'd imagined, by scrubland bushes, but by a neglected apple orchard full of regulated, stumpy trees. Slowly he rose to his feet and gazed around him.

His view was restricted by the unpruned branches, but in the distance, on a south-facing slope, he could see a house, like its orchard ramshackle and on its last legs, but far enough away to cause him no disquiet. He decided to ignore it and started walking towards the sun, already climbing rapidly. After three hours trudging across open bush and crossing a couple of indifferent, unmade-up roads, he saw in the distance, distorted by the newly formed heat haze, a Dinky Toy-like lorry with a long, high trailer apparently cruising three feet off the ground. It took another hour's slogging through the dust to reach the main road.

Flynn tried to read the tattoos on the beefy lorry driver's arm and shoulder but the rolls of fat and creases pulled them out of shape. It didn't matter. He was a chatty fellow, and not stupid. He also spent a lot of time bellowing into a CB system microphone that seemed to click on and off with the volume of his voice.

Flynn closed his ears to the on/off clicking and atmospheric annoyance of his driver's contact. He had more important matters on his mind. It took a period of silence to bring him back to the air-conditioned, refrigerator-like cab, and when he turned his head sideways he found the driver staring openly at him; his ear, apparently, was looking after the road.

'You ready for some brekky, mate?'

'I'm buying.' Flynn could afford to be generous. 'Where?' There was nothing in sight, the road disappeared into infinity.

The driver shrugged his bare shoulders and his neck vanished like a tortoise's head retreating into its shell. He didn't answer the question. Instead he bared his teeth in what could have been a grin.

'Ta, mate. You know the police are looking for yer, do yer?'

Flynn tried to look disinterested. It was difficult. 'What's that?'

'There's a bloody great police roadblock about fifteen kays north of here. One of me mates has just crawled through it.'

'What makes you think they're looking for me?'

The fat Australian allowed the grin to broaden, and then thought he'd better have a look at the road for a moment. The huge artic wasn't particularly concerned, it stuck to the road as if it were on a centrifuge; it only needed a driver to stop and start it. The grin didn't move an inch, it was still there when the face returned to Flynn. 'They're looking for a tall skinny guy with an Irish accent. You're tall and skinny and you've got an Irish accent. They're looking for a guy about six one, like you. Black hair, like yours. Brown coat, like yours; faded jeans . . .'

Flynn remained comfortable, one foot on the dashboard, his head back on the leather-covered sponge headrest and his eyes focused on the distant skyline. 'Could fit hundreds of blokes, a description like that . . .'

The driver's grin remained in place. 'Probably heading north on the Hume Highway?'

Flynn shrugged unconcernedly.

'What they want you for, mate?'

'It's a Brit problem.'

'Ah.' The grin faded. 'You're one of them, then, are yer?'

'One of what?'

'The Irish thing. Yer been clobbering the Pom then, 'ave yer?'

Flynn nodded. He was on safe ground with this one; he could have been on the A5 out of Dublin.

He wasn't far wrong.

The driver studied him for several seconds, then, belying the new grin that creased his chubby chops, became serious. 'Look, you wanna be going the other way – into Melbourne, not out of it. All these roads are being done over by the cops. They're not particularly concerned about things goin' in, and I don't blame 'em, only a flamin' idiot would go for the centre of the spider's web.'

Flynn stared at him.

'So take my advice, go into Melbourne, stay quiet for a week. They'll have forgotten you by then, and then you can winkle yerself out and go where the bloody hell you like.' He glanced at the windscreen to see where he was going and then turned his face on to Flynn again. 'You haven't said where you wanna get to?'

Flynn didn't respond. It was a phone he wanted, not advice from an Australian lard barrel who hadn't got a fuckin' clue what running was all about. But the lard barrel was still giving it.

'So, why not behave like a bloody idiot?'

Flynn stared at him out of the corner of his eye, his head still resting on the back of the seat. 'Thanks. What about that breakfast?'

'Forget it. There's a place about ten kays up the road. It'll be full of trucks at this time of the day. I'll find you one to take you into town, but don't do anything on yer own, let me do it. When I give yer the nod, go straight for the one I indicate. Don't do anything fuckin' stupid or you'll end up over the bonnet of a police car with yer bollocks tied up in a knot. Don't forget yer dealing with Aussie cops here, not fuckin' Poms.'

'Sure, and thanks again. I'll come in with you and have a cup of tea.'

'Are you fuckin' mad? It's a flamin' watering hole we're talking about. The Aussie coppers are not fuckin' stupid. There'll be at least two narks sitting in there with eggs and bacon on their plates and two-way radios up their flamin' arses just waiting for you to go in and get yerself a cuppa tea. The next roadblock after this is about six kilometres on the other side. They'd let you 'ave yer cuppa tea and pick yer off down the road. Do as I fuckin' say and yer'll get away with it. Anything else and the bastards'll castrate you. OK?'

'Thanks.'

'Don't thank me, mate. Any pain in the arse the Pom gets suits me, and anyone ducking the cops is my sort of bloke. Best of luck to yer.'

Flynn changed hitches twice more on the way back, just in case. The first changed his direction towards Adelaide and the second took him into the suburbs of Melbourne from the west. It had taken him less time than he'd expected, but then there were no road checks. His early-morning friend had been right, this was a doddle. He could have ridden in on an elephant draped in orange, white and green and the police wouldn't have noticed him – they were all on their toes looking to the north. But Flynn didn't find it funny. There was nothing funny in being on the run, not here, not anywhere. It was even less funny when he stood, just after opening time, in the phone booth in Footscray's Central Post Office, his hand full of coins and the realization hitting him that he had no idea how to make contact with 'Galloglass'. *I'll ring your Melbourne contact number at nine minutes past nine three days from now. If you don't answer I'll do it again three days after that . . .*

'Bloody hell!' He kicked the bottom of the cabinet in anger, drawing a sharp glance from one of the women behind the counter. But her disapproval had no effect on Flynn. He swore violently under his breath at his reflection in the glass side of the box, then tried to remember Jacko Sullivan's number. That didn't come either. Sullivan had been Doyle's boy; it was Doyle who'd known where he lived and where he jumped . . . Flynn bit his lip in vexation. Just a bloody minute! A quick flip through the international pages of the directory: 0011 44 . . . The rest came from memory and he was talking to a very bad-tempered Stephen Slattery in Belfast. But it didn't help.

'You must be out of your tiny fucking mind! If you want "Galloglass" you don't get him from here. And no, it's fuck all to do with me what's going on in fuckin' Australia. You sort that one out for yourself. Don't say anything more on this bloody phone. You ought to know fuckin' better. If you've got anything I ought to know, bring it, don't fuckin' talk about it.'

'Slattery –'

'Take your orders from Galloglass. I don't want to know!'

Flynn slammed the dead phone down into its cradle with another explosion of anger and stormed out of the post office before the lady who didn't like noise had apoplexy. But he wasn't getting anywhere and he was losing his grip. *Where the fucking hell did Sullivan live?* He stepped into a shoddy Italian café and drank a cup of indifferent cappuccino while he sorted himself out. Think! For Christ's sake, think!

The cappuccino did its stuff.

Doyle's emergency contact number. The bloody police'd be there . . . His fuckin' contact number, not his bedroom . . . The Irish Club. Close as bloody oysters. Even to another Irishman? Even then – the suspicious bastards! He glanced up at the clock on the café wall. Quarter-past nine. Give 'em a ring . . .

'My friend Vinnie Doyle!' he began.

'Fuck off!' Word had already got there.

'Just a minute. You can check me out.'

'I don't wanna fuckin' check you out!'

'Well, put me through to his mate Sullivan. It's home business. Seriously. Please, it's urgent, a matter of life and –'

'Whose fuckin' leg you pulling, mate?'

'I've gotta get hold of Sullivan.'

It must have been Flynn's lucky day.

'What Sullivan's that?'

'Jacko. Get in touch with him, please, and tell him to ring me urgently.'

The pause was significant. Jacko was obviously not a big enough name for a lengthy cover, at least not from an Irish face that knew names. 'Ring him your fuckin' self, then. Here, you'll get him at this number . . .' The digits thumped into Flynn's ear like bullets, but he hung on to them like a dying man to a priest's absolution and recited them over and over as he stuck his finger on the telephone cradle and then dialled the number. It was only when he'd finished dialling that he realized his hand was shaking and he was sweating like a dog.

Jacko Sullivan was feeling very pleased with himself as he led his new girlfriend by the hand up the stairs to the one-room flat on the first floor of the dingy apartment block in Stillman Street, Richmond. It had been hard work pulling this one and she'd shown nothing but reluctance since he'd begun the foreplay just after two this morning. Six long glasses of Tooheys Blue followed by a bloody expensive Chinese and a new line of bullshit and more drinks in a packed Molly Bloom's Irish pub in Port Melbourne before she'd given in and, his hazel eyes blinking in the unaccustomed raw sunlight, he'd steered her into the home stretch. This was it! By Christ he'd worked for it. And she was going to pay for it. By lunch time she'd think she'd spent the last four hours in a cement mixer.

'Jacko?' A door opened opposite the communal pay phone and an unshaved, unwashed face peered, bleary-eyed, through the gap.

Sullivan didn't slow down. 'Yeh?'

'Some guy's been ringing you all bloody morning. Quarter-past nine the bastard started. Don't your bloody mates realize some of us are up all fuckin' night?' The head lowered and its eyes studied the girl's ankles, rode up her legs, lingered on the hard round little bottom just above the hem of the short navy blue skirt, and decided not to go any further. The eyes didn't move even when Sullivan slowed and let her go in front.

'Did he leave a number?' It had to be Vinnie Doyle. Probably wanting help to bury the bloody Brit . . . 'Or a name?'

'None of that, mate. But he's got a bloody rotten temper, I'll tell you that for fuck all! Specially after the sixth call. He said he'd ring once more at ten, and if you came in, you weren't to fuckin' go out again until he's spoken to you – his words exactly.'

'And no name?'

'Like I said. But if he does ring again, Jacko, tell the bastard to watch his fuckin' language when he's talking to gentlemen! Better still, I'll tell the bastard myself.' He removed his eyes from the little backside and glanced over his shoulder, then back again, this time into Sullivan's narrowed eyes. 'If you wanna put anything into that, you'd better do it bloody quick. It's ten to flamin' ten, and like I said, he sounds a mean bastard.'

'Thanks, mate.'

'No probs.' The head vanished again and the door closed.

Sullivan stared at it for a moment, then at the pay phone on the wall. He contemplated taking the phone off the hook for half an hour, but decided against it. This didn't sound like Doyle's style. It sounded like something was wrong. Worse, it sounded like that psychopathic mongrel friend of Vinnie's . . . It sounded like trouble.

But it didn't put him off his stroke. She was on the bed, miniskirt screwed up round her neck and legs flailing helplessly, when a hand slapped noisily against the door.

'Fuck off!'

'It's your mate from Buckingham Palace. Get off her and get out here. He sounds like a fuckin' lunatic to me!'

Sullivan collapsed in a limp heap and allowed himself to slip slowly off the edge of the bed. He lay there, exhausted, for several seconds as his nervous energy drained out of him. The little girl couldn't make up her mind whether she'd had a lucky escape or missed something very special. Jacko Sullivan had that effect on them.

He let Flynn get it all off his chest before running out of patience. 'D'you mind getting to the bloody point, Flynn. The last time I saw you, you told me to get the car out of the way and duck out of sight. You didn't say sit by the bloody phone on the off chance you might ring!'

There was a long pause while Flynn swore silently and fluently to the back of the phone box. It was a long enough pause for Sullivan to light a cigarette. The whoosh of expelled smoke brought Flynn back down to earth. 'I wanna get out to Canberra, Sullivan, as soon as possible and without any fuss. When's the best time to move around?'

'From about now on. They'll all be coming into the city, not many going out, which might make you a bit obvious, but there are ways of beating the system. The cops can't block every road, they're more likely to concentrate on major routes into the country. But just a minute . . .'

'What?'

'Where's Doyley?'

'Fuck Doyley! Listen.'

But Sullivan wasn't in the mood; he didn't like the sound of what he was hearing. 'No, you fuckin' listen. Has something gone wrong? What's happened to Doyley?'

'Jesus Christ! I've had enough of this! Listen, you fucking little toerag, I'm on the friggin' run, and I don't want to say any more until I'm looking you in the face, got it? Just bear in mind that bad news for me means worse news for you. Now, go on about getting me out of fuckin' Victoria.'

He got another heavy whoosh of smoke in his ear, then a silence; not a phone cut-off silence, a breathing, live silence. Sullivan was thinking. But Flynn hadn't got time to hang around while Sullivan thought.

'Wassa matter with you, Sullivan?' Then suspiciously, 'You still there?'

Sullivan had finished thinking. 'Yeh. OK. Where are you?'

Flynn told him, reluctantly.

'OK. Come to my place. Get a tram or taxi.'

'No. I don't want to move – not yet. First thing, go and get some wheels, either rent or pinch, but get something, and meet me in half an hour in the car park under the railway arches – the big one at the bottom of Flinders Street, know where I mean?' He didn't wait for Sullivan's response. 'Don't be too particular. Whatever you bring, we'll change it for something else in the car park. Approach it from the station end of Flinders Street. I'll be on the lookout for you.'

'Flynn.' Sullivan managed to stop the flow of words. 'You're going over the bloody top. This is Australia. You're in Melbourne, not bloody London or Belfast. We don't have to piss around like that over here.'

'Just do as I say! Get a car and meet me where I said – and don't be late!'

The phone went down with an angry clunk and Sullivan grinned with satisfaction as he dropped his own phone into its housing. He drew deeply on his cigarette. Volunteer Fergal Flynn, the Belfast hotshot, the Provo hard man, the cold Irish killer, sounded as rattled as a little girl lost in a cemetery.

19

Reason listened in silence to the bad news. When Barlow had finished, he let out a whoosh of breath down the phone. 'Jesus Christ, Harry! How the fucking hell did you let that happen? Sixsmith! Christ, he was the bloody kingpin of the fucking structure! You should have sat in his bloody lap, Harry. The game was running.'

'These things happen, Clive.'

'Too fucking right they do, Harry, but they shouldn't. We're in big bloody trouble here. I know Flynn, and so ought you. He's a very, very dirty player and one of the best they've got.'

'They're all bloody bad news as far as I'm concerned,' said Barlow, 'and finding him's exactly what I'm trying to do. But in the meantime, think about it. Even if Flynn talks to his principals, they're not going to take an awful lot of notice of him until he comes in with something to substantiate his wild ravings – and that's all they'll be, wild ravings.'

'By the sound of it, Harry, he's got all the substantiation he needs. He's got that bloody disk. That's the good news, but he's also listened to Sixsmith's bloody version . . .'

'Plus a load of other interesting operational stuff.'

'Christ! Isn't there anything in our favour here?'

Barlow stared blankly at the wall in front of him. There wasn't. There wasn't a bloody thing in their favour. But he wasn't going to tell Reason that, not in Reason's present mood.

'What I want to do, as soon as I can get going, is run Flynn down and speak to him so that we can get a clear picture of who he's talked to and what he's said. The Irish have to have a full-blown contact over here, probably Embassy-based.'

'They have,' interrupted Reason. 'A top player, goes under the name of Galloglass. He works out of the Irish Embassy in Canberra.'

'That's not his real name?'

'No. But we're working on it. He's kept his fingernails nice and clean so far. Could be the bloody Ambassador for all we know!'

'Stranger things have happened across the street ... Look, I think I'd like to see David Murray out here, and I'd also like a rundown on these characters: the late Doyle, I don't know the rest of it but I think he's a Tyrone boy; Fergal Flynn we know about; and somebody Sullivan. I haven't got close to this last one yet.'

'David Murray's in Hong Kong. He can be with you in a few hours. Leave it with me. I'm coming too. No reflection, Harry, but if there're going to be any more balls-ups, I want to be there, on the spot and in a catching position. OK?'

'Doesn't worry me, Clive. When'll you get here?'

'I'm coming RAF. I'll be in Canberra tonight. I'll let Thompson know my contact point when I get there. Ring me as soon as you can. OK?'

'Fine. Can you tell David to have his stuff carried out diplomatic bag to the consul at Melbourne? He can stay with Mike Thompson. When I need him, I'll ring him at that number. One other thing. Knowing David's penchant for putting his foot in other people's mouths, I suggest you warn him that in official circles there's no "special relationship" for us over here. We're not in the group of most favoured people in Australia generally, and Canberra and Melbourne in particular. Tell him they won't understand his sense of humour. I'll be in touch.'

'Just a minute, Harry.' Reason had been thinking. 'This woman you mentioned – she part of the system?'

'ASIO.'

'So you said. OK. Use her; use their system. Let her, and them, find Flynn, but don't let her talk to him. You do the talking and then make sure he doesn't have anything left for them. David'll come in handy there. But watch her . . .' There was a long pause. Barlow let it run. Then Reason came back again. 'You don't think she's holding your hand for any other reason?'

Barlow didn't have to think about it. 'None that I can see. I think her motives are pure. She's not doing this under Canberra's orders. As far as anybody in the know was concerned, and that included Grant, I was just a Sixsmith watcher hanging about to find out what he was writing about. Sophie Ward's understanding is that I'm going for Flynn because he's got Sixy's computer disk. That's all it is as far as she's concerned, a recovery job on British Government property.'

'Ain't life complicated?' Reason's anger had evaporated.

'Bye, Clive. Do I know you if we meet?'

'We'd better have a nodding acquaintance, nothing intimate.'

'Heaven forbid! Bye!'

Barlow replaced the telephone with a wry smile. He made himself a cup of instant and sat down in one of the more comfortable chairs in Sophie's little flat.

He couldn't have timed it better.

Sophie let herself in with hardly a sound. It looked as if she was hoping to catch him doing exactly what he had just finished doing. She hadn't been gone long, but she'd done everything she set out to do. She dropped Barlow's holdall on the floor and stared at him accusingly.

'What have you been up to?'

'I fell asleep.'

She kept her feelings off her face and glanced suspiciously round the room. Nothing looked out of place. 'Your stuff's all in here,' she said after a moment. 'Don't spend all day over your bath. Leave the door open and I'll tell you what's going on.'

He raised his eyebrows, but didn't move except to lift the mug of coffee to his lips. 'Tell me now,' he said.

She moved over to the kitchen unit and began shovelling real coffee into a percolator. When it was on its way, she propped herself on the Formica counter and said, 'Flynn's started a bigger manhunt than Ned Kelly. Victoria hasn't had three killings in one go for a hundred years! The whole state's wobbling with activity – roadblocks, mobile patrols, helicopters, the lot.'

'Do they know what they're looking for?'

'Vaguely. Based mainly on what you told me and what I told Special Branch. The state police are organizing the show, but SB are running a special sideline themselves – a bit of a monkeys' picnic if you ask me! Then there's Dubrovnik, over there in Canberra, jumping on and off his desk with frustration because they wouldn't let him flood the place with ASIO teams with blackened faces and woolly masks! Did I say a monkeys' picnic? You've never seen anything like it!'

'What about you?'

'Ah! Never mind me. Now, how about getting in that bloody bath so that we can get on the road?'

Barlow drained his mug, stood up and placed it beside the popping percolator. 'I'll have one of those when it's ready. See you in a minute.'

'Leave the door open.'

'I'm shy!'

'Don't be so bloody silly! Leave the thing open. I can't talk to you through two inches of bloody wood! Now listen, before you go, Dubrovnik wants to keep you out of the hands of the police.'

'I thought he wanted me chained to a dungeon wall?'

'That was at one-thirty in the morning. He's had time to think about it and at last contact he was burning up priority wire to London to have you identified. He reckons he knows all about you now. For the moment you're going to be temporarily answerable to one Heros Dubrovnik for liaison and identification of suspected terrorists in the state of Victoria! But it's worse than that, mate. He's placed you under my nominal charge. As far as you're concerned, you haven't got a passport and you do as I say! You like that?' She looked at him challengingly. When he didn't reply, she shrugged. 'Well, it doesn't matter whether you like it or not. That's what you've got. Enjoy your bath.'

Barlow didn't move. 'So what does Dubrovnik want you – and me – to do?' he asked. 'Are we going to go looking for Flynn or are you going to sit and stare at me soaking in your bath for the next couple of days?'

'You're getting on my nerves, Barlow!' But she said it without rancour. 'I'd have thought that was fairly obvious.'

'Not to me, love.'

'OK. Dubrovnik's not happy with the situation as a whole. Not just Toby Grant's groundwork and Six-smith's and Robertson's deaths, but the whole bloody works. He thinks there's more to this than meets the eye. He thinks you Brits are crafty, underhand bastards – his words not mine, although I wouldn't dispute them – and anything that involves you lot over here is suspect. He wants me right up close behind Flynn and you right up close behind me because you seem to be the only person in Australia who's looked Flynn closely in the eye and walked away from it. You are our identification. Have you got that? You point him out and I pick him off. But he stays upright, Barlow. If he doesn't, you go up the bloody spout, and that's a promise from Dubrovnik passed on by me! Dubrovnik wants to have a good long chat with Flynn about matters general before handing him over to SB or the police. That's it in a nutshell.'

Barlow smiled, then turned his back on her and went into the bathroom. All in all it was a fairly satisfactory state of affairs; it was just a question of allowing her the first move, then easing himself into the command position. As Reason had said: use the system. He almost whistled with contentment as he turned on the taps.

There was no conversation over the sound of rushing water, but when he'd lowered his body gingerly into the bath and made himself comfortable, he raised his voice to carry through the gap in the door and said, 'Those "matters general" you mentioned?'

Sophie's head appeared round the corner. He wasn't embarrassed, he was beginning to accept her as one of the chaps.

'Dubrovnik's?' she asked.

'Yeh. What did he mean by that?'

She stared at him briefly, as if wondering whether the partnership was ready for this sort of confidence, then, purging her mind, said, 'He thinks Flynn might know something about a new drug problem that seems to be occupying his thoughts at the moment. He thinks the IRA might have designs on Australia as a major holding depot and there's a development towards serious international organization on those lines. Christ knows where he got that idea.'

Barlow knew. He kept his face expressionless as he began soaping his arms. 'And he thinks Flynn's running that sort of show?'

'He thinks he might have a few pointers to offer. He probably visualizes the answers on the inside of Flynn's fingernails. Hang on a minute . . .' Her head disappeared and a minute or so later she called out, 'Black or white?'

'White, two sugars.'

'You're not worried about that then?' She returned with two mugs and jerked her chin in the direction of his submerged waist. But it was only small talk, as if she reckoned she'd told him too much and was heading for a change of subject. She flipped the lavatory lid down, sat on it with her legs outstretched, and balanced one of the mugs on the edge of the bath. She studied the top half of his body critically as she sipped from her own mug. 'Where'd you get those?' Her eyes lingered on the two old misshapen and puckered bullet entry holes just above his left nipple.

He glanced down instinctively, smiled, then shook his head. 'One of the perks of the business. Do you want to see the others?'

She glanced immodestly into the bath and raised her eyebrows.

He shook his head. 'No, that's all OK. Round the other side.'

'I don't think I'll bother.' But there was a new tone in her voice, respect perhaps for someone in the same line of business who'd sat the exams and passed the physical. She leaned back against the cistern and raised the mug to her lips again. 'Toby said your reason for being in Melbourne was to get a look at the stuff Sixsmith was putting into his computer. I don't suppose you got anywhere near it?'

Did she know Grant had given him a copy? He guessed

not. Bloody good job he'd got rid of it. It was the easiest thing in the world to lie, it was part of the business, almost as natural as getting the best part of half a magazine of .40 S&W fired into your chest and back.

'Toby was going to ease his way into Sixsmith's flat and make a copy of whatever was going. I never got to see it. Flynn got one, and that went into your handbag, remember? Have you still got it?'

She ignored that part of the question and raised her eyes, frowning at the condensation-covered wall above his head. 'Toby wasn't playing quite straight with you, Barlow,' she said, almost apologetically. 'He got a copy and sent it to Dubrovnik. They've all seen it up there in Canberra. The stuff that was strewn across the kitchen floor was probably the only other copy in existence, and that's been expropriated by the Melbourne Coroner's Office pending enquiries. Sorry!' She lowered her gaze and studied his features for a reaction. There wasn't any. She continued: 'It would appear that the only way you and the British Government will get a chance of reading it is if his next of kin decide to publish.' She was still studying his face, 'Did he have any next of kin?'

'No idea.' Barlow replaced his mug on the edge of the bath and reached for the soap again. It was like playing Trivial Pursuit and liar dice at the same time. 'What happened to the Canberra manuscript?'

'Your guess is as good as mine. But I wouldn't advise trying to get at it. It doesn't exist as far as you and your people are concerned, and as for trying to get hold of the Melbourne one, I don't think you need reminding of the last time you British tried to do something like that through the courts! As far as Dubrovnik's concerned, I should imagine he's stashed it away until he needs a bargaining chip against your people, or, even closer to home, against you. You Poms don't have a monopoly of the dirty-tricks game, Barlow –' She was about to expound on the dirty-tricks business when the telephone rang.

Barlow hauled himself half out of the bath and strained his ears. The conversation must have been totally one-sided.

She came back into the bathroom in a flush of excitement. 'I forgot to mention,' she said, 'that Sullivan's car had been found abandoned in a backstreet in Richmond. On my suggestion nothing was done except to place a watch on it.'

'Good advice.'

She gave him a look. 'That's what I thought! It seems the thing's on the move again!'

'Bloody hell!' Barlow was halfway out of the bath and reaching for a towel, heedless of Sophie's appraising glance.

'D'you think Flynn's in the car?'

'No, definitely not,' replied Barlow, struggling with a large white towel. 'From what I've seen of this bloke Flynn he's a pro, a serious player. He wouldn't be caught in the same town as a dodgy car. This has got to be down to the guy who drove it away from Craigieburn, and I'll bet you half a ten-dollar note to a second-hand Mars Bar that his name's Sullivan.'

'You sound like a copper. Is that what you are, Barlow?'

Barlow ignored the question as he threw on his clothes. 'Who's tracking that car?'

'Special Branch. They'll ring me when it goes to ground. We can wait in my car. The radio's on the circuit; it'll give us a start. Erm, one thing before we go . . .'

He didn't hang on her words. Dressed, he moved towards the front door, waited a moment and pulled out the Smith & Wesson and checked the chamber. It was still fully loaded.

'I said "one thing", Barlow.' There was an edge to her voice. He recognized the symptom; it was called pre-battle nerves. He softened his expression and looked attentive.

'I can listen just as well as we go down the stairs. I can even talk at the same time!'

'Don't get bloody smart, Barlow. You're not going anywhere until I say. Now stand still and listen! You're coming along as a friend of the family, not charging through some bloody jungle with a gang of SAS cut-throats! Remember that, and remember this: that gun's for saving your life if some mad Irish bastard's got you in a corner with a gun jammed in your ear. You're not to take any action without my say-so, and you stay in the background – got it?'

'May I speak without being spoken to?'

She tightened her lips and shook her head in exasperation. 'Cut the bloody comedy, Barlow. I'm not in the mood. Go and talk to yourself on the way down, I'll meet you outside.'

The radio was hissing angrily when they climbed into the car. There was no way of telling how long she'd been on call, but it seemed to be losing patience. Sophie flicked the button and a voice cut through the hiss.

'For Christ's sake, Sophie, where the flaming hell are you?'

She glanced at Barlow, pulled a face, then picked up the handset and said, 'Forget it. Go on, what d'you want?'

'They've lost the target.'

'What! They've lost the bloody car?' There was more than disbelief in her voice.

'That's the only target we had!' came back the laconic response. No apology; it seemed like an everyday matter.

But not to Sophie Ward. 'How the bloody hell –' She

glanced again at Barlow. His face was impenetrable. She turned back to the phone, but it didn't help. 'How the flaming hell did that happen? Jesus Christ! Never mind. Where'd they lose it?'

20

Flynn melted into the bustling morning crowd that made Flinders Street Station resemble the main exit at Melbourne Cricket Ground on the day of the Victoria Football League grand final.

He waited for a lull around the telephone bank and then darted into one of the booths in front of a startled female who dropped her handful of coins in protest at being bundled to one side. But that was all happening behind Flynn's back. He was busy dialling the number of the Irish Embassy in Canberra.

He knew before he started that he was going to get nowhere. It wasn't difficult to imagine the conversation.

'I'm looking for a Mr Galloglass, an Irishman who lives in Canberra, or rather I think he lives in Canberra, that's where he said he came from . . . Can you help me, please?'

'Is this a joke?'

'Have you got a Mr Galloglass working in the building?'

'We don't reveal the names of anybody working in the Embassy.'

'Then screw you right up your arse!'

He abandoned the idea even before the operator came through with the Embassy phone number and dropped the receiver back on to its lugs.

Try Slattery again? He knows of Galloglass. He must be able to give me a bloody clue . . . Of course he fuckin'

*knows of him. Like I know of Bobby Sands, but it won't
help me dig the poor sainted bugger up, and I stand more
chance of getting him to help than fuckin' Slattery! So,
who the bloody hell do I tell that the Brits have got a
scheme going? More than that, who the bloody hell will
listen to me? Nobody in fuckin' Dublin, that's for sure.
So there's only one thing for it: go to bloody Canberra
and hang around the bloody dead letter box until Mr
bloody Galloglass makes a move in its direction . . .*

Flynn left the phone booth and rejoined the milling
crowd. He glanced up at the clock and watched the big
hand judder through another minute, then made his way
out of the station and walked down Flinders Street
towards the World Trade Centre. He could study the
Queen's Wharf Road car park long before he reached it.
Three-quarters of the area was spread out into the open
with rows of cars brewing up in the morning heat, while
the luckier ones were tucked tidily under the railway
arches. There were plenty of spaces in the open waiting to
be filled. Flynn walked casually across the road at the
traffic lights and cut through the car park. It was a forced
casualness. His eyes were everywhere and his senses
itched with impatience to be out of Melbourne and into
the country. There was no Sullivan. Just cars – dozens
and dozens of empty cars. He glanced down at his watch.
He couldn't wander around the middle of a Melbourne
car park looking up and down Flinders Street like an opti-
mistic whore touting for business.

Grunting an obscenity to himself, he retraced his steps
back towards Flinders Street Station, all the time studying
each car that came from that direction. When he reached
the Banana Alley vaults he slowed down and gazed, without interest, in the window of a physical-fitness centre. A
dark-skinned girl with muscles bulging out of her neck
studied him blankly from the back of the scruffy, over-

equipped gym. When their eyes met he turned away, looked at his watch again and gritted his teeth. It wasn't good enough. He moved further along the vaults until he came to one with a menu on a blackboard and easel parked outside its front door. He went in and ordered himself a coffee, then sat staring out of the window at the traffic coming down Flinders Street.

An hour later he was still there.

The wait wasn't doing his nerves much good. By continuously glancing at his watch and refilling his cup, he was becoming obvious, attracting attention just by being there — everything that went against the grain of a man who'd lived in the shadow for all his adult life. Jacko Sullivan was going to get the hairs torn out of his bloody ears if he didn't have a bloody good reason for putting him through this ordeal. But another quarter of an hour passed. He left the café and moved towards the car park again.

He waited on the kerb for the traffic lights to change.

'Fucking hell!'

The beaten-up Holden eased slowly through the lights in front of him and, in a convoy behind three other cars, stopped by the barrier to the car park.

Flynn tried not to believe his eyes. It wasn't possible. It couldn't be. But it was. And then he saw Sullivan's well-scrubbed face beaming around as if he was the ice-cream man.

'Oh, Jesus Christ. Oh, sweet Jesus! I don't fuckin' believe it!' Flynn's instincts urged him to turn and get away, as quickly as possible, in the opposite direction, to lose himself among the station-users. He started moving, crossed the road, then waited again, studying the road sign on the other side. Without staring, he watched Sullivan crawl up the line of parked cars until he found a vacant slot. It was unbelievable.

Sullivan stepped out of the car and leaned his arms on the roof, gazing about him. Flynn didn't move. He was watching the other cars – and the people. He saw nothing to cause the scowl on his face to diminish. But he still didn't move.

Sullivan got back into the driving seat of the old Holden, lit a cigarette and through half-closed eyes stared out of the side window, over the park at the river beyond. There could have been a thousand eyes watching him, he wouldn't have noticed them.

Another ten-minute stroll towards the World Trade Centre and Flynn made up his mind.

Moving in the opposite direction to Sullivan and the Holden, he cut round the car park and, from the other end, strolled innocently along the lines of parked cars three rows ahead of the lane in which the Holden was parked. When he was level with Sullivan he gave a quick sideways glance without making eye contact. It wouldn't have mattered. Sullivan, who was almost asleep, was only half-seeing what was going on around him. He didn't see Flynn, bending as if to open the door of his car, suddenly go down on his knees and duck out of sight.

Flynn waited a few moments, then sidled to the rear of the car and, still crouched double, waited for Sullivan to look in his direction.

It was not a long wait, but it was long enough for Flynn to imagine himself pummelling the Australian's face into a red pulp in his frustration. It helped pass the time until something jolted Sullivan's primeval instinct and he suddenly turned his head and stared straight into Flynn's eyes. Flynn had anticipated the movement and his finger was across his lips as Sullivan started, then scrabbled to open the door. Flynn willed him to look again. It worked, and he bared his teeth and stabbed his finger in a stay-where-you-are gesture as, still on his haunches and covered by the cars on either side and the bulk of the Holden in front, he edged his way to the passenger side of the car.

'Why didn't you pinch a fuckin' police car?'

Sullivan wasn't in the mood. 'There was nothing else handy. Why should I walk the bloody streets looking for an open door when this was already available? Jesus! You bloody people like making trouble for yourselves. You've always gotta find the hard fuckin' way of doing anything. You make my bloody balls ache! Now where d'you wanna go? And what d'ya wanna do?'

Flynn controlled himself. He needed this Australian, loud mouth and all, but the minute the gate opened and he could run free the cocky bastard would really know all about aching balls.

'Let's get rid of this bloody thing to start with,' he grunted. 'As quick as you like. Get out and have a look for something – and make sure it looks like every other bloody car.' He gestured to the left with his chin. 'Go down there, away from the road, and find something with four good wheels. Nothing flash, something that'll fit in. You got any money?'

'Why?'

'Don't keep answering with a fuckin' question every time I ask something. Have you got any money?'

'Yeh.'

'Good, because I haven't, and we'll need some more.'

Sullivan looked at Flynn with disdain. 'Why bother with banks? We'll walk into a shop and pinch some. It's like I said, you carrot tops always look for the hard way!'

'Go and get a fuckin' car.'

It didn't take Sullivan long. There's always one waiting for it in every car park. After checking it over, Sullivan strolled back to the Holden openly and casually. When he caught Flynn's eye he merely nodded and inclined his head, then cut back the way he'd come. Flynn crawled out of the door. Before moving, he managed a quick, professional survey of the car park. There was nothing out of the ordinary. Sullivan had been lucky. Flynn moved off in his wake, the ease with which the change had been effected worried him. Something wasn't quite right here, and his edginess showed as he joined Sullivan in the year-old Nissan. 'Don't try anything clever,' he said as he stared around. 'Drive carefully, obey the rules, no squealing tyres, and don't go over the limit. What's it like for petrol?'

'Half a tank. Where we going?'

'Where I told you on the phone – Canberra.'

'Fuckin' hell! That's nearly seven hundred flaming kays!'

'Listen, you dumb bastard, we walked into a load of bloody shit last night. The bloody thing blew up in our face and now the fuckin' police are after me. We've gotta get out of here, and quick, no fuckin' around! Got it?'

Sullivan almost smiled. He took his eyes off the busy traffic and glanced at Flynn. 'So you're on the friggin' run? Great! Where's Vinnie? Where we picking him up?'

'Just fuckin' shut up, will you!' Flynn's explosion wasn't controlled. He was beginning to lose it. Sullivan decided it was best to drive. He manoeuvred the Nissan out of the car park and headed east out of the city.

'Get on to something that takes us to Canberra,' ordered Flynn. 'Keep off the main roads but don't lose time. You know the bloody country, try some of the little dirt tracks that'll keep us in the right direction but out of the limelight. What the fuckin' hell are you doing?'

Sullivan had jammed on the brakes. They squealed in agony as with a violent twist of the wheel he spun the protesting car off the main road and into a down-at-heel Richmond side street and stopped dead. His jaw was set, his lips white and compressed. He kept the engine running.

'OK, you fuckin' Irish git!' he spat. 'That's it! I've had enough of you. I'm bloody pissed off! You're not in bloody Belfast, or even fuckin' London pulling the pissers off Brit pongos, you're in my bloody country and I'm not taking any more of your bloody crap. You wanna get to Canberra? You fuckin' ask me, not tell me. But before we go another bloody yard, you answer some fuckin' questions. Have you got that, Flynn? We're gonna sit right here until I know as much as you about what's going on. And Flynn, don't take me for a flaming idiot!'

Flynn had recovered from the violent manoeuvre. He sat unmoving, listening to the hysterical outburst of the only man in Australia he could rely on. Sullivan had got it all off his chest, but he'd shortened his life span, and in the not-too-distant future he was going to learn what a lot of other men who'd joined the Republican glory trail had learnt to their cost. It was simple and straightforward: you don't show your feelings to a Volunteer when he is on the job, least of all to a Volunteer of Fergal Flynn's stature. Flynn folded his arms and turned sideways in his seat to face the Australian. He looked cool and calm. It should have been a warning to Sullivan.

'Doyle's dead.' As simple as that.

Sullivan's jaw dropped. The anger and the truculence vanished as if a windscreen wiper had zipped across his face. For several seconds he could only stare uncomprehendingly into Flynn's stony eyes. Then, as if doubting his hearing, he said in a hushed voice, 'Dead?'

Flynn said nothing.

Sullivan repeated the word, and then, 'Christ! Bloody Jesus Christ!' It was an awed gasp. 'How?' He wished he hadn't asked; he'd been quite fond of Doyle, good mates. This wasn't how things should go. It was the Brits who were supposed to get the bombs and bullets and the coffins, not his lot, not his mates . . .

Flynn knew by the expression on the Australian's face what was going on behind, in his head. It gave him a few moments of pleasure, then he told Sullivan how Doyle had ended his military career.

'Who was this guy doing the killing?' asked Sullivan.

Flynn shook his head. 'No idea, or how he got into a position to blow Doyle away. He must have followed us. Christ knows how, or why.'

'Maybe he's a Pom minder,' whispered Sullivan, 'someone sent over to look after the old geezer we bagged in the flat in Melbourne.' He stopped short. There was the other thing he hadn't yet been told about. 'What've you done with him, by the way?'

'Topped him,' said Flynn lightly.

'You mean you killed the old bugger?' Sullivan was getting used to death. 'What for? Did he tell you anything?'

Flynn reckoned he'd said enough. 'Nothing that mattered. It was all a bloody waste of time when you add up the score. Just another dead Brit – one out of fuckin' millions.'

Sullivan wasn't interested in the mathematics of terrorism but he didn't want to let go yet, not until his knees had stopped behaving like jelly. 'How did you make it out of Craigieburn then, with this other guy gunning for you? And what about the coppers? How did they get into the act so quickly?'

Flynn frowned. He ought to have considered it himself. How had the bastards got on to him so quickly? Even thick Australians hit the button sometimes, and this stupid bastard had asked a question he hadn't even considered. How had the police started moving so quickly? And the angry bastard who knew how to use a .38 – there was no mistaking that bloody accent. He must have been

Sixsmith's minder. Some bloody minder! But the bastard had failed to keep his man upright and now he was in trouble too. What a bloody mess! It wasn't enough to have the fuckin' Australian police on the warpath, now they'd got a bloody Brit shooter in the game . . . And that was one thing he hadn't bargained for.

'Let's get on with it.' Outwardly, Flynn remained calm. This was almost his element, he felt at home. If the signs were right, for once in their bloody history the Brits and the Australians were hand-in-bloody-glove looking to nail Fergal Flynn's bollocks to some dungeon wall.

Sullivan nodded slowly and with his lips pursed made a dry nervous little whistle. He'd never had bullets hissing round his ears; for him running with the 'boyos' was still exciting stuff. London had been fun, but then the Pommy police were just one big bloody laugh; they never were going to catch up over there. And even if they did get lucky and the dice fell badly, it was a gentle tap on the shoulder, so the 'Home'-based boyos said. Bullets weren't on offer, not from the Pommy coppers. So it was still a game . . . Poor old fuckin' Doyley!

'It's going to be a slow one if you want to avoid the hard roads,' he said out of the corner of his mouth. 'You sure you don't want to take a chance and push through on the highway?'

'There'll be roadblocks. Just do what I said.' Flynn flipped open the glove compartment and emptied its contents on to his lap.

'What'ya looking for?'

'Maps.'

'Here.' Sullivan reached down beside him and pulled a bundle of dog-eared maps from the door pocket. 'Looks like we got ourselves a roamer. When you find the map you're looking for, I'm taking the minor road to Dandenong, then I reckon we bear down towards the coast, by which time the coppers will have lost interest in you and we can get on to the South Gippo Highway and make up for lost time.'

Flynn made no comment as he riffled through the wad of maps. When he found the Victoria State map, he threw the rest back in the glove compartment, opened it, and with his head bowed traced Sullivan's suggestions with his finger. Surprisingly, he agreed with them.

They'd been driving for two hours, mainly in silence, each with his own thoughts, when Sullivan glanced down at the dashboard and tapped the petrol gauge with the back of his finger. The needle remained where it was – almost on empty.

'We need petrol,' he said, still tapping the gauge.

Flynn didn't move. His eyes were half-closed, his thoughts fluctuating between the semicivilized streets of West Belfast and the rural killing grounds of County Tyrone. Flynn was homesick. 'They've got petrol pumps in Australia?'

'Sure. Got any money?'

'I said I haven't – haven't you? You said in the car park–'

'I've got five bucks and some change.'

Flynn controlled his temper. 'Got a credit card?'

'Don't be fuckin' silly.'

Flynn didn't reply. He knew what had to be done, but it was a bloody silly thing to have to do now that they'd beaten the cordon and were on a free run. He didn't trust himself to speak. Sullivan put it into words for him. Simple solutions posed no problems for Sullivan.

'We'll pinch some. We'll find a petrol pump, fill up and fuck off!' He grinned. 'After we've emptied the till.'

'And then we'll be back where we started with half the bloody Victoria Police Force screaming up our arse. Unless . . .' But Flynn didn't put it into words. Anticipation

wasn't Sullivan's strong suit; he'd probably start screaming and wet his knickers if he knew what was on Flynn's
mind. 'Keep your eyes open. The first place you see give
me good warning.' And with that he closed his eyes and
let his head fall back against the headrest.

Mrs Patterson's petrol station looked like one of those
TV advertisements that have absolutely nothing to do
with selling petrol. In the middle of nowhere, her nearest
neighbours were twenty-five kilometres north in a very
flashy new-age service station on the South Gippsland
Highway. The petrol people, and her decamping neighbours, had told her she was wasting her time trying to sell
petrol on a deserted road. She agreed, but she stayed; it
was her home and she made a bare living with two pumps
for petrol and one for diesel. Still she was happy. Far happier than the anxious fortune-makers who'd elected to sit
astride the Gippsland Highway.

The shop was a hut. A whirling table fan provided the
air conditioning whilst a freezer kept the Coca-Cola
chilled and a protected cabinet kept the flies and insects
off the home-made pies and cakes. If you wanted a cup of
tea you only had to ask; payment for the cuppa was a bit
of gossip and chat while the tea went down. Resting
against the wall in the corner beside the modern till was
her only concession to isolation; an ancient, rusting
single-barrel, twelve-bore shotgun. It was there for protection. She'd been on this site since the end of the war –
the proper one, the big one, when half the young men of
the country had gone away for something that wasn't
their business and got themselves killed or captured in
Singapore – but she'd never had cause even to think of
picking it up. In fact, it had been there so long it had
become a fixture. She no longer noticed it.

She lived behind the shop, up some steps hewn out of a

rocky slope, through a thick hedge, and into the neat and clean kitchen of an old-fashioned Australian settler-type house. No husband, no children, no interfering neighbours, she was happy. And today was another day. Well, not quite another day.

Sullivan broke the silence that had endured for the last three or four miles. 'Like a bloody water hole in a desert,' he grunted to the somnolent Flynn.

'Whassat?' Flynn's eyes flicked open. He was wide awake.

'Up ahead – a garage.'

Flynn took over. 'OK, look and behave natural. Give the guy your usual idiotic grin when he comes out and tell him to fill 'er up. I'll do the rest. You just go along with everything I say, but above all, be natural.' Flynn was no stranger to highway robbery. Petrol pumps in Northern Ireland were legitimate sources of ready cash; for people of Flynn's persuasion, they were almost as convenient as cash dispensers in a bank's wall. There was no reason why it should be any different in Australia. Driving slowly under the inadequate metal overhang, Sullivan stopped by the first pump.

Mrs Patterson had seen it coming almost from the time Sullivan had broken his silence way back along the stretch of road that faded into her almost limitless horizon. She studied the car for a moment, then got to her feet and waddled out to the forecourt.

The grinning head that watched her come gave her the willies rather than reassurance.

'How much d'ya want, son?'

'Fill 'er up please, ma.' The grin had locked into place on Sullivan's face. It looked as if he had a deformity, a sort of painful stricture that twisted his mouth into this unlikely grimace, but her attention was distracted by the offside door opening and the passenger slowly unwinding from the seat and stretching himself.

'Have you got a toilet, ma?' No please, no conversation, no pleasantry. There was no grin on Flynn's face.

She pretended she hadn't heard. She flicked on the electric pump, stuck the nozzle into the tank and set it on automatic. Only when she straightened up did she turn her head to Flynn, studied his unfriendly features for a moment, then jerked her thumb over her shoulder. 'Go round the side of the shop, through the garage, and you'll find a door marked toilet. There's a wash basin in there as well. A dunny in the desert with all mod cons!' She grinned humourlessly and went back to pumping petrol.

Flynn's eyes were all over the place as he walked past the shop and through the garage at the back of the forecourt. He'd spotted the shotgun propped against the wall. His eyes had been drawn to it like a magnet. As far as he was concerned it was already tucked under his arm and ready to go. The garage yielded the rest of the stuff he wanted: a length of thin wire, rusty, but with its core unimpaired, and two five-inch nails. In the lavatory he attached the nails to each end of the wire and tested its flexibility with a couple of whiplash jerks. Then, gripping both nails, he wound the wire around his wrist, put his hand in his pocket and strolled back to the front of the garage.

Mary Patterson was ringing the charges through the till when Flynn came into the shop. She still didn't like the look of this one. 'Sixty-five, eighty,' she said.

Flynn shrugged and moved to the other end of the shop, where he stood in front of the food cabinet and stared down at its contents. Without looking up, he said, 'I'd like a couple of these pies, if they've got meat in 'em, some sandwiches and two slices of this cake.' Still no 'Please' and no effort to help himself. He looked a surly, unpleasant bastard.

Mary Patterson's instincts were playing hell with her commercial feelings about these two. She allowed herself a quick glance out of the window at the car still standing by the petrol pump. The glance brought another idiotic grin from the driver and she turned away quickly and went to deal with the man by the food cabinet. She moved in front of him and opened the chiller door.

She gave only a gasp and a strangled cough as the wire went over her head and tightened round the loose muscles of her neck. Flynn took up the slack quickly, crossed his arms and pulled the wire tight. With his knee in the small of her back, he pressed her body against the cabinet until her knees gave away. Still hanging on to the nails, he lowered her flailing body to the ground and with both knees now grinding into her back, held her there and waited for her to die.

It took all of four minutes before her heart stopped beating.

Flynn straightened up and, leaving her where she'd dropped, picked up the plastic bag she'd brought for his purchases. He filled it with most of the food in the cabinet and threw in half a dozen tins of cold drinks from the fridge. He appeared to be in no hurry; his breathing was almost back to normal and his adrenaline count had hardly risen. This had been an easy one. He didn't give Mary Patterson another glance as he moved round the counter to the till. She'd left it open, but what was in it was hardly worth taking. Fifteen dollars, a few coins and three cheques made up the day's takings. Flynn scowled to himself as he stuck the money in his trouser pocket, then he lifted the shotgun from its corner and inspected it with disgust. Still in no hurry, he didn't even bother looking out at the forecourt or up the road. He seemed to have it all worked out.

'Flynn!'

He glanced over his shoulder and at the car with annoyance. Sullivan, with the front door open, was hanging out of the car. 'Flynn?' he bellowed again.

'Shut your fuckin' noise!' bellowed back Flynn. 'Start the car and get ready to go.'

'. . . something to eat.'

Sullivan's plaintive words went over his head as he turned back to the desk and broke open the shotgun. The breech was empty. 'Stupid old cow!' murmured Flynn as he dropped the unloaded gun and began rummaging among the shelves. 'There must be some bloody thing around. A gun's no fuckin' use without something to shoot from it. Even a silly old bitch like –' He stopped talking to himself when he opened the table drawer and picked out a plastic-covered cartridge. He snatched the drawer out and emptied it. Another cartridge, this one in green plastic, rolled across the floor. He picked it up and studied its end. No. 6. Birdshot! And probably a hundred years old, damp and useless! Stupid bloody woman, he mouthed again as he slid the cartridge into the breech and stuck the other one into his pocket. Picking up the plastic bag, he walked out of the shop and back to the car.

'How d'ya get on? What about the old woman? D'ya get any cash? What happened?' Sullivan shot the questions out like bullets, his eyes bulging into Flynn's unconcerned face.

'Stick that in your face and eat it,' said Flynn by way of reply. 'And drive. Stay on this road. I'll tell you when to turn off.'

'You've got a gun!' It sounded like an accusation.

'Eat your fuckin' pie and drive,' snapped Flynn. No money, a doubtful weapon, dodgy ammunition, and a bloody talkative, inquisitive Australian as a partner. Flynn's mood was black as he slumped back in his seat and considered the prospects.

21

Sophie shoved the handset back into its slot in the car, her lips tight. She didn't start the engine, but settling back in her seat glanced at Barlow out of the corner of her eye. 'You heard what the stupid bastard said. With all the resources at their beck and call, they lost a flaming car in the heart of Melbourne.' She didn't give Barlow a chance to respond, but leaned forward again and slapped the dashboard with the flat of her hand. 'I wish you hadn't had to hear that,' she said after another second's mental flagellation. Embarrassment wasn't a normal facet of Sophie Ward's character and she glanced again to see if he was gloating.

He wasn't. He shrugged unconcernedly. 'Sounded all very normal to me! Everyday stuff in the UK. Plod's always ballsing up unballs-upable situations!' It gained him an ally. 'What happens now?'

Sophie pulled a face, then wrinkled her nose. 'I'm not sure. We'll just have to wait.'

Right on cue the radio crackled into life again.

'. . . Sophie? This is Dick –'

'Special Branch,' she murmured to Barlow.

'I've got a couple of guys with the police. They were hanging around Queen's Wharf Road car park. They just had a guy reporting a stolen car. Over!'

'Happens all the time, Dick.' Sophie wasn't impressed.

'D'you want to hear the story, Soph?'

'Go on, then.'

'Another guy said he'd been dozing in his car and saw this character hanging around the stolen vehicle. He answers to the description of the guy the police lost at Swanston Street junction. There was another man, but he didn't get much of a look at him. Why don't you go down and talk to this bloke who saw it all?'

'Thanks, Dick. I'm on my way.'

22

Flynn threw a half-eaten home-made minced beef and onion pie out of the window, washed his mouth out with a swig from a tin of chilled Coke and stared out at the rolling Victorian countryside.

The road was a twisting one, winding through uninhabited country, a steep, almost vertical hill on one side and on the other a slope covered with a thick growth of gum-trees. Beyond the trees, vanishing into the skyline, was the pale emerald-coloured Tasman Sea, serene and calm, hardly disturbed by the barely visible white-speckled breakers.

But Fergal Flynn wasn't interested in white-speckled waves, or any other aspect of the view; Flynn was only interested in getting rid of the information that was burning like an ulcer in his gut. The man who called himself Galloglass was the only man who could relieve him of what was, to him, the awesome responsibility of preventing a major blood-letting within the New Executive. Even Flynn, and he'd be the first to acknowledge his limited horizon where politics within the Movement was concerned, could see what would happen when Sixsmith's planted memoirs wrapped inside a hard cover thumped on to the kitchen table in the Official HQ in Dublin. Blood-letting would be the understatement of the year. He tapped his pocket for reassurance. There was the answer, Sixsmith's confession, his own words spoken through broken teeth, his willingness to put the matter right.

Blood-letting? Christ! You must be joking! This tape'll turn the Sixsmith memoirs, and his MI masters, into the laugh of the bloody century! But what if Mr Galloglass has buggered off out of the country? Who else is there? Forget the flappy-mouthed Slattery in Belfast and go to the centre of things – Dublin? Give 'em a ring. Give who a bloody ring? Danny Breen? Niall Loughron? What the fuckin' hell good will that do? They'd ring up bloody Slattery and ask him what the bloody hell was going on . . . Go to the top – the Executive? D'you think they'd stop picking their bloody noses for a second to listen to what Volunteer Fergal Flynn in Australia had to say? Jesus, they'd think he was a fuckin' Brit tout. He shook his head and drew a comment from the casual, relaxed and generally disinterested Sullivan.

'Whassa matter, Fergie? Got a bit of the old lady's pie stuck in your throat?'

'Fu –' Flynn choked back the expletive.

Sullivan's head shot back to the front and saw them a fraction of a second later.

Two policemen, one standing at the edge of the road smoking and gazing over the expanse of tree tops at the distant sea. Hatless, he looked hot and sweaty and was staring longingly at the white triangle of a distant yacht. His partner, also smoking, leant against the bonnet of the patrol car and watched curiously as Sullivan, jamming his foot on the brake and ramming the gear into reverse, managed to stall the car.

Without moving his head, Flynn hissed through the side of his mouth: 'Start the fuckin' motor and carry on towards them.' Sullivan, hands shaking, knees like jelly, shot him a sideways glance. Flynn was cold and calm, his eyes locked on the two policemen. 'Go on, you silly bastard! Go forward.'

Sullivan did as he was told and moved the car hesitantly on. Out of the corner of his eye he saw Flynn's hand drop to the shotgun and raise the barrel so that its muzzle lodged on the armrest just below the window.

The policeman by the patrol car flicked his half-smoked cigarette into the road, ground it out with the toe of his shoe, and straightened up. Without taking his eyes off the car crawling towards him, he reached through the window behind him, brought out his cap and, using both hands, arranged it on his head at the correct angle. A quick glance into the wing mirror, a minor adjustment, and he stuck his arm out to bar the road, waiting for the Nissan to reach him.

Sullivan's jelly-like knees did it again. One of them went nervously to the brake pedal, the other did nothing, and the car stalled again.

The policeman on the other side of the road, his arms folded across his chest, grinned as he watched his straight-faced colleague walk slowly towards the Nissan, studying the registration number before raising his eyes and searching the faces of the two men staring at him from behind the windscreen.

Flynn didn't wait for him to speak. If he had he would have saved himself a lot of trouble. It was pure curiosity on the policeman's part. Neither the stealing of the car nor Mrs Patterson's murder had been broadcast yet and he shouldn't have been there anyway. This was a little side trip, a quiet stretch, the radio switched off for a moment's relaxation and a smoke before returning to the highway. It was a short break that had become a routine for the two patrolmen.

Standing at the passenger door the policeman frowned into Flynn's uncompromising face, then looked down. His eyes bulged as he focused on the gun and, as if in slow motion, watched the barrel rise into the open window and rest on the sill. He was given no time to think about it. Flynn squeezed the trigger and everything was blotted out as the gun exploded into his neck and chest.

His partner hesitated for a fatal second as the explosion was replaced by his partner's drawn-out scream and Sullivan's frightened bellowing.

And then he recovered. Not short of guts, he brought out his pistol and fired wildly at the Nissan. It didn't matter who or what was in it; that was where the explosion had come from, that was where his bullets went.

Flynn remained calm – this was his element. He broke open the shotgun, clawed out the empty case and jammed the other cartridge in its place.

'Go! Go!' he bellowed at Sullivan. 'Start the fuckin' car and go! Quick!'

The explosion of the windscreen shattering as one of the policeman's shots found a target, and the crack-crack-crack as he emptied the rest of the revolver's chamber, brought Sullivan to his senses. Ducking, he turned the key. The engine howled, the tyres hissed and squealed and spun in a shower of smoke and chippings. With his foot hard down as far as it would go, Sullivan, hunched over the wheel, sent the skidding car sideways into the crouching policeman.

The wing of the Nissan caught him and threw him over the edge of the road, but even as he flew through the air he still managed to hold on to his empty revolver. When he came to rest, he scrambled out of his belt the spare six-round moon-clip. With his back against a tree he fumbled the clip into the chamber, snapped it shut and then dragged himself up the bank to the edge of the road and began firing at the moving car. Anger had replaced the earlier fear, the shock and the pain, and he took his time aiming, double-handed, each shot into the car.

As he squeezed off the sixth round the car stopped.

There was a moment's stillness, a sudden deathly silence, then a graunching of gears and the Nissan began a slow erratic return.

The policeman watched, mesmerized, as the car stopped alongside him and Flynn climbed unhurriedly out of the passenger seat. He waited for a second by the door, gave a cursory glance at the first policeman's now still and grotesquely outspread body and then, with the shotgun held one-handed in front of him, moved warily to where the injured policeman waited.

Flynn stared down at him and pointed the shotgun. The policeman stared back, then raised his revolver and aimed at Flynn's face. Flynn shook his head in admonishment. He'd counted twelve shots, the chamber and the spare clip. If he'd had any more he'd have been shooting still.

'You should have saved one . . .'

The policeman's reply was drowned by the roar of the shotgun and his face disintegrated from the close-range shot. He was dead before his head slammed into the ground.

Flynn didn't hang around to study his handiwork. Holding the barrel of the shotgun with both hands, he hurled it with all his strength and watched it curve out of sight over the tops of the trees. He listened for a moment as the tree branches recovered from the disturbance before turning to the first policeman. He pulled him on to his back and dragged the unused pistol from its shining leather holster. He removed the full moon-clip of ammunition from its housing and dropped it in his pocket. As he turned away from the body he clicked open the pistol. All the chambers were loaded. He closed it and tucked it into his waistband. It didn't show on his face, but Flynn was a contented man. The blood was coursing through his veins, his breathing was back to normal. He'd killed,

228

and he was armed with a proper weapon. It was like the real times again, and as he walked back to the Nissan he could have been strolling down the Springfield Road on a sunny afternoon.

But he wasn't home yet.

'OK, let's go.' Flynn climbed back into the car without a backward glance at the two bodies behind him. 'Come on, get your fuckin' finger out and get us away from here.'

But Sullivan didn't move.

Hunched over the steering wheel, his head resting on his arms, he appeared to have gone to sleep. Flynn jabbed him with his fist. 'I said –'

Sullivan didn't raise his head. His voice was muffled and laboured. 'That bastard hit me . . .'

'What d'ya mean?'

'I've got a fuckin' bullet in my gut – one of that bastard copper's fuckin' bullets!'

'Jesus!' That was the extent of Flynn's consolation. Bullets were part of the business, even your lot got one, sometimes. 'Get into the back. I'll drive.'

'No!'

'Sullivan, we've gotta bloody get out of here.' Flynn glanced over his shoulder. 'Quick, come on, stop fuckin' about. Let me drive!'

'I can manage – '

'You need a doctor.'

Sullivan looked up, stared bleary-eyed at Flynn, then shook his head. The pain was making him bloody-minded. The movement set up a judder of pain that forced a cry of agony from between his tightly clenched lips. He blinked away the tears and gritted his teeth as, reaching forward, he turned the key in the ignition and then, with the same hand, searched the area just above his belt. It came away wet and sticky with blood. Flynn watched curiously as Sullivan studied the hand, wiped it on his trouser leg and nodded at the opaque, shattered windscreen. 'Don't just fuckin' sit there,' he groaned. 'Clear a hole in that bloody thing.' He waited until Flynn had made a large opening with his elbow, then stuck his foot hard on the accelerator. The car juddered and bucked for fifty yards before Sullivan managed to control the muscles in his leg. Then, with another tortured squeal of tyres, the Nissan roared down the middle of the road.

'Jesus Christ!' Flynn was thrown forward, then dragged back in his seat as they took off. 'Jacko!' he bellowed over the pained howling of the Japanese engine and the whistle of air through the jagged windscreen. 'Are you going to be all right? Can you manage this fuckin' thing? Why don't you –'

'Shut up!'

They were the last words Sullivan said for the next hour. It took all his willpower and a new gutsy determination he never knew he had to keep his eyes open and his hands gripped on the wheel. He'd forgotten the man beside him. There was only one thing in his life, and that was keeping the car under some sort of control whilst going as fast as his reflexes would permit.

Beside him, Flynn tried to look unconcerned as the car's progress became more and more erratic, gaining speed along the straight sections of the rough road, and then tyres protesting round the sharp bends as the back of the Nissan forced itself nearer the road's offside edge. As the wind rushed through the missing windscreen, hammering against his eyelids, Flynn was, thankfully, able to close his eyes without appearing nervous. But every so often he forced them open to study his partner. There was nothing reassuring in what he saw.

Sullivan was feeling none of Flynn's trepidation. He was fortunate that the road was not even a secondary one and that so far, apart from the police patrol car, theirs was the only vehicle on it. He was not aware of his speed. Every few seconds a new wave of pain seared upwards from his stomach, blotting out his vision with a red-streaked mist. He wasn't even driving by instinct – he was driving by luck. And then it ran out.

With his eyes battered by the intensity of the inrushing wind, all feeling gone from his leg and foot, and a sudden intense shock of pain that welled up from his stomach and into his brain, he blacked out. His foot was jammed down hard on the accelerator as he went into the bend. It was a sharp one. He made no attempt to control the already out-of-control Nissan and, dead to the world, knew nothing as it roared off the road. It hurtled, as if aimed, between two of the large white-ringed trees protecting the bend, flying through the air at over 160 kph.

Flynn began to scream as the car dropped like a shot bird through the canopy of branches below. The impetus carried it forward and it carved its way down the wooded slope, bouncing from trunk to trunk, until, meeting something more solid than itself, it thudded to a dead stop. It remained suspended, as if trying to make up its mind which way to fall, and then everything gave way and the wreck overturned and disintegrated. Flynn felt as if a giant hand had thumped him in the back and another had reached through the windscreen and pulled him by his head. He was flying through the air. It was a weird sensation but then everything went black, as though his eyes had been plucked out. And he died. Or thought he had.

23

There was almost a spring in her step when Sophie rejoined Barlow in the Queen's Wharf Road car park. 'At least we know what car they're driving,' she said as she slid behind the wheel of the Ford Falcon. 'A navy-blue Nissan. We've got the number as well, but that's about as far as it goes – the solid stuff, that is.'

Barlow turned in his seat. 'What about the unsolid stuff?'

She didn't answer immediately, but started the car's engine and began manoeuvring out of the parking slot. 'An old woman's been killed at a petrol station south-east of Melbourne.' Barlow's face remained blank as she glanced at him. She shrugged. She didn't really fancy it herself. 'It just seems to fit in. The owner of the Nissan reckoned he'd only got about half a tank of petrol.'

Barlow almost laughed. Flynn wasn't the type of gangster to balls up a simple thing like robbing a petrol station.

'Is that it?' he asked.

'It's all we've got. I think we ought to go and have a look.'

Barlow didn't argue. He settled back in his seat and tried to relax as she forced her way out of the city centre. She was driving fast, too fast, and he had no desire to risk impairing her concentration until he saw a fairly straight section of road when they entered the South Gippsland Highway.

'How was this petrol station done?' he asked, without taking his eyes off the road unwinding, fast, in front of them.

'He emptied the till, probably filling the car up with petrol first, and then carried on.'

'If that was Flynn,' mused Barlow, 'I'm surprised he didn't put a torch to the place. That's normal procedure for these mad bastards. They've just discovered that fire destroys all sorts of incriminating evidence.'

'He probably didn't want to draw attention. They were unlucky to have another car call in so soon after they'd left. I'm told it's against the law of averages to have more than one car every two or three hours on that road, especially this time of the week.'

'How was this woman killed?'

'He nearly took her head off with a bit of rusty wire. A garrotte, Mason's man said. Nasty.'

'Ahh!'

'What?'

'That sounds savage enough for our man.'

'Thanks.'

'What for?'

'For showing some enthusiasm at last. Is that the sort of thing they do over there, then, garrotte old women for a tankful of petrol?'

'Everything goes. The sort of Irishman we're looking for has never been choosy about what he uses to kill with. So, yes, that sounds right up his street, but it's only an assumption that the killer was Flynn. You haven't said anything yet that puts him in this part of the country and on that particular road. Australians have been known to commit the odd crime or two.'

She took her eyes off the road to look at Barlow. 'Like I said, it's all we've got.' She slowed down briefly to turn off the highway, wriggled through Koo Wee Rup, then

233

joined the secondary road signposted Catani and put her foot down again. She took another moment off to glance at Barlow to see how he was enjoying it. He looked relaxed. 'But I wouldn't put money on – ' The crackling of the radio coming to life cut her off in mid-sentence. She leaned forward and turned up the sound.

'I should have done, shouldn't I?' she said, dry-voiced, when Dick finished telling her of the murder of the two policemen.

'Should have done what?'

'Put money on it.'

Barlow leant against the side of Sophie's Falcon, legs crossed, arms folded, and gazed over the canopy of trees at the distant horizon where the Tasman Sea joined the sky.

Even that far away the sea appeared very welcoming, but the odd pyramid of white sail reduced to little more than a speck on a blue-green cloth did nothing for him. Barlow was a land man. The sea had little to commend it apart from the attraction of its cool embrace followed by yielding warm sand in the shade of an umbrella, with a heavy tumbler full of clunking ice cubes and gin and tonic in his hand. He gave up the sea and turned his head towards the group just along the road.

Sophie was there, among her own, standing in conference. A group of State policemen, ambulancemen and miscellaneous odds and sods of the violent-death brigade murmured to each other, the stunned expressions still ingrained on their faces after their initial curious glances under the two plastic sheets.

After a moment, Sophie extracted herself from a serious-looking and obviously senior group and picked her way through the parked cars and vans to Barlow.

She looked pale. He remembered she wasn't very good

with the uglier side of the violent-death business. 'One of them had hung on,' she said grimly. 'He didn't say anything and apparently died in the ambulanceman's arms. They've decided it has to be the Irishman.' She propped herself alongside him. 'I agree with them. This sort of thing fits in with yesterday's killing. The pattern matches. It's got to be Flynn and his mate.'

Barlow turned his head slightly and gave her a sad smile. 'Can't they find anything there to blame it on the British?'

She studied his face, tight-lipped. She wasn't amused, and she told him so. 'It's not a funny game, this, Barlow. There are two young men lying over there brutally murdered by a callous bastard with no pity. I don't see anything in that to be flippant about.' She paused, and thought about something. 'Although that Special Branch man, Mason . . .' She jerked her chin in the direction of the taciturn individual Barlow had last seen in the car park at the bottom end of Flinders Street. He was in his element, and had the happy expression of a funeral director studying a job lot. '. . . puts all this down to Pom skulduggery. He quoted Sixsmith at the State Commissioner and got him to agree that if the murders were done by the Irishman, it was because he'd been pushed over the top by you Brits!'

Barlow lost interest in Mason and turned his head to stare at the sea again. It seemed more sympathetic. 'Anything turn up that's not obvious?'

Sophie nodded. 'One of the troopers walked straight into the shotgun. He was probably going to ask what they were doing on an almost deserted road that leads nowhere in particular. His face is missing. So is his gun. The other boy had a go – used up all his ammo and did away with their windscreen. He might have hurt them, we'll probably never know.' She shrugged absently. The image

235

of pulped faces was still there, fresh and clear, in her mind. She was definitely going to have problems with her dinner and sleep tonight – and probably many other nights as well. 'They ran the poor sod down to start with. Both legs were broken, but he still had a go at the bastards. He reloaded – there were empty cartridge cases all over the place – and must have given them everything he'd got, then sat back against a tree and waited.'

'I've got the picture.' Barlow's face was blank. This was nothing new. He'd had more than twenty years' association with people like Flynn; Sophie, after two days, was just finding out what it was all about. But he couldn't stop her now, she was in the confessional – or the exorcist's shed. She was going to cleanse her soul of it one way or another.

'The bastard with the shotgun must have stood above the boy and given him enough time to think about what was coming and then pulled the bloody trigger – the fucking sadistic animal!'

'The PIRA,' said Barlow softly, 'never did put great store on playing games according to the rules. The women are just as bad, probably worse, but that's neither here nor there.' It was time to get Sophie back to work. He gazed up at the sky. 'If we can get our hands on Mr Flynn and friend first, you'll be able to have a few minutes alone with him.'

Her lips were still set on a last mouthful of invective, but she didn't enlarge on it. 'A bullet in the ear is what he's likely to get if I clap eyes on him first.' Like Barlow she studied the sky, then the horizon. 'I wish I knew where the hell he's heading.'

He climbed into the passenger seat of the car and waited until she had made herself comfortable behind the wheel. 'I suppose there's always the chance that one or the other's got contacts out here.' Barlow was quiet for a moment, then said thoughtfully, 'If that is the case, and that's where they'll be going to ground, Flynn'll dig himself in for a while – not long, but long enough for the police enthusiasm to die down. What I can't make out, though, is why they're leaving a bloody trail that a blind man could follow. It's not like Flynn's type. I don't get it!'

Sophie started the car. 'I don't want to keep arguing with you, Barlow, but personally I think they're trying to get out of the state. If they were going to settle again in Victoria, I don't see even a crazy Irishman making such a bloody mess of the countryside. I reckon he's put his head down and is running for the line.' The car moved off with a mild squeal of rubber on windscreen fragments and she waved to the faces at the side of the road. Nobody waved back. 'There's a new general bulletin gone out about a blue Nissan looking for a new windscreen. He's sure to know that, and could have ditched the car somewhere semi-civilized and picked up another. But we'll have a go at that theory later on.' She glanced sideways. 'You OK for a bit of speed?'

'Please yourself. I'm the perfect passenger.' And he pulled the seat belt tighter round him and closed his eyes to prove it.

24

Flynn lay still whilst his brain came to join his other problems, and then carefully, tentatively, he moved his arms. They worked. Confidently he raised his head, and held back a shriek of agony as an axe seemed to cleave it in two. He touched the top of it. He head was matted and sticky. He brought the hand down and held it, shaking and shivering, in front of his eyes. He had difficulty focusing – it looked like somebody else's hand. It was as if it had been plunged into a tin of red paint. He wiped it on his trouser leg and explored further. His fingers sank into a gash in his scalp that extended from one side of his head to the other, and with horror he could feel the hard bone of his skull. He nearly passed out again. He continued exploring. There was no real pain, not yet, just a cloying numbness, and in his confused state he decided this was a good sign. He abandoned further inspection of his head – that it was still on his shoulders was enough for Flynn – and moved on to inspect the rest of his body.

His clothes were in shreds and one bloody knee jutted out of a tear that ended at the bottom of his trousers. More blood. He moved his feet around and then his legs. Nothing broken, but nothing unbruised, and the pain was beginning to come through. Slowly and agonizingly he dragged himself to his feet and leant against the trunk of the nearest pine while he looked around.

He became aware of the deathly silence, broken only

by the tick, tick, tick of part of the car's engine cooling away the punishment Sullivan had given it. It wasn't far off. The main part of the Nissan was crushed up against a solid, larger-than-average pine and at first glance looked like a busted, rusty oil tank. He moved his eyes around. There was nothing more. The chassis and wheels had gone somewhere else and this bit, with part of the engine, was all that was left. Flynn stared at it for several minutes. There was no movement in the busted box. He bared his teeth. It wasn't meant as a smile – Flynn was never going to smile again, at anything. But he continued staring as if expecting to see Sullivan pop up with a grin on his face.

He spat out a mouthful of blood and tried out his voice. 'Jacko?'

It came out as a hoarse gurgle. He couldn't even hear it himself. He tried again.

'Jacko!'

That was better, louder, and it sounded human. But there was still no response, no echo, nothing, only the metronomic ticking of the cooling engine. He pushed himself away from the tree and staggered to the side of the wreck. Leaning against what had been a door window, he poked his head inside.

His stomach came up to his throat before he had a chance to pull back, and the whole of his last two meals splashed heavily on the remains of the Nissan's back seat. This was Fergal Flynn, the hard man; the man who'd laughed as he touched the switch on the transmitter detonating the huge mine by the side of the road; the man who'd grinned cheerfully as, defying orders, he'd descended from the safety of the Republic side of the hill and gone to the roadside carnage just to grin happily into the faces of the dying and mutilated young British soldiers he'd blown up at Ballygawly. They still talked about Fergie Flynn's guts in the pubs in Tyrone. He drew back from the wrecked Nissan, went down on his knees and, still spewing, dropped his face into the contents of his stomach.

It took him a long time to recover, and then he went back to have another look at what had offended his stomach.

Sullivan's head still grimaced at him from what had been the back seat. Just his head, nothing else. It lay in a mess of blood and gore, but the face was as clean and untouched as if it had still been attached to its body. Flynn stared mesmerized. And where was . . .? Where the bloody hell was the body? He spat his mouth clean of bile and wiped his eyes with the remains of the sleeve of his coat. Then he looked again, this time objectively. There was no body to be seen – anywhere. It must have gone through the door on impact, leaving the head, jaggedly detached, to bounce off the roof and on to the back seat.

For a moment, Flynn considered the freak. There was no remorse in his manner now that he'd recovered from the initial shock of meeting Sullivan's head. He put it into perspective. As a partner, Sullivan had been just a bloody nuisance, and once he'd got the bullet in his gut his usefulness had expired. And talking about bullets . . . Flynn straightened up and felt around his waistband for the dead policeman's revolver. But he knew before his hand went anywhere near where it had been that it was no longer there. He ran his hand forlornly round the back of his trousers and then, with his legs regaining their strength, searched the area where he'd regained consciousness. Nothing. He studied the undergrowth about him and shook his head in despair – when he most needed, his luck had deserted him. The pain from the sudden movement nearly made his eyeballs pop out and, grasping a low hanging branch, he stood with his head drooped on to his chest, swaying like a drunk until it had subsided.

He must have hung there for nearly half an hour before he felt strong enough to continue. It gave him time to assess the situation, but that got him nowhere; however he considered it, there was nothing to commend it. Being on his own didn't bother him. Losing the car was unfortunate. But the loss of the revolver was a serious setback. Weaponless he was impotent, and he was going nowhere without something to balance the odds. He staggered back to the car's shell and, ignoring its gruesome passenger, went down on his knees to inspect the interior. Still no revolver, but with a grunt of contentment he found an unopened tin of Coca-Cola. He clicked it open. It exploded after the battering it had taken, but there was still enough for him to swill out his mouth. He spat it out, then drank half of what remained. It thudded into his empty stomach and almost gushed straight back up again, but he gritted his teeth and held it down. The rest of the tin he poured on to his handkerchief and dabbed it on the gash in his head. It seemed to do some good. He moved round to the back of the car and peered into what had once been the boot. There was nothing of interest except, strangely, a perfect tyre on a perfect spare wheel still locked into place. He turned away in disgust. He didn't know what he'd expected to find but he knew what he'd have liked to see: a self-loading pistol with a thousand rounds, or a stubby, lethal Heckler and Koch. Anything . . . A bloody spare tyre was no bloody good at all!

He leaned against the back of the wreck and kicked the ground in exasperation. He wished he hadn't and held back a bellow as his toe stubbed something solid. He glanced down, only mildly interested. There was a lot of rubble – bits of the car and other rubbish that had fallen off it – but this was different. He put his foot under it and lifted it out of the long grass. It wasn't a Heckler and Koch, but it was enough to bring a gleam of interest to his

241

hooded eyes. It was a dark blue canvas holdall. Pristine, it looked as though it had never been used. It probably hadn't – the car had been less than a year old.

Flynn went down on his knees and with shaking fingers untied the tapes binding it. His optimism drained. The wallet contained nothing lethal, just a good-quality tool-kit. Probably a birthday present from the little woman. Or a satisfied girlfriend. Flynn's lip curled as he pulled out a screwdriver. Very ordinary. You could stick it in some-body's gut – if he allowed you to get that close. He threw it to one side and pulled out another handle. Ah! This was better, a grown-up screwdriver, a man's tool, thirty centi-metres of bright German steel, a good solid handle, and the business end tapered to a lethal sharpness. He gripped the handle and gave one or two practice jabs. It wasn't perfect. His lips parted in a grimace. But it *was* a weapon. And there was more to come. Upending the holdall there thudded at his feet a forty-centimetre length of stainless steel, four centimetres wide, and a centimetre thick. He picked it up and, balancing it in his hand, studied it. What the hell would you want this for in a car's tool kit? He didn't bother trying to answer the question, but instead slapped the piece into his open hand. It gave a very solid and healthy thwack and brought, once again, a look of intense satisfaction to his grubby, bloody features.

He dragged himself to his feet. He'd got two weapons, close-quarter ones, enough to defend himself or give someone a very nasty few minutes while he considered his future.

But Flynn wasn't happy. He wasn't even contented. And he hadn't the foggiest idea where he was going from here. But one thing he did know. He took the plastic-wrapped packet from his inside pocket and inspected its contents: a C90 cassette – Greville Sixsmith's last testa-ment – and one high-density 3.5 floppy disk with

somebody's death wish at the end of it. They were un-
damaged. He was still in the game. The Brits weren't
going to laugh yet, not while Fergal Flynn had two legs to
walk on and a tongue to finish what he started.

Flynn took the downhill passage. Not out of choice, he
had no option, his state of health dictated the route. He
moved slowly, passing himself from tree trunk to tree
trunk and stopping every four or five paces for a rest. He
could have been in the Amazonian rain forest: nothing
moved, there were no roads, no tracks. After a while he
could hear, through the canopy of branches, the muted
whoomph, whoomph, whoomph of a police helicopter
overhead. It hadn't taken them long. He moved off again
as fast as his battered body would allow.

The first of the tins of Cola went quickly. After that he
rationed himself to a mouthful at every third stop, and
with no idea of where he was going and how far down the
densely covered slope he'd progressed, he finally arrived
at the edge of a sizable, unmade-up track. The helicopter
had lost interest and moved away, leaving a heavy silence.
Nothing moved. He crawled on to the road and inspected
the depressions on either side. Not quite ruts from frequent traffic, but enough evidence to show that it was
used. He stood up gingerly and, narrowing his eyes,
studied the landscape to his right: nothing, except perhaps, a suggestion of the sea through a gap in the trees.
Either that or his eyes, like every other part of his battered
body, were playing tricks. He turned his head and peered
in the other direction. Same view. He blinked and stared
again. Not quite. Another gap. Definitely water – and
something else!

He crawled out of his cover and moved noiselessly
along the track. It was much smoother underfoot when
he got going, but it didn't please him; smooth roads

meant traffic, and traffic was something he didn't want to meet. Not yet. He'd covered about two hundred yards when he came to the thing that had caught his eye. And his eye hadn't deceived him. Unmoving, but beckoning, in a small deserted basin a tall, silver finger pointed sternly at the sky. Below it, moored snugly against an old, decrepit wooden jetty and shielded from the afternoon sun by the shadow of a derelict building, slumbered a large, sleek yacht.

He tucked himself under cover and stared down at the yacht. This was the answer. He tilted his head and from the side of his mouth spat out something that tasted of blood. It didn't help.

Boats didn't need roads, and you didn't get roadblocks on the water. You went where the bloody hell you liked. But boats had crews. Flynn shrugged and almost groaned with the pain the movement brought. He swore under his breath. But crews, with a bit of coercion, did as they were told – particularly if the coercion was pointed at someone's head and the hammer was pulled well back on a hair trigger . . . Flynn closed his eyes for a second. It was a good theory that one, except for the limitations. The limitations . . .? He opened his eyes and against his better judgement almost smiled. Yeh! The fuckin' limitations being that he hadn't got any coercion! He'd got bugger all! Nothing – less than nothing if he took into account his state of health.

He continued studying the yacht. Nothing moved. It was as quiet as the grave. Maybe it was the *Marie Celeste*!

It was time to move.

He worked his way through scrublike hedge, slid down the grassy bank to the harbour area, and, at a crouch, waited at the foot of the slope. He took the long screwdriver from the packet and moved stealthily into the shadow of the derelict warehouse. There, squatting, his back against the building, he settled down to wait for some life on the boat. With luck, it'd be a crew of Boy Scouts.

He had no idea how long he'd been crouching in the shadows. But he knew his time was running out; he needed proper rest, food. Something would have to happen, and soon. For an exotic second, he felt his eyelids begin to droop.

But they didn't quite make it.

Suddenly he was wide awake.

He stared across the narrow expanse of jetty.

The boat had moved.

And he hadn't imagined it. He sat up and watched closely, listening. He'd stopped shivering with pain, forgotten all about his tiredness and hunger.

The boat knocked softly against its rope fenders, setting up a small sympathetic tapping motion along the length of the jetty and starting a tiny ripple of movement on the water that lapped wetly against its side, sending the yacht's rubber dinghy with its heavy outboard engine, bouncing up and down like a small black rollercoaster at the far end of the jetty.

Flynn waited tensely.

The noise of the sliding hatch opening sounded abnormally loud. It grated against the silence and bounced off the water to echo noisily around the small harbour. Before the echo had died, a head and shoulders appeared. The head turned sleepily round, studying the harbour and the state of the boat. It was a head disturbed from its afternoon nap and looking, to Flynn, ready to go back to it. The rest of the body appeared and, like a sleepwalker, staggered to the far side of the yacht. It stood still for a second. Then the heavy splashing of water hitting water reverberated around the harbour.

Flynn slowly unwound and tensed the muscles in his stiffened legs. The heavy splashing continued. It masked the rasping of disturbed gravel as Flynn moved cautiously, half crouching, towards the edge of the jetty and the yacht.

He stopped just short of the boat and studied his target.

The man was huge. Nearly six and a half feet tall and wearing only light-coloured boxer shorts, he was built like a brick outhouse. With his back to Flynn he stood relaxed, head bowed, as he gazed at the water below. His legs, as solid as two healthy tree trunks, were wide apart, his attention centred entirely on the destination of the contents of his bladder. Flynn could hardly believe his luck.

He changed the screwdriver for the heavy metal bar and moved.

He was one second too soon.

As his foot touched the deck an indistinct voice from the depths of the vessel rose above the sound of disturbed water.

'For God's sake, Roger! You'll wake the children!'

Female. The voice echoed hollowly round the deserted little harbour. Children? The words were music to Flynn's ears.

And the man hadn't moved.

Flynn ducked under the heavy boom and covered the distance between himself and his target in three quick strides. As the boat canted with his weight, the large man suddenly came to life. It was as if the deck had suddenly started burning. He straightened up and was halfway round by the time Flynn's rushing feet were upon him. But he was too late, and slightly more than a fraction of a second too slow. He had the size, and the weight, and his guts were in the right place, but he was beaten by surprise. He'd come up on deck for a pee, not some roughhouse.

246

Flynn's first blow was decisive. The heavy metal bar landed with a vicious, merciless crunch across the bridge of the man's nose. The bone cracked and his eyes filled with water; he was blinded with pain and shock and Flynn had all the time in the world for his next blow. The man hadn't a chance. Sightless and unable to breathe, with both hands clutched instinctively to his face, he offered Flynn a free go. Flynn took it. He hit him again, hard and accurately, across the back of the head. It landed with a soggy thwack, then a crack that sounded as if it had gone straight through his skull.

Throughout the activity, the only sound apart from the metal bar striking home came from water slapping against the side of the boat. This increased with the boat's erratic movements, setting up a small tidal wave of ripples that shimmied across the harbour basin, rebounded off the far wall, and returned to give the hull little playful smacks.

Then, from below deck, came the woman's voice again. 'Roger! What's going on?' A pause – and then a cry of alarm, a scrabble of movement and the frightened calls of a child. Flynn didn't look round. He took a half-step backwards from the swaying man, unhurriedly measured the distance, and with a ferocious, well-timed swing, brought the iron bar down with sickening force on to the base of the man's skull. Again something cracked noisily and he slumped lifelessly to the deck.

By now the sleek yacht was behaving like a fairground roller coaster. It strained, groaning, on its lines as it rocked back and forth, and the big man's dead weight going down on one side dramatically upset the delicate balance and sent it crashing against its fenders with alarming force. The bucketing prevented the woman from reaching the deck and she struggled to stay on her feet. It saved her life.

Flynn placed his foot on the man's shoulder and pushed. The body hit the water like a sack of potatoes and disappeared in a shower of spray that spluttered on the deck like a rainstorm.

The noise of the splash echoed round the secluded little basin and the waves from the disturbed water hit the already pitching yacht, sending the unprepared Flynn staggering and stumbling backwards until he crashed with a grunting, painful yell against the open hatchway. He hung on to the half-open louvred door, riding the motion of the bucking yacht and struggling for his balance before clattering awkwardly down the companionway and roughly knocking aside the woman who was scrambling urgently towards the deck. Her cries changed to a drawn-out yell of fright as she crashed against the bulkhead. She shook her head in bewilderment, turned, saw Flynn's face, and continued to scream, louder and in panic, then choked as the scream almost died in her throat. Flynn clambered towards her, pulled himself to his feet and rammed one foot into her side. She started screaming again, uncontrollably, on a higher, piercing note of sheer terror, and tried to pull herself away, but Flynn, his balance restored, pressed his foot harder into her side. She was jammed tight against the bulkhead and could go no further. She stopped screaming. But now she could hear what Flynn was saying. It made her want to start screaming again.

Flynn was icy calm. He spoke in a low, grating voice: 'Shut up!' He held the steel bar under her nose and waved it about. It was sticky with her husband's blood and strands of hair hung obscenely from its tip. 'Don't say anything, don't make a sound. Do as I say, nothing more, nothing less!'

She closed her eyes. It was a nightmare.

'How many children?' he asked

'Children?'

'How many children are there on this boat?'

'Two.'

'Anybody else?'

'My husband.'

'Can you sail this boat on your own?'

'Wha – ?'

'Answer the fuckin' question!'

'Yes.'

'Where're the children?'

'In their bunks.'

'Where's that?'

She pointed with a shaking finger towards a narrow, louvred door in the bows. 'P-please – '

'Shut up! Go and join them.'

She struggled to her feet and did as he ordered. He followed her through the door and glanced quickly, but without interest, at the two children sitting up in the large bunkbed. They were wide-eyed and tearful with fright and when they saw that it wasn't their father, they began to scream.

Flynn glared over their heads and said to the woman, 'Shut them up! You stay here until I tell you to come out. No noise – not a sound. Got it?'

'My husband . . .?'

'You haven't got a husband. And if you don't do exactly as I say, you won't have any fuckin' children either!' He slammed the door shut, rammed the catch home, and stretched himself out gratefully on the upholstered bench that ran in two sections down the side of the saloon. He looked at the clock on the wall above. Twenty to six. Plenty of time till the sun went down. Later he would clean himself up, then he would eat, and when it started getting dark she would sail him out of the trap he had worked himself into. But in the meantime – rest.

25

At just about the time Flynn was making himself comfortable in the boat's saloon, Sophie Ward pulled off the main road and into a service station. After she'd filled the tank with petrol she parked the car and told Barlow to meet her in the cafeteria. She joined him about twenty minutes later, bringing with her two large cups of coffee. She squeezed round to Barlow's side of the table and spread out an ordnance map of the south-eastern half of Victoria. She lowered her head and studied it while she sipped her coffee. After a moment, she tapped the map with a ball-point pen and ran it, with its nib retracted, along the thin red line of the Gippsland Highway towards the east.

'I can't make out what the hell Flynn thinks he's doing,' she said, without raising her head from the map. 'If they were tourists I could understand. That's a scenic route that takes them out of Victoria to New South Wales, and then, although I can't for the life of me understand why they'd want it, easy access to ACT.' She suddenly realized she was rubbing shoulders with a foreigner. ACT would mean as much to the average Pom as 'Australia Fair'. 'Australian Capital Territory,' she explained. 'Canberra . . .'

But Barlow wasn't interested in Canberra. He was studying the vast coastline that ran the length of the State of Victoria, over a hundred miles of it, dotted with a thousand coves, deserted beaches, inlets, outlets, the lot. 'Maybe Sullivan, if he's a local boy, knows people with boats.' He took a cigarette out of the packet on the table without raising his eyes from the map, but before lighting it ran it from the centre of the bottom of the sheet to the end of the page. All coastline. 'He could go anywhere he wanted from any point along here.'

Sophie snorted and he raised his eyes. She wasn't impressed with his logic. 'The police would spot a boat in a minute.'

'And what would your helicopter be looking for?'

She thought about it for a moment, then tightened her lips. 'You're just bloody nit-picking.' She grimaced. But she knew what he meant. There were hundreds of craft moving along the coastline. 'How about a police patrol boat?'

He spread his hand over the Tasman Sea and lit his cigarette. 'In an area like that during the war, you could have lost a Japanese battle fleet! If Flynn takes it into his mind to go sailing you can kiss him goodbye.'

Sophie's lips tightened as their eyes met. 'Thank you. That's cheered me up enormously.' She stared at her cup of coffee for a moment and decided against drinking any more. 'I'll meet you out at the car.' She looked tired as she stood up and, with a little nod, walked out of the otherwise empty cafeteria. Barlow followed her retreating figure with his eyes. He'd built up a fair amount of sympathy for her, even though sympathy wasn't something Sophie Ward was openly receptive to. But he thought he knew what she was going through. He'd had worse, but it had been a long day; a rotten day for her, and she was getting more than her fair share of violence and death. She looked fed up and depressed. She had every reason to be. And the day still had a long way to go.

She drove for several miles in silence. Barlow made no

effort to break into her thoughts; she did that herself after fifteen minutes: 'I rang Central Coordination in Melbourne,' she said, without taking her eyes from the road. 'Flynn and his mate have completely disappeared. No sightings, nothing. It looks like they've dropped into a bloody great hole and pulled the lid down over them. All roads in this area as far as Orbost – that's a fair-sized town getting on towards the NSW border – are blocked at intervals. Everything's being checked at the point of a gun, nobody's excused.'

Barlow studied her closely to see whether she expected a smile, but Sophie wasn't joking. He had a vision of the good traveller taking in Victoria being dragged out of his car and thrown across the bonnet with his arms hoicked round his back. No half-measures with the Victoria police. They'd lost two of their own by behaving like civilized policemen, now they'd tasted terrorism, and they were reacting accordingly.

If Sophie noticed his scrutiny she didn't show it. 'Two helicopters have been farting around up there since dawn but haven't seen anything to get excited about. Bloody funny. They must be holed up somewhere in the trees, but the bastards have got to come out sometime.'

'Let's hope your people don't get too bored and give up.'

'No chance of that,' she snapped. 'It's bad enough two policemen being murdered at any time, but to be done in by a Pom on the run? No chance!'

'I thought only Englishmen were "Poms". Do the Irish come into that category as well?'

Any sense of humour she had, she'd left with her almost untouched coffee back in the service station. She took her eyes off the road, stared at him for a moment, then bristled. 'Are you trying to be funny?'

'No.'

She gave him the benefit of the doubt. 'Everybody's a bloody Pom when they get up to this sort of thing.' But she didn't smile. She couldn't find anything in this business to smile about. She hadn't yet come to terms with Barlow's casual manner, his phlegmatic acceptance of every obstacle and setback, but Sophie Ward, like the rest of her countrymen, hadn't had twenty years of being shot at and shat on by a bunch of scraggy-arsed gunmen from across the Irish Sea. Barlow had. He was almost used to it. It didn't worry him, but he had a feeling that she, and a few other Australians in this part of the country, might have a different attitude about the Irish boyos from now on. Still he kept his expression bland.

'Sounds like a waste of a telephone call.'

'Not really.' Her lips almost moved in the direction of a smile. 'You remember the name Dubrovnik?'

'I'll never forget it.'

'You'd better not. I've just had a chat with him as well. My status has been established with the local authorities. He's given me a free run at Flynn. He's gone to the top. The police get Flynn when I've finished with him. I get first go. But Dubrovnik's not very pleased about how this thing came about. He wants to know who put Flynn on to Sixsmith and what his mandate was.'

'To kill the poor sod, I'd have thought,' murmured Barlow.

'It's more than that. Dubrovnik's convinced himself that somebody fingered him to the Irish and said to Flynn, "Watch and find out what he's doing . . ." He's still not convinced that Sixsmith was as pure as he was made to appear. I think he's got ideas that your people were playing some sort of game in Melbourne. He doesn't like you, you know.'

'He doesn't know me.'

'Not you personally. All of you. Brits – the whole

bloody lot of you. English to Dubrovnik is like everlasting damnation is to the Pope. He doesn't trust you, thinks you're a nation of shits. But if you want to be personal, he wants you either arrested for complicity in Sixsmith's murder or your arse booted out of the country once you've identified Flynn and made your statement.'

The rest of the journey was as fruitless as Barlow could have told her it was going to be. He had a feeling about these unscheduled chases across uncharted territory. He knew all about them; he'd done them before. It was confirmed by the time they had reached, and been stopped at, their fifth roadblock.

The police were efficient and hard-faced. Flynn would have been pinned to the nearest tree if he'd hit one of these blocks and tried his tricks on the bored but angry troopers. But Flynn hadn't tried. That was the surprising thing and, for Sophie, the disappointment. Barlow shrugged his shoulders. Flynn, or anyone else, would have had to be sitting up in his pram to continue on this state highway after the little bit of mayhem down the road to Yarram. But they couldn't see it. Neither could Sophie. They seemed to think that Flynn, an experienced Irish terrorist, would make life easy for them.

'I'm going on as far as Sale,' she announced, 'and then I'm going to turn round and have a look at the likely offroads on the way back. He might have holed up down one of the creek inlets until boredom sets in.'

'Wouldn't the police have checked that?'

'They'd start with the obvious. I'm going to do the others. You haven't lost interest have you?'

He had. 'You want my advice?'

'Anything to relieve the boredom. I'm fed up with sitting here on my own.'

'Go home and forget about it. He's broken out into the

254

country. He could be anywhere. I'll tell you where he isn't, though.'

'I thought you might. Go on then, where isn't he?'

'Anywhere on this road – or in the district. I reckon he's doubled back to Melbourne and gone to ground with the help of his Australian chums. When all the cheering dies down they'll help him grow a moustache and spirit him out of the country to wherever he was trying to go in the first place.'

She took her time mulling over Barlow's words. She had already admitted to herself that he knew exactly what he was doing, and he certainly knew what he was talking about, but it was the feeling that she was allowing herself to rely on his judgement that disturbed her. That wasn't Sophie's way with men. But she wasn't being honest with herself. It wasn't Barlow being right or wrong that was troubling her. It was the sudden surprise that being with Harry Barlow was beginning to cause a little murmuring somewhere inside her. She was enjoying his company. Sophie was both surprised and confused. She hadn't noticed it creeping up on her. It wasn't fair. It was unkind and it was something she could do without. She shoved her feelings abruptly to one side. 'So where d'you think Flynn was heading for?'

Barlow kept his face devoid of expression. No bloody question! Flynn was making for home and a fireside chat with the flat-faced boys who counted, Dublin somewhere, or just outside, with a tape recorder and a glass of Bushmills to steady their hands when they heard how they'd nearly gone down the road with their thumbs in their ears and their brains set on killing a couple of their own – and all laid on by the fuckin' oily Brits . . .

'I've no idea. I was hoping he was going to tell us. I was hoping he was going to tell us why he wanted to kill a helpless old sod who only wanted to write his memoirs in peace.'

Sophie looked at him for a second from the corner of her eye. It didn't sound right. The gentle tingling under her left breast subsided. *Get your feelings under control, Sophie! Forget the man. Dubrovnik's right, there's more to this Sixsmith thing than they're letting on – and Harry Barlow's not here to help you, the bugger's here to help himself – and whoever's pulling the strings. Watch it!*

'I don't agree with you,' she forced herself to say. 'I still think he's around here somewhere. I've got a feeling . . .' Then she smiled. It transformed her features and showed what a beautiful woman she was when she stopped being the serious secret-service man. But it didn't last long. 'And, I'm afraid, Harry Barlow, you're stuck with my feelings. You can't even get out of the car and walk, otherwise you'll be rolled up in a plastic bag by those guys on the roadblock back there and dumped on Dubrovnik's doorstep.'

Barlow didn't respond. He was thinking about how many large whiskies he and Reason were going to pour into their ears on the plane home as they totted up the cost of losing this particular game. Sanderson wasn't going to be too pleased with them. He continued staring at the road as it unwound in front of them. Sophie was still talking.

'But as consolation I'll pay for dinner.'

He didn't reply. He'd stopped caring.

Sophie did everything she'd said she was going to do. As a geographic exercise it had been most interesting. The road back from Sale had so many side tracks and off-shoots it looked like a kipper's backbone. And Sophie investigated every one.

She was turning off the main road instinctively. By now the headlights were cutting a swathe in front of them. The roadblocks were still in place but the enthusiasm had gone. Barlow dozed on and off and let her get on with it. But it was he who noticed she'd missed one. He opened his eyes as the car's lights glanced over the dip in the road and Sophie's tiredness showed.

'Don't you fancy the one we've just passed?'

It took her a few seconds and two hundred yards to drag her mind to the question. She jabbed her foot on the brake, allowed the tyres a few gurgled squeals of complaint, and stopped in the middle of the road. 'I didn't see anything.'

'A track,' murmured Barlow. 'Not much, no road, but a usable track. You've been up worse.' He turned in his seat and showed his teeth in the semidarkness. 'When your enthusiasm was at its peak.'

'Oh, shut up!' She wasn't in the mood. She slammed the gear into reverse, jabbed her foot on the accelerator and, swerving erratically, hurtled backwards until she'd overshot the entrance. She studied it with the headlights, then reached up, switched on the interior light and, for the umpteenth time, dragged out the crumpled military ordnance map. She stuck her finger on the thick red highway and ran it up and down where the track should have been. 'Not marked,' she pronounced and stared at the track again.

Barlow was feeling sorry for her. 'Neither was the last one, Sophie,' he said, gently, 'and that one could have been the next state highway . . .'

She didn't look up. She didn't need consolation. 'There's water further down there.' She ran her finger to the left boundary of the map; she could have been alone and talking to herself. She continued studying, then glanced up at the track entrance. 'In the old days, some of these inlets were big enough for small drifters to bring cargo and unload it into warehouses and then on to horse carts. Just the sort of out-of-the-way spot for some un-pleasant bastards to park their car while the rest of the country gets bored looking for them.'

'How would an Irishman find his way down there, par-ticularly as he was going hell for bloody leather on the other side of the road in the other direction? Come on, Sophie, give it up.' Barlow was getting tired and bored as well. It had been a long day.

'Don't depress me, Harry, I've had a bad day. I'm going to look at it.' She switched off the interior light, threw the map over her shoulder on to the back seat and started cautiously down the track – no argument. Barlow sat back and let her get on with it.

The track should have featured on the map. After a couple of hundred yards, it widened out into a sizable roadway. She nodded to herself, said nothing to Barlow and put her foot on the accelerator, roaring along the pot-holed gravel road as if she had the only car left in Australia. It went on and on, with a high, steep bank on the right and a fall on the left with occasional glimpses of water in the thin light of the rising moon. But no parked Nissan, no sheds, no warehouses, no Irishmen camped round billabongs; even Sophie had almost had enough. And then the road ended.

'Shit!'

She stood on the brake pedal; the nose almost bit into the dirt surface and they were enveloped in a cloud of orange dust as their slipstream caught up with them and they peered into the dark void underneath the beams of the headlights. The road had ended. Not just ended, it no longer existed. Without warning, it just dropped away into a bottomless nowhere. But somebody knew about it. As Sophie sat shaking and gripping the steering wheel with white knuckles, Barlow took off his seat belt and opened his door.

'Where you going?' she asked huskily.

'To look at that house up there.'

'Christ!' She turned in her seat and switched off the lights in the same movement. 'Sod it!' she swore again. 'I didn't see it.'

It was a summer house, modest by Australian standards, but somebody's pride and joy, and with good views. The unsociable bastard who owned it had stopped the road from completely disappearing. But it didn't take long for Sophie Ward and Barlow to discover that, for this time of the year at least, it was empty – no Irishmen, no helpers, no cars. The place was totally deserted. Sophie's depression returned.

'Have a cigarette,' said Barlow. They sat on the verandah with their backs against the wood-panelled wall and gazed out over the scrub-covered slope to the distant sea.

'I don't smoke. I'm bloody fed up.'

'Just the time to start.'

Barlow lit one himself, his firm features outlined for a brief moment by the flickering flame of the match, then held out the packet. She was tempted, but shook her head. 'Finish that,' she said, 'and we'll go back. I've had enough. I want a bloody hot bath, a strong drink and bed.' She turned her head and studied his profile. 'I'm reluctant to have to admit it, Barlow, but you were right about the chances of finding Flynn. Me? I've given up. The bastard's ducked us. He's either back in Melbourne or, as you say, he's darted upcountry. He's probably in the bloody bush by now, or halfway to Christ knows where. Sod it, Harry! Sod it!'

He reached out and put his arm round her. Nothing serious, nothing sensuous, nothing suggestive, just a comforting arm. But initially, she stiffened. It was an instinctive reaction. Then she relaxed and moved closer. She rested her head on his shoulder and snuggled up warmly against him, waiting whilst he finished his cigarette.

*

259

The owner of the bungalow had cut into the overhanging cliff so that he could turn his car. Sophie gingerly eased the Falcon away from the edge of the drop and began the long ride back to the highway. She was in a hurry for that bath and strong drink, and it was Barlow, with his arm on the back of her seat, gazing out of her window at the occasional moonlit glimpse of reflected water, who saw it.

'Stop the car! Quick!' he snapped without warning.

The shout went straight to Sophie's foot. She stood almost upright on the brake, and immediately found herself fighting with a whirling steering wheel and a bucketing, skidding car sliding from one side of the gravel road to the other as the tyres locked on to the rough, loose surface.

'Bloody hell!' she screamed as she brought the Falcon under control. But Barlow didn't stop to hear the rest of it.

He threw open his door and shot out of the car before it had stopped and ran back down the middle of the road. Crouched low, his pistol drawn and held out in front of him, he disappeared rapidly out of the perimeter of light thrown from the Falcon's rear lights and moved into the shadows on the side of the road. The moon chose that moment to slide behind a cloud, casting a dark grey shadow where before had been a silver glow. Barlow disappeared.

Sophie grabbed the lightweight Glock 17 automatic from her bag and threw herself out of the car. She followed Barlow, cocking the weapon as she ran.

The cloud moved again, letting through a shimmer of moon just at the right moment. It was enough for Sophie to make out Barlow's form in the gloom, She saw him suddenly veer off the road and disappear into the grass verge. She followed cautiously, holding the Glock before her. As she straightened up she almost fell over him.

Barlow was on his knees, gazing intently, in the flickering half-light of an unhelpful moon, at a pale figure lying in the shallow dry ditch. It was the body of a large man. She peered over Barlow's shoulder. Lying on his back, his face was at an unusual angle, pressed into the side of the ditch. She stared at the lacerations and scratches across the man's chest. He was dressed only in a pair of light-coloured boxer shorts.

'I saw him out of the corner of my eye.' Barlow looked up at Sophie, who was staring intently at the body, expressionless. She was getting used to dead men. This time she didn't look as though her lunch was going to end up on the grass verge.

'How did you see him lying down here in this light?' she asked tightly.

'He wasn't. He was kneeling, and as we passed he fell backwards.'

'Is he dead?'

'I don't know. Here, see what you think.' Barlow stood up and slipped the S&W into his trouser band.

'Flynn . . .?' murmured Sophie as she knelt down beside the body.

Barlow nodded. 'He's got to have something to do with it, hasn't he? Unless it's an old Australian custom to strip your guest after he's had his dinner, drive him into the outback and toss him into the bushes.' He peered over Sophie's shoulder. 'Are you getting anywhere with him?'

Sophie had conquered her revulsion. She put her hand on the man's neck, waited a second, then leaned over and placed her face on the cold, wet chest. She strained her ear against the man's heart, but after only a few seconds raised her head and said, 'There's nothing there. He's as dead as – Just a minute!'

A faint rumble came from the body's throat and Sophie lowered her head again and stared closely into the man's face. It wasn't a pretty sight. The top of his nose was smashed to a pulp, and the bare edges of flesh and skin were white and wrinkled as if the whole area had been pickled in salt water. His lips were blue, and drawn tightly together, but his eyes were suddenly wide open and glaring fiercely at Sophie.

'He's still there.' Sophie glanced at Barlow over her shoulder. 'But only just. Put your coat over him, then get round the back of him and lift his head.'

'How about getting him to hospital?'

'Let's see if he's got anything to say first. I don't think he's going to hang on long enough for that.'

Barlow looked sharply at Sophie. This wasn't the girl who'd taken one look at Greville Sixsmith and rushed out of the bungalow with tears in her eyes and her stomach heaving in shock; Sophie had joined the war; the feminine edge had hardened into professionalism. Her face was set tight. Barlow knelt and put his hand under the man's head – and withdrew it almost immediately. He stared intently at his palm by the diminishing light of the erratic and almost faded moon, then muttered from the side of his mouth: 'The back of his head's a bloody sight worse than his face. It's completely staved in. It feels like an overripe melon.'

Sophie stared at him for a moment, then shrugged her shoulders and put her lips to the man's ear.

'We've come to help you,' she said harshly. 'Can you talk?'

She reversed the position, putting her ear to the man's lips, and listened to a watery cough and a series of short, gasping breaths. But nothing that sounded like words. Sophie shook her head at Barlow again. 'Nothing,' she said hoarsely and sat back on her heels, staring intently at the man's face. 'If he's not dead, he's not far off it.'

'Give it another go,' said Barlow. It was a forlorn suggestion; he'd known it was futile when he'd felt the back of the man's head, but you never knew . . . 'Try shouting.'

'Bugger you, Barlow!'

Barlow tried to move her away. 'Let me have a go.'

'Piss off!' She lowered her head again and in a high-pitched voice shouted into his ear. After a moment she took her mouth away and looked closely into the man's face. The words had touched something. The man's eyes shone with an intensity that animated his face with something very close to life. His mouth opened and closed as he struggled to do something with his vocal cords, but nothing came out, nothing except a rasping death rattle, while all the time the eyes glared brightly, appealingly, as if he were speaking through them.

'Go on,' Sophie urged him. 'Say it. We're listening, we're going to help you. Don't give up.'

The eyes filled with tears and closed; then they opened again and his chest heaved several times with an effort that came from deep inside as he tried to get words on to the back of his tongue. The effort must have been too much. He shuddered convulsively and his eyelids dropped, leaving just a thin strip of white eyeball that seemed to shut out the last vestige of life.

'He's dead,' said Barlow.

'No, he's not. Hang on a minute. Don't let go of his head yet.'

The man's eyes remained three-quarters closed, but tears suddenly welled from under the lids and his lips moved.

'Charlotte,' he said quite clearly. Then: 'Jayne . . .'

After each word he paused to build up strength for the next effort, then tried again, but his voice sank to a rough wheezing whisper.

'Boat . . . Girls . . .' He almost managed to string the last two words together, then, with a superhuman effort, he filled his lungs and shouted the last three words he was ever going to say: 'Help them! Help . . .'

'Go on, don't stop now.' Sophie pummelled his chest in

exasperation, then lay across him and spoke urgently into his ear. 'We'll help them. Where are they? Where?'

'If you want to talk to him any more you're going to have to do it through a medium.' Barlow laid the man's head down and wiped his hands on the damp grass. 'He died after he asked you to help them. Whoever they are.'

The two straightened up and stood looking down at the pale shape in the grass. 'No question in your mind, I suppose,' said Sophie, 'about who gets the points for this little bit of butchery?'

Barlow didn't hesitate. 'None whatsoever,' he murmured. 'With Flynn on the loose around here I'd blame him if a little old lady came hobbling down the road complaining about sore bunions.' He touched the corpse with his foot. 'The sort of going-over this poor bugger's had would be right up his street. One bang's not enough for Flynn, he has to try and lead-bar the poor bugger's head right into his shoulders. Nope. There's no question in my mind who did it. What's puzzling me is why?'

Sophie looked up from the ditch and gazed along the quiet road, deserted except for the rear lights of the Falcon glowing through the beginnings of mist. 'What odds would you lay on him having been bundled out of a car?' she asked Barlow.

'Long ones.' Barlow retrieved his coat and shrugged himself into it. He spoke over his shoulder while he studied the undergrowth at the edge of the ditch. After a while he stood up and stretched to look over the rough hedge, where, in the corner of a dark landscape, his eye settled on a small triangle of reflected light. He stared steadily downwards, then grimaced to himself and turned back to Sophie. 'He came by water. Boat was what he said, and that's where it floated. He dragged himself up here, Christ knows how. Look.' He pointed to the reflection. 'Flynn did his brain surgeon's act on the poor sod down there. He threw him in the drink, not caring whether he was dead or not, and pinched his boat and took off with his women.' Barlow's bland expression showed even in the thin moonlight as he stared into Sophie's face. 'And if they're women with any spunk in them at all, we'll find them floating face down on that pond over there. That evil bastard'll give them boat room only if they're submissive, or useful. I hope for their sakes they're not as tough as him.'

Barlow nodded down at the dead man. He wasn't being callous. Everyone had a place in life, but to Barlow dead was dead and once you'd gone nothing was going to hurt you again, least of all words. He stared at the body for another second or two, then shook his head slowly and jerked his thumb over his shoulder. 'The boat was down there. God knows what this guy and his women were doing with it here, but that doesn't matter now. The sea's over there, so with your vast experience of the area, how about making a guess on what direction Flynn's going to take?'

Sophie made no reply. She continued staring in the direction of Barlow's thumb, then frowned and said, 'Harry, would you mind going back to the car and getting a torch? It's under your seat somewhere. I think we'd better go down to the water.'

Barlow managed a tight smile. Not only was he being used as the errand boy by this contrary Australian, but he found she was prone to winding herself up and down like a wooden yo-yo. He was beginning to enjoy the company of Sophie Ward. 'For an Aussie, Sophie,' he grinned, 'you're a real bundle of contradictions. How d'you do it? A few minutes ago you were flat on your face, you'd given up, you wanted to go home and have a bath – remember? Look at you now. You're like a bloody cat in a bag.'

'Go and get the torch, Harry!'

He did as he was told.

When he got back Sophie hadn't moved. Nor had her mood changed. She was still gazing down at the triangle of water and her jaw was set firm. Barlow stood beside her for a moment, then turned and touched the corpse lightly with his foot. 'What are we going to do with this?'

She didn't turn. 'Leave him where he is. I don't think he's going to complain about the cold. Not to us he isn't. I'll sort things out with the local people when we get back on the highway. They can tidy it up in their own time. First, I want to go down there and have a look around.'

Sophie and Barlow moved in silence along the side of the hedge, until, by the light of the torch, they were able to trace the dead man's tortuous progress through the dew-covered undergrowth. In this manner they arrived, as Flynn had earlier, at the side of the derelict warehouse.

Barlow, in the lead, held up his hand and pointed to the left. 'Go and have a look there,' he whispered to Sophie. 'I'll go this way.' He nodded in the direction of the jetty, now deserted and covered with white fingers of mist that crawled out of the water and spread like molten lava towards the more solid ground. But he took only one step. He stopped, rocked back on his heels and touched Sophie's arm.

'Listen!' he hissed.

Sophie strained her ears.

The faint chug of an engine carried across the water on a sudden breeze. It broke the still quiet of the harbour. The sound came out of the now impenetrable blackness on the other side of the harbour wall, a shallow earth and stone-built crescent that swept round the tiny harbour entrance to form a crude breakwater.

Sophie dug her fingers into Barlow's arm. 'I had a feeling there was something still there . . . Damn the bloody thing! Damn my bloody stupidity! And damn you, bloody Barlow!' He didn't ask her what she was damning *him* for, but grabbed her by the hand and took off.

'Come on! Run!'

Throwing all caution, and stealth, to the wind, he dragged her round the corner of the building and they ran along the hard stone surface of the breakwater until they came to the narrow opening. Beyond this lay a channel into the lake and then the open waters of the Tasman Sea, and then anywhere. They could go no further, and from where they stood the chugging noise was louder and quite distinct. Out there, in the blackness, no more than two or three hundred yards from the harbour entrance, were the bobbing lights of a boat heading out into slumbering waters beyond.

They stood and watched the receding lights without speaking. A minute and a half passed in silence, then wordlessly, Barlow handed Sophie a cigarette and, cupping his hands tightly against the pushy sea breeze, held out a lighted match.

Sophie lit the cigarette without thinking, sucked in smoke, spluttered and threw it away. With narrowed eyes, she nodded towards the disappearing but still audible boat. 'One thing I'll say about your bloody friend Flynn,' she coughed, 'he's one of the luckiest sods I've ever come across.' She didn't move but continued staring out to where the lights of the yacht now looked like coloured pinpoints on a sheet of dark grey paper. Her shoulders sagged, some of her new-found ebullience had gone. Barlow stared with her. He didn't move and in the dark nothing showed on his face.

'Maybe it'll sink,' he said without conviction.

26

Barlow chewed his steak slowly. It was nothing more than you'd expect from an off-the-track motel kitchen at eleven at night. They'd done him a favour, although they shouldn't have bothered – overcooked and almost inedible, it would have been tough even had it been minced into a shepherd's pie. He gave up on the steak halfway through, but managed most of the greasy, undercooked chips.

Sophie had gone to bed with a large Rémy Martin. She'd had enough of this day and decided she wasn't going to be good company; in fact, she wasn't going to be any sort of company, not in this mood. He didn't try to stop her.

He left the darkened, deserted dining room and returned to the bar. He ordered a large whisky and water and took it to a table near the area that doubled as a foyer. The man behind the bar went back to his stool in the corner and picked up the thick paperback he'd left on the counter. He promptly forgot his only customer.

Halfway down the glass of whisky, Barlow stood up slowly, took his time lighting a cigarette and, leaving the packet and matches beside the half-empty glass, moved casually to the door. Without opening it he could see, through an unfrosted section of the door, the length of the building housing the chalet-type rooms, sombrely bathed in a discreet security light from somewhere overhead. The light in his own room shone a welcome through the thin curtains and the lamp over the door beckoned him to bed. But he wasn't ready yet. He moved his eyes three doors to the right. There was just a dim light behind Sophie's curtains. He watched for a few moments. She was probably in her third or fourth nightmare by now.

He turned away from the door and glanced at the pay phone on his way back to his table. The barman stubbed his finger in the book to mark his place and looked briefly across the room at his customer.

Barlow met his eyes and offered him a friendly smile. The barman wasn't interested. He nodded and lowered his head, but before he could dive back into his fantasy world, Barlow said, 'Does the phone out there take money, or does it need a card?'

The barman thought about it for several seconds. 'Card,' he said finally, 'but you can ring from your room. It'll go on the bill.'

'I prefer that one. Let me have a couple of cards, please.'

'Suit yerself, mate.' The barman reached into the till and brought out a wad of phonecards. 'D'you want me to put these on yer bill?'

'No thanks, I'll pay cash.'

'Suit yerself,' he said again. His vocabulary was limited, even for an Australian barman. He flicked two cards across the counter, collected the money and went back to wherever his book was taking him.

Barlow picked up his drink and cigarettes, moved over to the pay phone and dialled the Melbourne number Mike Thompson had given him.

'Mike, it's Barlow,' he said when, after a long wait, the phone was finally answered. 'Have you got a guest staying with you?'

'I'm expecting one,' replied Thompson, 'but not until early morning. You got a problem?'

269

'D'you know anyone in our line of business who runs a fairly fast boat?'

'Seagoing – that sort of thing?'

'Yup.'

'Leave it with me,' said Thompson. 'Where you calling from?'

Barlow told him. 'D'you want anything else?'

'Nah.' Thompson was a man of few words. 'I'll ring you in the morning. Is that it?'

'Yeh, thanks …Oh, just a sec. D'you know where sonny boy is at the moment?'

'Yeh, Canberra. Says to tell you he's playing it straight. He's using the political card – real name and number, all above board. Room 168, the Hyatt. Hang on a second and I'll give you the number, save you looking it up.'

Reason had brought his frustrations with him to Australia.

'Bugger it, Harry! The whole bloody thing goes up the spout if Flynn gets the stuff back to his control and talks them through the disk. It was a tricky scam at the best of times. It's a pity you couldn't have done something with Sixy before his mouth went walkabout. Now listen, I've been thinking about this bloody thing since I spoke to you yesterday – I've been thinking about bugger all else! Now I want *you* to have a good think. Did Flynn take anything other than the disk with him when he broke out?'

Trust Reason. Barlow hadn't got that far in the analysis. He dragged his thoughts back to the chaos of the house at Craigieburn and ran a series of still pictures through his mind. Click, click, click, click, click … Back it all came: Sixsmith hurtling across the kitchen table with two pounds of fresh mince for a face … The sheets of manuscript showering all over the floor and scudding around the kitchen like giant confetti … And something more solid. The clicking stopped and his brain fine-focused. Crashing down with the paper and sliding in Sixy's wake ... Something solid. Click again, stop. A FUCKING TRANSISTOR RADIO WITH A TAPE FACILITY. Grundig! He could see the name as clearly as if it were balanced on top of the pay phone in front of him. And the cassette flap open – and empty.

'Harry?' Reason knew what he'd triggered but he hadn't the patience, not at the moment. All he'd got at the moment was effing, bloody jet lag. 'Talk to me, Harry.'

'Fuck it, Clive! I've just remembered – he had a tape. The bastard taped Sixy's ramblings! That's why he's running. He's got a leader here in Australia who set him on to Sixy and he's going to play the bloody thing while the guv'nor's reading the script. That's what it's all about, Clive. That's why Flynn's doing this bloody course.'

'Why doesn't he drop it in the post?'

'It's got to be authenticated. Flynn's going to put his arse on the line by swearing on his mother's grave that the voice is that of the author. Even a hobnail boot like Flynn can see that it's one of their top players they're being invited to shove up against the wall.'

Reason didn't have to think too long about it. 'You're quite sure it's Flynn who's pinched this boat?'

'It's got to be, Clive. It's like a bloody jigsaw – this is a definite piece. I'm going for it. I just hope Thompson comes up with something that'll catch this boat.'

'He will. You still got that ASIO woman with you?'

'Yes.'

'Is she going with you?'

'It's her show, Clive. I can't do a bloody thing without her. But I do need Murray, and when I spoke to Thompson he hadn't arrived.'

'He'll be there. Look, when you get to Flynn, you've got to find out whether he's spoken to anyone about this.

271

If he's waiting for an eye-to-eye with his control, it could work in our favour. But remember what I said: don't leave anything for the Australians. If you do turn him up, can you keep this woman out of the way while you finish the job?'

'I don't know yet. I'll have to somehow. I'm going to have to play it by ear. I'll think of something.'

'If she's going to be a nuisance, perhaps she ought to get in Flynn's way when you've run him down? Murray could sort that out for you.' Reason pronounced Sophie Ward's death sentence without a change of tone. He could have been suggesting a gentle tap on the wrist.

Barlow's jaw tightened. 'I said I'll think of something, Clive. About Flynn —'

'What about him?'

'The Australians'll want to see something at the end of the day, even if it's only a corpse. So what do you suggest happens to him after David and I have finished with him — assuming I ever catch sight of the bastard again?'

'Think positive, Harry. Things could be worse!'

'How?'

There was a long pause while Reason ran over the possibilities. 'Oh Jesus, Harry! You've made me bloody depressed now.'

'What about Flynn, then, Clive?'

'Get rid of him.'

'And the game?'

'Stays on track. I'm meeting this guy Dubrovnik tomorrow to try and hurry things along a bit. But that's not your concern. Just get bloody Flynn out of the way.' He yawned noisily into the phone. 'I'm going to bed now, Harry. You ought to do the same. See you!'

Barlow dropped the dead phone on to its hook, recovered his card and went back with his drink to the table in the corner. The barman gave him a brief, disinterested glance. The book was still holding his attention and his head remained bowed over it when Barlow drained his glass and went out into the night air. The light still burned behind Sophie's curtain as he passed it. He hoped she was having a good night. But he doubted it.

It was that doubt that made him turn back. He knocked gently on Sophie's door.

'Who is it?' Her voice was not muffled. She wasn't in bed.

'Barlow,' he whispered. 'Are you all right?'

'The door's not locked.'

She was sitting in one of the two armchairs, her bare feet propped on the round coffee table and her head resting on the back of the chair as she stared up at the ceiling. She made no move when he came through the door, or when he closed it and came across the room.

'I thought you were tired and wanted to go to bed?' he said gently. He knew what the trouble was. It had got to her, the killings, the mutilated horrors of violent death, the chasing, the tension, and the underlying fear. It was a kind of delayed shock. She might one day become used to it, but he doubted it. No one ever did; it was just that some showed it less than others. 'And how about that bath?'

'I found the one unappealing,' she said dryly, 'and the other I just didn't have the energy for. Enjoy your dinner?'

'No.' He glanced around the room. 'I'll leave you to it, then. See you in the morning.'

'Don't go, Harry.'

He looked across at her without expression. She didn't look back, but continued to stare at the ceiling. There was no underlying invitation in her request; nothing to be read in it. It was an appeal not to be left alone. Her dark eyes turned slightly and studied his. There was a softness, an almost shy appeal in them. She was very close to tears. 'Come and sit down.'

'In a minute,' replied Barlow. 'First I think you'd better get out of those clothes and have a bath. You'll feel much better. I'll go and get you some coffee.'

'At this time of the night? You'll be lucky!'

Barlow managed a genuine smile. It was almost relief. 'I'll run you a bath. Jump in and I'll be back in a few minutes. Here, shove this on.' He handed her a towelling bathrobe he'd found on the back of the door. 'Be in the bath by the time I get back. OK?'

'Don't let this become a habit, Barlow.' He recognized the tone, but the eyes were still full, probably more so, and the mouth was soft. Sophie's professional attitude was proving hard to maintain. 'No tears' wasn't part of the job specification.

'Don't let what become a habit?'

'Ordering me about.' She didn't smile, but she wasn't serious.

'See you in a minute.'

He was lucky, he caught the literary barman just before he put his head down for the night. Surprisingly he made no problem out of producing a large percolator of real coffee. Barlow also bought a bottle of Rémy Martin. When he returned to the chalet, Sophie's clothes were stacked neatly on the luggage rack and the bathroom door was closed. No sound came from inside.

'Sophie! You all right?' He put his ear to the door.

'Will you stop asking me whether I'm all right! There's nothing wrong with me. I'm tired – nothing else. Go and drink your coffee. I'll be out in a minute.' There was no truculence in her voice, but there was a slight hiccup when she said there was nothing wrong with her. Barlow stood at the door listening for a moment longer, but there was still no sound, not even a splash. He turned down her bed, then, after lighting a cigarette and pouring himself a cup of coffee and a large measure of Rémy Martin, lowered himself into the other armchair. It was only when he settled back that he realized he, too, was tired.

They'd finished the coffee and were on to their fourth Cognac when Sophie, after a reflective silence and a glance at the turned-down bed, said: 'What sort of woman is it that walks out on a fellow as house-trained as you?' Anticlimax, an hour and a half of inconsequential chitchat, Cognac, and a feeling of partial wellbeing made for familiarity. It was a question that had to come from a woman like Sophie.

He didn't respond.

'Why'd she do it, Harry?'

Their eyes locked. 'Perhaps because I was a bastard,' he said.

She studied him knowingly, with a woman's knowledge of what would constitute a bastard, formed a conclusion, and shook her head. 'I doubt that, somehow. Tell me about it. What was she like?'

'Attractive, scatterbrained, good fun.'

'And you?'

'The middle one!'

He lit another cigarette and wished he hadn't stopped to see how she was. She didn't know what she was doing. It was like having the stitches pulled out of an unhealed wound. But then, perhaps she did know what she was doing.

'Go on,' she urged, softly. 'Tell me why.'

For the first time since it had happened, he felt he wanted to talk about it. But why Sophie? He had no idea. He didn't even think, he just started talking – it was the Cognac again. He topped up their cups with lukewarm coffee, lit a cigarette and exhaled with the suggestion of a deep sigh. It was like an exorcism, slow and difficult to begin, but once started, the bitterness, the sadness and the unhappiness came out. At first he was embarrassed and hesitant, then like corn out of a burst sack, it gushed out.

'I joined the army when I was eighteen. I suppose that was the fault of my father. He gave me a hundred pounds when I reached seventeen and told me to bugger off and not come back. He'd just found himself a new wife – she was about six years older than me.' Barlow's mouth twisted into the semblance of a smile at the memory. But it didn't last. 'So, I suppose you can understand him not wanting me hanging around! Anyway, the army seemed an interesting thing to do.'

Sophie stared at him, her mouth open in disbelief. 'I don't believe it! Your father threw you out?'

'Changed all the locks in the house as well.' Barlow grinned. This was another one that sounded funny in retrospect. It hadn't been at the time. 'That was about 1968. Liz and I were married in 'seventy-five.'

'Hang on! You're not getting away that easily.' Sophie leaned forward and refilled both their glasses. She was a different woman from the one Barlow had walked in on. She was wide awake now. She pushed his glass across the table. 'I want to know how you met her.'

'Boring, Sophie. I'd known her all my life. We used to play with our toys in the sandpit together. I just happened to bump into her during a leave. I was spending a lot of time in Northern Ireland then and I really hadn't got the time, or the inclination, for marriage. But this is what happens, isn't it? It just comes up and jumps on your back and there's nothing you can do about it. It happens that way. Doesn't it?'

'No idea, Harry. It's never happened to me. Perhaps I've never wanted anything to jump on my back without knowing exactly what was coming out of it.'

'You're older and wiser than I was, then. Let's hope you can control it when it happens.'

'Sure. So you got married . . .'

'That's right. And we moved into an army quarter in Hereford.'

'Isn't that where the SA —'

'That's right,' he interrupted before she developed that line of query. 'And we were deliriously happy until —'

'Any children?'

Barlow shook his head. 'Until the Falklands. When I came back, she'd gone.'

Sophie stared at him. 'Just like that?'

Barlow nodded. 'Just like that. Oh, there was a note. She'd gone away with some guy who played in a West Indian steel band . . .'

'Oh, Harry! For God's sake! And you hadn't a clue what was going on?'

'No. Apparently it happened about four months into the war. I suppose she was bored, lonely.'

'Oh Christ, Harry! Don't be so bloody English! Why are you looking for excuses for her? Deliriously happy women don't get lonely after four months on their own – at least they don't go swanning off to get themselves laid whilst their husband's fighting his balls off in a war. There must have been something wrong with the woman – was there?'

Barlow pulled a face and shook his head. 'Not that I knew of. I never did find out why. But then I wouldn't have noticed anything, would I? Men in love don't notice whether there's anything wrong with a woman. We only notice that she's different, nicer, kinder, more passionate – wouldn't you?'

'We're not talking about me, Harry,' Sophie said gently. 'Go on.'

'I've never really bothered to think too much about it. I

277

suppose our inadequacies are one of those taboos, one of those things we'd rather not know too much about.'

'So you said to yourself, OK, that's it, best of luck, darling, in your new life! And that was it? Christ, Harry, you're not going to leave me stuck up here, are you?'

Barlow smiled at Sophie's expression, but it faded even before it got going. He drained his glass of brandy without taking his eyes off her. She didn't move, she didn't blink. She stared back in her oversized towelling robe, her legs tucked under her and her arms hugging herself as if she were cold. She gave a slight shiver. But it wasn't the temperature; it must have been Barlow's expression – or the story of his life – that caused it. When he didn't reply, she said angrily, 'Did you go for this bloody bongo drummer, or whatever he was?'

He nodded slowly and thoughtfully. 'Of course.'

'And?'

'You want blood, Sophie?'

'I want to hear the end of the story.'

He broke contact with her eyes and stared at the framed chocolate-box print on the wall just to the side of her head. 'What I had to do for my own peace of mind,' he said hesitantly, 'was to go after her. And I found her. And him.'

'What did you do?'

'Beat his face into a pulp, ignored her, went home and got blind drunk, cried my eyes out for two days, then got over it. I had a bloody good bath and then volunteered for extended duty in Northern Ireland.' He topped up his drink again and held the bottle over Sophie's. She shook her head, picked up the glass and held it to her lips. For once she appeared lost for words. Barlow looked into her eyes again. 'Was that what you wanted to hear?' It was unkindly said and it was totally unwarranted. He watched the effect with regret.

'I'm sorry, Sophie.'

But it was too late. The hurt showed. She bit her lip and closed her eyes for a moment. When she opened them they were moist. She lowered her head so that he couldn't see her face, and studied the contents of her glass. After a minute or so, and without looking up, she said softly, 'Don't be unkind, Harry. I didn't mean to open a wound. I'm sorry. I shouldn't have pried.'

He hadn't seen her like this before; in their short acquaintance, he'd never imagined Sophie Ward as capable of being so sensitive. But he was wrong – again. Sophie Ward was a very sensitive woman – when conditions dictated. 'It's OK,' he said. His eyes were dull. The memories hadn't done him any good at all; the exorcism wasn't working, the hurt was still there. But he didn't tell her; nor did he tell her that it was Clive Reason who had restored his sanity, who had stopped him trying to throw his life away and given him a new future. Clive Reason who'd picked him out of the gutter and set him on his way again. That wasn't for Sophie's ears.

'So much talk, Sophie,' he said harshly, 'and all it does is make us both feel embarrassed.' His jaw tightened as he slowly forced himself up from the depths of his chair. 'This hasn't done either of us a lot of good. It's time you got some sleep.'

But Sophie wasn't embarrassed. The tears that filled her eyes were of a different sort. She stood up, her bare feet making no sound on the carpet as she moved around the table. She stopped in front of him, looking up into his grim, sad features, and grasping his elbows, raised herself on to her tiptoes.

'Harry . . .'

It was a very natural thing to do. His face relaxed and he kissed her waiting lips very gently. They were moist and salty. It was like nectar. Then he kissed a little harder.

But it wasn't hard enough for her. Her arms went round his neck and her hands, grasping his head, pulled his mouth hard on to hers. No words were spoken. They parted for a second and stared into each other's eyes, and then her bathrobe slid to the floor, whether intentionally or otherwise neither cared. Barlow pushed her away slightly and stared at her naked body. Perfect. She was like a ballet dancer, slim and firm, with boyish hips, full thighs and long tapering legs. Her breasts, not large, were well shaped, with hard, dark pink nipples pointing aggressively forward. She remained unmoving, her thighs pressed modestly together, watching his eyes feast on the perfection of her body, until they both ran out of patience and, locked together, gasped their way to the bed and struggled as strangers do in a passionate tangle of arms and legs and mouths and moans as if to get the sex over and done with so that they could concentrate on making love. But it was over all too quickly, and breathlessly they lay together, gazing into each other's eyes as they recovered and tried to work out how it had happened.

It was a short respite.

After the second time they were able to look at each other, to touch and admire. Sophie Ward was a beautiful woman. She had a beautiful body. And she enjoyed making love with Harry Barlow, as she demonstrated throughout what remained of the night.

It was early morning when, waking from a brief, fitful doze, she stirred and felt herself imprisoned in his grasp. It was a nice feeling of security; soft, warm and exhausted. She opened her eyes. The sun was struggling on its uphill path and glimmered weakly through the curtains, allowing her to study the outline of his face. After a moment a tiny smile, then, stretching across him, she lightly kissed his chin, his nose, the side of his mouth. She worked her way down to his neck, brushing all the way with her lips. Drawing her head back fractionally, she studied him with a puzzled expression. She thought he was asleep, until his arms tightened round her, and in a smooth, gentle movement she found herself on her back, spread-eagled and the weight of his hard body on her. He kissed her softly.

'Harry?'

'Hmmm?'

'I don't want you to read anything into this . . .'

'Into what?' His eyes were still tightly closed.

'This. You know what I mean. We had too much to drink. It was late. We'd had a tough day. It was my fault, but it's a one-off, Harry, nothing more than that. Therapy . . .'

'OK.' Barlow kissed her again, long and deep, then, opening his eyes and raising his head, he studied her face as he entered her willing body. But she hadn't finished.

'I m-mean it, Harry,' she said, jerkily, 'this is not the b-beginning of anything. I don't want it – I don't n-need . . . Oh, Christ!' The cry came from deep inside her. She closed her eyes and, pulling her outstretched arms out of his hands, grasped the back of his head and pulled his mouth to hers. 'Oh damn you, Harry Barlow!' she groaned. 'Damn you!'

Reason didn't waste time on trade chitchat. He came straight to the point.

'Mr Dubrovnik, I understand that you have some property of ours that you would like to return discreetly.'

Dubrovnik's black eyebrows moved fractionally towards each other. Sophie Ward would have recognized the expression. 'Where'd you get that information from?'

Reason played the Pommy dummy card. 'The bit about you having our property or the whisper that you wanted to return it?'

But Dubrovnik didn't buy it.

'Don't come the clever arsehole with me, mate. Somebody's telling tales, and I've got a bloody good idea who, but let's hear it from your lips.'

Reason ignored the invitation. 'It's a manuscript of about a hundred and twenty thousand words – in your language, that makes a wodge of something like four hundred pages, just in case you were wondering what it looks like – and it belonged to a former employee of D16, that's British Secret Intelligence Service –'

'You're not going to get anywhere with pomposity, son, not with me you ain't.'

He could have been talking to the wall for all the notice Reason took of him. 'Who hasn't been released from his Official Secrets Act commitments and has possibly broken some of the constituents of that Act. I'm here officially on British Government business to claim any part of Mr Sixsmith's property that might belong to HM Government.' Reason felt like smiling but kept it to himself. 'D'you mind if I smoke while you think about it?' He brought from his pocket a pack of Rothmans and flipped open the lid.

'Yes, I do,' snapped Dubrovnik. 'And I see it quite differently.' He sat back in his chair and held the fingers of one hand up to his face, as if noticing for the first time that he'd got four of them. 'First of all . . .' A finger curled out of sight. '. . . we have here a pack of paper, the beginnings, if you like, of a book of reminiscences written by a legal resident of the sovereign territory of the State of Victoria – if you really want to play hi-de-hi and ho-de-ho.' Another finger vanished. 'If he wants to go ahead and publish his words in his adopted country, then as far as this department's concerned, he has every bloody right to do so.' He narrowed his eyes and met the cool dark ones of Clive Reason. Reason smiled. It didn't lighten the atmosphere, it just made Dubrovnik's eyes harden, as he smelt mockery. The delay cost him the advantage.

'But he doesn't want to publish,' said Reason lightly. 'The poor bugger's dead. He died in his adopted country by having his face blown off by one of his adopted countrymen –'

'That's not been –'

Reason didn't allow the interruption. 'While another of his adopted countrymen, one employed, presumably, by the sovereign State of Victoria to look after his welfare, sat outside in the garden watching it happen and didn't raise a finger to help the poor sod. I'm not going into the whys and wherefores of an official minder being tacked on to Sixsmith, and to whose advantage it was supposed to be, but it might take a lot of explaining when my people officially ask what the hell was going on.'

'I'll tell you what the bloody hell was going on . . .'

Dubrovnik's fingers were still waiting for a few more items, and his feeling of superiority was deteriorating by the second. A smooth, Pommy bastard laying down the law in his office was always going to be a nonstarter, and this big, black, self-assured Pommy bastard was likely to find his arse being kicked up and down the corridor if he carried on like this.

But that was exactly what he did do. The big, black, self-assured Pommy bastard smiled at him as if he'd just taken over. 'I can imagine what the bloody hell was going on,' said Reason, evenly, 'but instead of raising all sorts of complicated yes and nos, I'm giving you a simple cutout. You can either hand the Sixsmith manuscript to me on a friendly, cooperative basis, which, incidentally, will guarantee reciprocal cooperation in the UK should you ever need it, or I can apply to the Federal Court for –'

Reason stopped.

Dubrovnik was smiling.

'British Government agents asking an Australian court for judgement? You've got to be bloody joking! You guys have got very short memories. Have you already forgotten the bloody nose you picked up the last time you went down that road?'

Reason didn't smile back.

And Dubrovnik's didn't last. His raised fingers had long since dropped out of sight and his hand had formed a clenched fist that now rested on top of his desk. The knuckles were white. Dubrovnik was having a difficult time keeping his voice even. When he got really angry his origins played havoc with his hard-earned Australian accent; he felt this gave him a disadvantage and he fought against it. It made it worse.

'I think, Mr Reason,' he said grittily, 'you'd better go out and have a walk around the lake to remind you you're in Australia and not Whitehall. Different ways, mate, different attitudes. When you come back, come back with a clean and open mind and we'll start this conversation from the beginning again.'

Reason didn't move. He kept his eyes firmly on the craggy features on the other side of the desk. He was happy with the way things were going, but kept his satisfaction off his face. He'd got the Yugoslav boiled up and looking for ways to score points off the simple Brit. He'd succeeded. Dubrovnik had bought it. By the time he was finished, cooperation of any kind was going to be a dirty word with the Yugoslav. And that was exactly what he and Harry Barlow wanted. This hard-faced bastard was going to do everything in his power to make sure that anything the British wanted was going to be bad news for the Australian security industry, and, by the look of it, he was going to see that every stop was pulled out to make sure they went home with red eyes and fuck all in their handbags. Reason was content. The Sixsmith memoirs were in good hands; they were never going to be quietly handed over to the British Government for burial. Not by this fellow. He was going to hang on to them until some bright lawyer came along with a possession order from a local publisher acting on behalf of the Sixsmith estate – no matter how long that took. Heaven help the first British lawyer to come trundling along with a note and a suppression order from the Downing Street Cabinet Office.

Reason climbed down graciously. Dubrovnik, content with grinding the Pom into the dirt, relaxed, as magnanimous in victory as his newly acquired Anglo–Saxon philosophy dictated, and reapplied a smile, although like others that had sat unconvincingly on his features, it had no warmth in it.

'Let me give you a little bit of gratuitous information, Mr Reason,' he said coldly. 'I've got one of your MI people on temporary attachment helping a senior member of my staff to look for the man who killed Mr Sixsmith. You might know him . . .'

Reason raised his eyebrows.

'A guy named Barlow?'

Reason turned his eyebrows into a frown, concentrated for a moment, then slowly shook his head. 'Barlow? Nope. Who does he work for and how does he find himself working for your people?'

Dubrovnik studied him closely. 'MI5,' he said at length. 'You sure you don't know him?' He carefully avoided the second part of Reason's question. It suited Reason for the time being; he didn't pursue it. 'My number two, Grant, did – and he knew *you* too.'

Reason had no difficulty with this line of questioning. He was one of the best liars in the business. His expression didn't change. 'MI5's a very big club – it's almost an industry. Six is probably bigger. You didn't say how this . . . er . . . Barlow got into the act.'

Dubrovnik told him. Then, in a fit of confidence, he added, 'I'm not even sure he's real MI5. He could be something on the side. His master's a guy named Sanderson and you get at him through the channels. He's the one who authorized Barlow's attachment – an open one at my discretion . . .' He stared hard at Reason as if waiting for him to query the extent of his discretion, but nothing came. Reason kept his face devoid of expression, allowing Dubrovnik to continue. 'The agreement is that he stays under my control until this Irishman's put away in the cupboard. But forget about him. How long are you staying?'

Reason pursed his lips. 'I haven't decided. If you won't hand over the manuscript and the rest of Sixsmith's effects to my department, I'll have to wait here and see what London wants to do about it.'

'What do you mean by that?' Dubrovnik asked coldly.

'It means that I'm going to hang around until Arthur Gunne advises you to start helping rather than hindering us.' Reason stood up. 'Until then I don't think there's an awful lot more we've got to talk about. Perhaps you'll let me know when Flynn's been run to ground – if he ever is.'

Dubrovnik got to his feet slowly. His unfriendly expression didn't soften. 'Am I supposed to read something into that last remark?'

Reason ignored the question. 'On my way out I'll let your secretary know where I can be reached. I'd appreciate being kept in touch if anything crops up.'

'Sure, but don't forget the British don't own this place any more, Mr Reason. You're a guest, and if you want to do a bit of walking around outside ACT, let me know before you book your bus ticket . . .'

He didn't offer to shake hands, he didn't even ask how he knew that the man who'd killed Sixsmith was named Flynn; he took it for granted that, being English, anything underhand, anything crafty, was all part of the business. The clever bastard knew as much about what happened in Melbourne as he did. He waited for Reason to close the door behind him, then sat down and lit a cigarette. After a moment he glanced at his watch. Give the bugger half an hour. He'd tell him the good news when he got back to his hotel and put his feet up.

But Reason didn't go back to his hotel. He had better things to do than sit in the Hyatt with his feet up. He crossed over Kings Avenue Bridge, turned into King Edward Terrace, and cut across Parkes Place to Commonwealth Avenue and the British High Commission. He glanced round occasionally. Nothing ominous, it was habit, but after the bruising session with the family friend it was hard to feel relaxed and comfortable in a country

287

where the prime minister's outlook towards Britain appeared to be less friendly than Saddam Hussein's. Surreptitiously, he looked over his shoulder again before entering the High Commission building; he'd have felt more at home in West Belfast.

The ten hours' time difference seemed to make no difference to General Sanderson; whether he'd just woken up or was about to go to sleep, he sounded the same. He even sounded pleased to hear Reason's voice.

'Richard,' began Reason. 'We've got ourselves a hell of a problem . . .'

'That's why we're so well paid, Clive – to overcome these little difficulties. If you didn't want problems you should have stayed in the army!'

'OK, that's the repartee over with, Richard, now here's the sticky bit.' Reason wasn't amused; he'd used up his ration of humour for the day in Dubrovnik's office. 'Sixy's taken the long jump. He ain't going to be able to carry out his part of the contract –'

'I know all about that, Clive,' interrupted Sanderson. 'Tell me about the problem. And don't bother going into detail over Barlow's new paymasters. I've already had a complicated session with an inarticulate kangaroo named Dubrovnik – Dubrovnik! I ask you? I don't know what the country's coming to. They all used to be called Smith or McClusky, or Bradman. One felt as though one was talking to one's own . . . But Dubrovnik!'

'Well done, Richard.' Reason managed a crooked smile as, one-handed, he tried to work a cigarette out of its packet. 'You're just the sort of guy they love to talk to here. They'd make you feel very much at home! Here's the problem. This uncooperative bastard whose name you've just mentioned has got the only official copy of the Sixsmith life story and he isn't going to release it to a publisher.'

'So, what are you doing about it?' asked Sanderson.

'We've ground to a bit of a halt in that direction, but I'm thinking about it. And, that's only part of the problem. The other part is that the guy who's put Sixsmith down and can throw this whole plan out of the window is a PIRA hotshot named Fergal Flynn. He started his song-and-dance act with the Tyrone mob. Nastier than average and more intelligent than most, he's one of the best they've got at this sort of work. He worries me. And he worries Harry too. He's the sort of bloke who could pull it off for them.'

'He's a long way from home – is he doing this on his own?'

'No, he had a team, not first-rate, but adequate. His backup was one Vinnie Doyle from Springtown. Australia's like one bloody great holiday camp to these people, every gutter you splash through has one of the fuckers swimming up and down in it.'

'Get to the point, Clive.'

Reason waited for the time gap, blew a mouthful of smoke at the ceiling, and rested his feet on the corner of the Second Secretary's desk. 'Harry took Doyle off the list, but, according to Harry, Flynn did a bunk, taking with him recorded highlights of Sixy blowing our bloody thing sky-high ... Have you got that, Richard? This Flynn is making his way to Christ knows where with a pocketful of audio cassette which, played into the ear hole of the right Provo mandarin while he's gazing at the unedited manuscript of the Sixsmith saga, will mean that we go right back to the beginning again. And we haven't got the time. Have we?'

Sanderson's voice remained unaffected. 'No. If Doyle's gone, what help is this Flynn getting to move the cassette around?'

'You mean apart from people like Dubrovnik and three-quarters of the Australian population?'

'It's not that bad, Clive. Tell me what you know, not what you imagine. We can't afford the luxury of upsetting our kith and kin over there, so let's keep our thinking on an even plane. Tell me how the man's keeping out of Barlow's way.'

When he spoke again, there was no contrition in Reason's voice. There was a lot of bloody difference between sitting round the fire in Chelsea with a large glass of whisky and high ideals about the old Australians and actually being here face-to-face with a long-abandoned blood relationship. He took his feet off the desk and stubbed out the cigarette. 'He's now in tandem, it seems, with an Australian who's been doing a bit of freelance mercenary stuff in London for the Provos. He's got no pedigree of violence, just a whisper that he made the tea and did a bit of dicking for the people who tried to burn down Windsor Castle. He's of no significance, but he's giving Flynn a free run. Harry reckons he's close to them, but he's got this Australian lady –'

'Did you say "lady"?'

'Yeh. She's a tough guy who runs the Melbourne shop for Dubrovnik's office and, apparently, has a personal interest in running Flynn into the ground. Another problem here, though. She wants him intact, Harry and I want him under the ground. It's a sort of conflict of ideals and, erm, methods of dealing with mad dogs. When we run Flynn into a corner, I think she'll somehow have to be eased to one side while we attend to him. Our intention is that Flynn doesn't walk once we've finished with him. We'll sort out his Australian helper's destiny when the time comes. I think he'll probably have to go the same way.'

'I thought it was a question of "if" you catch up with Flynn rather than "when"?'

Reason pulled a face to himself in the mirror. Logic supported Sanderson's observation; Reason's experience agreed with it. But he wasn't letting on. 'If we thought like that, Richard, we might just as well throw the idea in the bin and come home now. We'll catch the bastard – I'm sure of that.'

'Good.' Sanderson didn't sound convinced. 'But, whatever happens, don't make any ripples, Clive. We don't want an Australian *Rainbow Warrior* lookalike, and I don't want to have to explain to our Leader that he's got to grovel to the chief dingo because we got caught blowing some bloody Irishman's ears off in the holiday camp.'

'Do I detect a shadow of doubt in your voice, Richard?'

'It's the time and distance, Clive.' Sanderson paused. Then, 'Have you got something else to tell me?'

'No – to ask you.'

'Go on, then.'

'Can you have someone drop a hint or two in places that matter that there's speculation about another *Spycatcher* problem in the offing, with some fairly serious implications for British intelligence interests in Ireland?'

'Is that wise?'

'I'm not sure, but I'd like to give it a go. There's not enough speculation about Sixsmith's revelations; everybody seems to be playing this thing too close to their chests. Nothing from Dublin, nothing from London. I think it's time the name Sixsmith, what it's thought he's been up to, and his former occupation, came out, gently, into the open. A sort of build-up to the finale, if you know what I mean.'

'Provided you catch up with Mr Flynn before he goes on air with his side of the story!'

'Of course – provided that.'

'Bye, Clive. Keep your nose clean.'

'Don't worry, I'm the only honest one here. Harry's on their side, temporarily, and Murray's not on anybody's list. If the shit hits the fan, Harry'll make sure nothing comes in our direction. Trust me, Richard . . .'

'I was hoping you weren't going to say that! Goodbye, Clive.'

Staring at the blank ceiling, Reason finished his cigarette and lit another before he picked up the outside line and dialled Melbourne.

Murray didn't say a word; he gave a little click of his tongue to announce that he was there and waited.

'David?'

Murray recognized the voice. 'Yeh.'

'Have you spoken to Harry?'

'Not yet. He rang Thompson last night asking about a fast boat. Thompson has done that and is waiting for Harry to call back —'

'I know all about that,' interrupted Reason impatiently. 'What else is happening?'

'Buggered if I know. I only got here this morning. Thompson couldn't tell me much, even if he wanted to. It seems that only Harry Barlow knows what's going on.'

'Thanks, David! That's great news! I could have saved a bloody telephone call. I thought I was depressed after I'd spoken to Harry last night — you've made me fuckin' suicidal! You staying there, at that number?'

'Until Harry tells me otherwise.'

'OK. I'll be in touch. I'm at the Canberra Hyatt if anything breaks and you want me — and please God it does, and you do! See you in church, David.'

'Bye, Clive.'

When Reason got back to the Hyatt there was a message at reception asking him to ring Dubrovnik — urgently, it said. Reason glanced at his watch. Half-past eleven. It was just about two hours since he'd left Dubrovnik's office. Two hours in the underhand business was a lot longer than Harold Wilson's week in politics. But he let it

292

bubble, it was good for the adrenaline. He stripped and stood under the shower with the cold needles thrashing his muscular body like pine switches in a Swedish sauna. He stood it for ten minutes, then clad in an emperor-size white towel padded across the room, poured himself an ice-cold Carlsberg from the miniature fridge and picked up the telephone.

Dubrovnik sounded pleased with himself, even answering the phone. His happiness went up a couple of octaves when he recognized Reason's voice. 'I've solved one of your problems, Mr Reason,' he said. 'You don't have to waste any more time hanging around here. Sixsmith's manuscript and his other stuff has been claimed by a Mrs Fiona Campbell. She's also taking possession of his body when the coroner gives the word. She's going to have him cremated in Melbourne as soon as she arrives and clears the formalities . . . Are you still there, Mr Reason?'

'Yeh. Who's Mrs Fiona Campbell?'

'I'd have thought your people would have told you. She's Sixsmith's next of kin, his daughter.'

'Well, thanks for the information, Mr Dubrovnik, that was very thoughtful of you.'

The silence at the other end was more than satisfying to Reason. But it didn't last. 'Just a minute, Reason! Is that all you've got to say about it?'

'Yup. Thanks very much. Goodbye.' Reason put the phone down thoughtfully.

Mrs Fiona Campbell . . . Good news and bad news. Why the bloody hell haven't we run this one to ground in London? We could have worked her, or even replaced her with one of our Fionas. Is this one going to play with us, or is she going to stamp her little high heels and do what she thinks is right? Let's hope she's not a Union Jack fetishist, a patriot, heaven help us! Fuck it, Richard! You could have done something about this before it got to this stage . . . And that's only the bad news.

Reason swigged his beer, gritted his teeth and let his sinuses settle down from the ice-cold impact before restarting the thinking processes.

On the other hand, she could be one of those straggly haired, ashes and sackcloth and oversized flat-sandal types of interfering bitches who feel that British secret-service matters should be open and in the public domain – and too fuckin' bad if it helps THEM! Reason took his glass over to the bed and propped himself against the headboard. *That's the good bloody news! Let's hope she turns out like that . . .*

He finished his beer, lit a cigarette and rang the British High Commission.

28

The rays of the sun were like two red-hot pokers probing his eyes. Barlow turned over on his side.

'Bloody hell! What time is it?' He reached out for Sophie. She wasn't there. And then he was wide awake. He looked around the room. Her clothes had gone, everything was neat and tidy, even his own clothes, which he'd thrown around the room in the first rapturous assault, had been collected and neatly folded on the luggage rack. It wasn't a dream. He looked down at the crumpled bed beside him where she'd lain. His heart was thudding, but not from exertion. Something had happened. Not a one-night stand; not a drunken wrestling match with one of the local whores: love, not sex. Something had definitely happened. Barlow felt light-headed; he felt twenty years younger.

And he looked it as he walked into the motel dining room after he'd showered, shaved and put on a clean shirt.

Sophie looked radiant. Something inside her had been released as well. But she also looked pensive as she watched him approach. Should he kiss her? He wanted to. Touch her? Bury his face in her neck and savour the sweet fragrance of her body? Christ! How did you keep your hands off her? He did none of these.

Harry, I don't want you to read anything into this . . .

'Good morning,' he said. It sounded as though he was speaking through a mouthful of chocolate.

'Morning. Coffee?'

'Thanks.'

'I spoke to Dubrovnik last night. I forgot to mention it . . .' She was Head of Station again. She paused. Their eyes met. Not quite Head of Station. 'Other things were happening at the time.' Their eyes locked as they each remembered those other things. Barlow gave in first and reached for his cup of coffee. How the hell could you work under these circumstances?

Sophie could. 'The boat that Flynn hijacked is named the *Charlotte* something or other, and Jayne's the name of the dead man's wife. Those are the two women he mentioned.' She sipped coffee without taking her eyes off him. 'The man's body was collected last night and it's now in the mortuary with the rest of Flynn's victims. They're an English couple sailing the world. They reached Sydney, liked it and decided to stay for a bit. For the past six months they've been sailing this stretch of coast, exploring all the inlets – like the one where he got killed – and coves and beaches. They probably know this stretch of coast like the backs of their hands. Maybe they were looking for somewhere to settle.' Sophie lowered her coffee cup into its saucer and wrinkled her nose. 'What rotten luck to come all this way to meet someone like Flynn.'

'Didn't he mention some other women being on board?'

Sophie's generous lips tightened. 'Those other "women" are children, twin girls aged seven.' She paused to allow Barlow to consider the implications. 'Children! Two of them. Think about it, Harry. One woman and two little girls. The dead man's name was Roger Clarke, but that's neither here nor there. You thinking about it?'

Barlow didn't need to, he was way ahead of her. 'What else did your Mr Dubrovnik have to offer?'

'Not a lot. He's arranging for a helicopter but has left its deployment up to me. It'll be standing by in half an hour, awaiting instructions.'

'What about a boat?'

'He doesn't see what use a boat could be. Neither do I. I'm all for the chopper, though.'

'And what do you think Flynn will do when he sees a police helicopter hovering over his head and going wherever he goes?'

'I don't follow you.'

'Try. The first thing he'll do is break the arms of those two kids and throw them over the side. Those'll be the starters. And if the helicopter doesn't take that as a hint to bugger off out of his way, Mrs Clarke'll follow them, but with her head staved in like her husband's. Sorry, Sophie, I reckon you should have another long hard think about helicopters.'

Sophie didn't respond for a moment. 'OK. I've thought about it. What would you suggest we do, then? Sit here drinking Pimms and hope everything will sort itself out?'

'Not quite,' said Barlow. 'Flynn doesn't know we've found him – he thinks he's ducked out of sight and is running free. That's worth an extra card to our side.'

'What d'you mean, found him?'

'Figuratively speaking.' Barlow couldn't resist it any longer. He reached across the table and laid his hand on hers. The tingling went right to the base of his spine. She let it stay there for a second, then gently withdrew hers and let it rest in her lap. Business, her gesture said, is business. Barlow took his hand back without rancour and lit a cigarette. 'Will Dubrovnik find you an unmarked boat and unrestricted use of it?'

'No way!'

Sophie's answer didn't entirely displease Barlow. He'd laid the ambush; she'd walked into it. 'What if I could lay my hands on one?'

She glanced up suspiciously, but didn't put her suspicions into words. She picked up her mug of warm coffee and sipped, studying his eyes as she did so. 'Keep talking,' she said.

'We know this *Charlotte* thing's a sailing boat and has a good engine, but neither of those methods can compete with a powerful motor launch. We get one of those and head towards Sydney –'

'Why Sydney?'

'Just a hunch.'

'Barlow, are you being entirely frank with me?' Barlow winced. It was back to 'Barlow' – last night's 'Harry' had been put into suspension. 'I don't think I like the way all this planning and conjecture is coming off the top of your head. It doesn't sound sufficiently ad lib to me. It sounds more like something you've had worked out for some time. Tell me, and convince me, that I'm being unduly suspicious.'

'Nothing like that, Sophie,' said Barlow with a straight face. 'It's all part of the training. Trust me. I've had a lot of practice at this sort of thing.'

She studied his face for several long moments. 'Why do I get the feeling I've known you for years?'

What was this leading up to? Barlow frowned. A joke? Hardly. 'I have that effect on gullible women . . .'

It wasn't a joke. 'Is that how you see me? Well let me tell you something, gullibility apart, I'm still not sure I trust your motives in this business. But go on, for the time being I'll buy it. But a little warning, Barlow. If things go too pat, I'll have more than second thoughts, I'll have a big boy with a cricket bat come and ask you a few questions.' Her eyes sparkled for a moment to show that she didn't mean it, but the fleeting smile was quickly replaced by another searching glance. 'OK, assume you've got a fast boat – what then?'

'We run up to the yacht and board it.'

'You're joking!' But Sophie could see in Barlow's face that he wasn't. She shook her head. 'Or bloody mad!'

Barlow acknowledged the compliment with a little tilt of the head and the beginnings of a smile. 'Listen, Sophie, Flynn doesn't know we're on to him, and it'll stay like that unless something silly like a chopper starts buggering around over his head. Do it my way and the only bloodshed will be from Flynn and his mate, Sullivan. Any other way, it'll be the kids and a woman. Hostages, Sophie. Doesn't that word mean anything out here?'

She didn't react as she would have done yesterday. 'Tell me,' she said softly, 'where, at short notice – or no notice at all – are you going to get hold of a fast boat that doesn't' mind ramming yachts in the middle of the Tasman Sea?'

'Everything's possible! Let me make a short phone call to a friend in Melbourne –'

But this was different. Her head came up suspiciously. 'You've got friends in Melbourne and I've only just heard about them? Come off it, Barlow!' She continued staring at him. 'Australian friends?'

He shook his head. 'Friend – singular. And no, he's English. Where can a boat pick us up?'

'Show me that map.'

The telephone had no protection. Barlow felt exposed. He glanced over his shoulder and met Sophie's accusing eyes. He stared for a second, then half-smiled and turned back to the phone. Thompson told him he'd arranged a boat and it was on its way to a landing jetty about half an hour's drive from the motel. It would take the boat about an hour to get there, Thompson reckoned, and gave Barlow explicit instructions on how to find the jetty. 'The driver's name is Burne Harris,' he concluded. 'He's a New Zealander who came out of SBS –'

'Our SBS?'

'British,' replied Thompson laconically. 'And one crew member named David Murray. Anything else I can do?'

'No thanks.'

'Have a good trip then.'

Barlow replaced the phone, opened the door and breathed a deep lungful of fresh air as he made his way back to the table. Sophie was getting impatient. She glanced at her watch as he sat down and began buttering a slice of toast.'

'Harry, it's ten o'clock –'

'We've got half an hour,' he told her. 'Have some more coffee.'

'Half an hour to what?' she hissed. 'What the hell's going on?'

'Relax.'

'Just cut out the bloody games, will you, and tell me what the hell's going on.'

He told her what he thought she ought to know about the boat and where they were meeting it. She wasn't convinced everything was open and above board, but she let it run – for the time being. If there was more to it than Harry Barlow was letting on, she knew of at least one way to get the rest of it out of him. Sophie studied Barlow's face as he talked and consoled herself with the axiom that there was a time and a place for everything, particularly divulging confidences – or secrets. She stood up. 'OK,' she said. 'Half an hour. I'll meet you at the car.'

'Where are you going?'

'I've left some things in the room. Have you got your stuff?'

'It's in the car.'

He followed her outside. The sun was hot even under the trees that bordered the narrow path running the length of the row of chalets. When she turned into the open door of the one they'd slept in last night, he went in with her. Inside it was cool and the still-drawn curtains diffused the bright sunshine, leaving the room pleasantly in the shadows.

Sophie stopped just inside the door and stared around as if it were the first time she'd seen the room. Barlow moved alongside her, closed the door with his foot and took her in his arms. She didn't resist, but there was a slight stiffness in her manner, as if she were reinforcing her warning that last night was not the beginning of anything. There was no melting of an eager body. Perhaps it *had* been the Cognac?

Even so, it was a long and tender kiss. When their mouths parted she leant against the door, but kept both hands clasped round the back of his neck and pulled her body tightly against his. He felt her hard, firm breasts pressed against his chest through the thin cotton of his shirt and the gentle swell of her stomach as she leant against his groin. Barlow closed his eyes, gratefully. Half an hour? He was almost back to last night. She brought his head forward and kissed him again, quickly, then leaned back and stared into his eyes. 'Harry,' she said huskily, 'are you playing some sort of game with me?'

Barlow looked hurt. It was genuine. 'What do you mean?'

She looked down at their fused bodies, her legs slightly apart, his between them, demanding. 'This. Is it all part of whatever's going on between you and Sixsmith and Flynn? Are you using me, Harry?'

He didn't answer. He studied her eyes, accusing and slightly moist, then lowered his mouth to hers. But just before he made contact she pulled away fractionally.

'Answer me, Harry.'

He continued searching her eyes until her lips tightened aggressively. He said softly, 'I don't think what I'm going to say is what you want to hear, Sophie.'

Her stomach fluttered, then went cold. She stiffened and tried to withdraw from him, but the door was pressing into her back and there was nowhere else to go.

'You bastard!'

'I love you.'

'What?'

'I love you.'

Her knees felt weak; the silence seemed to go on for ever. Then she found her voice. 'No, Harry, don't – it's too quick!' She stared at him, confused, and then added, timidly, 'And that's no sort of answer.'

It was time to lie. 'I'm not playing games, Sophie. I'm not using you . . .' And then came the truth that had hit him when he saw her in the dining room: 'I love you.'

This time she didn't pull her mouth away, but it was with a thoughtful, eyes-wide-open kiss that she responded.

The half-hour drive that Thompson had mentioned turned out to be nearly an hour. Barlow left Sophie with her thoughts and the driving while he sat and considered the next move.

Surprisingly, she hadn't mentioned Flynn's welfare for some time, and she'd given up warning Barlow of the consequences of any grievous bodily harm caused to the killer of, so far, three Australians, and the kidnapper and possible murderer of God knew how many more. Once again the kissing had finished. Before they'd left the hotel she'd been very willing, very soft and feminine, but she hadn't mentioned love. And now it was back to business for the second time that day – and it was still only ten-past eleven in the morning. But she'd made it quite clear. She wanted first claim on Flynn's body – 'upright, standing and *compos mentis*', according to her last words on the subject. But she hadn't met David Murray yet!

'What sort of weapons d'you think we're up against?' Sophie asked casually as she came out of a thoughtful silence.

Barlow didn't open his eyes; he didn't turn his head. 'We'll soon find out,' he murmured.

'You can do better than that, Harry.'

He sat up and turned to face her. She looked tense. 'Hard to make an assessment, Sophie. We know one of them had a shotgun in his hand a short time ago, and they've also the trooper's gun and a spare clip of ammunition. There are some other odds and ends to consider, judging by the appearance of Mr Clarke. Will that be enough for you?'

Sophie pulled a face but didn't take her eyes off the road. Barlow warmed to the subject. 'I think you can eliminate your boy Sullivan from this scene. Flynn's the mad dog, he's the one with the form card, and he's the one we've got to worry about. A guy with Flynn's experience could make a lethal weapon out of a cheese straw. Improvisation is part of the upbringing . . .'

Sophie glanced at Barlow out of the corner of her eye. 'He didn't make that mess of Mr Clarke with a cheese straw.' She said nothing for a moment and then tightened her lips. 'But he's got something else, hasn't he? Something more potent than weapons.'

'What d'you mean?'

'He doesn't need things that go bang to persuade ladies to sail him around the Tasman Sea – he's got twin girls to do that. Those children are probably the sole reason why Mrs Clarke is taking Flynn where he wants to go. Without them as gambling chips she would probably have told him to get stuffed – and ended up on the slab with her husband. Still could, I suppose . . .' She broke off and pointed ahead to a rickety wooden jetty that stuck out a few yards into a small private harbour. Alongside the jetty rode a sleek, powerful-looking motor launch. 'This is the place they told you, and I think that's what we're looking for.'

Sophie drew the car alongside the jetty and stopped.

When Barlow got out he could hear a steady throb bubbling up from the launch's stern as the engines ticked over under the eye of the only man visible. He had obviously heard the car arrive, but took no notice. He remained leaning over the side of the boat studying the exhaust bubbles, and it wasn't until he heard the footsteps creak on the wooden jetty that he stood up, studied the new arrivals for a moment, then invited them on board.

Up close Burne Harris was a fine specimen. Over six feet tall and well built, he carried no surplus weight. He had fair, almost blond, hair, and the lower part of his face was covered with an unruly curly beard that made his age difficult to define. But he wasn't old – mid-thirties. He didn't look all that friendly. He wiped his hands with a wad of grubby cotton waste and reached out to take Barlow's hand in a firm grasp.

'Harris,' he said. 'I know – you're in a hurry! We can go as soon as you want. I'm ready, and so is the boat.'

'What about crew?'

'You're looking at it. There's another guy, but he doesn't know much about boats. But don't worry, it's a lazy bugger's boat, everything works by switches.' He studied Sophie as he spoke. Barlow followed his gaze.

'This is Miss Ward. It's her show.'

'Sophie,' she interjected and held out her hand.

'Hi, Sophie.' Harris enveloped her small hand in his, held it briefly, then gave it back to her. He turned to Barlow again, moved him casually away from Sophie and lowered his voice. 'Your friend's down below cooking himself an early lunch. I've never known a bugger eat so much. He hasn't stopped since he came on board. Shall I give him a shout? D'you want to see him?'

'No, leave him where he is. He'll come up when he's ready. Can we go now?' asked Barlow abruptly.

When he cleared the harbour entrance, Harris opened the throttles fully and stood back. There was no more talk as Sophie and Barlow hung on and watched the launch dig its stern into the water and charge eagerly at the open sea.

Nobody kept a note of the time. The roar of the engines and the continual thump-thump-thump of the hull as it crashed on to the choppy water cut out the need for small talk as Harris concentrated on keeping his boat on the course he'd set for it. After a while, he eased the throttles slightly and looked intently through the clear section of the smoked-glass windscreen. He studied the sky, then the horizon from right to left, and then, finally, straightened up and smiled at his audience dispersed around the cockpit.

'It'll get rougher shortly,' he said cheerfully, alternating his gaze between Sophie on one side of the cockpit and Barlow on the other. 'How close d'you want to get to the yacht when we reach her?'

Barlow answered him. 'We're going to board her,' he said. 'Didn't Murray tell you?'

Harris shook his head. 'He said you wanted a lift out to a boat named the *Lady Charlotte* that had left her anchorage somewhere between here and Margaret Island late last night. He said he didn't know where she was making for, but you would and if you didn't you'd have a bloody good guess. What's it to be?'

Barlow didn't bother answering.

Harris continued: 'But just in case, and while I was waiting for you I laid off speculative courses for a boat heading for Sydney – which seemed a reasonable place for it to go under the circumstances – and, as a wild possibility, New Zealand. There shouldn't be a great deal of variation between the yacht's ideas and mine, but if there is we'll still have enough strength to cut backwards and forwards until we make a sighting. Whatever you decide to do then, you can count on me.'

Barlow glanced over at Murray, who'd appeared, almost unnoticed, in the cockpit. He had two thick slices of bread bulging round half a pound of crisply cooked bacon in one hand, and pressed against his side under the same arm was a condensation-covered tin of Powers bitter. He looked at home as he held on to the side with the other hand and swayed to the rhythm of the boat's movements. A man of many talents was David Murray, and obviously no stranger to the sea. He studied Sophie and undressed her with a glance, but otherwise didn't acknowledge her. She'd met his type before. She gave him the same treatment. Murray wasn't the least bit abashed and continued munching on his sandwich. After a moment he propped himself against the side of the cockpit and took another large bite out of his sandwich and chewed. Melted butter dribbled on to his chin and he unselfconsciously flicked it away before sliding down on the bench seat, making himself comfortable and closing his eyes.

Harris studied his recumbent form for a moment. Maybe there was a touch of envy, but he hid it as he took a cigarette from a crumpled packet lying on the shelf by his shoulder. He stuck his finger in the opening to inspect the contents and pulled one out for Barlow. He tossed the packet to Sophie, who was studying a small, round, television-type screen set into the main consul. Sophie caught the pack one-handed, threw it back at him and continued inspecting the dials and knob settings of the elaborate system.

'State of the art,' bellowed Harris. 'Just had it installed. D'you know anything about it?'

Sophie nodded and ran her fingers over the switches on the set. As she watched it come to life, she raised her voice and said, 'It's a useful gadget, this one, but we probably won't need it.'

'Why's that?' asked Barlow.

Sophie didn't look up. 'I've got a feeling Flynn and his mate are going east – the same way we're going. I reckon he's fairly certain he's got a clean run now. Make Sydney, drop off anywhere around there – the bloody place's got more yachts than fish – and just get lost in the crowd . . .'

'So what's your point, Sophie?' They were both interested; even Murray opened his eyes and looked at her.

She wasn't embarrassed at having an attentive audience. 'If we do the same thing we're almost sure to pick him up with a pair of binoculars.' She tapped the top of the radar. 'All this does is give us a bit of luxury. We can drop off to sleep if we like and still bump into him – in the dark if necessary! Isn't that so, Burne?'

Harris nodded, but he was only half-listening. He put his face closer to the windscreen, then looked away and blinked – then back again to the windscreen.

'Pass me those binoculars – quick!' he snapped.

He stared at the horizon for the best part of a minute, then handed the binoculars to Barlow. 'That's her all right,' he said emphatically. 'That's your *Lady Charlotte*.'

'How can you tell at this distance?' asked Barlow.

'I had a word with a friend who has a book. She's in it.' He didn't look smug. 'Take my word for it, that boat is the *Charlotte*. We've made good time,' he said grudgingly, studying the dial on the large chronometer he wore on his wrist. 'Just over four hours – not bad for an old tub like this!' He stopped admiring his watch and looked towards Sophie. 'The people on that boat,' he said. 'Good sailors, are they?'

Sophie shrugged. 'I've no idea. Harry!' she called. 'Is Flynn a sailor?'

Barlow lowered the glasses and looked through the windscreen with his naked eye. He could see nothing in the distance. He didn't turn for her question. 'Ask him,' he said and waved his arm in Murray's direction. 'He'll tell you anything you want to know about Irishmen.'

Murray answered before she asked the question again. He had to shout to make himself heard over the noise of the slapping of the boat's hull on the choppy water. 'The nearest thing to sailing the Flynn I know ever did would've been on a paddle boat on Lough Neagh and the ferry to Stranraer.' He picked up another sandwich and inspected it preparatory to his next bite. He raised it to his mouth, held it there, and added, 'But Flynn won't be sailing that boat, Harris, if that's what you're worried about. He'll be standing close to Mrs Clarke with something unpleasant stuck in her ear to make sure she does the right things at the right time. Somebody's going to have to blow his arm off when we get close enough.'

Sophie, having made a point of ignoring him so far, studied Murray with new interest. 'Who are you?' she asked.

Murray shrugged. Harris's eyes briefly met Barlow's and got the message. 'He's a friend of the owner of this boat,' Harris told her. 'Comes from Ireland. He's here to make sure I don't scratch the bloody thing – untrusting bastards, aren't they?'

Sophie stared at Harris in disbelief, then at Barlow, waiting for him to say something a little more intelligent. When nothing happened, she narrowed her eyes at Murray. 'How do you know about Flynn?'

'It's a habit of mine,' replied Murray through a mouthful of bread and bacon. 'I collect Flynns.'

'Another clever bastard!' snapped Sophie, but she

didn't pursue the matter. 'I'll pretend I didn't hear that bit about blowing people's arms off,' she said. 'Let me remind you what I told your friend here – if he is your friend. This is not a bloody tiger shoot! I want that man Flynn alive and walking beside me when I step off this boat. I hope you're all listening – you in particular, Barlow!'

Nobody took any notice of her.

Harris interrupted. His voice was hard but cool. 'We're closing fairly rapidly. Have you decided how you're going to act this out?' He looked from Barlow to Sophie, then back to Barlow.

Sophie said nothing, but followed his glance.

Barlow said, 'You're the naval person, make a suggestion.'

Harris scratched the back of his head, then ran his fingers through his straggly beard. 'There's only one way to tango on this sort of water,' he said slowly. 'And that's to roar up alongside, jam our bows into her side and board her before anybody realizes what's happening.'

'You sure you'd be able to hold tight into her long enough for me to make the jump?' asked Barlow.

Harris nodded. 'This boat'll stick. I can keep her in touch as long as you like – that's the easy bit. Yours is the hard part. You're going to need split-second timing when you let go of us because the two craft'll be bobbing up and down like empty bottles – and at different heights and directions. Not easy!' His teeth gleamed through the blond beard in a grimace. 'Personally I'd rather watch than have to do it, but if you've made up your mind I suggest you start getting ready. We'll be in range very shortly.'

'What d'you want me to do first?'

'How about saying your prayers?'

'Let's save the funny routine for the ride home. D'you want me to ask again?'

Harris's beard closed over his smile and he looked down at Barlow's shoes. 'Those aren't suitable to start with. Take 'em off, and your socks, it'll make it a bit easier for you to get a grip when you land on the other deck. I think remaining upright is going to be your first problem. But we can help there.'

'What do I do?' Murray threw the remains of his sandwich overboard, washed his mouth with a long swig of Powers and tossed that away as well.

Harris pointed forward with his chin. 'You can provide cover from there, and if I keep us close into their stern, we'll be able to see the whole of the other cockpit and keep things under control if he goes sprawling on his arse.'

Barlow sat down beside Murray and began to untie the laces in his shoes. Out of the side of his mouth he said, 'I'm going for Flynn. I'm going for kill. You keep your eyes peeled for the other guy and make sure he doesn't survive. I don't want either of these two bastards walking away with an arm round Sophie Ward's shoulders. Got it?'

Murray nodded. 'Are you sure there are two of them?'

'They could have split up,' said Barlow, thoughtfully. He hadn't considered that possibility before, but it was too late now. 'I'm going in with the expectation of having to deal with two. If there's only one, that'll be a bonus.'

'There's not much else you can do, Harry,' said Murray, then, after a quick glance at Sophie, 'but what about her?'

'What about her?'

Still with his eye on Sophie, Murray put his head close to Barlow's and said, out of the corner of his mouth, 'Having heard what she had to say about the programme just now, I'm inclined to agree with sonny boy about keeping her out of the party. What d'you say? She could slip over the side if you like.'

Barlow turned on him. His voice was cold, his face set tight. 'Don't even look at her, David. She's my problem, I'll handle it my way. Is that clear?'

Murray wasn't put out. But he did give Barlow a deep, thoughtful look before nodding. He'd read the signs. He glanced quickly again at Sophie. Not bad – well done, Harry! Murray understood.

'I mean that, David. Don't touch her.'

'OK. What're you going to do about the woman on the boat and the kids if they get in the way?'

'Tough . . .' Whatever it was, he didn't finish it. 'And what the hell d'you think you're doing!' he shouted at Sophie.

Sophie had taken off both her shoes and was fastidiously rolling her jeans up to her knees. She took no notice of Barlow until she'd finished both legs, then, carefully pulling the jeans tighter round her waist, she looked up and raised her eyebrows.

'What was that?' she asked.

'You know bloody well what it was! And you know what I meant. Cut it out, Sophie. This is man's work, not a bloody woman's.'

Sophie got up slowly from the bench seat, moved unsteadily across the cockpit and stood over Barlow. Murray leant back out of the line of fire, a tiny twitch of a smile beginning in the corners of his mouth.

'I thought it was something like that,' she hissed, 'but I was wondering whether you meant the insult, or whether it was an unintentional slip.'

'What are you talking about?'

'I'm talking about you, Harry Barlow! Don't you dare tell me what's man's work and what's woman's! That's your first error. The second one is that you happen to be in Australian territorial waters and you've forgotten who's in charge of this affair.' Sophie Ward was very

311

serious. She jabbed a finger into her chest. 'It's me, I'm in charge, and you'll do exactly as I say.' She stepped back a pace, her lips drawn in a tight straight line. She was angry, a real, genuine purple anger, and she pointed her finger at Barlow's face. 'Don't ever dare try a line like that with me again, Harry!' She lowered her voice. 'I mean it!'

Barlow stared into Sophie's serious face, then looked sideways at Murray. Murray stared straight ahead; it wasn't his argument.

'Sophie, listen –'

'You haven't heard a bloody word I've said, have you? This is bloody Australia, not England! We don't have boy and girl syndromes in our service, so just back me up, will you, and I'll thank you when I get back. Otherwise . . .' She left it unfinished, and before Barlow could try another, more diplomatic argument, a third voice entered the conversation.

'We're almost within screaming distance of your boat,' shouted Harris, and pointed through the windscreen. 'About seven hundred metres.' He picked up the glasses again and focused them on the *Lady Charlotte*. 'And it's a woman at the helm,' he said. 'I can't see anybody else on deck.'

'Have another look,' Barlow broke in. 'There's got to be a couple of men lurking there somewhere.'

'They're probably down below.' Harris peered through the binoculars again. 'I don't think she knows we're here yet. I haven't seen her turn her head since we started closing in. Strange!' Harry tossed the binoculars to Barlow. 'Come and see for yourself.

Barlow braced himself against the buffeting of the waves whilst Harris reduced his speed to match that of the *Lady Charlotte*, and focused the glasses on the trim figure standing in front of the big chrome wheel in the cockpit. Something must have nudged her shoulder blades as Barlow refocused on the back of her head. She gave a casual glance round, stiffened, then, shielding her eyes from the sun, turned fully and stared at the big motor launch. Barlow stared back.

Her expression was hardly inviting.

'Mrs Clarke,' he told the others without lowering the binoculars, 'is a very frightened woman, which is, I suppose, under the circumstances, a highly normal state for her to be in. A couple of mad dogs each with a twin daughter under his arm, and part of her husband's head stuck to a lump of iron in the coat pocket of one of them – I think I'd be bloody frightened too! The trouble is that it's not Flynn or the other one she appears to be frightened of – it's us!'

'One of your men could be standing just out of sight,' offered Harris. Nobody responded.

Barlow handed the glasses to Sophie. She took them without a word or a glance and studied the *Lady Charlotte* briefly, then dropped the binoculars on to the bench behind her. She picked up her bag and drew out the Glock, cocked a round into the breech, and, with the safety catch on, jammed it firmly into the tight waistband at the back of her jeans. As she turned away she caught Barlow's eye. She wished she hadn't. She bit her lip and looked away, then moved to the side nearest the *Charlotte*. Barlow moved across and stood beside her. 'Sophie . . .?'

'Make it brief.'

'Let me do it – please!'

'Shut up!'

'For Christ's sake, Sophie,' Barlow exploded. 'You've never used that bloody thing in anger.' He gestured with his chin at the Glock. 'It's not bloody easy –'

'I said shut up.'

'Oh, bloody hell!' he said angrily. 'OK, go and get

yourself killed then.' Their eyes met. Hers softened momentarily at the anguish in his, then she shook her head kindly. 'Don't worry,' she mouthed.

'Sophie –'

She tilted her chin.

'OK,' he said resignedly, 'then listen. Don't take any chances with Flynn. If he's got anything on that boat that shoots bullets, kill the bastard on sight – don't give it a second's thought. And I mean that. Forget everything else. Just shoot the bastard, or he'll kill you.'

She smiled. It wasn't a real smile. This one was a contraction of the muscles around her lips. It failed. Harris and Murray studied her closely. The nerves were getting to her. These men knew what was happening, they'd all been there, and it never improved, the nerves would always twang. But nobody's face gave a flicker of what was going on behind the eyes. She turned away, hesitated, then came back and pinched Barlow's arm. When he lowered his head to her she put her mouth to his ear: 'What you said, back at the motel . . .'

'What did I say?'

'You said something about love, and I made a mistake. It's not too quick. I love you too, Harry,' she breathed.

'Oh, Jesus Christ! Sophie . . .' But there was nothing he could do except stand and watch. She gave his arm a final pinch and, gazing round the cockpit but catching no one's eye, she called, 'Harris?' When he looked up she said calmly: 'OK, let's go for it!'

Harris opened the throttles and moved the launch up until he was riding in the yacht's delicate backwash, then throttled back so that he was closing the gap between the two vessels by inches.

He jabbed Sophie sharply with his elbow.

'Move up to the bow on the port side,' he told her, 'and stay low until we touch. When I give you the word, move to the other side, and when I say jump, jump!'

He didn't take his eyes from the yacht, still slipping through the water just ahead, but now beginning to yaw away to starboard in an unconscious slide to avoid the inevitable embrace. But Harris went with her, like a determined bridegroom, breaking his concentration only to bark at Sophie: 'Go on – now! MOVE!'

Sophie lowered herself to the deck. She moved on all fours to the front of the boat, keeping the cruiser's raised forecabin between herself and the yacht until she could go no further without being seen from the other vessel. When she peered round the corner she saw that she was almost level with the *Charlotte*'s stern, and that the two vessels, although bobbing up and down like two corks, appeared to be standing still. She looked up at the yacht's huge mainsail, flapping and cracking with uncertainty as the helmswoman, apparently with only one thought in mind, veered the yacht across the wind in an effort to avoid contact with the menacing stranger. By Sophie's inexperienced eye – and stomach – she seemed to be doing it successfully. The gap appeared not to be narrowing.

It was an illusion. It was closing by fractions of an inch.

Harris knew what he was doing. He ploughed on, ignoring the frantically waving arm of the woman at the helm, and turned a deaf ear to the incomprehensible words she screamed across the narrow strip of water. He gave Barlow a quick sideways glance before opening the throttle for the final closing burst.

Just before they touched, he picked up a small cream-coloured handset.

'Ahoy, *Lady Charlotte* . . .'

His words boomed out with a hollow, echoing, metallic roar.

'. . . Australian Immigration . . . I am coming alongside to inspect you. Do not alter course.'

They all heard Jayne Clarke's shriek. She turned her

315

head towards them and screamed into the wind: 'No! Don't come any closer. Keep away! Please!' She didn't pause for breath. 'He'll kill us all if you don't go away.'

The expression of terror on her face matched the urgency in her voice.

Harris said out of the corner of his mouth: 'What d'you think? Shall I abort?'

Barlow stared impassively at the yacht. His eyes never left the woman's face. She appeared to be staring directly at him, as if she knew, and seemed to be addressing her plea to him alone. His lips barely moved.

'Take your orders from me, Harris, not her! Move in now, and tell Sophie to go aboard.'

Jayne Clarke looked imploringly at the open door from where Flynn's eyes bored accusingly into hers.

His head, barely visible below the top step of the companionway, turned between her and the vessel bearing down on them. His face wore an expression of quiet but calm menace; it was almost as if he'd been expecting the launch.

She glanced quickly over her shoulder again, then back, even more quickly when his voice said coldly: 'That's it, you're doing fine. Keep 'em away from us or . . .' He raised a screaming child, his hand over her mouth, just high enough for Jayne to see her terrified eyes. It was enough. She looked over her shoulder at the enemy again, quickly – very quickly – and stifled a scream. They were almost touching.

When she looked back at Flynn he produced the boat's Very pistol, which he'd found in the locker, and rested its muzzle against the side of the small head.

Jayne tried to scream again but there was nothing left in her throat to cope with the new horror. She bit into her lips and stared in disbelief. There was nothing in Flynn's face. She knew he'd do it. Her mind almost died. She closed her eyes to blot out the nightmare, but Flynn put it into words for her.

'Keep them away!' he ordered. Instead of finishing the sentence, he pulled the pistol's hammer back with a loud metallic click.

Harris gave the engines the extra little jolt they needed and swung the nose of the launch firmly into the *Lady Charlotte*'s side.

There was a jarring, tooth-gritting screech as the two vessels met, joined, and hung together. Harris swung the wheel round hard and ground his bows firmly into the yacht, holding it in tight with his powered strength and following it round as the yacht gave way under the pressure.

Sophie shot a quick glance over her shoulder and nodded briefly at the fiercely gesticulating Harris. She moved away from the security of the cabin roof and ran at a half-crouch across the wet, canting deck to the edge of the cruiser. She paused for a fraction of a second, then launched herself over the rail. She'd timed it perfectly. She landed with a slithering crash on the afterdeck of the yacht.

As she hauled the Glock from behind her back, she looked straight into the face of the woman at the helm. She was staring at her in stark horror, her mouth wide open, screaming without stopping for breath, the hysterical howling drowning out the flip, flap, cracking of the empty mainsail and piercing the roar of Harris's revving motors. And it was all for her. . . . No, not quite. First her, angrily, accusingly; then, as she swung her head sharply towards the open hatch, her voice became pleasing, conciliatory. Sophie blinked, quickly. It was all wrong.

Sophie lowered herself into a crouch, arms outstretched in front of her, the automatic secure and rock steady in both hands as she shifted her weight rhythmically in time with the movement of the deck.

But Jayne Clarke could contain herself no longer.

Without warning, and still screeching at the top of her voice, she abandoned the large wheel, twisting her body protectively in front of the companionway entrance.

Then Sophie saw it. The outline of a man's head at the bottom of the entrance, tucked down, almost out of sight, protected by the waving arms and legs of Jayne Clarke's spread-eagled body. It was briefer than brief, but it was enough for Sophie. Flynn's face was as clear as the ridged foresight nestling so sweetly in the V of the Glock's backsight. She aimed to hurt – a shot halfway between his eye and his chin. She held steady before squeezing the trigger, then paused.

It was a fatal hesitation.

The woman looked down the barrel and threw herself deliberately into her line of sight. It allowed Flynn to duck below the step. He'd seen all he wanted to see.

Sophie kept the pressure on the trigger and shouted across the deck: 'Come out, Flynn, hands in front of you, empty, or I'll blow the top of your head off!' And then, desperately, in a hoarse, overloud whisper: 'For Christ's sake, woman, get out of the bloody way!'

But Jayne Clarke took no notice.

As if in slow motion, Sophie saw the ugly metal orifice of the Very pistol appear from behind Jayne Clarke's legs and point directly at her face. She had no warning, no chance to duck or move. Like a fiery red arrow, the projectile came straight at her. Missing her face by a fraction of an inch, the flash of the exploding phosphorus filled her vision before the projectile continued on its way like a maverick rocket, zigzagging, fizzling, still burning and smoking until it steamed into the water two hundred yards away.

Sophie's scream died in her throat. The pistol dropped from her hand with a clatter and slithered across the cockpit. Momentarily blinded, she instinctively ducked, lost her footing and staggered sideways like a puppet that had lost some of its strings and didn't quite know where to go. Again instinctively, she brought her arm up to protect her face as she sensed rather than saw the approaching loose boom swing towards her head. With a crack like another gunshot and a thwack that carried across to the remorseless, thrusting cruiser, it snapped her protecting arm like a brittle stick. Sophie screamed. The boom swung away, then came back with a screech of tackle, and before anybody on the cruiser could move or shout a warning, with a sickening crack it caught her a full-bodied blow to the side of the head. The force of the blow carried her further across the sloping deck until she met the guardrail with her back. There she balanced lifelessly for what seemed to the horrified watchers on the launch an eternity, before splashing, legs and arms in all directions, into the crested wake of the two locked vessels.

Barlow stared in disbelief, the S&W in his hand pointing uselessly towards the yacht's cabin while his eyes focused on the disturbance where Sophie's body had entered the water. The tableau lasted no longer than a fraction of a second. From behind him came a shout and the sound of running bare feet, and from the corner of his eye he saw Murray catapult himself from the cruiser's well and hurtle over the stern, legs and arms flailing as he surfaced and cut through the water.

Harris turned with a shout, but his movement was arrested by a firm command.

'Get back!'

Barlow's eyes were glued once again on the bucking yacht.

'Get back to that wheel and keep this thing in place.'

Harris bellowed, 'The girl . . .' but Barlow's harsh command brought him back to the wheel. With one hand he detached a life belt and hurled it over the stern. He watched it skim over the water until it touched down and bounced out of sight in the shallow waves. After that he had no time to plot its progress, though he thought he saw Murray's arm rise near it in the troughy water. But he wouldn't have bet money on it. He turned quickly back to the wheel to maintain the cruiser's glue-like hold on the sliding yacht.

Without a helmsman, the *Lady Charlotte* wallowed and yawed dangerously in the wind, and then the current began to take control of the boat's direction.

But Harris hung on tenaciously.

Barlow fought the bile that rose in his throat. He lowered the revolver and shouted over the roar of the engines: 'Hold her steady, Harris! I'm going over!'

He leapt from the cockpit on to the upper deck and balanced himself for the jump on to the *Charlotte*'s deck. The Very pistol boomed out again and exploded, this time in a searing white flash a few yards away. He watched as it came for his head and swayed very slightly out of its path, following its passage as, bent by the slipstream, it skimmed snake-like over the launch to fall in a sizzling splash into the sea a hundred yards beyond. He straightened up, his eyes firmly on the gap on the other side of the woman's body from where the shot had come, and timed his moment to jump.

He could see clearly into the yacht's cockpit.

Apart from Jayne Clarke, lying in a crumpled heap in the well of the boat, the deck was clear. But her body was still pressed protectively against the companionway entrance. To hell with her! He bent his knees to launch himself on to the deck – and got no further. He stopped as if frozen.

A small girl had suddenly appeared on the top step of the companionway. Thrust upwards from the dark depths like a toy out of a spring-loaded box, she stood blinking in the sunshine, only partly protected by her mother's still form.

The small body shielded Flynn's head and shoulders. His left arm encircled the child's waist and his right hand held the blunt pistol with its muzzle pressed firmly under her chin. She stood trapped and shivering in his grasp and cried silently in her own private little nightmare. Too silently for Flynn. He dug the gun barrel into her soft chin and forced her to stare up at the sun. She screamed once, loudly and piercingly, then stopped suddenly and, with her eyes screwed up in pain, stood silently and submissively, like a little cherub statue. Flynn had a way with children.

Barlow kept his face devoid of expression as he stared at the child. The arm encircling her waist and the hand under her chin were the only parts of Flynn visible to him. There was nothing that would take a disarming shot. Flynn had covered himself well. Barlow straightened up from the position he'd assumed – halfway to jumping, halfway to shooting – but kept the revolver pointing directly at the child's middle.

He froze at the sound of Flynn's voice.

'Take one step towards this boat and the kid's head gets blown off.'

Barlow made no sudden movement. He stood in the open, fully exposed, and searched for the mouth. But Flynn had left no gaps. They'd taught him well at Libya's advanced terrorist academy. The cool night air after the sun had gone down in an orange blaze; the smell of charcoaled mutton; the quietly spoken lectures on the survival of the strong among the weak. The simple lessons, the effective ones, easily remembered: *they* don't shoot through kids; *they* haven't got the guts; *they're* too soft.

But just in case this was one of the others . . .

He snuggled down behind the child and studied Barlow from behind the little ear. He didn't like what he saw, not the man or the serious weapon he held like a prop, pointing in exactly the right direction. He looked hard at Barlow but there was no recognition.

'You!' he bellowed. The loud voice in her ear sent the child into paroxysms of malarial-like shivers. 'You, on that boat over there. Can you hear me?'

Barlow nodded.

'Good! Then move yourself away from the edge of your boat and put that gun somewhere where I can't see it.'

Barlow dropped his arm, allowing the pistol to hang by his side. He took a step backwards.

'More than that,' shouted Flynn. 'Get yourself off the top of the boat and go and stand in the stern.'

Barlow did as he was told.

'Keep him talking,' muttered Harris behind his beard. 'We're slowly pushing him round. He's nearly pointing back the way he came. In a couple of minutes they'll be right into the wind and there'll be such an almighty banging and flapping up aloft it'll take his mind off it. They might even capsize!'

Barlow shrugged his shoulders and shouted at the top of his voice: 'I repeat what my colleague said earlier. Surrender or face the consequences.'

'Fuck off!'

Flynn had moved fractionally to one side of the little girl's shoulder, showing just enough of his head to accommodate a soft-nosed .38. Barlow abandoned the thought even as it was born. It was a long way up for the S&W to travel. Too much movement underfoot, a fraction out, and he'd never live with himself. Flynn was shouting again.

'Tell your man to take his boat away from me. Go back where you came from, both of you, and if I as much as catch a whiff of you, or anyone else, following behind, this kid goes over the side!'

'I thought you said something was going to happen with that bloody boat?' Barlow growled at Harris out of the corner of his mouth. 'How much longer do I have to stand here talking to this bastard?'

'She's a good boat,' said Harris apologetically.

'What the bloody hell's that got to do with it?'

'Look! The woman . . .'

Jayne Clarke was pulling herself to her knees. There was blood on the side of her face where Flynn had tapped her with the muzzle of the Very pistol. She knelt in front of the cabin door, bemused and shaking her head, as though fighting herself back into the nightmare. Then, turning an ashen, terrified face in Barlow's direction, she looked directly into his eyes and appealed to him in a cracked, breathless voice.

'Please, please do as he says. There are two girls – twins. He'll kill them both if you don't go away. Please do as he says – go away!' She shook her head several times again and crawled towards the frighteningly silent child, whose tightly closed eyelids opened tearfully at the sound of her mother's voice. But not for long. They snapped shut again, like a toy doll turned upside down, when Flynn's unemotional voice sliced into her ear again.

'Shut your mouth, woman! And get back over there and start sailing this thing again.' He continued to stare unblinkingly at Barlow. 'I told you to fuck off. Just do that, will you!' He pulled back the hammer on the Very pistol with an exaggerated gesture to emphasize his warning. 'And don't forget what I said. I don't want to see you again!'

Jayne Clarke dragged herself to her feet and scuttled

back to the yacht's wheel in terror. Just in time, she brought the craft back on to a steady tack. At the same moment Harris disengaged his bows from the *Charlotte*'s side.

As they parted, he glanced at Barlow. 'Why don't I pull away,' he muttered, 'then turn and ram the bastard? We could sink him. He wouldn't have time to get off more than one shot with that flare gun.'

Barlow shook his head. 'It's that one shot I'm worried about. The kid's too close. Do as he says. Pull away and go about. Let's go and find Murray and Sophie and do something about getting them out of the water. Is that going to be a problem?'

Harris swung the wheel hard over. 'No. Murray would have got her, I think, before she went down.' He looked accusingly at Barlow. 'I'm surprised you let her do that job. She wasn't up to it, you know.'

Barlow's jaw remained set. 'Shut up, and let's find them.' He turned his head away and lit a cigarette while he worked out which part of Murray's body would get the first bullet if he surfaced without Sophie.

Harris stared at him. 'What about Flynn?'

'Later.'

It took another fifteen minutes before they spotted Murray's arm waving at them. The life belt thrown by Harris had found its mark, and after several deep dives Murray had brought Sophie to the surface and enclosed her in it. Fortunately the water was warm. Wrapping himself around her with his arms and legs, he'd kept her head out of the water by resting it on his shoulder. She looked in a very bad way. Apart from the near miss by the Very cartridge that had seared the side of her head and the horrendous cracks she'd received from the *Charlotte*'s boom, she'd taken in a lot of sea water. She was unconscious, which was a blessing.

They brought her gently on board. Her arm was broken, and with it strapped temporarily to her side, they laid her on her face on an improvised stretcher and rocked her up and down until most of the water had been cleared. She was young, she was fit, and she was healthy. Within minutes she was spitting and spluttering. But Harris wasn't happy. He shot down into the cabin and returned within seconds. He had a small needle in his hand.

'What's that?' said Barlow suspiciously.

'She's in pain,' snapped Harris. 'This'll do the trick. It's a vial of morphine – morphine sulphate.'

'Hang on a second. D'you know what you're doing with that stuff?'

'Yes. So do you. It's only fifteen milligrams. It'll knock her out for a bit. She'll be as right as rain when she comes round. Let's get her below.'

Harris stuck the needle deftly into Sophie's arm, then picked her up gently and carried her into the main cabin. Barlow, with an awareness of having been there before, carefully stripped her and thoroughly dried her. Harris hovered in the background. There was a certain possessiveness about the way Barlow kept his body between Sophie and Harris's interested scrutiny. But this wasn't the time for jealousy, or the place. 'Can you do something with that arm, Burne?' he said over his shoulder.

'Sure, leave it up to me. Nice body!' he observed as he moved in close.

'Just do the bloody arm, Burney,' growled Barlow. 'And then wrap her up and make sure she doesn't roll around on that bunk. Can you manage that?'

'No probs. How about your mate up there?'

'Look after her. I don't want her up and about for several hours. Can you manage that?'

'I don't think we'll be seeing much of Sophie Ward for

quite some time. But we've got to get her to hospital, you know – and not too late.'

'Get on with it.'

'You OK, David?' asked Barlow when he came on deck.

Murray was sitting in the cockpit with a towel draped round his waist, a cigarette in one hand and a large glass of something that looked very much like Harris's best Cognac in the other.

'I've done sillier things,' responded Murray with a tight grin. 'Is she all right?'

'She'll live. Erm, David . . .'

'I wouldn't bother, Harry.'

'Thanks. I owe you one.'

'Sure.'

When Harris reappeared he wasted no time on small talk. 'She's OK. She's sleeping. What now, Harry?'

'Find Flynn and the boat again.'

With a nod as acknowledgement, Harris stroked the throttles and the cruiser hurtled westwards like a frightened horse. He left behind two huge crested mounds of churned water as a goodbye kiss.

The noise from the fully stretched engines made normal conversation impossible. Harris had to shout at the top of his voice to make himself heard.

'You've got options now. We can crawl up on him from behind, as we did last time, or we can carry on at this setting and take him at an angle. We can even approach him from the direction he's heading if you like. Any of those. He won't be expecting us. If you don't fancy those, we can sit back and wait until he beaches and roll him up on land. Take your pick.'

'What do you think he'll do?' Barlow asked.

'I reckon he's going to find himself a fairly uninhabited

spot, make a soft landing and take up a land route to wherever he's set his sights on. That's my opinion. For what it's worth. What do you think, David?'

Murray, perched on the stern deck, had changed into a pair of Harris's scruffy white shorts. He looked sceptical. Apart from his still-wet hair, he'd recovered from his dip in the ocean and a prolonged period of having his body wrapped protectively round a beautiful Australian female. It had been the nicest part of his day, so far. He drew heavily on a cigarette and met the eyes of the other two men. 'Don't expect the predictable from Flynn. Expect the worst. He's a mad dog, an intelligent one, but still a mad dog.'

'But you reckon he'll go for land,' insisted Harris, 'now that he knows we're behind him?'

'No question about it. But he'll kill those people on that boat the minute they stop being useful as hostages.' Murray had an unfailing ability never to mix facts with sentiment – or to credit people with feelings that were totally alien to their character. He knew Flynn's type. He was speaking from long experience. 'And that includes the children. The minute Flynn gets to within jumping distance of that bit of land you mentioned, the woman and her children'll be put on the short list. They're going to be a bit more than surplus to his requirements. That has crossed your mind, I suppose?'

Harris nodded gloomily. 'Funny you should bring that up. I was just trying to visualize the bastard stepping off the boat with a nod of thanks to the woman and a cheerful wave as she skates off to the nearest cop shop! Not on, is it? I don't fancy her chances...' He shook his head doubtfully and looked pointedly at Barlow. 'Not unless you're in the mood for another boarding party – and a sore head like the one your girlfriend got.'

Barlow pulled a face and moved across the cockpit to

stare critically at the radar screen. It stared back at him, dull, lifeless and flat. He patted it as if it were a friendly mongrel. After a moment, he touched Harris's arm.

'What sort of range does this thing have?'

'What've you got in mind?'

'Can we pinpoint the *Lady Charlotte* on it and follow from behind without being seen?'

Harris nodded enthusiastically. 'No problem. But I'd want to locate her first from a visual sighting – a quick look from a distance, then drop back out of sight and follow his trace. Did you notice that small dish at the top of her mast?'

'Can't say I did – why?'

'That was put there to give us a fix on the boat. Mr Clarke was taking no chances. He wanted to make sure everybody could see him coming – and going. If only the poor bugger knew . . .'

'OK, let's find the yacht and we'll take up your first option. We'll follow him in. What d'you want me to do?'

'Take first watch with the glasses. I'll put us on a course that'll intersect his path – assuming there's been no radical change of direction since we made our last sighting.' He throttled the engines down, reducing both speed and noise. It made conversation easier. 'I suggest you stand up there and look over the top of the screen. Shout if you see anything interesting.'

Barlow made another wide sweep of the horizon, lingered for quite some time on a spot on the port skyline, then lowered the binoculars and picked up his cigarettes. 'Here,' he said, 'have one of these, and then tell me what you make of that speck at eleven o'clock.'

Harris propped his elbows on the upper deck and stared intently for several minutes at the dot sitting on the horizon. Without lowering the glasses, he lit his cigarette, blew a long stream of smoke from the side of his mouth and said, 'That's the *Lady Charlotte*.' He drew on his cigarette again. 'I'd recognize her if she were surrounded by a thousand of the same class. No question about it. Smashing!' He put the glasses down with a satisfied grunt. 'Move over and let me get a fix on her, then we'll mark her on the radar and drop back out of sight again.'

The two Britons sat in silence and watched Harris at work. The young skipper seemed to be enjoying himself and whistled tunelessly as he straightened up and swung the cruiser's wheel with a series of go, go, stop, go, go, stop motions until, satisfied with the direction they were now heading, he slapped it with his hand and nodded to Barlow.

'Are you happy with that?'

'Happy doesn't come into it, mate,' answered Barlow. 'And if I knew what you were doing, the answer would be the same. I leave it in your hands. Don't lose the bloody thing.' He stood up and, drawing heavily on his cigarette, stared at the lively circle of activity on the small round screen. After a moment he looked at Harris, searching his face for signs of unease. 'I wish I had your faith in this thing.'

Harris shrugged his shoulders, as if he wasn't too sure about it himself but tried not to let it worry him. He stared at the screen.

'That dot there . . .' He leaned over and put his finger on a minute black speck. '. . . is the only one we're concerned with. We're coming round behind them now. If we go any closer, we'll be staring right up the *Lady Charlotte*'s arse – I don't think you want that, do you?'

'Burne, I've just said, it's in your hands.'

'OK, we'll cool our speed down to hers and trickle along at this distance, just out of sight. That should do the trick. We can stay like this until Flynn decides on the bit of Australia he fancies. Then we'll move in. Does that sound about right?'

Harris stopped at the top of the companionway and pointed to the radar screen. 'I'm going below for a minute. Don't worry about anything else, just concentrate on that trace. This boat'll sail herself. I sometimes think she prefers it that way.'

Barlow put his feet up, accepted a cigarette from Murray and stared at the green screen. After twenty minutes or so he allowed himself to be mesmerized by the constant darkening and lightening of the machine as it made its scan. With the somniferous throb of the boat's engines and the warm, comforting sun on his back, it quickly became an all-out struggle to prevent his eyelids from dropping to a more comfortable position. He was on the point of giving in when the trace moved.

It was as if somebody had squeezed the trigger of a .45 just behind his ear.

He shot up into a sitting position, put both hands round the screen to shade it, and narrowed his eyes to concentrate on the *Charlotte*'s position. He watched it for thirty seconds.

'David, come and look at this.'

Murray peered over Barlow's shoulder and for a few seconds followed the shape at the end of Barlow's finger.

'Notice anything?'

'Nope.'

'Give Harris a shout,' said Barlow without taking his eyes off *Charlotte*'s trace.

'Harris! Get up here. Quick!'

'What is it?' Harris was beside them before the echo had died. 'What's happening?'

'I think this thing's changed direction.'

Harris was unflappable. 'Interesting,' he murmured. 'Let's have a shufty.' He spread his arms across Murray's and Barlow's shoulders and lowered his head between them to study the small screen. It was only a cursory glance, but it told him everything he needed to know. He tapped Murray's shoulder and pointed to the companion-way.

'There's whisky, and a tray of stuff to eat at the bottom of the steps. Help yourself while I sort this out.' He moved across the cockpit to the helm and gave a lot more attention to the compass setting and the automatic controls, then picked up the binoculars and made a wide sweep of the area where the *Lady Charlotte* ought to have been. There was nothing to see, but it didn't seem to worry him. After another search, he put the binoculars to one side and sat down to concentrate on the small screen.

Barlow moved back to his earlier position, poured himself a large glass from the blue-labelled bottle and studied the back of Harris's head. It gave nothing away.

After a moment's staring at the screen, and two or three fractional adjustments to one of the control knobs, Harris said, without turning his head: 'He's been running as near to the coast as he dare without attracting too much attention. By the look of it she's been made to run parallel while he looks for a likely spot to put in.' He tapped the screen with his fingers. 'According to this, he was moving east at a distance of about two kilometres from the coast and now he's suddenly turned and is heading out to sea. Interesting. I wonder what he's up to?'

'Guess,' ordered Barlow.

Harris didn't give it too much thought. 'Didn't fancy any of that coastline, so he's going out to turn that headland and come in again and try another stretch. What'll he do then?' Harris asked and answered his own question. 'Go closer in and swim for it? Anchor, then dinghy his way in? Any good to you?'

'I didn't see a dinghy on the yacht,' said Barlow. 'Come to think of it, I didn't give it a bloody thought. At the time I had other things on my mind!' He buttered an untidy lump of bread, wrapped it round an inch-thick slice of Australian Cheddar and handed it, with a glass of whisky, to Harris. 'But there was a rubber dinghy with a serious outboard tied to the jetty where the yacht was moored. Must have been used by the Clarkes for fishing or something. Anyway, they came away without it. I don't suppose Flynn would have known any better.'

Harris bit into his bread and cheese, washed it down with a large sip of Johnny Walker's special, and said pensively, 'There was another one. A little one, no engine, but it'd have a couple of small oars. It was tied up tight on to one of the starboard cleats. It seemed to me at the time a strange thing to do for an experienced sailor. But when you think about it, there's been a lot of bloody funny things going on on that boat. Mrs Clarke probably didn't have time to ship it on board when she was rushed out of harbour this morning. But it's not important. What is important is that Flynn, whatever he decides, can't just leave the yacht riding on the edge of nowhere. He's got to tuck it out of the way somewhere.'

'We'll stay with him until he does.' Barlow stood up. 'I'm going down below to see how Sophie is. Give me a shout if anything changes.'

Harris took a large mouthful of sandwich and looked up when Barlow joined him and Murray on the settee. He glanced down at his watch. 'Look, Harry, it's an hour since the yacht changed course.' He swallowed. 'I'm not very happy . . .'

Barlow and Murray looked at each other. 'You've lost it,' said Murray accusingly.

'No-o,' said Harris unconvincingly, 'I'm just not happy about it. D'you want my advice?'

Barlow leaned forward and began to make a sandwich. He didn't look up from the tray.

'That's what we're paying you for!'

'I think we ought to pull the tit out and get within looking distance of the *Lady Charlotte*, just in case.'

'Just in case of what?'

Harris filled up his mouth again. 'Just in case. Leave it at that.'

'OK.' Barlow closed his two pieces of bread and looked up. 'I hope for your sake there's still something out there to look at.'

But Harris wasn't listening to him. He was staring at the radar, his last mouthful of sandwich bulging the sides of his cheeks as he frowned at the screen. He balanced his glass carefully on the shelf above the console and leant towards the screen, staring intently as his face got closer and closer.

Then Barlow noticed it too.

The *Lady Charlotte*'s trace was no longer there.

Harris turned his narrowed eyes to Barlow. 'It's gone,' he said in a voice muffled by the unchewed, forgotten sandwich. 'The bloody boat's vanished into thin air.'

Barlow continued sipping his whisky. 'Flynn's probably found himself a little hidy-hole.'

Harris shook his head. 'I don't think you're with me, Harry.' He flicked a switch and the screen filled with radial-distance features. He stuck his forefinger between the lines where the *Charlotte*'s trace had been. 'Look. The boat was six kilometres out to sea. The only thing that can vanish like that in the middle of nowhere is a bloody submarine!'

29

Flynn stared at the Victoria coast simmering in the distance and made up his mind.

He moved from where he was sitting at the stern of the boat and stood just behind Jayne Clarke at the helm. He held Sophie's Glock 17 automatic loosely at his side.

'Can this thing sail itself?' he asked.

She didn't look round. 'Yes.'

'Make it.'

'Why?'

'Just do as I bloody say!' He moved to the side of the cockpit. 'Take the sails down and switch the engine on, and when you've done that come over here.'

'Why?'

Flynn ignored her question but watched what she did. When she stood beside him, he said, 'Get up there, turn round and face the other way.'

Puzzled, she did as she was told. Swaying with the movement of the boat, she tried to look at him over her shoulder, but she almost unbalanced and only just stopped herself from falling.

'D'you mind telling me . . .' she began hesitantly.

He didn't allow her to finish. 'Patience, Mrs Clarke, patience, and all will be revealed!'

'I don't understand.'

'It seems that you and I have run out of topics of mutual interest. We're about to part company.'

'I still don't understand.'

'You will.' Flynn reached up and placed his hand in the small of her back. As soon as she felt it she understood and instinctively swayed backwards. But it was too late. And then it didn't matter. He thrust one hand between her legs and pulled her off balance whilst the other thumped her forward and she hurtled over the side and into the water.

He straightened up, looked over the stern and watched where her head broke the surface. She was already some distance from the boat and was floundering around, turning in his direction as she tried, ineffectually, to swim towards the boat. Flynn studied her progress for a few more minutes, then, with a final bored look at the orange blob, now some distance away, cursed himself for not removing her life jacket. But it was a big water, he consoled himself, and with the way her luck had been running, she'd float all the way to Fiji before anyone saw her.

The idea brought a little smile to his lips and he cocked his head as he turned away. He thought he heard a distant scream; his smile broadened.

But just as quickly it faded.

He eased the throttle forward until the engine was just ticking over and waited until she was barely making way. Then he set about sinking her.

He leaned over the side and studied the dinghy dancing skittishly in the boat's gentle wash. The tiny vessel, looking as frail and vulnerable as an old orange box, did nothing to reassure him. As an option it was pathetic – but he was becoming used to pathetic options.

He glanced across the cockpit at the companionway, then again at the floating orange box, and assessed its carrying capacity. One or both kids? He wasn't home yet; somebody was going to have to keep him shielded until the door closed behind him. But two queens were better than one ace – until the water slipped over the edge of the rowing boat with the weight, that was, and then one of them was going to have to get out and learn how to swim. He'd start with two.

He walked across the cockpit and kicked the companionway door open.

'Come on up here, you two!' he bellowed. 'And make it bloody snappy or I'll send you down with the boat.' He didn't wait for them to surface.

He lifted the engine-room hatch and dropped down on to the floorboards. He prised up one of the boards and attacked the keel with an axe. It needed half-a-dozen strokes to produce a small hole, and as he watched, a steady rush of clear sea water gushed busily out of the hole and began to fill the bilges below the engine-room floor.

Climbing back up to the deck, he shielded his eyes with his hand and studied the hazy coastline shimmering in the distance on the boat's port side. His face was expressionless as he turned and gazed seaward, but then he frowned, went to the wheel and stared hard at the autopilot mechanism clicking ominously as it maintained the course Jayne had set for it. How the fuck did she do it? He swore aloud and moved his finger to within an inch of the block with the two arrowed buttons, one arrow pointing to the right, the other to the left. 'I hope the fuckin' thing doesn't self-destruct!' He placed his finger gingerly on the right-hand button and pressed. Nothing happened. He pressed again. The belt on the wheel tightened, there was a frightening click, and with a whirl the wheel responded to the first press and the bows came round. He watched fascinated, as it responded to the second and the yacht settled on its new course. He pressed again. The bows turned another ten degrees. He kept pressing until the *Lady Charlotte*, sluggish with the lack of headway, was pointing directly out to sea. With a final glance at the magic of the autopilot, he left the wheel and looked over the side again at the dinghy. The closer he inspected the tiny craft the less he liked it. His doubts affected his voice.

'Get in, you two,' he snapped, without turning round. 'And sit yourselves at the –'

There was a hollow sound about him; he had the feeling he was talking to himself. He stopped and looked over his shoulder. He *was* talking to himself. There were no children on deck.

'CHRIST AL-BLOODY-MIGHTY!' he shouted at the top of his voice.

There was no response.

'Where the fuck are you, you stupid bitches?'

Without moving from the dinghy, he leaned backwards and, peering down the companionway, found himself staring into the faces of the two terrified children cowering halfway up the steps.

'And just what the fuckin' hell d'you two think you're doing?' he exploded. 'You stupid little bitches, get your bloody arses up here now or I'll close this door and send you down with the fuckin' boat!' Flynn's anger, bubbling near the top of the glass, was fuelled by his unfamiliarity with the sea and a rapidly rising, bladder-straining urge to get off this sinking coffin and into the uncertain security of the insubstantial dinghy. Insubstantial dinghies were more secure than sinking yachts. 'I'm not waiting any bloody longer. Come on, you little fuckers. Out!'

'Where's Mummy?' one of them managed, wild-eyed with fear.

'Sod your bloody mummy! Come on, quick!' Flynn softened his approach; he knew how they felt. He was afraid too. 'Come on, you'll be all right in the little boat.

We're going to the seaside.' He raised his voice for the last time. 'But for Christ's sake hurry up, I'm not waiting any longer!'

He moved away from the top of the stairs and looked round the deck. The *Lady Charlotte* already seemed to be listing slightly. He opened the throttle halfway and scuttled towards the dinghy, gingerly lowering himself into it.

Suddenly, the *Lady Charlotte* lurched unhappily.

It seemed to be a message the children understood.

With a terrified scream and a scampering of feet on the ladder, the two girls emerged from the hatchway like two little corks from a bottle. In their unsophisticated minds the lesser of the two evils had to be human. They'd learn differently when they grew up.

'Come here, bugger you! Quickly! Get in before the bloody thing pulls us with it.'

'What about Mummy?'

Fu —' began Flynn again, but decided it wasn't going to help. 'Never mind about her, come here.' He stepped reluctantly out of the dinghy and balanced himself on the now sloping deck. He kept the dinghy's painter securely in one hand while he lifted first one girl, then the other into the small tender. He nearly turned it over in his anxiety to get back in, but steadied it, and without another word, or thought, unshipped the oars and rowed towards the coastline.

After pulling some two hundred yards, he rested the oars and blew on to his already sore palms. He sat and watched without emotion as the elegant yacht, now some distance away, sluggishly pulled herself to where, desecrated and abandoned, she could slip discreetly below the white-crested ridges of the sea.

30

Harris looked up from the radar set, his eyes blinking with the effort of studying the flickering screen.

'Vanished into thin air!' he said in a loud whisper.

Barlow put his glass back on the tray and leaned forward. 'What d'you mean, vanished? Things don't just vanish. This is the Tasman Sea, not the bloody Bermuda Triangle.' He stared at the screen, then at Harris. Harris stared back, his mouth still bulging with sandwich. He shook his head slowly, but said nothing.

'So what are you going to do about it?' demanded Barlow.

Harris hunched his shoulders and swallowed the remains of his mouthful of sandwich. 'Go and have a look. He's either hit something or, for reasons best known to himself, pulled the plug out and sunk the bloody thing!' He stopped talking and opened the throttle. 'Take the binoculars,' he shouted. 'And keep your eyes on the water in that direction.' He waved his hand straight ahead. He looked like something out of a silent movie, his eyes rolling and his mouth opening and shutting, but the words ending up fifty yards in the stern. He was used to it and pitched his voice higher, but he still managed only a poor second against the crash of spray that splattered thunderously against the smoked-glass windscreen.

'What am I looking for?' shouted Barlow.

'Anything! Debris, people . . . People mainly. But if he's

put the boat down deliberately, I'm prepared to bet a pig's arse to Madonna's left tit he's sent the woman and the kids down with it.' He glanced at Barlow out of the corner of his eye. 'Let's assume he's done that, sunk the boat, thrown the surplus cargo overboard, and is now rowing for a strip of sand.'

Barlow continued staring ahead. He said nothing.

'The nearest strip to where that dot flicked out.' Harris slowed the launch and engaged the autopilot.

Murray, lying flat out on the soft bench, the top part of his face covered by a damp towel, said, without moving: 'D'you think that sudden right turn they took an hour ago has any significance?' He raised his head and lifted the towel, and with his hand shielding them, wrinkled his eyes in Harris's direction. 'Maybe that was just a little manoeuvre for us. I told you Flynn was nobody's bloody idiot. Maybe he got off there, pulled the plug out and sent the boat on its way on auto, inviting us to do exactly what we're doing – follow the bloody thing until it sinks?'

'What would he do with the woman and kids?' asked Barlow. He didn't know why he bothered. He knew as well as Murray what Flynn would do with anybody threatening to hold him up.

'Kill 'em.' Murray had been in the game too long to mince words. He raised himself up, lit a cigarette and, resting his elbows on the back cushions, stared at the frothy wake behind them.

'Harris?' Barlow stared at the bearded skipper.

Harris met his gaze steadily. 'I have to agree with David. I'm setting a new course for the earlier sighting, then I'm going to draw some lines, check some figures and come up with the shortest and quickest line an inexperienced rower in a toy dinghy would take to touch a bit of Australian rock.' He took a large swig from his glass, then ducked out of sight, leaving Barlow and Murray to stare helplessly at the Victoria mainland, now only visible on the distant skyline as a long black line of paint on a half-finished canvas.

Murray leaned back as he sipped from a half-filled glass of Johnny Walker's finest and gazed moodily at the engine's backwash. This was boring. He'd rather have been somewhere else, like peering over the wall into a Republican back garden in Ballymurphy. Anywhere there wasn't more than a gallon of water. After a moment he changed his position, sipped another mouthful from the glass and stopped. He stared, then stood up.

'What d'you think that is, Harry?' He pointed over the launch's swirling wash.

Barlow turned and followed the direction of his finger. He looked, but saw nothing. 'What's what?'

'A long way back there. Something orange. I can't see it now. Come up here and look.'

'Just a minute . . . HARRIS!' Barlow lowered his head into the companionway.

'What is it?' Harris appeared at the foot of the stairs with a pencil stuck between his teeth. He looked like a dog with a troublesome bone. His eyes crinkled into slits as he looked up out of the shaded cabin and into the sun. 'What is it now?' He grimaced as if in pain.

'How do I slow this thing down and turn her round?'

'You don't, I do. Why?'

'Murray thinks he saw something in the water.'

Harris bounded up the steps and nudged Barlow to one side. He took the helm and whirled the wheel round in a series of spins and stops until, without having reduced speed, they were facing the direction from which they'd just come.

'Take the glasses and go up there,' he said.

But Barlow was already clambering up to the fly-bridge.

'Slow down,' he shouted as he tried to focus on the choppy water ahead.

'OK!' bellowed Harris. 'But I'm in your hands. I can't see a bloody thing except water down here. Tell me where you want to go.'

Barlow waved an acknowledgement, then lowered the glasses and turned his head. 'Don't get too enthusiastic, Harris. He's probably seen an ice-cream wrapper floating in the water!'

'Very funny, Harry.' Murray continued staring from under his hand. 'There it is again,' he said calmly. 'Orange, like a life jacket, two o'clock, about four hundred yards.'

Barlow brought the glasses up again.

'Got it. You were right, David. Sorry! It is – and there's someone in it.' He raised his voice. 'Burney! Slow down, you're right on course. There's someone floating around, dead ahead. Can you see it?'

Harris leaned to one side of the cockpit and stared at the water as he eased the throttles to dead slow.

'What've you got?' he asked. But he knew what they'd got. 'The woman from the yacht?'

Neither Murray nor Barlow acknowledged him. He tried again. 'Is she on her own?' He put the engine into neutral and moved up front, where he stood watching Murray and Barlow.

They were closing rapidly on her now. Harris waited another second, then thrust the gear into reverse as Barlow stretched over the gunwale and put both hands under Jayne Clarke's armpits. With Murray grasping her by the waist and legs, they lifted her easily on to the boat.

She looked dead but the instant her back touched the solid deck her eyes shot open. She stared straight into Barlow's face. recognition was instantaneous.

'You're the im-immigration p-p-people?' she stuttered through cold wet lips. 'The ones who s-s-stopped us . . .'

342

Barlow nodded briefly.

'The twins?' she whispered hoarsely. It was all she could manage before she was violently sick over the deck.

She recovered briefly. 'My children?' she hiccuped. Nobody replied. She tried again. 'Are my daughters still with that animal?'

Murray and Harris exchanged glances before Murray, with a grimace at Barlow, darted below in search of towels and blankets.

But Barlow had no such reservations. He put his arms round her and held her in a sitting position while he began removing her life jacket. 'We don't know, Mrs Clarke. I'm sorry. The only thing I can say is, if he didn't throw them over the side with you they're still with him – hopefully.' His face was set and his voice harsh with sympathy and concern. The anger he'd felt for the part she'd played in Sophie's last act had long since worked itself out of his system. But it didn't sound sympathetic enough to Mrs Clarke.

The little touch of colour that had returned to her cheeks vanished. 'Why, you callous bastard!' she hissed.

Barlow shook his head sadly. He understood. She must be suffering seven kinds of hell – but someone had to do it. 'Please tell me what happened to Flynn and the boat,' he asked her gently.

'What about my children?' Her voice was getting stronger. She'd stopped coughing and spitting up salt water and was full of aggression and anger for the man standing before her. It had to be somebody; Barlow would do until she caught up with Flynn.

'Mrs Clarke,' insisted Barlow, 'can we talk about your children later? At the moment we don't know what's happened to them. Tell us about the boat. Did he sink it?'

She struggled free of Barlow's arm, stood up and accepted a towel and blanket from Murray. She wiped her face with the towel and tried to say something but nothing came; instead she closed her eyes and retched silently. It must have done some good. 'I don't know what he's done. He threw me over the side and that was the last I saw of him or the boat.'

'OK, Mrs Clarke, go down below and get some rest. We're going to do everything we can, but first tell him,' he pointed to Harris, who had returned to his place at the helm, 'what you think Flynn's intentions are and exactly where your boat was when you left it.'

'After you've told me about my husband.'

'Your husband's dead. I'm sorry. He managed to get ashore. He was the one who told us what had happened to you.'

It was confirmation of something she'd already prepared herself for. She didn't cry, she didn't faint, she didn't have hysterics. She stared hard at Barlow, and then disappeared below.

Harris moved to follow her but was stopped by Barlow. Murray had lost interest. He was back in his earlier position, gazing once more over the stern. There was not enough action here, it was making him nervous.

'Forget her,' Barlow told Harris. 'How far do *you* reckon we are from where that boat changed course?'

Harris waved his glass in a ninety-degree sweep. 'Anywhere around there. But I think the important factor to consider at the moment is that.' He directed his glass at the coastline, still hazy but now quite prominent. 'Flynn's had a good, favourable tide, and we've wasted a lot of time buggering around. With all our going back and forth and God knows what, we've allowed him to disappear. He could be anywhere.' Harris looked hard at the distant coastline again as he lowered the level of whisky in his glass by a good half-inch. 'He could be anywhere in a ten-kilometre strip from there to there.' He ticked off two points with his finger. 'We'll just have to look for the most likely spot. But it won't have been easy for him. His hands'll be blistered to hell'.

'Well, that's something.'

'He'll also be tired. All he'll want to do is lie down. And then, of course, he won't want to move around till night-time, so once we've located his hole –'

'But he'll see us coming.'

Harris shook his head and sipped from his glass. 'We'll have to take that chance.'

Barlow didn't reply, he was scrutinizing the chart laid out on the table. 'Can you find me on this a deserted little cove, or an inlet, that might have caught Flynn's eye?'

'This coast is full of 'em, Harry, it's going to be impossible to choose one from another.'

'Not to me it won't.' Jayne Clarke entered the conversation from the top of the companionway. 'I know this stretch of coast,' she said. Her voice was clear and firm. She'd recovered quickly. 'Roger and I have been exploring it for the last six months. If there's anything likely to hide a dinghy full of children, I'll find it for you. Have you got any more binoculars?'

'Help yourself.' Harris pointed to one of the lockers. 'How close d'you want me to go?'

She looked at the coastline for a few seconds, then said, 'About a kilometre.'

'There's something you haven't been told, Mrs Clarke,' said Barlow as Harris adjusted their course.

She stared hard. 'If it's about the boat disappearing, don't bother, I already know.'

Barlow shrugged his shoulders but she gave him barely a glance. Harris pointed his finger at the coastline, then slowly moved it to the right. 'Give or take a kilometre or two, I think we'll find him somewhere in there.'

Jayne nodded in agreement. 'Keep on this course.' She

continued to stare straight ahead. 'And sail slowly against the tide. I'll tell you what I'm looking for when I see it.'

Some time later, Jayne Clarke put down her glasses, moved behind Harris and pointed her arm over his shoulder. He sighted along it. 'That promontory,' she said.

'At ten o'clock,' he murmured. 'Got it.'

'Go round it, and follow the line of coast as it goes.'

'What exactly is it you're looking for?'

'Something that fits the description you made earlier. I've just remembered it – it's perfect.'

'A secluded cove?'

'Better! About half a mile round this headland there's a shallow inlet. A mile beyond that is a narrow channel that runs into a creek. This current . . .' – she waved her hand in an arc – '. . . would drag the dinghy right past the inlet.'

'Does the creek go anywhere?' Barlow joined in the conversation. He picked up his glasses again and followed the line she'd indicated.

'Yes. There's a small silted-up harbour with a concrete jetty and a couple of derelict Nissen huts – leftovers from the war. We checked it out. It appears the navy kept some sort of radar installation there. When the war ended they took everything away except the huts – they left those to rust and become an eyesore. It's not really a harbour, it's nothing more than a muddy estuary –' She stopped before completing the description and pointed over Harris's shoulder again. 'There!' she snapped. 'It's coming up now. D'you see what I mean?'

Barlow raised his glasses again. It didn't take long.

'Got it! Harris?'

Harris nodded.

'Carry on round this next bit of headland and tuck us out of sight of that big tree we're going past now.'

'Right!'

'And don't do anything obvious.' Barlow pointed to the heavy-duty inflated dinghy lashed below the transom. 'When you've anchored, get that thing in the water, cut your engines and don't make a sound until we get back.'

'D'you want me to come?' Murray stood up lazily and flexed his arms, but he wasn't pushing himself. He'd followed the conversation, he knew what was coming next – or what ought to come next.

Barlow exchanged glances with him; it was all that was necessary. Murray slipped below. When he returned he was wearing a pair of Harris's frayed navy jeans and battered canvas deck shoes. His shirt, hanging outside the jeans, barely concealed the bulge of a .45 Colt automatic snuggled in the small of his back.

'Mrs Clarke knows the place,' said Barlow, and stared at Jayne. 'Unless you'd rather just Murray and I . . .?'

She shook her head. 'I would have insisted.'

With the outboard barely ticking, the dinghy slipped past the inlet. There was nothing to see through the overhanging branches, but the flow of water from the inlet was obvious. Flynn would have been drawn to it like a magnet if he'd reached this far. Jayne was convinced he had.

They hid the rubber inflatable in amongst the undergrowth and covered it with broken branches.

'David, there's no point all three of us barging around the place. I'll go with Jayne – she knows the place. If there's any trace of him, she'll come back for you. If you hear shooting, you know what to do.'

Jayne stared in horror at the large Colt that had appeared in Murray's hand. To him it was a natural appendage when trouble was in the air; to Jayne it posed a threat.

'That thing . . .' she said, glaring at Murray's hand. 'I

347

hope you two haven't forgotten that man has my children with him?'

Murray ignored her. He glanced at Barlow, raised his eyebrows slightly and moved silently into the undergrowth.

'Don't worry,' Barlow assured her. 'If the children are here, we'll bring them out safely – you have my word.' And then he had a vivid recollection of this same woman throwing herself across the deck of the *Lady Charlotte*, and, even more vividly, of Sophie with a red ball of flame searing towards her face. This woman's fault. His jaw hardened. 'But if anything happens, please don't get in the way,' he finished lamely. She had a good idea what he meant but made no reply. 'Come on,' he said in a whisper.

A few hundred yards inland, Jayne pointed out an overgrown concrete road. 'This is part of the system that used to serve the base. It runs straight up to the empty Nissen huts. We can either walk up it and take a chance that there's nobody there, or use it as a guide and crawl through the undergrowth.'

'Let's be daring,' whispered Barlow, and eased the S&W from his waistband. 'But no noise. Don't talk unless I say.'

Jayne stared at the revolver in the same way she'd stared at Murray's Colt. She looked more concerned than she'd been with him. 'D'you think . . .?' she began.

Barlow shook his head. He'd had enough of Mrs Clarke's gun phobia. He placed his finger on her lips. 'Shhh!'

When they reached the fringe of the harbour they left the road and cut through the undergrowth to the edge of the muddy pool. Jayne was right – it wasn't much like a harbour.

Barlow crouched and pulled her down beside him.

There was nothing but a fringe of thin seedlings and high grass between him and the abandoned base.

The two Nissen huts were both in the last stages of dereliction; their doors hung drunkenly on rusted hinges, half open and at different angles and most of the wire-reinforced glass panes that made up their top half had jagged holes in them, as if something on an orgy of destruction had been to work with a fifteen-pound hammer.

Jayne touched his arm lightly.

'He's not here,' she whispered.

'Did you expect to see him sitting on the patio in a deck chair?'

'I can't hear anything either. Just a minute!' She sucked in breath and gripped his arm. 'Look at that!'

Barlow turned his head slowly.

She was pointing to a length of light varnished elm – a short oar – caught up in the undergrowth and swaying gently in time with the barely moving flow.

'What about it?' he mouthed.

'It's one of the oars from my boat's tender.'

He looked again at the piece of wood. 'Are you sure?'

She nodded emphatically. 'And I can reach it. Give me your hand.'

Barlow hung on to her, at the same time staring with renewed interest at the two huts standing side by side some twenty yards across open ground. If that oar was from Jayne's boat, Flynn was here. In one of those two? Probably. But which? He glanced down at the piece of wood in her hand. 'Is that thing what you thought it was?'

She wrinkled her nose and pointed to the name *Lady Charlotte* branded into the wood. 'He must have sunk the dinghy,' she whispered, 'and neglected to secure the oars.'

'OK,' said Barlow, 'so at least we know now he's been here. He could have moved on, but I don't want to take chances. I'm going to have a quick look at the inside of those two huts. Stay here, out of sight, and don't interfere.'

'What d'you mean?'

Barlow tried a kindly smile. It didn't really work. 'If you hear or see anything out of the ordinary, no matter what it is, get out quickly, and go for Murray, then bring him back here. D'you understand that? Don't do anything, just go for him.'

She didn't have time to respond. He was gone.

It took ten minutes' crawling through the wood to circumnavigate the old harbour area and arrive at the rear of the first hut.

It was empty.

Retracing his steps, he entered the cover of the undergrowth again. From its protection he measured the distance of open ground between the two prefabs. It wasn't reassuring. There was no cover, just bare gravel-type soil, noisy stuff, and about twenty feet of it. And all the time the question thumped him between the eyes: did Flynn have Sophie's gun or only the Very pistol? It wasn't going to be long before he found out . . .

He wasted no more time on speculation. He took a deep breath, and at a crouch darted across the gap. Nothing. Just a deathly silence. He threw himself the last few feet and rolled into a position below the first window at the rear of the hut. He raised himself quickly into a crouching position with his back to the wall and the S&W pointing to the sky, ready for a shot to the right or left. He counted to ten, slowly. There was no reaction, no movement, no noise. It was like a cemetery.

He eased away from the wall and inspected the window. He could have bet money on it. It was the only one in the camp with a perfect set of unbroken panes. He moved cautiously towards the front of the building. The next window along was a gem – all but one of the panes were cracked or holed.

He chose the lower right-hand corner. It was a big hole and allowed him a clear view from one end of the interior to the other.

Barlow stared through the broken glass. He saw them immediately – two bright-orange-coloured bundles huddled in the right-hand corner by the door. He swept his eyes over the debris in the centre of the concrete floor – it was just debris – then on to the end of the hut. Nothing there. Then he came back to where he'd started and did it all over again.

It was obvious by the dust and cobwebs that the place had not been disturbed for years. There was no sign of Flynn. Barlow looked away from the hole and inspected his surroundings again. Flynn had been there. He was probably still there. But where the bloody hell was he?

He shook his head to displace the globules of sweat that had collected round his eyes and ran the back of his hand quickly across his forehead. Then he returned to the hole in the glass.

This time he stayed a fraction longer on the bundles in the corner, allowing his eyes to adjust to the darker area, but no matter how hard he looked, he couldn't bring them to life. There was no movement, nothing. Mrs Clarke's twins were there all right, both of them, but if they weren't dead, they were doing very well with the imitation. He left the window and moved soundlessly towards the front of the hut.

It was still deathly quiet. He eased his head round the corner of the building to survey the front end of the hut, and then the overgrown vegetation on the far side of the compound. It was quite clear. There was still no sound. And still no movement.

351

He edged the rest of his body round the corner and noiselessly covered the few feet to the half-open door. He paused for a fraction of a second, a final look at the surroundings, then stepped quickly through the doorway into the cool, musty-smelling Nissen.

He held the revolver loosely at his side as he took the few steps to the huddled figures. He looked down and gently touched the nearest of them with the toe of his shoe.

The small heads were resting on the orange life jackets, and as he looked closer, he could see that one of the children was sleeping – or appeared to be. Her eyes were firmly closed, clenched in fear, or tiredness – or death. The other twin, the one he'd touched with his foot, lay frighteningly still. But her eyes were wide open and she watched him, silent and staring and unmoving – even when he bent down towards her.

'Don't be afraid,' he whispered. 'I've come to take you home.'

The brown eyes regarded him gravely. She could have been a long-haired doll, the sort that blink on command, and that was the only thing she did – she blinked, as if to confirm she was alive. But nothing else, no acknowledgement, no gleam of happiness or joy in the blank eyes. He might just as well not have spoken.

He tried again.

'Where is the man? Has he gone away?'

She looked beyond him – and her eyes snapped shut.

'No. He's right behind you, with a gun pointing at the back of your head.'

Flynn's cool, unemotional voice, whispered from the doorway, had the right effect.

Barlow froze solid, like a snowman in midwinter, but he couldn't stop the instinctive tightening of his grip on the revolver. The flat Irish voice spoke again.

'Don't do it! You'd be dead before you were halfway round.' Flynn kept the tone conversational. 'Put the gun down gently on the floor and kick it away.'

Barlow ran the instruction quickly through his mind. It wasn't a bluff. Or was it? Flynn had to be armed, but with what? He conjured a quick mental picture of Sophie hurtling over the end of the yacht, the blast of a Very pistol . . . What would it do to the back of a man's head at this range? Flynn wouldn't want the S&W kicked away if he was bluffing. He'd want it placed where he could pick it up quickly without moving. *Come on, Barlow, make up your mind. Take a chance or not?* Barlow flicked his eyes to the right. A quick dive and an underarm shot as he landed? Better than having your head taken off by a flaming ball.

Flynn read his thoughts.

'You've only got the two choices: drop the gun – or die.' The lazy inflection in his voice changed with a sharp note of impatience. 'Be quick, mister! Make your choice.'

Barlow remained crouched over the child. Her eyes were open again, staring at him, blank and unblinking, like a china doll with its eyes jammed open. He made his choice and lowered the revolver the few remaining inches to the concrete floor. He left it there and took his hand away slowly.

'Now kick it away, hard, down to the end of the hut.'

Barlow stood up slowly and stroked the weapon with the inside of his shoe. It slid heavily and solidly across the dusty floor, raising a small cloud of white powder before it clunked against a broken breeze block halfway down the room. There was nothing more to be done, except regret the ease with which Flynn had picked him off, and wait for the bullet.

Flynn sounded relaxed. He allowed himself a little patronage. 'I like a man who behaves as well as you do.

Let's see if you can keep it up, eh? Now, for your next trick I want you to stand perfectly straight – slowly now, very slowly – and put your hands out wide, just like the Man on the Cross. That's it. You've done this before, haven't you? It's all right, don't bother answering or moving anything. OK. Now bring your hands together on top of your head. All right. Stand still. Don't move.'

Barlow did exactly as he was told. He caught the little girl's eye as he straightened up; she closed both hers quickly, as if she'd been caught doing something wrong, and then Flynn's voice cut through the tension again.

'Don't move any more than that or I'll blow your spine apart.' The voice was fractionally closer and Barlow felt a hand run lightly over his back and legs.

The handful of spare .38 rounds from his back pocket hit the concrete with a rattle and scattered across the dusty floor. Next, the hand came round the front and removed the packet of Rothmans. This also went flying across the room.

'You can turn round now,' invited Flynn. 'No, no! Don't be silly! Keep your hands where they are. OK, turn yourself round – that's it! Stand still!'

Barlow entwined his fingers on the top of his head and turned slowly. Sophie Ward's grey Glock automatic, held rock steady in two cloth-wrapped hands, pointed unwaveringly at his midriff.

'Well, well, well!' Recognition brought a gleam to Flynn's lacklustre eyes and he actually smiled as he looked Barlow up and down. 'You're a persistent bastard, I'll say that for you. And you've gotta be Brit. You couldn't be any-fuckin'-thing else! What are you?' He studied Barlow, and waited. He didn't expect a reply. He didn't get one. He grinned humourlessly. He knew bloody well what Barlow was; and Barlow was already a dead man. But curiosity first. 'I might ask in a minute how you found me here.'

Barlow stared back, po-faced.

'I'll ask you again, who are you?' Flynn stared hard into Barlow's face. 'You've got ten seconds to answer.'

Barlow still held his silence. He gazed directly into Flynn's eyes and willed himself not to look over the Irishman's shoulder, not to take his eyes away, not even for a blink, for outside in the sun-drenched harbour things were happening.

From the corner of his eye as he stared at Flynn, Barlow could see, to his horror, Jayne tripping across the open ground on her tiptoes. Clutched in her hands, outstretched like a rifle and bayonet, was the totally unwarlike wooden oar she had dredged from the harbour.

For Christ's sake, you stupid bloody woman! Go and get Murray! Put that fucking piece of wood down and go and get fucking Murray!

And still she came.

Flynn searched Barlow's face with suspicious eyes. Something wasn't quite right about this man, his blank and lifeless stare was having a disturbing effect. How about a bullet in the knee? That should wake him up and start his tongue wagging. Flynn took half a step backwards and lowered the Glock until it pointed at the lower part of Barlow's stomach. Ignoring the pistol, Barlow continued to gaze stolidly into Flynn's face. Flynn frowned. This wasn't making sense. His finger tightened on the trigger.

She hesitated – second thoughts – almost stopped, then hunched her shoulders and moved forward again.

Stupid bloody woman!

Do something, Barlow.

He timed his moment carefully – and crucially – and began to answer Flynn's questions noisily and rapidly. This was more like it! Flynn relaxed. But not his finger.

That remained delicately caressing the Glock's hair trigger.

It wasn't lost on Barlow. He dropped his gaze from Flynn's eyes as Jayne approached the open door and blocked out the light.

And still Flynn didn't turn.

Barlow blinked quickly at Flynn's whitened forefinger and braced himself for the bullet that was going to splatter its way through his stomach if Jayne lost her nerve at the last minute. And even if she went all the way – *Go on, Jayne, be a sport!* – there was no guarantee what Flynn's finger was going to do when he felt an oar scrape up and down his backbone.

Barlow continued talking rapid nonsense into Flynn's increasingly suspicious eyes. *For Christ's sake, Jayne, come on. Hurry up! And don't forget – it's a lump of bloody wood, not a feather duster. Hit the bastard! You hate him! Hit the bastard's head off his shoulders. You've only got one chance – so have I – and you can't see where that bloody gun's pointed. But I can!*

Barlow's jaw locked with the strain.

The message was passed. She didn't falter.

She came hurtling through the open door – and slipped on the loose gravel lying just in front of the entrance. It helped. It added the extra impetus to carry her forward at speed, and as she stumbled and lost her balance, the sharp wooden edge of the oar's blade, instead of landing, as Barlow had feared, like a feather duster on Flynn's head, took him squarely between the shoulder blades.

The roar of the explosion from the Glock 17 echoed round the metal-constructed building like a salvo from a battleship. But there was no target for it. The bullet missed Barlow by half an inch, bounced off the concrete floor and tore through the rusty arched roof. And then came another, and another, all bouncing harmlessly through the thin-skinned walls as Flynn jerked the trigger again and again, trying to regain his balance. But he lost his tightrope act. He was on his way down, and as he hurtled past, out of control, Barlow caught him a glancing blow with the edge of his hand. It was badly timed. It did no damage. Flynn barely felt it as he crashed to his knees with a bellow of pain.

He wasn't disabled.

Shocked and numbed by the attack, it slowed him down for only the briefest of seconds. When he hit the concrete floor, the sharp jolt, instead of crippling him, cleared the confusion from his brain. Just in time, he managed to drag himself out of the way as Barlow landed beside him in a flying leap.

Barlow crunched into the rough, ridged concrete floor on his elbows and felt the skin grate off his arm. But he recovered immediately and threw himself forward, clamping Flynn's outstretched hand and the firmly held Glock to the floor. But Flynn wasn't finished. He squeezed the trigger again. Another ear-shattering explosion and another bullet skidded harmlessly across the floor and punched its way through the wall to lose itself amongst the trees outside.

Still Flynn hung on, his finger wrapped round the trigger as he tried to squirm from underneath. Another shot rang out, but before he could fire again, Barlow thumped his knee into the base of Flynn's spine, pressed down hard on his fist with one hand and pulled on his wrist, backwards and forwards over the rough-finished concrete. Flynn bellowed in pain. It was like grating nutmeg over rice pudding. The skin of Flynn's knuckles, tight as they would go round the butt of the Glock, disappeared with the first scrape.

Flynn's screams reverberated around the room.

The second and third scrapes dragged off the rag serving as a temporary bandage for his blistered palm, and with it came the rest of the skin from the back of his hand and fingers. But still he refused to let go. He was hanging on to the Glock from memory. Barlow gritted his teeth and pulled again. There was nothing left. The exposed bones of Flynn's knuckles and fingers rasped on the floor. Flynn's screams were becoming maniacal when, just as another thunderous shot rang out, Barlow caught a flash of movement over his shoulder and a pair of rope-soled shoes moved towards his head.

The feet danced round, in and out of his vision, tripping and balancing like somebody learning the steps of a complicated *pas de chat*. The dance seemed to go on for ever. Then it stopped, the dancer's feet wide apart, and he felt a rush of displaced air and winced as, with a sickening crunch and the sound of splintering wood, Jayne's oar whistled past his ear and thumped into the back of Flynn's head.

Flynn grunted and went still.

Immediately there followed another rush of air and another jarring crack. Flynn stopped struggling, and the bloody hand, with Barlow's fingernails embedded into the wrist, went limp and died.

Without moving, Barlow stared at the back of Flynn's head. It was at a funny angle. A steady stream of thick blood poured freely down the side of his face from a nasty gash above his ear. Another, older gash had shed its plaster and joined in the flow of blood. Flynn looked dead. Barlow leaned closer and, turning the bleeding head to one side, studied the little bubbles of air appearing in the stream of blood now coursing freely just below Flynn's nose. Flynn's luck was still holding, he was still breathing. But that was all.

Barlow rolled on to his back and looked up at Jayne.

She stood above him, legs apart, her damp hair drooping over her eyes and her mouth wide open. Her breasts rose and fell with exertion, and she gulped in air as if it were liquid. Her arm hung limply at her side, and in her hand, held loosely like a tennis racket, was a two-foot length of varnished oar. The bottom of it was jaggedly splintered where it had snapped across Flynn's head, twice.

Barlow looked up into her eyes and tried a smile. It didn't work.

'Thanks!' he rasped.

'I wonder why you get all the fun, Harry?'

Murray's voice sounded hurt. Leaning against the doorframe, he held the Colt casually in one hand whilst he lit two cigarettes with the other. He'd run fast and furiously from the beach and headlong up the concrete track just in time to see Jayne deliver the final blow. But he looked cool and collected. For Murray it could have been an afternoon stroll. He glanced at Jayne with a small, approving nod of his head as he entered the hut and placed one of the cigarettes between Barlow's lips. He looked at the crumpled heap behind Barlow and, with the hint of a smile, studied Flynn's battered face. 'You haven't left much for me,' he remarked after a prolonged study. He could have been referring to a bowl of tapioca pudding.

31

Barlow watched Murray steer the cruiser's dinghy loaded with Jayne Clarke and her children until it turned the headland, then went back to the Nissen hut. He untied Flynn's bonds, stripped him down to his underpants, then tied him up again, hands to feet, picked him up bodily and threw him on to his face. Flynn was still feeling nothing. The pain would come in a few minutes, when he woke up. Barlow studied the figure for a few moments before making himself comfortable in the shade by the door. He lit another cigarette and smoked while he went through the tattered remains of Flynn's clothes.

It was the jacket that held most interest and it didn't take much searching to feel the packet through the lining. He knew what it contained before he worked it through the torn lining and stripped it from its outer plastic wrapping. The 3.5 diskette and the C90 cassette were in remarkably good condition considering the punishment they had taken, but he didn't linger over them; that he'd found them was sufficient. He rewrapped them and worked them back in the lining before throwing the coat over Flynn's head.

Flynn was still twitching in his sleep when Murray reappeared at the door. He dropped a bundle on the floor and kicked it in the direction of Flynn's body. 'Bedding. What the bloody hell are you going to do, tuck him up and let him sleep it off?'

'Shhh!' Barlow put his finger to his lips, then stood up and touched Flynn's recumbent body with his foot. There was no groan or grunt. He was still out. Barlow motioned for Murray to follow him outside. 'I want to bundle him up so that he can't see what's going on. We're going to play games with Fergal, David, but he mustn't see the blokes who're playing with him. Not yet.'

Murray shook his head. 'You've lost me, Harry.'

'Sit down over there, David, light yourself a fag, and listen. As soon as he wakes up, you're going to have a little talk with him.' Barlow tried a smile, but didn't succeed. 'It's about time we did something useful with that funny accent of yours!'

Murray didn't smile either. 'Harry, I'm not in the mood to fuck around here. Flynn doesn't want talking to, he wants his bloody head kicked in, and that wouldn't cause me too many problems.' He stopped talking and studied Barlow's face. He could see he was getting nowhere. 'OK, Harry,' he resumed after a moment, 'I know, you're not in the mood and I don't want to argue with you. Clive said to find this bugger and stop him from talking. OK, we've found him, and as far as I'm concerned, there's only one sure way of closing his mouth – kill the bastard and drop him in the drink with a few rocks stuffed up his arse! He's a bloody Irishman, Harry, don't try using finesse, he won't appreciate it.'

Barlow shook his head. He still hadn't recovered his sense of humour. 'Your instincts, David, are forever basic.' He winced as a new area of pain made itself felt, but got no sympathy from Murray.

'OK then, tell me about *your* instincts, Harry. We're going to make him a bed – then what?'

Barlow leaned forward and peered through the door at Flynn's body. There was movement. Flynn was awake and testing his bonds. The movements were sluggish and tentative; soon his brain would be back to normal and someone would have to go and sit on his head. But Barlow reckoned he had a few more minutes.

'I'll tell you about it. First, go and do something with him, will you? Go and tap him on the head. Nothing drastic, just a goodnight kiss. I don't want the bugger too bright and cheerful yet. Tell him to go back to sleep for another half-hour or so.'

Murray put his hand on Barlow's shoulder and leaned forward to study the twitching body.

'What have you covered his head up for?'

'I don't want him to see your face. And David – don't talk to him yet, just send him to sleep.'

Murray nodded. He still didn't understand what Barlow was aiming at, but it didn't worry him unduly. Inside the Nissen, he gazed about him before bending down and picking up the remains of Jayne Clarke's paddle. He smacked the splintered end hard on the concrete floor until he was left with a length of solid handle. He tested the balance and tapped it several times in his hand as he walked across the hut, then stood and looked down at Flynn's body. After a moment he pulled the coat to one side so that part of the back of Flynn's head was exposed.

Flynn had plenty of time to worry about what was going on. He opened his eyes when he heard movement. Everything was black, but he felt the slight draught on the back of his head. He tried to work it out, but nothing came, nothing made sense; he decided the best thing to do was to stay out of it and, closing his eyes again, he feigned unconsciousness while he waited for the next move.

It wasn't long coming.

Murray straddled Flynn's body. Balancing himself on the balls of his feet, he addressed Flynn's head with the rough end of the paddle. He rested it lightly on a spot at the base of Flynn's cranium. Timing. He shifted his weight fractionally, concentrated on the spot, then, with a smooth, straight-arm stroke, like a one-armed golfer, he brought the club back, shoulder-high, held it there for a second, then, with a smooth, downward stroke, thwacked Flynn's head exactly on the spot.

Flynn grunted, and his body, tensed in semiconsciousness, flopped like a sack of water. Murray studied the effect for a moment, then, leaning forward and returning Flynn's head to its original position, removed the rest of the coat and exposed his face. Although his eyes were open, Flynn was seeing nothing. Murray raised the club, and with a back-hand stroke hit him again, this time just above the bridge of his nose.

Barlow was leaning casually against the doorframe when Murray, after a closer look at Flynn's bleeding face, looked up and nodded at him.

'Fifteen minutes a hit,' he said, and threw the paddle handle to the end of the hut. 'That makes half an hour's Irish kip! You going to tell me now what it's all about?'

'Let's wrap the bugger up first, then we can relax.' Barlow dropped his cigarette on the floor and ground it into the dust with the toe of his shoe. 'Get that sheet. Did you bring some rope?'

'It's all there. What d'you want that duvet for?'

'I don't. I asked for bedding – I just meant a couple of sheets. But it doesn't matter. He can lie on it. He might think he's in heaven when he wakes up.'

It took the two of them about three minutes to turn Flynn into an Egyptian mummy. 'Drag him over here and shove him up against that overhang. Lay that duvet down first.'

Murray shook his head. 'I don't know why we don't just switch his bloody light out, Harry, and go and have a couple of pints with Clive in Canberra. I don't like handling these bastards as if they were people.'

363

Barlow grunted noncommittally as he rolled Flynn's body out of the way, then straightened up and touched the shroud-like bundle with his foot. 'He'll be all right there for a bit. Come over here, have a cigarette and I'll tell you what I've got in mind.'

They made themselves comfortable in the shade, out of earshot of the white bundle, but not out of view. Murray was sweating freely. A Belfast boy born and bred, he was a man of overcast skies, a drizzle-lover, at home with wet, glistening pavements with overhead orange lighting, cars with dipped headlights in the middle of the day splashing their way through puddled streets, people with upturned collars and squelching feet. Hot, cloudless weather didn't suit him, and standing around under a featureless sky talking about the welfare of a dead man was not Murray's idea of fun.

But Barlow sparked his interest.

'Flynn's got that stuff in his pocket. I left it there – it'll give him confidence when you go over there, once you've finished your fag, that is, and help him work himself free.'

'Oh yeah?'

'He was going to deliver that bloody stuff somewhere, David – Canberra's now my choice – and to someone who's of potato size among the boyos there, somebody who's been primed about the contents of Sixy's literary efforts by one, or more, of our Australian friends.'

'Maybe they've also been primed about the contents of that bloody cassette as well!'

Barlow let that one ride. He took a deep pull from his cigarette and smiled, mirthlessly, into Murray's face. 'Whatever they've been primed about, we're going to give them something – and you're going to deliver it to them.'

He didn't expect a reaction from Murray; he knew him too well. Murray never offered reactions, he just entered into the spirit of the thing. This didn't sound any funnier than most of the other things he'd become a specialist in since Belfast boys were invited to choose sides.

'Sounds fun. You're going to give the other side the tape of Sixy spilling his guts up?'

Barlow shook his head. 'No. If Flynn's reported to his team manager since he took to the road you might have a little problem convincing him that it got lost on the way, so I think we'll take the stuff back to Melbourne when we've finished here and use it as a guide to make one of our own. Can you do a convincing Flynn accent?'

'He's a Tyrone boy – they all sound like cats on the job. No problems there. Sixsmith's no problem either. They won't know his voice from any other Englishman's – even yours'd do for that! The mike'll be under your nose, not mine, so it won't be clear enough for them to do a proper voice pattern. They'll accept it. But how are you going to explain that he's not in a position to talk them through it?'

'I dunno,' said Barlow thoughtfully. 'Maybe we ought to get him to leave a little note saying he's had to bolt for the bush after delivering this stuff because he's got the Aussies breathing down his neck and he wants to lead them off the track. Get a bit of his handwriting and we'll write it for him. Thompson'll know a decent forger – he looks the type! D'you think they'll buy that?'

'Buggered if I know, Harry, but it's worth a go. D'you know where he's delivering the stuff?'

'Not yet. You're going to find out. You're going to do a job on him, David. When did you see anybody with a head in worse shape than Flynn's?'

'Living? Can't say I ever have.'

'Right, then the poor bugger can't be thinking in top gear at the moment, so we'll give him another bloody good hiding and then turn you loose on him. Tell him you're a friend – you know all about that sort of thing. Screw the bastard to the ground, confuse him, and then go along and help him to his feet, brush him down and he'll be all over you.'

'Not the Flynn I know!' Murray pulled another half-inch off his cigarette and inhaled deeply. 'If any of that works, it takes care of the disk. But what about the printed version?'

Barlow studied him for a moment. 'We haven't got a lot of choice here. The only official copy of Sixy's manuscript is being held by the Australian authorities for a Sixsmith enquiry, and so far I haven't heard of any signs that they're going to let go of it, so, for the time being, we'll have to concentrate on this end of the game. But at least we've got a chance of getting the disk going in the right direction. All we've got to find out now is who Flynn was going to hand it to.'

Murray flicked the ash off his cigarette and inspected the red ember. 'And who he's told that the bloody thing's a British put-up job!'

'Which you're going to find out.'

'Fine, Harry. But stand by for disappointment. We're not dealing with an onion here. Flynn's no bloody idiot. Even with the best will in the world, I can't see him buying this thing.'

'Flynn's just a sideline, David, so is the disk.'

'Yeh, I've gathered that. But whatever happens to this disk, the main talking point has still got to be the publication of these bloody notes of Sixsmith's and the kerfuffle in the Australian court over British objections to their publication on the grounds of national security. Right?'

'Right.'

'Stick this disk in the hands of the people who matter in Dublin and they'll read them and take note of anything concerning them. But, my dear old Harry, they won't give a fucking bit of credence to anything if the British don't offer a Peter Wright-type spectacle to an Australian court. In fact, second time round it's going to have to be even more realistic. If the last one cost ten million, this one's got to cost three times that. The fight for an injunction to take out the offending chapters is the only thing the Irish'll take notice of. They learnt the tactics, as we did, from the Peter Wright fiasco. The harder you fight, the more you spend, the bigger the splash, and the louder the yells of Australian – and Irish – derision when we fall flat on our face. But it means we tried seriously to protect the memoirs, ergo the memoirs contain sensitive stuff that the British'll kill for. What is that sensitive stuff? It's to do with us in Dublin . . . Is that the essence of the problem?'

'A very good summing-up, I'd say, David. It shows you the pen's mightier than the sword!'

'Bollocks. I could achieve the same object you and Clive are after with this,' he patted the bulge of the Colt, 'and another one of these.' He brought the pistol into the open and flicked the magazine out of the butt, absently checking what he already knew – that it was fully loaded. 'And I'd still have half of them left.' He met Barlow's eyes, serious for a moment, then grinned. So did Barlow. 'Now it's your turn,' he said.

Barlow flicked his cigarette into the sandy soil and for a few seconds watched it die, then he brought his eyes back to Murray.

'That's what was meant to happen, David. But when we lost Sixsmith, we lost the initiative. Now we've got to find another way of directing the Sixsmith memoirs to some Australian publisher's desk. At the moment the only people I can see helping us out are the people we're laying the bloody table for – the Irish. The Australians have got the only official paper copy, and they're not likely to put it back into circulation, not because they think they'll be doing us a favour by keeping it out of circulation, but because they don't want to go through a Peter Wright/ Turnbull affair again.' Barlow sucked on his cigarette and whooshed smoke out of the side of his mouth. 'But that – a beautiful humiliation in a Sydney court with all the world's press in attendance – is exactly what we want. So, can we count on the Irish, when they get this disk and read what's on it, to arrange with their Australian friends to go for publication?'

'I don't know.'

'What d'you mean, you don't know? You're a bloody Irishman – you ought to know.'

Murray grinned broadly. 'We're a very complex people. Never count on an Irishman doing what you expect him to do. It's also part of our charm. Now, if you don't want me to shoot him, tell me in simple terms what you would like me to do with Mr Fergal Flynn.'

Barlow studied Murray's face for a moment, then said, 'He's got to be taken totally out of commission. Physically. And he's got to know about it. He's got to know that even walking down as far as the water's edge would be totally beyond his capability. He's got to be convinced that any ideas about getting to Canberra, or anywhere else, are right out of the question.'

'Break his legs.' There were no half measures with Murray.

'I'll leave it up to you. When he realizes that he's not going anywhere, you're going to appear like the good fairy. After killing me, you'll whisper a bit of Irish in his ear and tell him you've come to solve his problems and carry the mail for him to wherever he wants it delivered. D'you fancy that?'

Murray did. He grinned. 'Provided he didn't get a good look at me from the boat.'

Barlow shook his head. 'I don't think you need worry

about that. He was too bloody busy. He didn't have time to take you in when he was trying to deal with the kids, Jayne Clarke, Sophie Ward, me, the two boats, Harris . . . Christ Almighty, David, how the bloody hell could he be interested in you? You were out of his sight most of the time. In any case, it doesn't matter. You could say you're an undercover guy who's worked his way into Brit intelligence out here.'

'He won't buy that.'

'You haven't tried yet. Christ, David – why not? You know enough people in his circle. You've got the names and you've done the opposite – you've worked on their side of the fence, been in their camp. He might even have heard your name mentioned. You've just got to be bloody convincing.'

'Underestimating your enemy, Harry, is the –'

'Oh, piss off!' But Murray had got a point. Barlow thought about it a bit longer, then shook his head. 'Anyway,' he said reflectively, 'that's why I wanted the bugger wrapped up like a packet of fish and chips. If I'd just covered his head and your voice appeared from nowhere, the first thing he'd do would be to start screaming "Foul!" This way you can chat him up as if you were his girlfriend sitting in the back row of the pictures. You only need to fumble around trying to find the end to uncover his face, by which time it'll be time to say goodbye. Of course, this is after, having been lulled into a sense of comradeship by your lilting Irish voice, he's told you who he's been talking to and the rest of his life story since he knocked off Sixy, and who, and where, he intends dropping the goods –'

'I don't want to appear like a half-cooked spud, Harry, but all this is going over my bloody head! Let's see if I've got you so far,' interrupted Murray. 'We make sure he's awake, then fire half-a-dozen shots at each other, you give a death rattle in his ear, having broken his legs before giving battle, and I crawl up to him and offer absolution in lieu of a dose of morphine to deaden the pain of these broken limbs – is that about right?'

Barlow smiled and lit another cigarette. 'One thing about you, David. You can't be faulted for perception. You've got the script to a T. There's only one thing out of sync . . .'

Murray raised his eyebrows. He didn't think he'd got anything out of sync.

'You do the nobbling.'

'Happy to oblige, Harry. Let's hope I don't get a touch of the vapours and mistake his neck for his legs. But there is another thing . . .'

'Go on.'

'It's so bloody weak, it's laughable.'

'It's all we've got.'

'Thanks, Harry!'

Barlow's jaw tightened. 'OK, I think we've wasted enough time on discussion. Go and kick the bugger awake and let's get it over with. We'll start playing as soon as you give the word.'

Murray nodded, his untroubled expression unchanged. He picked up the heavy Colt, studied it for a moment, then eased the hammer back all the way. Happy with the situation, he stood up and dropped his hand, allowing the automatic to dangle at his side. There was no need to check it; Murray knew more about the minute-to-minute state of his Colt than most people knew about the daily state of their wallet.

Watched by Barlow, he walked across the open ground and took up station beside Flynn's shrouded figure. He touched it gently with his foot. There was no reaction. He kicked. Still nothing. Flynn appeared dead to the world. But Murray knew better, he'd kicked far too many un-conscious bodies to be fooled by this one. He crouched down at the narrow end of the shroud and felt for Flynn's foot. He ran his fingers along the outline until he came to Flynn's kneecap. He fondled it for a moment, then moved his fingers about four inches down the shinbone and tapped the spot with his forefinger, making a shallow indentation in the shroud. Then he stood up and raised his hand to Barlow.

Barlow aimed the S&W three feet to the right of Murray's figure and fired four shots in succession. They thudded into the bank above Flynn's head, sending out a shower of soil and small stones rattling around the shrouded body. Murray waited a few seconds for the echo to die down, then fired two shots into the air. He watched Barlow empty his revolver into the same place, then run towards him shouting before diving forward on to the rough gravel surface, where he lay prone. Murray grinned in acknowledgement. Raising his hand again, he brought the Colt round and aimed at the tiny indentation he'd made in the material of Flynn's shroud. He moved his head fractionally out of the line of the blast and squeezed the trigger.

Flynn clawed his way back to life and tried to work out what it was all about.

He moved his head slowly from one side to the other, feeling the softness of the sheet drawn tightly against his face, then tried to move his arms to pull away the nauseating restriction. They refused to move. He tried his hands, and found he could wriggle his fingers about. Then he opened his eyes and, with the sheet pressing down on his eyelids, felt the first gentle pressure of panic: there was nothing there except a claustrophobic blackness. He lay still for a moment, then became aware of the soft, slightly yielding padding underneath him. His imagination clicked into gear. Flynn was many things, but he was no coward. His greatest fear – anybody's greatest fear – was to be buried alive. This was it. He began to scream. He was wrapped in a shroud. He was in a coffin and the lid was screwed down and the bastards had buried him alive. Holy Mother of God!

But there was no relief in the scream or the plea. Neither refused to leave his parched throat and in stark terror he tried to force himself back into the peaceful oblivion of unconsciousness, hoping to die before he woke up again. But it wasn't going to be that easy; the pain in his head and hands wouldn't allow him to sink. And then it all came back with a rush, the crunching blow, the screaming nightmare. But why would they bury him alive? Who would want to bury him? Who said he was buried? Flynn blanked out the horror and made his mind work.

First, how big was the box?

He bit back the pain that seared through his head when he moved, and, after several attempts, managed to swing his legs from the hips and reach upwards with his feet as far as they'd go. They failed to find anything solid above him. That was a measure of relief. His claustrophobia dropped half a degree. If he was in a coffin, it was a bloody big one, with enough room above him to put half a dozen more. He tried again, then again, and again, and each time failed to reach the roof of the overhang. Happier now, he moved his feet sideways, first one way, then the other, and met only a yielding softness, nothing solid, nothing like the wooden sides of a coffin.

He rested for a minute and breathed deeply to bring the rest of his senses nearer to the surface. On the third or fourth breath, he found on the sheet pressing against his face the lingering, almost imperceptible aroma of a woman's body. It brought no reaction from him. He managed to drag a mouthful of sheet into his mouth and started to chew his way through it, but within seconds the muscles of his battered jaw refused to answer his commands. There was nowhere else to go. The darkness, the pain, the restriction, thumped the message between his eyes: Flynn, you're going to die . . .

The pain in his nose and mouth finally got to him and, unable even to raise a decent scream at the searing message from his battered body, Flynn stopped fighting. He let his head drop back on to the soft duvet and, closing his eyes, gave up the struggle.

By Flynn's brain refused to lie down and die. After a while he opened his eyes and thought he could make out, through the folds of the shroud, a slightly lighter shade of darkness. He concentrated on it and lay quietly listening to the silence around him. He made another tentative assault on the cloth pressing against his mouth, but abandoned it after two mouthfuls. He spat the sheet out, wet and soggy. And then his heart almost stopped.

He thought he'd heard noises.

He held his breath.

He hadn't made a mistake.

Over the thumping of his heart he heard feet approaching. They came closer and closer, then stopped. It was a comforting noise. He was above ground at least. He prayed for more noise, and got it. He was back in the world.

He raised his head off the ground as far as it would go and tried to join in, shouting at the top of his voice, but nothing came out of his mouth. He tried again and managed a hoarse croak, he sounded like a frog in pain. Flynn was no dreamer. It was forlorn, and he knew it as he listened to the feet move around him, then stop; the crunching of gravel again, then silence. Who was there? What was going on? He lay still and let his breath return to a rasping, laboured normal before allowing his head to fall back again. Once more, the silence closed in around him. He was not far from despair.

But it was a strange silence, forced, unreal. He felt a presence, as if someone, or something, was near him, holding its breath, unmoving, and then, before the fear established itself in all its horror, something poked him in the side. He stifled a scream. Then something kicked him. Human, but not friendly – definitely not friendly. He remained unmoving, unyielding. He was dead. Perhaps they'd go away. Then something touched his foot. A hand. He resisted a shiver of fear as the hand crept up his leg and stopped at his knee. He'd stopped breathing and his heart thudded in his chest in time with the flashing red lights behind his closed eyelids as he waited for the next move.

He didn't have to wait long.

The gunfire almost jerked him upright. Then the explosions almost in his ear; the sound of running feet coming towards him. He cringed. Then the bellow of a man in pain, the crashing of a body, and another roar of gunfire close to his ear. He had a fractional sensation of his bladder emptying before the searing, unearthly pain of his shin disintegrating, almost tearing off his leg just below the knee. His brain told him to scream, but before his mouth could open to relieve the shock, barbed hooks tore round the inside of his head, dragging everything with them in a wild whirlwind of sheer agony until, mercifully, he died again.

It could have been an hour, it could have been a day. In fact, it was no more than twenty minutes before something woke Flynn up. The minute his brain came back to life he began to scream. The pain from his shattered leg crawled into his head again, and then, as he lay in his dark, shroud-covered world, it all came back. The gun battle, the shots almost in his ear, the drawn-out cry of a man hit on the run, the man dropping almost beside him, close enough for him to hear him die – as close as that. But what the bloody hell was it all about?

He thrust the pain, as much as he could, into the background of his brain. His ears were on points, and once again he picked up the sound of approaching footsteps; somebody walking lightly on his toes; somebody who'd been in action – and was coming to finish off the job?

The footsteps stopped, and after a second he heard the sound of something being dragged away. But not far. Then the metal-against-metal rub of a weapon's magazine being withdrawn and the familiar click, click, click of new rounds being inserted and the cocking of the weapon.

He cringed as the steps came closer, and once again held his breath, remaining as still as a dead man.

Suddenly, all around him was quiet. Like a tomb. Frightening. He bit back another wave of searing pain and clenched his eyes tightly together as he felt the unmistakable hard, round metal of a gun's barrel against the side of his head. He tried to scream. But again nothing came out, not even the earlier hoarse croak.

But there was no bullet, no eternal darkness, no everlasting easing of the pain. Instead:

'Flynn?'

The voice was barely a whisper. Perhaps he'd imagined it. He strained his ears. The desire to scream, the pain in his head, his hands, his leg, were shoved into the background as his ears took over.

It came again, a fraction louder.

'Flynn?'

He opened his mouth. 'Ahhh! Who . . .?'

'Shhh! Don't move. Don't make a sound.'

Flynn's heart missed a beat and nearly choked him, then raced like an overthrottled engine. His ears hadn't deceived him: an Irish voice! A Belfast voice! The miracle! He wasn't going to die – not this time! The realization of his impending salvation gave strength to his voice. It also brought a resurgence of the agony, and with it a strangled sob from between his clenched teeth.

'Jesus Christ!' he hissed. 'Who in God's name are you?'

Murray squatted himself comfortably on his haunches and stared unconcernedly at the blood-soaked sheet wrapped around Flynn's legs. His unconcern changed to fascination and he moved his head closer to observe what seemed to be a distinct welling-up through the cordite-blackened hole in the material. It looked like mud bubbles breaking air over a steaming, hot spring. He frowned at it for a second or two and wondered how long it was going to take to drain Flynn's eight-pint tank of blood. It gave him a sudden sense of urgency.

'Murray,' he said, and then a little louder, 'the name's Murray.'

Murray had no difficulty retrieving the accent he'd been born with. His Belfastness was more pronounced, more emphatic than Flynn's higher-pitched County Tyrone dialect. But Flynn was at home with Murray's voice; the accent of the bloody gutters of the world's saddest city was the passport.

'Then get this fuckin' thing off my face so that I can see you! Murray, you say? Where yer from, Murray? What're you doing here? What the fuckin' hell's going on?'

'Shut your mouth, Flynn!' snapped Murray. 'Keep quiet and listen. We're not out of the wood yet.' He made no attempt to uncover Flynn's face. 'I was on the boat – I was with that lot. But keep still, and quiet. I'll give it to you in a minute.'

Flynn made no reply.

'First, let me get this stuff off your face so you can see what you're dealing with.' He fumbled with the folds of the sheet without making any real headway. He and Barlow had done it deliberately; it was difficult to find the end without bouncing Flynn around like a half-cooked suet pudding, and he wouldn't like that, not in his state of health. 'I don't want to pull you around more than I have to,' he whispered into what he thought was Flynn's ear. 'You've got a very bad leg. It could turn into a gusher.'

'Get on with it. You said you were on the boat?' The covering round his face failed to muffle the suspicion in his voice. Murray almost smiled to himself.

'It's a long story, Flynn.'

'Then cut the bloody thing down, but talk!'

'The Brits have an intelligence network in Australia to counter our support here.'

'*Our* support?' sneered Flynn, then changed his tone. 'What's this got to do with you on that bloody boat?'

'I'm coming to it. I've managed to break into their set-up. I've been running with Brit intelligence over here for eighteen months. The guy controlling the network comes out of Melbourne. He's an anglicized Aussie –'

'Name?' This was the tester.

'Thompson. Ex-Aussie SAS, only one leg.'

'Where's he working from?'

Murray told him.

'OK.' Flynn filed Thompson's name and description. It sounded right. A bit far-fetched, but not impossible. There were three PIRA men working full time in London's Thames House, so what could be done in MI5 London had to be a distinct possibility for MI5 Melbourne. But he didn't throw his arms open yet.

'Galloglass . . .' murmured Murray.

'What's that?' Flynn wasn't ready for disclosures yet, but mention of the code-name was encouraging.

'You know of Galloglass?' repeated Murray.

'I know of fuck all at the moment. Get this stuff off my face before I choke to bloody death. Jesus!'

'What?'

'My fuckin' leg! Christ!'

Murray shrugged and took his time. 'I lost you for a moment back there. I thought that was the end of the road. The boat was a bloody good idea, though. Pity they caught on to you, otherwise you'd have been home and dry.' He tugged a bit more of sheet away and brought an anguished groan from Flynn. Murray lifted Flynn's head and found one of the ends of the sheet. 'There's a guy lying out there I've just coffined. He's a top Brit operator sent out from London to run the Sixsmith scam.'

'Well, they've fucked that one up!'

Murray waited for more, but all that came was another prolonged groan. He lowered his head closer to Flynn's. 'He's the bastard who just shot you in the leg. I wonder why he didn't put one in your head?'

Flynn was also thinking along those lines. But the man had been a Brit – those bastards were capable of anything and had their own reasons. Meanwhile, Murray's remark dispelled any doubt he had had about the wound in his leg.

'Christ knows!'

Murray smiled happily to himself and finally disentangled the sheet from Flynn's face. It wasn't a pretty sight. A suffusion of red and black bruising, with an indentation just above the nose that was soft and soggy and looked as if the slightest touch would go right through into his brain. The untouched patches of his face were white and pinched with pain. He looked very close to death as he stared back into Murray's face and studied his features.

'Do I know you?'

'Ever been down Oldpark Road?'

'Belfast, Ardoyne?'

'You've got it. Third Battalion.'

'There was a guy named Murray running in that outfit in 'eighty-eight. What's your first name?'

'David.'

'It wasn't that.'

'The guy you're thinking of was Cathal Murray.'

'What happened to him?'

'Killed by the Brits on the mainland. He was my kid brother.'

That was it. Murray had answered all the questions correctly. There was no condolence for the loss of a 'kid brother'; no regret for the late Cathal Murray, least of all from Murray, who'd been instrumental in blowing his namesake, and no relation, out of the game. But it satisfied Flynn – he'd got a friend. But it was time to come back to Australia. He groaned inadvertently and closed his eyes. He didn't want to look any more, but he wanted to know. 'Me leg?' he grunted.

Murray transferred his eyes from Flynn's face to his leg, studied it for a moment, then sucked air in through his teeth. 'It's bad,' he said. 'You can't walk on it. I'm going to have to get you to a doctor or a hospital. You can't hang around too long with a wound like that.'

'Forget it, Murray! Get me into a car and I'll be all right. I've got to get to Canberra. I can't hang around here wasting time waiting for bloody doctors. Wrap something round the soddin' thing to stop it bleeding and let's get going. You got trans – Jesus Christ!' He tried to sit up but it didn't work and he dropped back, his head cracking on to the ground like a falling coconut.

It took him several minutes to recover, then he was back into action. 'Where's that Brit you killed?'

Murray jerked his thumb over his shoulder. 'Still out there.'

379

'Let's have a look at the bastard's body.'

Murray smiled coldly and put his arm round Flynn's waist, raising him into a semisitting position. Flynn studied Barlow, still lying comfortably where he'd gone down.

'You killed him?' He swivelled his eyes and studied Murray.

'Yup.'

'Good. Go and put another one in his head. He doesn't look dead enough to me.'

Murray stared into Flynn's cold, black eyes for a few seconds. He'd been right about one thing – Flynn was a hard bastard to convince. 'A waste of a bullet, Flynn. He's as dead as a bloody doornail.'

'Get on with it.'

Murray pulled the Colt from his trouser band and slid open the breech. A round flew out and bounced into the dust and another slipped smoothly into its place. It was an unnecessary action. Murray was playing for time.

'Quick!'

Murray strolled across the open space to where Barlow was lying on his face. The Colt hung by his side. 'Flynn's still testing, Harry,' he murmured without moving his lips. 'He wants to see some more bullets go into your head.'

Barlow's eye studied Murray.

'Don't worry, Harry, you won't feel a thing!'

'Fuck off!'

'Jerk your head when I fire.'

'Murray!'

BOOM!

The heavy bullet seared past Barlow's neck and into the ground. He felt the heat of its passage, but even as the explosion thundered in his ear he jerked his head and shoulders off the earth like a wooden doll that had been kicked behind the ear.

'Give him another one!' shouted Flynn. From where he sat the performance looked perfect.

Murray fired again. Barlow's head came off the ground and Murray bent down, as if to inspect his handiwork at closer range.

'Bloody good job you're not knocking off my wife, Harry!' he muttered. 'If I had one!'

When he returned to Flynn, he told him he was going to get him into the shade. Flynn didn't argue. Murray half-pulled, half-carried Flynn out of the broad sunshine and into the shade round the back of the Nissen hut. Halfway there, Flynn passed out.

He was out for several minutes, but it didn't affect his brain. 'Did you go through the Brit's pockets?'

'Not yet.'

'Go back and do it.'

'You looking for something in particular?'

'A plastic packet. Go and get it.'

Murray moved out of Flynn's vision and joined Barlow, who'd given up playing dead and moved into the shade. Without speaking, he lit another cigarette, winked at Barlow and stuck his thumb up. Barlow nodded in return and rubbed his ear as he made himself more comfortable on the heavy paving stone he'd found to sit on. After a decent interval, Murray returned to Flynn and, crouching beside him, said, 'No plastic packet.'

It took Flynn the best part of a minute to run through his extensive vocabulary of swearwords while Murray sat quietly smoking his cigarette. When Flynn, exhausted, closed his eyes again, Murray reached behind him and said, 'Is this your clobber, Flynn?'

Flynn opened his eyes and stared hard at Murray. Was it possible? No, of course it bloody wasn't! Even the bloody Brit couldn't be that fuckin' stupid! Or could he? 'Jesus! Is me coat there?'

'This one?'

'Give it here.' He worked his arms loose from the enveloping folds of the sheet and ran his fingers urgently round the lining below the right-hand pocket. When he felt the packet, the animation drained from him and he collapsed backwards on to the ground, closing his eyes as if in supplication. He looked like a dead man – a contented dead man. Murray watched him and waited for the next move.

It didn't take Flynn long to recover. He ripped open the lining, took out the packet and held it up to his eyes. There was disbelief in them, then suspicion. 'Why didn't he take it?' he asked himself. Murray waited until he repeated the question, then offered an answer.

'Maybe he didn't know you had it, whatever it is.'

Flynn stared into space for a moment, then accepted Murray's theory. 'The stupid bastard!' he grimaced. The grimace changed to suspicion again. Flynn had never taken the smoothest road; he wasn't going to start now. 'Then why the fuckin' hell was he so determined to run me down?'

'You know the Brit,' said Murray condescendingly, 'you know him probably better than anyone. Who ever knows why he does what he does?' Murray paused to let that little bit of home-grown philosophy take root before adding, 'You killed his mate. Maybe he wanted to hurt you.'

Suspicion again. 'How d'you know I killed his mate?'

Murray was ready for him. 'I told you, I've been with him since he commandeered that boat, but even without that, when did you last read a paper? When did you last listen to your trannie? You're big time now, boy – big news.'

But Flynn was busily thinking out the next move. First things first. He had to kill the pain that was disfiguring his thinking, find some transport and drop the stuff in Mr Galloglass's lap, and then start heading for home. He reckoned he'd outstayed his welcome in Australia, but now, by the grace of God, he wasn't alone. This boy was Irish. One of the lads, the Ardoyne Battalion, he knew what running in front of a hunting team was all about. Murray from the Ardoyne was a different proposition to the whining, soft-gutted Australian who'd left his head on the back seat of the car. The comparison warmed him to Murray.

'Do something with me leg, Murray. Tie it up, stop the bloody pain, do something with the fuckin' thing. I want to get to Canberra, and I wanna do it today.' Flynn had sorted himself out, he'd taken charge.

But Murray didn't move.

'Have you seen your leg, Flynn?'

'Fuck my leg!'

'Look at it.' Murray put his arm round Flynn's scrawny shoulders and raised him from the waist. With his free hand he pulled the blood-soaked sheet away from Flynn's legs and let him have a good look.

The right leg was hanging on by shreds of skin, splintered bone and gristle. The blood had stopped pumping and was oozing like thick treacle. Flynn regarded it for a second, then fainted.

It took a few slaps around the face to bring him round again.

'See what I mean?' said Murray.

It was a different, spiritless Flynn who stared back at Murray. 'Jesus!' he whispered. 'Jesus Christ! I'm going to die. Get me a priest. Get me a bloody priest – quick!'

'I don't think you'll find many priests sitting round here reading their beads, Flynn,' said Murray light-heartedly. 'If you die out here, you die alone. But don't worry, you're not going to die. Look, I've tied your belt round your thigh, the bleeding's almost stopped. But your head's something else, Flynn! Christ, it's something else. I've never seen the like of it before. You've got more bloody cuts in it than a joint of meat. And it's getting to you, Flynn. You're a fuckin' sick man, you've got to quieten yourself down. If you stop buggering around and trying to jog to Canberra, you might be all right, you might even pull through. Hang on and in a minute I'll go and get a doctor. We've got a couple on the circuit here. One of 'em will fix you up and keep you quiet until the dogs are called off. But Flynn, for Christ's sake stay still and don't move.'

'The tape –'

'Sod the bloody tape! Don't worry about it. You're the important thing, Flynn. We can't afford to lose you over a fucking tape.'

'Jesus, Murray! Look, getting this tape to Dublin means a lot to me. I couldn't rest in me grave . . .' He searched for Murray's eyes and held them. He saw nothing but sincerity there. 'Murray, will you deliver these things for me?'

Murray appeared reluctant. He took his time lighting two cigarettes and when they were both going, stuck one between Flynn's pinched lips and the other in his own. He drew deeply, and exhaled a mouthful of smoke with a whoosh. 'I'm not sure, Fergal.'

'Do it!' Flynn shoved the packet into Murray's hand, as if the action absolved him from further responsibility. 'Here, take it to Canberra. It goes to a drop. Be careful, this is very special. It's a flat in a place called Kingston. It's been rented for one month only in the name of Mr Galloglass. It's thirty-seven, Fitzstephens Road. OK? Mr Galloglass. The package'll fit in a box in the water cistern in the lavatory. Place the packet and leave. The key'll be hanging on a string behind the letterbox. Put it back where you found it and then get lost.'

384

Flynn tried to get up and look round the corner at Barlow's body, but couldn't make it and collapsed back against the wall of the Nissen. 'I suppose killing that guy out there's blown your position in Melbourne. You won't be able to go back there. But that's not my fuckin' problem. You can sort that one out yourself.'

Murray shrugged Flynn's observations to one side. 'Who's collecting?'

'Galloglass, but you're not interested in him. Your job's finished when you close the lid on the cistern. Murray . . .'

Flynn reached out and grabbed the top of Murray's hand. Murray didn't pull it away. There were the beginnings of tears in the corners of Flynn's eyes, tears of pain – Flynn wasn't capable of producing tears of any other sort – but they had no effect on Murray. He extricated his cigarette, transferred it to his other hand and carried it to his mouth. His whole attitude was one of casual interest. He gave the impression that he had all the time in the world. It impressed Flynn.

'Murray,' he repeated, 'I wish to hell I'd met you at the beginning of this business. I wouldn't have been in this bloody state if I had . . . But listen, they'll hear about you in Dublin – the top people. This won't be forgotten, mark my words.'

'We all have to do our bit, Fergal.' Murray brought from his back pocket a brown leather-covered diary and opened it at last December's pages, then laid it in Flynn's lap. Flynn studied it for a moment, frowning.

'What's this for?'

Murray slid a Biro between Flynn's fingers. 'I want a testimonial, Fergal. I want something that authorizes me to act on your behalf. Come on, nod your bloody head. I'm undercover, nobody knows me here. What if Galloglass is watching this box? What does he think when I turn up instead of you? You want me to stick my neck out for you, then you bloody well write something, otherwise . . .'

Murray left the threat in the air and watched Flynn stare blankly at the open diary before picking up the pen in a shaky hand and commence writing. He filled two pages before dropping the pen and collapsing back with the effort. Murray picked up the diary and stowed it in his back pocket, then decided to take Flynn's mind off it for the moment. 'Tell me what you know about this guy doing the collecting. Where's he from? When's he expecting the drop – just in case?'

Flynn looked up from his lap and stared at Murray. He held Murray's eyes for several seconds, then cast his reticence away like a pair of worn-out shoes. At this stage, Murray could have been the Pope taking his confession. He told him everything he knew about the man called Galloglass, plus what conclusions he'd formed about him. Nothing was sacred. 'My bet is that he's something in the Embassy. He looks the sort – never heard a fuckin' gunshot at close quarters or heard a nine milly being cocked in his ear. Trench warfare? The fucker wouldn't know, would he? But he's a brain, Murray.'

'Takes all sorts, Fergie. What's he look like? Has he got dirty fingernails?'

'Has he fuck!' Flynn gave a perfect description of Thomas Collins, Head of the Joint Official and Provisional Intelligence Network Far East.

'Have you told him what's on the tape?'

'He's expecting a bloody pile of paper. But it's all bullshit. The tape explains why. It's a bloody Brit spilling his guts on a Brit trick. No, Galloglass knows fuck all about the tape; he thinks the paperwork's genuine. This'll change his bloody mind.'

'So who've you spoken to about this trick?'

'No fucker would listen to me. Nobody knows about the bloody thing.'

'You mean you haven't told anybody about this bloody trick, anybody at all? You're the only guy who knows about it?'

'Yeh – I've just fuckin' told you!'

'Just making sure. Er, Fergal, before you make yourself comfortable again, let me introduce you to the chap who's going to put you out of your misery.'

Flynn looked up in surprise. 'The doctor? You've got one with you?'

'Sort of.' Murray tightened his lips over his teeth and emitted a low-pitched whistle.

'What d'ya mean, Murray?' Flynn's eyes narrowed. Something wasn't quite right about this. 'What d'ya mean, a sort of doctor?'

'Hang on . . .'

Barlow strolled round the corner and stood at Flynn's feet. He gave a professional glance at the shattered leg before nodding at Murray. He ignored the startled expression on Flynn's face.

'OK, David?'

'Sure, Harry.'

Still squatting, Flynn's hand still grasping his, Murray met Flynn's eyes and gave a tiny jerk of the head. 'That's it, Fergal. Looks like you've come to the end of that road you've been talking about.'

'What d'ya mean? I don't get it, what's going on?' He glanced down at his hand clutching Murray's and snatched it away as if it were one of the devil's hoofs. He transferred his gaze to Barlow and stared in bewilderment. 'This bastard's dead – you killed him! You fuckin' said you'd killed him! I watched you put two in his bloody head just now –'

'Sleight of hand, Fergal, now do shut up, there's a good

chap!' Murray reverted to his normal accent. The change from Belfast sewer to tea and crumpets couldn't have been more pronounced. It sent a cold shiver up Flynn's spine and, for a moment, silenced him. Murray got to his feet, reached down and removed the cigarette from Flynn's fingers, crushing it under his foot. He did the same with his own, then collected the folds of the sheet and began wrapping it round Flynn's body, retying it so that his arms were pinioned to his sides. Flynn recovered his tongue.

'You're a fuckin' snout!' There was total disbelief in his voice.

'I told you to shut up!'

'You'll pay for this!'

'Tell him to be quiet, David. If he won't shut up, shove something in his mouth.'

Murray lifted Flynn's head and wrapped the sheet around his face as it had been earlier, but Flynn's imprecations, although muffled, went on unabated. Until he ran out of breath and listened to the two men talking. His blood ran cold.

'What d'you think, Harry?' he heard Murray say. 'A bullet, then drop him in the drink?'

'No,' said the other voice – the big bugger. 'I wouldn't want to chance him coming up again when the fish start nibbling. These bloody Australians are sniffy buggers, all hell'll break loose if they find him in this state. They know I've been running up his arse. It wouldn't take 'em long to put me in the sack with him. No, we've got to do something clever here. We've got the game going again. We can't afford to lose the pieces a second time.'

'So what do you suggest?'

'Bury him.'

Flynn stopped breathing.

Murray didn't agree. 'Fuck that for a game of soldiers,

Harry! I'm not digging a bloody grave in this climate, not for a shit-head like this.' He kicked Flynn's side with his foot. 'Don't they have piranhas in these waters?'

Barlow grinned fleetingly. The thought of Flynn being nibbled by hungry little fishes was a very pleasing one; it went conveniently beside the one of Greville Sixsmith appealing to Flynn not to hurt him and getting his face blown away for his trouble. 'No digging necessary, David. Did you notice that slab I was sitting on out there?'

'No.'

'It moved. I had a look under it. You'll never guess what it covered.'

'You're right about that, Harry.'

'A borehole.'

'Surprise me. What sort of borehole?'

'This used to be a RAN post. You know the navy, sticklers for hygiene. It's a bloody shithole – a borehole latrine. Goes down about twenty feet in a straight line.'

'Full of shit?' Murray was definitely interested. 'After all this time?'

'No, bone dry. I dropped a stone down it. Hard as concrete.'

'Pity. Will this bugger fit in it?'

'Just about. It'll be a tight squeeze. He'll probably get stuck halfway down, but I don't think I'm going to worry about that. What leg was it you damaged?'

'The right. What a bloody good idea – burying a shit-bag in a shithole.' He raised his voice and kicked Flynn's shoulder again. 'D'you hear that, Flynn? We're going to bury you in a shit-hole! Don't you think it's a bloody good idea?'

Flynn came to life. 'I wanna priest!' And then he began bellowing, first in pain when Barlow picked him up by his left leg, and then in fear as Murray took his head and shoulders. He struggled and kicked and arched his body, his right leg with its dreadful wound bouncing and scraping in the dust as it was dragged across the uneven ground, relegating his other aches and pains to the background of his nightmare. And all the time there was the uncontrollable high-pitched scream that he knew would eventually wake him up from the nightmare.

But it wasn't a nightmare. This was real. He felt his legs being threaded into the hole and when the restraining hands under his elbows were removed, he dropped. But only as far as his shoulders.

'Jump on him, David.'

He felt shoes on his shoulders as Murray balanced himself, then, with the extra push, his shoulders cleared the opening and he felt himself sliding down a gun barrel. Another fifteen feet and he jammed again, and all the time he was deafened by the horrible sounds coming from his throat, a mixture of screams and shouts and baby-like crying. And then, suddenly, his ears detected a change. It was a different sound, hollow, unreal and echoing, as if there was no exit for the noise he was making. He opened his eyes again. The pale light, diffused by the covering over his face, had vanished. They'd covered the hole. It was jet black. Everything was black, pitch-black. He was jammed halfway to nowhere, unable to move his head or anything else, nothing, not even a finger. He choked on his screams, clenched his eyes as tight as they'd go and let the tears run unchecked down his face as he waited for something to happen.

PART THREE

32

Dublin, January

Tom Collins shrugged the collar of his raincoat higher round his neck and risked a glance upwards at the overcast sky. The rain, heavy and cold, thudded on to his face and unprotected head, then sloshed gleefully on to the wet pavement before joining the torrent in the gutter rushing to swell Dublin's underground lakes. Another half-hour to midday, the cars were swishing past with orange headlights as if it were midnight. The gloom suited his black mood and fuelled the overpowering gut feeling of a man looking for a decent bit of wall to be shot against.

Ignoring the taciturn figure in the soaked navy-blue donkey-jacket and torn pale blue jeans splodging beside him, he put his head down again and, with his hands thrust deep into his raincoat pockets, waded on in silence until a jab at his elbow brought his eyes sharply to the right. Without waiting, the jean-covered legs quickened their pace and crossed the road into a tree-lined but shabby row of working-class dwellings.

Collins caught up with his companion as he dived down a narrow alley that cut between the monotonous, featureless houses. He took in the twitch of a curtain from a window on his left and a pair of flat, inquisitive eyes that gave the two of them a brief, experienced examination before allowing the curtain to fall back into place. Collins wiped the rain from his face with the side of his arm and splashed down the narrow alley in the donkey-jacket's wake until halfway along the six-foot-high fenced alley, he went through a rickety door and, without looking round to see whether Collins was still with him, continued at the same pace through a concrete yard. He swung open another gate, took two or three paces, and stopped on the step of a half-glazed back door.

The door opened before he had raised his hand to knock and he stood back and motioned Collins forward. His job was finished. With a curt nod to the woman holding the door, he turned on his heels and, with his head bowed, squelched back the way he had come. He hadn't said a word to Collins from the time he'd picked him up at the rendezvous in Grafton Street.

Collins smiled politely at the woman. She didn't respond. Smiling strangers were nothing to do with her. She leaned forward and, out of habit, watched Collins's guide disappear through the yard gate, then closed the door and stood back, her ungainly man's carpet slippers making no sound on the shiny linoleum floor. She motioned Collins with a cold nod of her head and led him through the kitchen. He squeezed past a large pine table covered with a grubby, stained cloth and the remains of a fried breakfast. He wrinkled his nose. The room had the smell of a Chinese takeaway.

Glad to get out of it, he followed her along the short, narrow passage and into the front room. She didn't stay. She said nothing. Her expression hadn't changed from the moment he'd stepped through the door. It was a working-class welcome for a stranger with a suntan and a tie. And it was never going to change. It was always going to be like this – backstreets, corner-watching from behind double-thickness lace curtains, meetings in working-class kitchens in working-class slums. Safety first. It was the only place they felt safe. They wouldn't feel at home without the smell of last night's kippers and this morning's fried bread. Wet, snivelling, snotty-nosed kids pressing themselves against the wall with dull, cunning eyes, and even over the thumping of the rain, raucous voices, male, and female, shouting in never-ending arguments, added to the grim quality and the uninspiring squalor of life. But it was *their* way of life, and they wouldn't want it any other way. Collins had barely time to work that one through his mind when the door closed behind him.

The three men in the room filled it. Two sat round a rectangular 1930s dark oak drop-leaf table, whilst the third sat upright in an uncomfortable-looking wing chair by the pale green tiled fireplace. A single bar of the electric fire glowed bright red. The room was oppressively hot and full of cigarette smoke, but the men in the room appeared to suffer no discomfort and watched him in silence as he shrugged out of his sopping raincoat and dropped it in its own puddle by the door.

'Sit down, Tom,' said the man in the armchair and frowned at him from under bushy grey-and-white eyebrows. A man in his early seventies, he had cold, pinched features, all the expression having been driven from his face by sixty years of doing things the hard way.

Eoin McNeela was a relic of the Irish past. One of the more respected of the remaining old guard of Republican Army chiefs of staff, he'd gained nothing from sixty years of hatred of the English, of conspiracy, murder and scheming. He was still as poor as the day he'd signed his Volunteer papers in 1938. Ex-chiefs of staff of the official IRA are not granted pensions or directorships. But his poverty, in a strange, Irish rationale, improved his status. No money, no savings, meant he was not corruptible and therefore his judgement was safe. Fifteen years in Durham Prison on explosives charges and eight in his own Portlaoise for possession of firearms, gave him all the qualifications necessary when it came to studying and pronouncing on evidence of treachery in the Republican hierarchy. Collins had pledged his life to a safe, reliable pair of hands.

Without taking his eyes off Collins, McNeela jerked his head at the table and said, 'You know Jack Kearns?'

Who didn't know Jack Kearns? A pale, sickly death's-head on a six-foot-three frame that looked like a navy-blue suit hanging on a garden rake. The same age as McNeela, he looked as though he'd been dead for the past fifteen years and had been dug up for this meeting. Jack Kearns, the most feared and ruthless of a line of feared and ruthless Republican intelligence officers. This man's speciality had been interrogation. Heaven help you, innocent or guilty, had you found yourself in a decrepit farmhouse kitchen with your ankles chained to the table leg and only a flickering candle for you to see that Kearns was sitting opposite you. Collins met his strangely colourless eyes, not watery, as his age should have dictated, but flat and staring, like two river-washed pebbles under a high, creaseless forehead. Like his friend, McNeela, there was no expression on his face. Collins looked away with a nod.

'And Patrick Fleming?'

Collins sat down beside the third man and glanced sideways at him. He looked different. His face was almost that of a normal man. He lacked the slightly haunted look of the born Irish Republican, the shifty over-the-shoulder glance of the guilty and the hunted. He could have been foreign. He certainly wasn't Irish. He'd looked up only briefly when Collins had come into the room before returning to the well-thumbed sheets of typewritten paper in front of him. Collins made himself comfortable – as comfortable as was possible on a 1930s straight-back chair with a hard, imitation-leather seat and his knees jammed under the drop leaf of the table – and glanced, blank-faced, at the man by the fireplace. 'Is the name Patrick Fleming supposed to mean something to me?' he asked and waited, sensing a further inspection by the man on his right. 'I thought I stressed the danger of bringing third and fourth parties into this business. I thought it was going to be just you and me?'

'When you put your troubles and worries in my hands, Tom, you do just that. From now on, I choose who shares the problem. Don't worry about these people. I'm the one you're concerned with. Now, tell them what you told me about this computer disk you picked up.'

Collins stared for some time at the top of the bowed head of the man sitting beside him until prompted again by McNeela.

'Tom, I said forget them. Jack Kearns has done more for the cause in his life than you, or any of those blood-thirsty bastards up North, will do if they live to be ninety-five.'

Collins still wasn't happy. 'I'm not worried about Jack, Eoin, I'm worried about this one – Fleming.'

'He's American, CIA.'

'Bloody hell!'

'I said forget it. He's as Irish as you are, he just lives in another country. He's my sister Mairead's boy. Now get on with it and tell them about this bloody disk. Go on from when you put this Fergal Flynn on to the English-man.'

Collins studied the old man for a moment, read his eyes and was satisfied. He told the three men how he'd learned of the Sixsmith project, of Flynn's background and brief, and of collecting the packet at the drop in Canberra. He told them also of the hornets' nest Flynn had disturbed with his series of seemingly wanton killings. Fleming, who had been preoccupied with the manuscript of Six-smith's memoirs, stopped reading to study Collins's face as he told of the events. Nobody interrupted and the small, dingy room was silent except for Collins's voice and the regular scraping of matches as cigarettes were lit.

'Was this drop a regularly used one?' asked the American during a brief pause.

Collins glanced at McNeela. He was still having difficulty relating to Fleming. McNeela nodded curtly, impatiently, and Collins frowned in recollection. He answered Fleming's question, but he answered it to McNeela.

'It was a secret drop. A one-off specially arranged for this purpose. Only Flynn and I knew its location and you know Flynn – they could blow his legs off and he wouldn't even tell them the colour of his hair. But Flynn had problems, serious ones. He had on his tail one of the biggest hunting packs in Australia's security history. There was much more to it than has come into the open. A lot of underground stuff. They still haven't stood down the search party. When I left yesterday, Flynn was still on the run, and still being chased. They've lowered the profile, but they're still serious. After he used the drop, Flynn would have taken the pack in another direction. But you can forget what you're thinking. No one else could have used the drop because no one else knew of it. I've got faith in Flynn. He'll turn up – if he hasn't been buried.'

'OK,' said McNeela, 'forget the drop for the moment. You picked up the disk and this tape. Go on from there.'

Collins nodded. 'I had the disk copied at the Embassy in Canberra and, in strictest secrecy, made a print-out. You have it,' he said to McNeela and pointed his chin at the sheets in front of Fleming. 'That's it – the whole works.'

'Who was with you at the time?' It was the first question from Kearns. Even his voice sounded dead as he locked eyes with Collins and effortlessly picked up his former role. Many men had dropped their guard at the sepulchral voice that came out of the death's-head. It sounded as though it was going to be an effort for it to get to the end of the sentence. But Collins wasn't deceived.

'No one. The only person other than myself – or so I thought – who's seen the contents of the disk is Eoin McNeela.' Collins's accusatory tone wasn't lost on Kearns.

'But you already knew of the contents, or, rather, of the subject of the Englishman's writing, before it came into your possession.'

'That's not quite true. I heard through a third party of the existence of the manuscript.'

No change of expression. No movement. The dead eyes locked on to Collins. Heaven help him if his voice wavered.

'An English third party?'

'An Irish third party –' He stopped, then qualified it. 'Irish/Australian, a member of ASIS, the Australian Secret –'

'We know what ASIS is. How reliable is this Irish/Australian person?'

Collins stared back. 'Unimpeachable. What are you getting at, Jack?'

Kearns crushed his cigarette out into the saucer of his tea-cup and then lit another. The other two men looked on and listened without expression. They were like spectators watching a craftsman at his bench. 'What I'm getting at, Tom, is the suggestion that you've been nominated by the British to throw this bundle of shit at the organization so that the Army Council, with the New Executive in its sights, does exactly what you proposed to friend McNeela they do. That is – '

'Don't be so bloody silly!'

'Watch your language, Tom! Remember who you're speaking to.'

McNeela jerked his head up angrily and his warning glance told Collins that whilst men like Kearns might be, for the time being, out of the front line and limelight, they still wielded enormous influence within the organization, and had votes that qualified them for a share of the financial bonanza when the revenue from the expanded organization was established.

But Kearns ignored the support. 'All right, Tom, then you don't think the British would like to see the members of Army Council at each other's throats on the eve of a highly complicated change of direction? And you don't think they know as much as you do about this change of direction?'

Collins wasn't overawed. 'I think all those things are possible,' he said authoritatively, 'but not in this case. The British haven't been in a position to direct events. It's the Australians who've been dictating the play all along, and as we know, the Australians are not generally recognized as lackeys of the British.'

Nobody laughed or sniggered. This was a serious matter and these were serious people, even though they, like the rest of the world, had enjoyed the previous British humiliation at the hands of the Australian legal system.

Collins glanced at Fleming out of the corner of his eye. The man was disturbing him. So far he had played no real part in the discussion – no real questions, no apparent interest. He hadn't even looked up from Sixsmith's manuscript when McNeela had introduced him. He was obviously sure of himself; he appeared to have no excuses to make for his presence. And that was the main thing that was niggling Collins; that and the way he occasionally raised his head at the exchange between the old and the new intelligence men. But he was listening, and taking it all in. He hadn't turned a page since Collins had started speaking. It was very distracting.

But Kearns hadn't given up.

'Did you notice any British intelligence presence there?'

Collins frowned in feigned recollection before speaking. Barbara O'Donnell had made a point of sitting in Dubrovnik's lap when the blood bath started. There hadn't been much going on that he didn't know about; the only small cloud of doubt was how much Dubrovnik was allowing Barbara to know, and how much of that was fluff. No love lost, she'd said, between the two departments; a certain amount of fluff would be very normal! Collins kept his voice low-key; there was no need to appear too eager to show how clever he was.

'There was a guy hanging around Melbourne at the time of the Sixsmith killing. It was whispered that he'd got his eye on Sixsmith and had been holding hands with an ASIO agent. The Australian agent was taken out of the scene and sent to Washington. He played no further part. But another, minor agent who came in as a Sixsmith watcher was killed. Flynn was suspected.'

'Let's hear about the Brit.'

'It was suggested that he might have had Sass credentials at one time and that he was on a watching, or nosing, brief for one of the MIs. He was certainly around when Sixsmith was writing that stuff.' He nodded at the manuscript and for the first time looked into the eyes of the man reading it. He was momentarily startled by their icy blueness. But Fleming made no comment and the contact was fleeting.

'After the Sixsmith killing a senior British official arrived in Canberra, but he wasn't on an active field role. My source says he was only interested in recovering the manuscript, claiming it was the property of the British Government. He was a black man, by the way.'

'Was his name Reason?' Fleming looked up and spoke for the first time. His accent was definitely American.

Collins, surprised, nodded.

'That complicates things,' said Fleming. 'If Clive Reason's sitting in on the game, it splits the options.'

'How?'

'Either the British are so anxious to get their hands on this Sixsmith thing and burn it before anybody in your corner gets a chance to read it, or it's what Jack here has been hinting at – they're trying a game. Either of those suppositions would explain Reason's presence. What was the name of the other guy?'

'Barlow.'

'One of Sanderson's people.' He gave a cold smile to Collins, and McNeela gave a nod of approval that said *See what I mean? We didn't even know such an organization existed.* Fleming continued. 'A funny crew. No holds barred, very un-British. They feel that winning the game is more important than taking part!'

'Very good, Pat,' growled McNeela, 'but it gets us nowhere. Tell us what you make of it. That's what you're here for – a bit of transatlantic advice. Who are these people?'

Fleming continued where he'd left off. 'You have to look at it this way. Barlow's a hard, bare-knuckle fighter. He'd be the man they'd move in to spy on a rogue ex-MI man. They took an expensive lesson with that Wright character.' He gave a wry smile and paused while he reflected on the Wright character. 'If this,' he tapped the part manuscript on the table in front of him, 'is allowed to run its course, in spite of British efforts to suppress it in an Australian court, then I wouldn't put it past Barlow to have put Sixsmith away himself. In fact, the more I think about it, I reckon that's exactly what happened.'

Kearns picked him up quickly. 'Would a man like this Barlow be given such a mandate?'

'It's all changed, Jack,' Fleming advised him. 'Nowadays British intelligence people like Harry Barlow make their own mandates. They also make their own rules as they go along. They don't like being good losers any more, they play to win. They're hard bastards now. They've come a long way since Anthony Blunt.'

Kearns shook his head. The debate was now between him and Fleming. Collins sat back and listened to the two intelligence experts as he waited his turn. 'This Sass man, Barlow,' said Fleming, 'running loose in Melbourne on a watching job almost puts a seal of veracity on this bit of writing. But who told the British their man had found himself a place in Australia and was writing his memoirs? What made them sufficiently worried to launch a man of Barlow's status in Sixsmith's direction? And then, all of a sudden, they rush out an even more senior operative to make a song and dance about some so-called Government property. There's something doesn't ring right. There's a bit of overelaboration somewhere . . .'

Collins sat forward. 'But Reason, the team leader – if it is a team – came after Sixsmith had been killed, and according to my source, whose people had him covered, the only contact he had until the time I left was with top officers of ASIO in Canberra. His only interest, it seems, was the recovery of Sixsmith's papers. There was no recorded, or observed, linkup between Barlow and Reason. The pair of them being in Australia at the same time could be coincidence.'

'Coincidence is not a viable option, Tom,' hissed Kearns, and then changed track, careful not to slow the momentum. 'This disk? Was it hard to come by?'

Collins knew what he was getting at. 'Flynn picked it up in Sixsmith's flat. It was probably hidden, but Flynn would know all about persuading people to come up with things like that. I wouldn't say they had an easy passage. It cost Sixsmith his life, along with Vincent Doyle – '

'The Belfast nutcase?' interpolated McNeela. 'Was he there?'

'You knew him?'

'Fuckin' madman, not the full shilling. Somebody blew the bastard away, did they?'

'Yes, but nobody was named as the man who put him down. I wouldn't scrub Barlow off my list for that little gem, but as I was saying, as well as Sixsmith there was an Australian special agent, Doyle, a garage owner, a couple of Australian policemen, the owner of a yacht – and those are the ones we know about. There could even be more. But that's what it cost to get that disk into your hands.'

'People get killed in war, Collins.' The dry, husky voice coming out of Kearns's tight-skinned face reduced seven deaths to a simple equation. 'Did you talk to Flynn when he delivered the disk?'

'No. He dropped it, then went out of circulation.'

'So you didn't see him?'

Collins paused significantly. Three pairs of eyes studied him. 'No. But Flynn was no fool. He made a recording of part of his interrogation of Sixsmith which bears out the authenticity of the memoirs.'

'Why would he do that?' asked McNeela.

'I should have thought for the reason it serves. That if anything happened to prevent him presenting the disk in person, the tape would prove that Sixsmith's project was on the level.'

'Have the voices been verified?'

'Flynn's has. Indistinct, but the source says yes. Nobody knows what Sixsmith sounded like, but if you asked me to guess what an English desk man sounds like, that's what it'd be!'

Kearns sniffed. It wasn't apparent whether the sniff signified acceptance, but he didn't pursue the point. 'Anything else?' he asked.

'There was a rough note with the stuff explaining why he couldn't hang around. He reckoned the Aussie SAS had been brought in.'

'So when did you last see him?'

Collins shrugged. 'When I gave him his instructions. I didn't want him sitting on my doorstep at any time. I'd got my own cover to consider, so I couldn't run along with him pointing where he could and where he couldn't go, or what he could and couldn't do. Once I'd briefed him, I had to leave him alone. I didn't think he was going to do an Attila the Hun across Australia, otherwise I'd have thought more than twice about giving him the brief. He was recommended as the safest pair of hands in the business by the person who instructed me.'

'Who was?'

'Michael Fitzpatrick.'

'Chief of Staff, Chairman of the New Executive?'

Collins didn't reply as the two older men exchanged glances. Fitzpatrick was the man who fitted Sixsmith's barely concealed description of a British agent. But nothing was said. Not yet.

'OK,' said Kearns. His eyes narrowed. 'How did you know Flynn found this disk in Sixsmith's flat if you haven't spoken to him since he started pushing the ball around?'

Collins bridled. 'I don't think I like the sound of that question. You're not thinking of sticking a bag over my head, are you?'

Kearns stared at him stolidly. There was nothing to be read in the two dull pebbles where his eyes should have been. 'So?'

'What?'

'The disk?'

Collins shrugged indifferently. 'You've forgotten the taped interview and Flynn's note. One has to surmise that's where he picked it up.'

Kearns didn't show whether he was satisfied or not. He continued his flat stare. 'Forget that for a moment. Tell us something else. How did your source come to know what was in these papers before your retrieval operation began?'

'I've already gone into this in detail with Eoin,' replied Collins.

'Then go into it again, in detail, with me and Fleming,' rasped Kearns, without rancour. 'But briefly, and stick to the facts, not what you surmise.'

Collins looked pointedly at McNeela before replying, then, getting a nod of approval, told the other two men how Barbara O'Donnell, whose name he didn't mention, had brought Sixsmith's activities to his notice.

'And you passed this to the Foreign Department in Dublin?' interrupted Fleming.

'I work at the Embassy in Canberra,' replied Collins, tartly. 'I'm employed, ostensibly, by the Foreign Department abroad. It would have been foolish not to. Besides, I wanted a read-out on Sixsmith's credentials before committing myself and the organization to an all-out recovery operation. My initial reaction, like yours – ' he stared at his two interrogators '– was that the British were playing the joker.'

'And you changed your mind?'

'The circumstances dictated it. They couldn't carry out a scheme like this. In England maybe, and with difficulty, but in Australia? Never! I think the stuff's genuine.'

Fleming leaned forward with his arms on the table, then turned his head and looked Collins in the face. 'So, what would you do, Mr Collins? Follow Sixsmith's finger and take out the top man in the New Executive and stick him up against the wall? What do we do after that? Poke around and see if we can come up with another bunch of executives who are reasonably clean and don't come from Whitehall?'

Collins didn't react, but McNeela did. 'Steady, lads,' he

said grimly, then stood up, opened the door and called for his daughter to bring tea. They weren't asked whether they wanted it. It was tea or nothing. Some of the tobacco smoke hanging over the table like an army blanket shivered in the draught, but there was no marked improvement in the atmosphere. McNeela left the door ajar and came back to his place by the fireside. 'Things are bad enough as they are. If we start pissing over each other, we might as well pack up now.'

The only thing that moved was Fleming's head as he transferred his attention from Collins to McNeela. It sounded as if the summing-up was on its way. Somebody in a high place was going to have his face blown in.

'But the trouble is we can't,' McNeela continued. 'We can't pack the thing in now as if nothing's happened. We've got this fucking tiger's tail in our hands and we've just got to pull the bastard until we've laid it to rest. Which is easier said than done. But first, before we start shoving black bags over people's heads, we make absolutely sure that the story's straightforward. Tom – ' He swivelled his eyes in Collins's direction, but before he could add to what he'd already said, Kearns butted in.

'Eoin, apart from Fitzpatrick, you've got another two on the Executive who need looking at. You know all these people better than anyone, they came up through you, so tell me, could you finger any one of 'em and say, yes, he's a slippery bastard – he's our bloody man?'

Instead of answering immediately, McNeela lit another cigarette, trickled the smoke from the first drag down his nostrils, and then filled his lungs again. Fleming watched the operation and coughed in sympathy.

'Did you ever hear of Stephen Hayes?' McNeela asked him.

'Can't say I have,' replied the American.

Kearns had, but he kept quiet. So had Collins.

'Nineteen forty-one, he was Chief of Staff, the big job, the top man. I was a boy, nineteen. I loved the man, would have followed him into perdition at the crook of his finger. He was the best leader I ever served under. That was Stephen Hayes.'

'So?'

'The fucker was a British spy!'

'Who said so?'

'He said so himself. I was there.' McNeela jerked his thumb over his shoulder. 'Just down the road – Terenure. They had him hooked to the wall in a house there and I heard it from the bastard's own lips. A fucking British agent.'

'I'm surprised he could talk,' said Fleming.

'He could talk all bloody right. He was like a fucking budgerigar! Ever since that day I've trusted no fucker – not even my mother! So, as far as I'm concerned, the whole fuckin' Executive's in the pay of the British until it's proved otherwise.'

'What did you do with Hayes?' asked Fleming. He seemed to have a morbid interest in what happened to convicted British spies. 'Shoot him?'

'No. The morning he was due for his coffin, the bastard grabbed his minder's gun and legged it off into the town – down here, Rathmines. I never saw him again; nobody ever saw him again. Somebody reckoned he went into the British Army and became a major or something. I just hope the fucker got his legs blown off at Alamein or somewhere!'

'Very interesting,' said Fleming dryly. 'Now we've got Fitzpatrick in the frame, but that doesn't seem to be enough. Who else d'you think we ought to be looking at?'

'Assuming it can be established that Sixsmith's words are genuine?'

'I thought we'd just established that?'

McNeela moistened his lips with his tongue. 'No one but Michael Fitzpatrick.'

'You're quite sure?'

McNeela moistened his lips again. The memories of a nineteen-year-old's disillusionment had dried his mouth out. He hawked quietly and swallowed whatever it produced before nodding.

'I'm sure.'

Jack Kearns watched him through narrowed eyes, the cigarette gripped between his lips forgotten as its smoke rose like a sinuous grey silk rope to join the blanket hovering under the ceiling. The silence that had descended on the room seemed to be waiting for Kearns to break it. He turned his head away from the table and blew down the side of his cigarette. The ash shot on to the threadbare carpet like a bullet. 'I think we've got to tread bloody carefully here,' he said at length. 'And don't forget he's still Chief of Staff as well as Chairman of the New Executive ... Christ, Eoin! The fuckin' man walks on water. He's untouchable!'

'I feel the same way as you do, Jack, but this thing is too bloody clear cut – everything points his way. But even with this lot, he won't admit a bloody thing. I know him too well. It's going to take something very special to break Michael Fitzpatrick.'

'I'll have a word with him,' said Kearns. His cadaverous expression almost lightened at the prospect.

'No, you won't!' barked McNeela. 'Nobody's having any words with anybody until I say. Nothing's to be said about what's gone on this morning until we meet again, here, in this room. Have I your word on that – all of you?'

After a pause, Jack Kearns nodded his head. The other two reluctantly followed suit, but it satisfied McNeela. At the same time the tea came. Fleming didn't touch his and left as if he'd an urgent appointment he'd just remembered. Collins gave him time to clear the district; it took half a cup of undrinkable brew, but he stuck at it stoically. When he stood up to leave, McNeela gave him an encouraging, almost friendly nod of farewell. Kearns ignored him. He looked as though he was enjoying his cup of tea. Maybe he thought it was his last.

'What d'you think, Jack?'

McNeela stood up and joined Kearns at the dining table. Kearns lit another cigarette and coughed. It went on for a long time, a wheezing, dry rumbling cough that scoured its way up his throat from ruined lungs. When he'd brought it under control, he wiped his mouth with a large handkerchief and turned his flat eyes to McNeela.

'They're too fucking smooth, these boys taking over the business. Fleming looks like a bloody bank manager, and Collins smells of politics . . . But about Collins, he's your lad, where's he going? Where'd he come from?'

'Forget Fleming, Jack, he's a sniffer dog, a bloody good sniffer, knows his way around the world and how to move, but that's all he is, a bloody sniffer dog. He's all right for us where he is. He's not going anywhere. But Collins? That's a different matter. His father was Hughie Collins, the same Hughie Collins who topped himself in Mountjoy at the time the boys were starving themselves to death in the Kesh. He did it to draw attention to the fact that there are as many injustices being done in the South as in the North. You don't get stronger faith than that. On top of that, Hughie was my best friend. We were together in Durham after the Manchester bombing campaign.'

Kearns wasn't a sentimentalist. 'I knew Hughie.' He didn't elaborate. 'But rolling along with the Sands bandwagon doesn't make his son an expert in the making of poteen. What's Collins done to earn himself a possible place at the top table?'

'You're a hard man, Jack Kearns. The Movement brought the boy along, paid for his schooling, working him into Government. He went into the intelligence service at the Movement's insistence. He's done us well. He's repaid our money a hundredfold with his work in London alone. He ran the whole campaign from the Embassy when he was there, and no one, theirs or ours, knew of his involvement. That's what he's done. He's been in Australia, working the place up for over a year now, and we reckon, all in all, he's earned his place on the reserve list for one of the top places on the New Executive.'

Kearns still wasn't impressed. 'You mean, if you're right about Fitzpatrick and he goes to the wall, this smartarse of yours'll move in to run the — '

'His chances are probably better than anybody else's,' said McNeela aggressively. 'He'll certainly go in at the first vacancy. You got some objection?'

Kearns was noncommittal. He lowered his eyes and studied the red ember at the tip of his cigarette. The whole thing was getting out of hand. They were no longer fighting the British in a war for a principle; they were fighting everyone for a drugs market and the chance to make money out of what had started as a crusade against the English. They used to have leaders who'd proved themselves in Armagh, Tyrone, the Lower Falls, Crossmaglen and all points North, and if they didn't die doing it, they'd come down South and sat on the Army Council because they knew what it was all about. Not any more. Now they went to university, learnt politics and how to stash cocaine and heroin, and then came down South to sit on the Army Council and wait for a place on the New Executive. Kearns shook his head. But he shook it to himself. No, he had no objections to men like Collins running the organization, because there was no fuckin' organization left, only a bunch of people splitting up sackfuls of

411

dirty money. He raised his head and looked his old friend in the eye. It was like two shuttered shops on either side of the road, neither showing the other what was going on behind. It was the way you survived when a change of allegiance was called for and a change of system was in the air.

Kearns shook his head slowly. No expression, no objection and another long pull on the cigarette. 'Give the Brits a month to prove themselves in Australia,' he said through a rumbling throat. 'This stuff,' he flicked the cigarette at the sheets of Sixsmith's manuscript left untidily on the table, 'has got to find a passage out. Somehow it's got to end up on a publisher's table and then we can sit back and see how the British dance. We have a precedent. If they don't like it, they'll fight. They'll kick and they'll scream to have it suppressed, and if they do that we'll know it was on the level. If they say nothing, do nothing, and watch the thing go through without a whimper, it'll be a set-up and Michael Fitzpatrick can remain an obstacle to your friend's boy running the New Executive.'

'I don't like the way you put that, Jack.'

'How would you have put it?'

McNeela studied Kearns's expression for a few seconds, then shook his head. He made no reply to the invitation, but said, 'OK, leave it at that. Give Collins and Fleming a month to stir things around a bit in Australia, and then we'll have another, closer look at how the British play this hand of cards. Agreed?'

Kearns waited a second, then nodded his head. It was barely noticeable. If McNeela hadn't been looking closely, he wouldn't have seen it.

33

Fiona Campbell was perfectly composed as she learnt of her father's effects. There was nothing to discompose her. Greville Sixsmith had been an absent father, a father in name only. She hadn't missed his fatherly ministrations; she'd last seen him at her wedding, and God knew who'd invited him to that. At least he hadn't appeared at the divorce party. That would have been more than her fair share of unwanted paternal sympathy. Next of kin apart, she was still wondering what she was doing here. First there'd been the telephone call, then the arranged air passage: 'Your father was a highly respected civil servant, Mrs Campbell. It's only right that you should be there to recover his private effects. Leave everything to us.' And she had. And here she was.

'Your father was writing a book, Mrs Campbell,' said Heros Dubrovnik. He'd introduced himself at the coroner's inquest and taken it upon himself to guide her through the formalities. The British High Commission official accompanying her had managed, not unusually, to mislay her charge and had returned to her desk, where she felt more at home. She wasn't good with death, or death's spin-offs. Mr Dubrovnik, whom she knew by sight from one of the Australian civil administration offices, had taken Mrs Campbell off her hands. None of the British contingent was unduly worried that Mrs Campbell had strayed into the enemy camp. In British

High Commissions, worry was a dirty word. Nobody worried about anything until the gin ran out or the beer barrel ran dry in the High Commission club.

'Perhaps you'd allow me to offer you lunch,' Dubrovnik had proposed to Fiona. 'Afterwards we can go to my office and I'll let you have the manuscript.'

'That's very kind, Mr – '

'Dubrovnik.'

'Thank you, Mr Dubrovnik.' She smiled as she pronounced the name. 'But – '

'Good, then that's settled.'

Dubrovnik's secretary wouldn't have recognized her boss. But Dubrovnik wasn't putting anything on. Fiona Campbell was an extremely attractive woman and Heros Dubrovnik wasn't averse to the company of attractive divorcees, even English ones. As for Fiona Campbell, in her mid-thirties, tall, with dark hair and a figure that commanded quite a few sidelong glances, she wasn't entirely indifferent to the attentions of an interesting and quite good-looking foreigner herself.

'I didn't know my father had taken up writing,' she said now, as she sipped her coffee after the meal. 'What do Whitehall warriors write about when they hang up their umbrellas?'

Dubrovnik stared at her over his after-lunch Cognac. This should have been a grieving daughter. It wasn't right, such frivolity. Dubrovnik wasn't quite into the English female's sense of humour. He brought the matter back to a proper Slav-like respect for the mourning period.

'It was a well-written documentation of his life in the British intelligence service.'

'Is that what he did, intelligence?'

'Didn't you know?'

She shook her head. 'Or care. We weren't father and

414

daughter in the accepted sense.' She sipped more coffee and frowned. 'Intelligence ... I suppose that would be why the man from the High Commission said he would be round to collect this manuscript when it was handed over to me.'

Dubrovnik's eyes narrowed. 'What man was that, Mrs Campbell?'

'He said his name was Reason.'

'Oh, did he?' The brandy glass thumped on to the white tablecloth with a little more aggression than Dubrovnik meant to show. 'And did he make any sort of threat?'

She smiled sweetly – a touch of nervousness? 'Threat? Good God, no!' She met Dubrovnik's serious black eyes and the smile withered and died. 'Well . . . ' she hesitated. 'I wouldn't have construed it as such, but now you come to mention it . . .' She paused again. Dubrovnik's eyes seemed to be urging her on to commit herself. 'Well, he did say that as a representative of the British Government he was empowered to sequestrate any of my father's effects, including manuscripts, pending clearance by the security service for which he worked. He said something about the Official Secrets Act.' She was still studying Dubrovnik's expression. 'Does that sound like a threat to you?' Dubrovnik's eyes didn't flicker. She tried again. 'Was he entitled to make such a statement?'

'No,' said Dubrovnik evenly. He was on dangerous ground here. Once it was released by the coroner's court, he had no jurisdiction over the Sixsmith manuscript. Worse, he had no reason to recommend that the manuscript be withheld by the Australian security organization for safe keeping. Once in this woman's hands, it would be floating. It wouldn't take much pressure by British Government people, Reason in particular, to shove it into a bag and confine it to the nearest incinerator. And they had every right to do that; it was none of his business. But

415

there was something niggling. Perhaps it was Reason's attitude; perhaps it was his antipathy to the British as a whole; perhaps he wanted their noses rubbed into it again. So what the bloody hell!

'My advice to you, Mrs Campbell,' he continued, 'is to hand this manuscript to a solicitor – I'll give you the name of one, if you like – for safe keeping until you decide whether you want to offer it for publication or not. My advice, and it's personal,' he tightened his lips to emphasize the next bit, 'and strictly unofficial, is that it should be published, if nothing else than as a gesture to your father's memory.' Dubrovnik treated himself to a little unnoticed sigh of contentment. He'd got it out. He'd got rid of his conscience. Bugger the English. Let them go to court and eat shit! 'But,' he continued, 'whatever you do, don't hand it to Mr Reason, or anybody else. Let them make their plea to your solicitor.'

'I wonder what my father intended doing with it?'

'There's no question what he intended doing. He was going to publish it, which is why he came here. The British wouldn't allow him to do it in England. I suggest you discuss this with the lawyer I recommend.' He picked up his glass again and drained it. 'By the way,' he said and lowered his voice, 'I'd rather you didn't discuss this conversation with Mr Reason. I wouldn't want him to think I'd advised you to go against your Government's wishes.'

'Is that what I'd be doing?'

Dubrovnik didn't answer. 'Would you like some more coffee, a liqueur, brandy?'

'No thanks, Mr Dubrovnik. I've enjoyed lunch enormously. And thank you for your advice. But if Mr Reason suggests the stuff my father's been writing might endanger the security of my country, I think I'd better do as he requests.' She smiled into his eyes as she touched the

416

napkin to her lips. There was just the suggestion of conspiracy. 'But I'd like the name of your solicitor just the same – if you wouldn't mind.'

Whilst Fiona Campbell was powdering her nose, Dubrovnik slipped into the restaurant's office and picked up the telephone. He dialled his own number.

'Mary,' he said when his assistant answered, 'don't ask questions, no clever stuff, no backchat, but get hold of that woman over at ASIS and ask her if she'd meet me in your office in half an hour. A matter of urgency, tell her.'

'O'Donnell.'

'Pardon?'

'Her name's Barbara O'Donnell.'

'Thanks. Get cracking.'

'I'll get you a cup of coffee, Mrs Campbell,' said Dubrovnik as he placed the wrapped bundle of manuscript on the table in front of her, 'while you're glancing through it.'

'Do I have to?'

He nodded seriously. 'You wouldn't want to sign for four hundred blank sheets of paper, would you? I'll get your coffee and then arrange for a car to take you back to your hotel. I won't be long. Take your time.'

Barbara O'Donnell, leaning across the table, was having a very serious conversation with Mary. She looked up when Dubrovnik came in. It was a look of impatience rather than of curiosity.

'It couldn't have been all that urgent,' she said and pointed to the corner of Mary's desk. 'D'you know what that thing is?'

'What thing?'

'It's called a telephone. We can tell each other things on it . . .'

Dubrovnik didn't bite. 'Sorry to have kept you. Would

you like to come outside with me for a moment?' He didn't wait for her to acknowledge but held the door open. 'A cup of coffee for the lady in my office, please, Mary – black, no sugar.'

He led Barbara down the corridor as far as the south-end window. There they could look out over East Basin and the Jerrabomberra Wetlands beyond. They could also talk without being overheard.

'D'you remember the name Sixsmith?' he began without preamble.

She went through the motions of recollection for a second. 'The Irish thing you were interested in a short time ago?' She paused and studied his face. 'And a mad Mick named Flynn who's been rampaging through Victoria killing everything in sight?'

Dubrovnik's eyebrows closed together over the bridge of his nose. It was his way of hiding his surprise. 'Six-smith wasn't connected with that,' he stated.

She turned to go.

'I haven't finished,' he said.

'I have. If you're going to play the Gay Hussar with me, Dubrovnik, I've certainly finished. Goodbye!'

'Just a minute! I deliberately kept Sixsmith's name out of the Flynn affair, it's not common knowledge. I didn't want the British landing in force to demand a share of the hunt. D'you want to tell me how you made the connection?'

'No. But now we know where we stand, let's keep it open. What about Sixsmith?'

Dubrovnik regained control of himself. 'I've got his daughter in my office. She's here to collect his effects and she's been granted leave to take possession of that manuscript I discussed with you – the one concerning the deaths in Ireland last November. Right. Now, there's a big black guy in town who wants that manuscript on behalf of the British Government. His name's Reason and he's a fairly high-powered Government agent. If he gets hold of it it'll go straight into the incinerator and that'll be the end of it.'

'What's your interest in keeping it out of British hands?'

'I want to keep it running for a while. There's a British MI guy named Barlow who wants it as much as Reason does. Barlow also knows Flynn. He's been looking for him, ostensibly on my behalf, but also for his own purpose. There are too many people chasing this pile of paper. I've said it before and I'll say it again, there's something not right about all this.' He tapped his forehead with his finger. 'I can feel it up here. There's a lot of bullshit going on and a lot of Poms forking it over. I want to see exactly how far they'll go.'

'Is this in Australia's interest, or purely to satisfy Heros Dubrovnik's curiosity?'

Dubrovnik gave Barbara one of his rare smiles. it was a genuine one. Barbara had read him; he gave her credit for it. 'Australia's interest. Any gathering of British Government and MI people in this country is, as far as I'm concerned, a threat to the security of Australia. And yes, Heros Dubrovnik is also curious!'

Barbara returned his smile. 'What do you want me to do about it?'

'Stay with her for a bit. Make sure the manuscript is lodged in Donald McKay's safe until she makes up her mind to have it turned into a book, or at least kept out of Reason's hands until a decision is made one way or the other.'

'Is McKay acting for her?'

'Not yet. I told her I'd give her the name of a Canberra lawyer who'd look after her interests. McKay's a Turnbull clone; he'll certainly do that. Anything antigovernment – anybody's government – and you'll find McKay breathing heavily at the bar ready to do battle for free.'

'And you think they'll go all the way with this one?'

'I've read it. They will!'

'Surely even the British wouldn't want their arses skinned twice. Old Peter Wright's barely stopped counting his good fortune since the last time they took on the Australian courts. They wouldn't try it again – would they?'

Dubrovnik didn't turn away from the window. He'd found something of great interest going on below in Sir Thomas Blamey Square. 'I think the British got out of that exactly what they wanted.'

Barbara looked sharply at the side of his face. But nothing showed. 'What d'you mean by that?'

He continued as if he hadn't heard. 'And I think they're up to something again. I think they're using us.'

'Bollocks, Heros! Nobody's that deep. They're going for another bloody ride if they chance their arm in a Melbourne court! No! Definitely not! They're not bloody devious enough to play games like that, not any more. They used to be, but no, not any more. They don't toss bloody lives away to make points.'

'What about those two guys you told me about who got blown up in Northern Ireland? They were supposed to be Brits, weren't they? Intelligence operatives, you said, and no responsibility claimed by the other side.'

'That's different,' said Barbara, slowly. 'I heard that Sixsmith had named names and pointed fingers at his own people tripping across the wire in Ireland itself. They wouldn't want that put out for general consumption. If they did, the Dublin people would have a field day. You're trying to be too bloody devious, Dubrovnik – like them.' He didn't notice that she'd gone back to surnames

420

after a brief sally into the friendlier use of Heros. But it was his turn to look at her sharply.

'And how did you know that?'

'Know what?'

'That Sixsmith had named names.'

'A little bird tweeted in my ear. Cut it out. I'm in the same bloody game as you. Don't take us all for bananas, Dubrovnik, we've also learned to put our ears to the wall. Anyway, I don't agree with you in any of those areas, but I'll do as you ask. I'll take the woman and have a quiet chat with her in the ladies' loo, and then we'll take it from there. But I'll tell you one thing for nothing, if that bloody pile of paper ends up on a publisher's desk, it'll be Sydney 'eighty-six all over again. The British'll fight. Take my word for it. I know the bastards.'

34

Harry Barlow took a taxi out to Canberra Airport. He told the driver to take him through Duntroon Military Academy. It was for the novelty. Duntroon had to be the only military establishment in the world that had public roads running through the middle of it. It was there for the taking, a gift, a terrorist's dream. He didn't look round, but he knew the same car was there tickling in his wake; they even had the same two heavies doing the job. He sat in the back of the Aerial Taxi and read his newspaper. That's what they'd expect; Poms would be too high and mighty to share the front with the driver.

No bags, but that didn't deter his watchers. One got out of the car at the far end of the terminal entrance and followed Barlow into the departure lounge. The car pulled away and tucked itself in the car park, where the driver switched off, got out, lit a cigarette and waited.

Barlow walked along to the café and bookshop, collected a cup of coffee and sat down at the only unoccupied outside table. The watcher hung around and studied the posters in the main lounge. He wasn't worried when, after a minute, Barlow put his open newspaper on the table beside his unfinished coffee and walked back into the cafeteria. As he walked straight through the shop and through the side door that led outside, just beside the taxi rank, Barlow had a gentle smile on his face. The driver of the watcher car hadn't moved. He was still enjoying his cigarette and leaving the work to his partner.

They knew he knew. Still they carried on with the charade. It wasn't really serious, just enough to make him feel welcome and wanted, and to know that all was not forgotten. It had taken him only a few minutes to draw the watcher far enough away from his partner to throw the team off balance, but it was only temporary. He climbed into a new taxi and twenty minutes later arrived alone at the Lakeside Hotel in London Circuit.

The trouble for anyone trying to meet Reason on the quiet, in public, was that he was going to stand out anywhere. Reason would be conspicuous in a crowd in Kwazulu. Which was why Dubrovnik was letting him run freely; he knew he could find him any time he wanted. It was Barlow who interested Dubrovnik, and who Barlow met. He'd tried to match him with Reason, it would have settled quite a lot of queries in his mind, but so far he hadn't yet made a definite connection between the two. He didn't know it, but he'd just lost his last chance.

Barlow found Reason sipping a cold Tooheys beer in the far corner of the Humbug Bar in the Lakeside's Cahoots Pub. It was an appropriate setting. The walls were covered with pictures, sketches and cartoons of Australia's finest leaders; politicians of every hypocritical shade of opinion, with every smug, complacent and self-satisfied expression, were gazing at Reason from every angle. He didn't appear to be put out by it; it wasn't affecting the taste of his beer.

'Murray's put a name to the guy who picked up the disk,' said Barlow, once the well-built German-Australian girl dressed like a man in black trousers and a starched white long-sleeved shirt had deposited a frosted glass and a huge bowl of assorted nuts in front of him and glided back to her place behind the large circular bar.

'Mr Galloglass?' said Reason.

Barlow nodded. 'Real name Thomas Collins. Third

Secretary at the Irish Embassy, which means he's a senior intelligence officer for the Republic of Ireland and looks after the Micks' many friends in the future Republic of Australia. That's his day job.'

Reason stared at him, but said nothing.

'The rest of the time, according to David's friends,' continued Barlow, 'he moonlights as a very senior member of this rearranged IRA/PIRA grouping and is a prime candidate for a place on the New Executive.' He studied Reason's face for a moment to see how he was taking it but, as expected, found no clues. Encouraged, he drank from his glass, winced as the cold liquid cauterized his sinuses, and went on. 'David fancied him and got the garden fork out. Apparently he typifies the new wave. He can write his name in proper ink, and has a couple of interesting degrees from Trinity College, Dublin, which I suppose you need nowadays to be able to cut cocaine to the infinite. David also tells me it's reliably whispered that he'll definitely go on the New Executive when they really get the thing going. A high-flier, who'll run the show one day. We've got a star in the making, Clive. Aren't you impressed?'

Reason lowered his glass but didn't place it on the table. Looking like a thimble in his huge hand, it remained ready for the next swallow. 'He's one of the two, Harry,' he said.

'One of the two what?'

'Ah! I forgot to mention, he's one of the two specialists briefed by the Micks' security council to look into the little bit of skulduggery you and Sixsmith have been up to. The other one's a guy called Fleming, an Irishman with an American accent who somehow got himself employed by the Cousins –'

'Just a bleedin' second, Clive!'

'Sorry, Harry, it's all jumped out of control. Collins

424

took his disk back to the fair city and went into committee with two of the grey heads who look after the Movement's archives. Two hard old bastards named McNeela and Kearns. They've accepted, in principle, your little effort and pointed the shillelagh at the present Chief of Staff and Chairman of the Executive, one Michael Fitzpatrick. Fleming, CIA, is coming to Australia to pick holes in our game. If, in his opinion it's all square and on the level, Fitzpatrick goes to the wall and Collins slips on to the committee. But before all that happens, Collins comes back to Oz to steer the Yank in the right direction.'

'Bloody hell!'

'Going to be fun, isn't it? Is Fleming going to find anything? Did you and Murray clean everything up behind you?'

'There was only one loose end, Mrs Clarke, but Murray and his consular mate at Melbourne have stuck a "Penelope" in her place who has all the conversation about Flynn.'

'Where's the real Mrs Clarke?'

'She and her children are back in England. I don't know where Sanderson's hidden them, and neither does anyone else. They're out of sight. No address known. It won't bounce. I don't think Flynn'll be found for the next thousand years, so your Fleming fellow can sniff to his heart's content. He won't blow this one into the open. But I've got a couple of questions . . .'

Reason raised an eyebrow.

'How did you get all this stuff about movements and decisions in Dublin?'

'Don't ask, Harry.'

'About Collins?'

'Same thing, Harry. Forget it.'

'But you won't mind me speculating?'

'Dangerous stuff speculation, Harry.' Reason looked Barlow squarely in the eyes. It was a look that invited Barlow to drop the subject. Reason emptied the contents of his glass and replaced it on the table. 'Murray's staying at Thompson's other place until we close down here. One never knows when David's particular talents might be required. When this game's run its course he can go back and finish what he was doing in Hong Kong. By the way, what happened to that woman Dubrovnik sicked on to you? I noticed she didn't obstruct you after all. Did David attend to the matter for you?'

'It sorted itself out, Clive. There wasn't a problem.'

No problem, Clive, she didn't get in the way! What she got was a nasty broken arm, concussion, and a knocked-out, morphine-induced delirium on the boat while Murray and I played the dirty on her. Apart from that, she got nothing for her troubles . . .

The hospital in Melbourne had been impressed with Harris's first aid treatment. He got a bollocking for the delay in delivering her, but they got over it and in no time Sophie had been sitting up in bed, arm plastered, hair brushed, make-up applied and eyes warm and welcoming. But the jaw hadn't lost its firm outline.

'You were right, Harry,' were the first words she said.

'Don't talk about it,' said Barlow. 'It's best forgotten.'

'I said you were right. Make a meal of it. I don't often admit my mistakes. You were right about using the gun. I was too slow, I should have ignored the woman.'

'You did exactly what I would have done. Murray might have found another option, but Murray's not like other people.'

'What happened to the woman, the children? What happened to Flynn?'

'I don't think this is the time, or the place – '

'Harry!'

'OK. We killed Flynn, but had to sink the boat doing it.'

'Oh, Jesus.'

'The woman and her children managed to get off in the boat's dinghy. We picked them up. They're being looked after until the woman can be debriefed by the police, then they'll all be flown back to England.' How easily the lies came. Barlow didn't flinch; even his eyes showed total sincerity. 'But this is no concern of yours any more. How're you feeling?'

'Sorry for myself.'

'Sophie . . .'

'No, Harry. Not just yet. Let's think about it.'

'You said – '

'I know what I said, but let's leave it for the moment. Harry?'

'What'

'What's England like this time of the year?'

'You fancy it?'

'I wouldn't mind a look around. Would you have the time?'

'Yes.' As simple as that. 'When?'

She glanced down at her arm and tapped it. 'About three weeks? Will you be around?'

'I'll make a point of it! I'll be waiting for you. Wild Irishmen couldn't keep me away!'

'Harry?'

'Yup.'

'Give us a kiss!'

When their mouths parted she held on to the back of his head with her good arm. Her eyes were soft; he'd never seen them softer. Her chin was soft, her mouth was soft, and her lips were moist. He kissed her open mouth

427

again, gently, and after a moment she pulled away fractionally and looked into his eyes. 'OK, Harry, let's not think about it just yet. Let's sort things out in England. You know I meant what I said on the boat?'

'Say it again then.'

'I love you, Harry Barlow.'

Barlow waited until Reason had settled back in his chair, then asked: 'What d'you want me to do now, Clive?'

'The game's finished here, Harry, you might as well go home. Don't sneak out. Pick the phone up and say goodbye to your friend Dubrovnik. Your departure'll give him something else to worry about.'

'What are you going to do?'

'Try and persuade Mrs Campbell not to publish her daddy's memoirs, and hope like bloody hell somebody else is doing the opposite. I'm sure Dubrovnik is full of advice, but we'll have to wait and play each over on its merits.'

'Maybe Collins could help out.'

Reason smiled sadly and stood up. 'There you go, Harry, that's what I said about speculation – you could get your fingers lopped off for trying to make four out of two and two. I'd cleanse my mind of such thoughts if I were you, Harry, particularly when you're sipping gin with Richard. Offer him anything like that and he's liable to think of removing something a bit more substantial than your fingers.'

Barlow looked up and smiled. It was a genuine smile. He knew a threat when he heard one, even when it came from as close a friend as Clive Reason. 'Wipe that troubled look from your face, Clive, you look like a Zulu general contemplating Rorke's Drift. Nothing'll ever be that bad again.'

'Don't count on it, Harry. See you in Chelsea for sundowners.'

Barlow watched Reason's tall frame until he disappeared round the corner. He ordered another beer, lit a cigarette, and after a few moments' silent communion got down to some serious speculation and some interesting thoughts about life with a beautiful woman lying in a Melbourne hospital.

35

Collins sat and waited for Kearns to say something.

It was three weeks since he'd been here last: three weeks spent digging and diving for these two hoary old sods who suspected everybody and trusted no one. Kearns looked as if he hadn't moved since Collins had last turned his back on him. He still stared blank-faced into his cup of tea, still wore the same old-fashioned, navy-blue suit, probably the same grubby shirt, its collar limp and curled like last week's lettuce. McNeela had at least changed his teacup for a glass of bottled Guinness.

'The Yank reckoned everything was above board,' conceded Kearns reluctantly. 'He couldn't find Flynn, but that doesn't worry me any more. My guess is that they turned an Australian SAS team on to him, and you don't need reading glasses to know that they're no different from their British mentors. The Brits would have buried him. With his record, they wouldn't have given him a chance. I reckon the Australians have done exactly that. Anyway, Flynn's outworn his usefulness. He'd just be a liability now. What does worry me, though, is why he went over the top like that – it's not like him at all. He must have thought he was a fuckin' Red Indian the amount of bloody killing he did. And who was this Australian he went running with? Sullivan? His body was found wrapped round a tree on the side of a bloody mountain. He had no fuckin' head! Did Flynn do that as well?'

'The state police reckoned that was an accident,' said Collins. 'Sullivan was wounded by one of the policemen Flynn killed, and it seemed he just drove off the road at high speed. Sullivan was a friend of Vinnie Doyle. Doyle was killed in a safe house on the outskirts of Melbourne. They reckoned he might have been done by Barlow, the SAS man. There was nothing ominous about these killings. Everything looked straightforward. Did Fleming comment otherwise?'

'No,' grumbled Kearns. 'He couldn't find a fault anywhere, and neither could I in anything he said. He's done a job, and done it well. Going back to Flynn for a moment . . .' There was something about Flynn that was still niggling the old interrogator. He seemed to want Flynn well and truly scrubbed off the list. 'Did you talk to the woman who came off the boat about him?'

'Yes,' responded Collins, patiently. 'She said Flynn dumped her and her kids on a bit of sand – God knows why he didn't kill her and make a clean sheet of it – and the last she saw he was heading out to sea on the boat's engine. Maybe he sank the bloody thing before making his way to Canberra.'

McNeela, excluded from the conversation for some time, lifted his head from his glass of Guinness and stared at Collins. 'If "maybe" is the best you can come up with, you'd be better off leaving it alone. Stick to facts.'

Collins took the rebuke in his stride. 'The police put in a high-profile search of the area. It's deep water. Nothing was found. But he obviously got away with it because he made the drop.'

Kearns gave him a quick sideways glance. 'You're right. I'm happy about that. Let's move on. How did the manuscript find its way to Hemisphere Publishing?'

Collins paused for a moment to adjust to the sudden change of tack. The two old men watched him closely. He

431

didn't keep them more than a couple of seconds. 'Along with the rest of Sixsmith's effects, it was claimed by his daughter, a Mrs Fiona Campbell. The head of ASIO's Room 24, Heros Dubrovnik, who'd been the instigator of the watch on Sixsmith, introduced her to Barbara O'Donnell, who – '

'Who's Barbara O'Donnell?'

'A senior executive running the Irish desk in ASIS. Apparently this Dubrovnik has an obsessive dislike of the British.'

'You can't fault the man for that!' Kearns's lips almost shaped themselves into a smile, but they weren't used to it. His face settled back almost as quickly to its taut, parchment-like death's-head. 'Go on.'

'He introduced her to – '

'We've had that bit.'

'Barbara O'Donnell, under my prompting, persuaded Mrs Campbell that the right thing for her father's memory was to publish his memoirs. She agreed, against enormous pressure from the British High Commission and despite the personal intervention of the British intelligence representative, Clive Reason, and deposited the manuscript with an Australian lawyer. He went through the motions with the publishers on her behalf and then it was almost as if they'd brought out the script of the Wright/Turnbull circus act again. An injunction to prevent publication until it had been scrutinized and anything prejudicial removed was sought by the British Government. This, as in the previous script, was opposed by the publishers. The British, as before, went over in strength and the Australian press geared itself for another spectacle of the British Government's legal hierarchy making a monkey's arse of themselves."

'What went wrong?'

'It seems the Australians got cold feet over another

British humiliation and appointed Mr Justice Jonathan Godwin, a Supreme Court judge, to conduct the trial.' Collins forestalled Kearns's interruption with his hand. 'Godwin was known for his fawning, pro-British leanings. He even had a CBE tucked away that he got before the Australians barred their citizens from receiving British honours. It looked a foregone conclusion that he'd grant the British stable anything they wanted. If they'd asked, he'd have given them Mrs Campbell's head wrapped up in the bloody manuscript like a fish-and-chip dinner . . .'

'Does this have a moral somewhere, Tom?' growled McNeela. He already knew the answer. This performance was for Kearns's benefit.

But Kearns wasn't in a hurry. He was taking in every word, analysing it and forming his own conclusions. He wasn't listening to a story, he was conducting an interrogation, seeking the flaw, waiting to pounce. 'Let him get on with it, Eoin,' he admonished McNeela without taking his eyes off Collins. 'Don't leave anything out, Tom,' he warned Collins. 'Go on about the judge.'

'There's nothing more to say about him,' replied Collins. 'He played no further part after he fell out of his boat whilst fishing and drowned.'

Kearns stared at him.

'Drowned?'

'That was the verdict.'

'Nothing suspicious?'

'How can you make anything suspicious out of an old boy falling out of his boat and drowning?'

'Where were these British people at the time – this Reason and Barlow?'

'Why don't you tell me what you're trying to make out of this, Jack, and we'll break it down as we go along?'

'Answer the question.'

'Barlow left Australia shortly after the Sixsmith killing.

433

Reason was in Canberra. The judge drowned in Port Phillip Bay, off a place called Mornington, south-east of Melbourne. It was an accident.'

'Anyone else die with him?'

'No. He was doing what he'd been doing for the past eight years – fishing alone. He didn't like crowds. But Jack, I think you've missed the point. This was to our advantage, it left the seat open for someone who didn't think the sun shone out of the British arse. It levelled the thing in our direction and offered the chance of the result going in the publisher's favour which, from our point of view blows away any sort of conspiracy theory we might have harboured against British MI. The Brits don't want the bloody thing published, remember? The old guy's death worked in our favour. What's wrong with that?'

'I don't know. Did we kill him?'

'No. It was an accident, Jack.'

'Too bloody convenient. The Brits could have killed him.'

'Why would they want to do that?'

'I'm not sure,' admitted the death's-head. Something was niggling away behind the expressionless eyes. 'Maybe they want this stuff published. Maybe they want us to put Fitzpatrick against the wall. Maybe –'

'Come off it, Jack!' implored McNeela. 'Nobody in their right mind would go to those bloody lengths to put a noose round somebody's neck. Christ, if they wanted Fitzpatrick out of the way there are easier methods than this.'

'OK,' conceded Kearns finally. 'I'll give you that one. But this old bugger throwing himself out of his boat doesn't sound right to me. There's a coincidence here that comes just right for us. I don't like coincidence, never did. Still, I'll take this one. So, how's the thing sitting now, Tom?'

'They're waiting for a new judge to be appointed and a new date to be set. The Brits are fidgeting around with faces as black as thunder and waiting for the bad news. I wouldn't be surprised if they don't throw their hands up and go home, because whoever's chosen to sit on this is bound to give 'em a bloody hiding. There was all hell to pay when Godwin's name was made public. The Australians don't like *faits accomplis* in their bear-baiting. They want a bloody good fight with the British losing by a knock-out in the last round. The Australian judiciary won't make the same mistake twice. Maybe they'll dig that other old bugger out again – what was his name?'

'Powell,' said Kearns. He never forgot a friend's name. 'OK, so we've got to make a decision. We accept that this thing is genuine and take the necessary steps, or we ignore it. Eoin?'

No hesitation. 'It's gotta be right, Jack.'

'Collins?'

'We've done everything possible to break the thing down and it holds up everywhere. There are no gaps, no creaks – this thing's bloody solid. The British have fucked themselves, they've blown the cover of the highest-placed infiltrator they've ever had. I go along with Eoin.'

'I'll have a word with Fitzpatrick,' said Kearns. It was the pronunciation of the death sentence. Collins shivered inadvertently as he stared at the skull on the other side of the table. He could almost hear the bell tolling.

McNeela broke the silence.

'I think we ought to make sure we've really got the right bloke. I wouldn't like to see an innocent man hanging from the Post Office balcony!'

The other two men stopped staring into each other's eyes and slowly centred on McNeela's. 'I thought we'd just established the man's guilt?' said Collins.

'We've established *a* man's guilt. We've surmised that it's Michael Fitzpatrick. I want to be sure.'

'You will be after I've had a talk with him,' intoned Kearns. He felt something slipping away. He'd decided who was guilty; now it was just a question of getting the victim to agree with the verdict.

'What do you suggest, Eoin?' asked Collins. Like Kearns, he'd made up his mind.

McNeela put his glass down, debated whether to call for another, changed his mind, and studied the other two men. He wasn't building up an atmosphere or setting a scene. Eoin McNeela had no use for subtleties, he knew only the direct approach. 'I've got a bit of news,' he said and touched the side of his head. 'Just me. They won't talk to the Committee, not since I told them we'd got a loose lip in the boardroom.'

'Which "they" are you talking about, Eoin?' asked Collins.

'Tripoli. I can keep it to myself or I can let it drop. Put in the right place, it'll be enough to pin the bastard's ears to the shithouse wall.'

'You want to tell me what "it" is?' asked Kearns.

'Yes, and Tom as well. But it'll be just us three – and Fitzpatrick.'

'Whatever it is, Eoin, it sounds like a hell of a bloody risk. These Tripoli people didn't tell you this bit of news to use to winkle out a snout, did they?'

'This is no ordinary snout we're talking about, Jack. If you kill Fitzpatrick and we find we're wrong, we're going to have to start again – and then again, and again. And until we pin the bastard down once and for all, we none of us are going to be able to look each other in the eye. It's getting to me already. At the moment the only people I'm prepared to say good morning to and not have the remark passed on to Whitehall are you and Tom. It's gotta be fuckin' finished *now*.'

'OK. But what if it's one of us?' asked Collins.

'Speak for your fucking self!' snarled Kearns. 'I don't need to – '

'See what I mean!' interjected McNeela. 'And we're the people who're trying to clear the fuckin' mess up. You two are clean – that's my word. Now listen, have you any idea what a billion dollars looks like?'

The two men at the table stared at McNeela as if he'd grown another head. They said nothing, just stared.

'When it's cut for the street, you multiply it by twelve and that's the size of the Executive's war chest being held on our behalf by Libya.'

'War chest?' queried Collins.

'Uncut cocaine. We don't touch it. It's collateral for the purchase of high-performance weapons from the former USSR and the Afghan arms market. But, basically, it's surety for one particular, very special item which, the way the Executive has planned to use it, will bring the British Government to its knees. Or better still, it'll bring 'em to Gerry Adams's kitchen door to discuss what arrangements he might want for a British withdrawal of interest from the Six Counties.'

'What's this "special item"?' asked Collins. 'Bearing in mind that twenty-five years of all-out armed conflict hasn't been able to get them to raise even an eyebrow in Adams's direction. It's got to be some bloody special item.'

'It's an Executive secret. You'll know soon enough,' replied McNeela enigmatically. 'Can I get on with this?'

'Sure.'

'When the war with Britain is finished, we'll expand our holding of this commodity and the prosperity of the organization will be based on the European drugs market. But for the future – '

'Why are you telling us this?' asked Collins. 'What's this got to do with British infiltration of the Executive?'

'I was coming to it. One billion dollars of pure cocaine. You know where it is?'

Collins and Kearns continued to stare.

'You don't. Nobody does. It used to be stored in a dozen or more small depots throughout Libya and only a handful of people knew the location of each depot. None of that handful lived in Dublin, that I can tell you. Right, well it's not like that any more. Thanks to the trust Tripoli places in our organization, they've had to shift the whole bloody lot to four secret, top-security locations. They've been at it day and night since I dropped the word and now the shift's complete. The only one outside Quaddafi's selected committee who knows of the location of all these new depots . . . ' He stared back at the two men for a moment. A lavatory somewhere in the house flushed noisily and then a door banged. But nobody moved. ' . . . is me,' finished McNeela. 'And I'm going to tell Michael Fitzpatrick where one of them is.'

The silence continued, then Kearns said softly, almost under his breath, 'That's fuckin' madness!'

Collins said nothing.

McNeela was unmoved. 'I told you it was going to take something special to move him. This will. This'll break the bastard wide open.'

'How?' Collins found his voice through a mouthful of sand.

'Because he'll have to tell the people who're pulling his fuckin' strings. That's what he's there for – to shove information up their arses – and they'll have to react. They'll go into a huddle with the Yanks and the next thing we'll have is a fucking SAS movement to take the place out, with Yank backup to get them in and out.'

'And we lose millions of dollars' worth of crap!' The greed showed in Kearns's face. He was almost animated over it.

'Better that, Jack, than losing the whole fuckin' lot when Fitzpatrick gets his head down over the map and pinpoints all four.'

'Can't you give him a dud reference?'

'Come off it, Jack! Tell him, Tom. I'm fed up with talking. I'm going to get myself a beer. You want one?'

Not at this stage. Kearns didn't touch it. Collins wanted a whisky, but he knew this house didn't run to that sort of thing. He swallowed a mouthful of saliva and faced Kearns's suspicious expression.

'If it's going to be done, it's got to be done properly. Fitzpatrick will pass the location to his people in London. They're not just going to fly Soldier "A" out and drop him in the desert. They'll pass the information to their American friends at Langley – the CIA –'

'You're not talking to a fucking dummy, Collins. I know the routine, *and* I know who lives at Langley.'

Collins carried on without missing a step. 'Who'll switch on their aerial surveillance tubes, and tell their cousins in London that yes, there has been, or no, there hasn't been, shipment activity in the area designated. Some of that American technology can read the tattoos on the arm of the security guard sitting at the entrance to the underground bunker and tell you what type of cigarette he's smoking. Above all, it'll tell the British that the information's good.'

Kearns's expression faded as he worked out the implications of modern technology. He continued staring into Collins's face but made no further comment.

'And then they'll attack it, destroy everything in sight and get out.'

'Happy, Jack?' asked McNeela as he came back into the room and sat down again in his armchair by the fire.

'I've a good mind to kill Fitzpatrick myself!'

'It's not been proved yet.'

'Then I'll wait till it is, and then I'll kill the fucker!'

'OK, this is the place he's going to be told about,' said McNeela.

'Christ! I don't want to know,' rasped Kearns. 'Tell it to Fitzpatrick, not me. I don't want the responsibility.'

'You've already got it, Jack. It dropped on your shoulders when you agreed to go into this thing with Tom and me. You've got to know the sequence. You're going to be standing next to Fitzpatrick at his court martial. It's got to be done properly. I trust you. And I trust Tom here. So find a corner in your head and sink this lot in it. Bettafal Oasis, just south of El Ergh – '

'Holy Mary! I don't like this.'

'Listen! It's about two hundred miles south of Ajedabya on the Gulf of Surt. This depot is the smallest of the four. It holds twenty-five tons of pure cocaine – untouched. That converts to a street value of several billion dollars. The British know what that sort of money'll buy and they'll pull out all the stops. Qaddafi'll do his bloody nut!'

'Is that what we want,' asked Collins quietly, 'for Quaddafi to do his bloody nut?'

McNeela looked at him sharply. 'No. I want fuckin' Fitzpatrick nailed to the bloody wall. That's what I want. Tom, you know how these great minds work. How long will it take for this thing to work its way through the grapevine? When will we know when to start blowing bits off Fitzpatrick?'

Collins pursed his lips. 'Provided Fitzpatrick *is* the man and does the business with the Brits, the first thing you'll know about it is when Qaddafi stops doing his nut and calms down sufficiently to tell you that a few billion dollars' worth of our collateral has gone up in smoke and the UN wants his guts for garters if he doesn't start doing something about the rest. Give it about three weeks.'

McNeela looked moderately pleased. 'OK, see you both in two weeks, then. Tom, you going back to Australia?'

440

Collins nodded.

'Right. Then you'd better start getting ready to give up that fancy striped-trouser job and prepare yourself for something serious. I'll keep you in touch. OK, Jack?'

Kearns almost nodded, but otherwise sat still, his eyes blank, his mouth vanished into the taut skin of his face. Then slowly he turned, looked Collins full in the face and said, 'When you step into Michael Fitzpatrick's shoes, Collins, I'll come and shake your hand and show you a bit of respect. Until then, I'm going to make it my business to follow your career. Make sure you don't fall off the kerb and into the gutter.'

36

Dublin, February

Clive Reason sat in one of the confessionals in the tourist-crowded church of St Francis Xavier and strained his ears to hear the whispering coming from the mouth pressed against the other side of the grille.

Reason didn't interrupt until the voice had finished, then, after a longish pause, said in no more than a whisper himself, 'If we go ahead with this, will it compromise you in any way?'

The voice hesitated for a second, then: 'No, the arrow's pointed firmly at Fitzpatrick. Apart from us, he's the only one knows about Bettafal. Me? Christ . . . ' A dry cough came through the grille. 'I'm one of the trusted three. I'm bombproof unless something hits the fan. But as far as Fitzpatrick's future is concerned, minds have been made up. His head rolls if the Bettafal Oasis is taken out. There's no way he can duck – he's dead.'

'OK. We'll give it a whirl. But if it rebounds in any way at all, we cover you and out you come. Agreed?'

'There's no way I can be blown now, Clive. You closed the hole when you put Peddy O'Dwyer down. There are no fingers left to point in my direction.'

'Don't get complacent, my friend,' whispered Reason. 'Not at this stage of the match.

'No chance of that. But listen, to get right into the guts of this New Executive we might need another head in the basket. Somebody could cramp my style. It's not critical at the moment. I'll let you know in good time.'

'You'd better let me – '

'Shhh!' The voice began intoning to itself as a penitent, anxious to get it off his chest, tried the other door. A few moments later the voice came back. 'Was it Murray did the judge in Australia?'

'What? Oh, that judge. Yes. Was it obvious?'

'Fishy! But we talked our way round it. I'm going now. Say your prayers, Clive! I'll be in touch. Same number?'

'Sure.'

Reason waited a few minutes before slipping out of the suffocating confines of the confessional and joining the rest of the throng staring up at the coffered ceiling. He moved with them towards the high altar and ogled it like any other sightseer, then satisfied that he wasn't attracting more attention than the lapis lazuli decorations, he made his way out of the church and began walking down Gardiner Street before cutting back towards Pribsborough, North Dublin, and catching a taxi for the airport.

'They've bought it, Richard. They've gone for the full set.' Clive Reason sat down in one of the heavy leather armchairs in General Sir Richard Sanderson's study and crossed his legs. 'D'you mind if I smoke?' He knew damn well that Sanderson minded but was far too well bred to object. Without waiting, he lit a Rothmans.

Sanderson watched the match flicker under the cigarette and waited until it was snuffed out by Reason's exhalation. 'Casualties?' he asked.

'None of ours, apart from Sixsmith,' said Reason casually. 'They didn't do so well, and they've got a few more to come. We have a bonus, too.'

Sanderson raised his bushy eyebrows. He was wary of Reason's casual attitude to death, there was always a catch somewhere. But he made the right sounds. 'Tell me about the bonus.'

'We have been invited to turn into ash . . .' He leaned forward and flicked the end of his cigarette into the glass ashtray on the table in front of him, then leaned back and met Sanderson's eyes. '. . . twenty-five tons of the purest cocaine. That's worth about several billion dollars on the streets of Europe, and Christ knows what to Moamar al Qaddafi in hurt pride. That's the bonus. But the net result of the bloody hard work put in by Harry and me over the past three months or so is, apart from losing Sixsmith, entirely plus to our side. All that remains is for us to go and say hello to Qaddafi's camel-watchers in Bettafal Oasis, watch another couple of Irish heads bounce into the gutter and we're in where it matters in Dublin and know what's going on before it goes on. More importantly, we'll know if the IRA's got the nuclear wherewithal to give London a gigantic new car park where the City now is, or whether it's another slice of Republican bluff. One way or the other, John Major'll be able to tell them to go and get stuffed, or give 'em everything they ask for.'

If Sanderson was delighted, it didn't show on his face. He sat opposite Reason, legs crossed and his chin balanced delicately on a two-fingered spire made from his clenched hands. Reason wasn't perturbed. He smiled broadly, sat back and allowed Sanderson his thoughts. The minutes ticked by, then, still without expression, Sanderson spoke. 'I'll give you full marks for deviousness, Clive. I don't think I've ever heard anything so bloody complicated in all my life! But that's what it's about, isn't it, complication, everybody trying to outdo the next gullible bugger. We're like a bunch of third-rate bloody cardsharps.'

'That's the soul-searching, Richard – how do you visualize the result?'

'You want to go all the way with it?'

'You're the general, is it feasible?'

'To take out the oasis? Certainly. It depends how much of a bang you want to make. Getting rid of one pile of muck from Qaddafi's larder is like trying to make a hole with a shovel in a silo full of grain. They'll replace it as soon as the smoke clears, and next time there'll be no surprise.'

'Next time, Richard, we'll know where it all is before it becomes an established fact. Remember? We're going to help run the show through the Executive's newest member. We can do all sorts of interesting things to the stuff over the whole run, from when it's first shipped, to where it's shipped to, and at all points of the process. We'll be informed of every new market and the routes and methods of distribution. We'll be able to pinpoint every major player right down to the street pusher. We won't be able to wipe them out, of course, not in one go, but knowing who, when, why and how is more than half the battle. We could even set up unofficial gangs of good guys to hit the pushers on the street. That wouldn't necessarily reflect our inside knowledge, and the other possibilities are limitless. You can't ask for better than that, Richard.'

'Provided your man doesn't make too much of an exhibition of himself, or get over-ambitious and decide that having a few million in his pocket is infinitely more desirable than being run like a poodle from London.'

'Any ideas like that,' said Reason firmly, 'and he'll find himself in bits and pieces. I don't think his mates'll take too kindly to being done over by us twice.'

'You'd blow the whistle on him?'

'Too bloody true – chapter and verse. But he's not silly enough to try double games. Besides, he'll get enough out of it to pay for a swimming pool in his back yard!'

'OK, so we've got Fitzpatrick on the rack. How're you going to finish him off? Don't expect him to go quietly. He'll scream at the top of his voice that it's a put-up, a conspiracy. He's nobody's fool is Fitzpatrick. He'll fight for his knees, you can bet your life on that, Clive.'

'He won't be able to duck out of this,' replied Reason confidently. 'Christ, Sixsmith's game went the distance – from our point and theirs. We tried to hide it – still are. We're fighting like little bantam cocks to keep the Sixsmith revelations out of the public domain. Even that's enough to send Fitzpatrick headfirst into the Liffey. This Bettafal thing'll be like sticking his feet in concrete before he hits the water. There's no way he can talk his way out of this one – he's stitched. Outside McNeela's back-room confessional, he's the only one in the game. When a few billion quids' worth of muck goes up in smoke, so will he.

'And the icing on the crumpet is that the Libyans have demanded that if they're to remain as the Executive's storekeeper, broker and arms negotiator, the next vacancy at the top goes to our man. They know him, they trust him. They want him over all others. Tripoli holds all the court cards at the moment and they're using them – they're laying down the rules. If they say they want something to happen, then by God, it'd better happen. They demand this new structure and if Dublin ignores them, it's their role in the lucrative European drugs cartel that's in peril.'

Sanderson kept his thoughts to himself. He was old enough to know all about the sort of things that happen to the plans made by mice and men. But there were other things to think about.

'What if this desert thing turns into a damp squib?'

'How is that likely, Richard?'

'I could think of a dozen reasons, but let's confine it to one. What if the Americans, who consider Colonel Moamar al Qaddafi their personal rubber ball, hear the same sounds that you've been generating and decide to try out their aeroplanes on him again? Or notice that some

British soldiers are being kitted out in desert gear and decide to get in the way? I can give you another half-dozen potential balls-ups, based on nearly fifty years of being involved in 'em, but take that as two.'

Reason stared at him for several seconds while he thought his way out, then shook his head. 'First of all, Richard, no contact – absolutely no contact at all – with the Yanks. No favours asked or given, no help in preparation – nothing. That takes away the biggest source of a possible balls-up, provided we put it together quietly with, above all, no political involvement.' He ignored Sanderson's frowning, shaking head. 'The only thing that offers the chance of a little bit of dice-throwing is the fact that we must let the Dublin Executive know we're going in, and where we got the information.'

'And how do you suggest we do that?' asked Sanderson. He didn't try to keep the cynicism out of his voice.

'Very simple,' said Reason. 'About twenty-four hours before we're due to roll in to Bettafal, one of your tame Westminster chatterboxes will whisper his suspicion of our intentions to a likely lad in one of the House of Commons bars. I'll point out whose ear it goes in, and I guarantee it'll be in Dublin before the wax settles.'

'Are you making this up as you go along?'

Reason shook his head. 'Oh no, Richard, I've been up all night working out every contingency – '

'Like hell you have. Have you worked out the contingency that when Dublin tells Libya what's about to hit them, they move in troops to dig in around Bettafal?'

'Not in twenty-four hours or so, Richard. The Libyan Army needs a week's notice to get a jeep's engine started. We'll have been in and out before they pull their boots on. Don't forget, the main thrust of this thing is not so much to destroy a few tons of stuff in a desert as to discredit a so-called British agent in an Irish organization. Don't let's lose sight of that.'

447

'Have you had a reconnaissance made of the Bettafal area?'

Reason's mouth tightened. It was as near as he dared allow his exasperation to show. 'Richard, let me make the point again: we're putting a small strike force into an unarmed depot. It's been pinpointed. I reckon that's enough. In and out, as I said. Bettafal Oasis, Richard, not the bloody bridge at Arnhem.' He paused to study the expression of one who was at the bloody bridge at Arnhem and gave a tentative smile. It was returned. No hard feelings. Sanderson knew he'd have enjoyed it. 'D'you want me to go on with the way the game is to be played?' asked Reason.

'I wouldn't be able to sleep tonight if you didn't.'

'Your man'll have to convince this ear he's whispering into that the information we're running on came from a high Dublin Executive source, so that they make no mistake over apportioning blame. Then, once the word's out in Dublin, we'll give the go-ahead and our people can hit the place with everything you give them.'

'Which won't be a lot.'

Reason lit another cigarette and tried to keep the disquiet off his face. Sanderson's enthusiasm didn't seem to be matching his own. 'D'you want to expound on that, Richard?'

There was no response. Sanderson merely looked. Reason tried again.

'Richard, for Christ's sake show me something! There's a lot of work gone into this thing! When we go in, we want to go in hard and get out intact. We've got to hit them with a bit more than a couple of old frying pans. We don't want anything half-cocked on this one, not at this stage.'

Sanderson smiled fleetingly. 'For a moment I was thinking about Arnhem.'

'Jesus Christ, Richard, this is not the time to sit there reviving old memories. Come back! D'you want me to start all over again?'

'I didn't say I wasn't listening, I said I was thinking. It's all relevant. We were too light at Arnhem, we're going to be the same at Bettafal.'

'You were fighting the bloody Germans at Arnhem, Richard. You're not comparing Libyan camel-keepers with a couple of divisions of battle-hardened SS Panzer Grenadiers, are you?'

'Weight is always a decisive factor in a battle, Clive, even with total surprise on one side. Anyway, we haven't reached that Rubicon yet. But numbers are important. If we put more than a hundred men into the field, some bloody politician'll want a share of it, particularly if it looks like a popular cause. So we come to one of the reasons for my misgivings. We have to do the thing on the cheap. If we bother MOD, the screams of financial anguish'll be heard in Tripoli before the first live round is issued. So, no, Clive, we're not going to have the bloody politicians wetting their lips over this one, either before or after.'

'How're you going to manage to put a force into the desert without telling anybody?'

'By keeping it in the family. Call it a fire-brigade exercise and we can keep it to ourselves. I'll have a drink and a chat with Nigel at Hereford and get him to bring in R Squadron, SAS, and make it look like a mercenary outing. R plus a mobility troop to take them across the desert, and half a regular Sabre Squadron hanging in the background in case they trip over their bootlaces. Harry'll go with them to make sure the thing's played in the right spirit.'

'Will he be able to keep up with them?'

'R Squadron's all reservists. Harry should feel at home.

It'll do him the world of good – them too. They like flexing their muscles occasionally and putting packs on their backs and burnt cork on their faces, it makes them feel useful. Leave it up to me.' Sanderson's earlier reticence had vanished along with his memories of Arnhem. Reason stared at him with misgiving. He looked as if he might be getting ideas about putting burnt cork on his face himself. 'They can trot in along one of the old wartime LRDG overland routes.'

'How will they get out?'

'We'll have a C140 stray off course during a mercy mission. Nobody'll notice it in the smoke.'

'What's the excuse if it goes wrong?'

'It won't, for two reasons: surprise, and the best soldiers in the world.'

'Sure, but what if it does?' insisted Reason.

'Who's going to say anything? Lieutenant Colonel Moamar al-Qaddafi? And what's he going to say? That a bunch of mercenaries came in out of the blue and took out twenty-five tons of uncut cocaine that he was looking after for a bunch of Irish ex-terrorists and future drug barons? Don't give it another thought. But Clive – '

Reason stood up. He was giving it more thoughts – many of them.

'Keep very close to Dublin for the next few weeks while we work this thing up. I reckon three weeks to get our people sorted out and on site – just an exercise between us and Hereford. The rest'll be up to you, but not a word until Harry's people are squatting in the dunes eating dates, swatting flies and admiring the palms. Only then do you start the whisper. I'll see Harry this evening and brief him. You and he can look for flaws tomorrow. Is that all right with you?'

Reason was non-committal. 'I'll let you know.' He thought for a moment, then frowned. 'Richard, I'm thinking about the Americans . . .'

'Well?'

'I'm having second thoughts – must be you talking about bloody Arnhem. Look, why don't we ask them to take a photograph of the area from the CIA's satellite, just to make sure the Libs are on the level with the Oasis? They can tell us whether there's been a bit of wheeled activity around there. I'd feel a lot more comfortable knowing.'

'Pre-battle misgivings, Clive – everybody has them. Better not worry our cousins, they'll ask too many questions and there are too many O'Caseys and O'Farrells in the industry. And apart from that, if there is something to be won at Bettafal, they'll want a slice of it. They're just as likely to arrange a divisional drop of their own people and grab everything that's going. That would bugger you up with the Dublin thing. No, it's got to be British – uniquely British – to have any credence over there. Forget the Americans, Clive. Keep it in our family – before and after.'

37

Dublin, March

Jack Kearns had barely lowered his shiny-trousered bottom on to the chair when McNeela slopped a mug of tea in front of him. 'Jack,' he said, 'there's more bloody information flowing out of this fucking organization than water out of a leaking tap. The bloody British have been given the word and the bastards are moving in on the Bettafal Oasis. That Brit MI man, Sixsmith, was right with his bloody writing. They are in amongst us, worse than we thought, and they're getting it all right.'

Kearns's flat eyes studied him for a moment. He hadn't touched his tea. There was no expression. His grey face made him look more than ever like one of St Michan's dried-up corpses that had crawled out of the vaults for an afternoon stroll. 'Don't go over the top, Eoin,' he said hoarsely. 'Fitzpatrick is only one man. That can be corrected. Once we've silenced him, things'll get better.'

McNeela stared back at him. 'Jack, I didn't tell Fitzpatrick about Bettafal.'

'You didn't what?' rasped Kearns. 'I don't believe this! What in the name of God, then, have you been playing at?'

McNeela's eyes remained steadfastly on Kearns's face. He looked relaxed, undisturbed. 'I gave it a lot of thought, Jack, and decided that the bastard had already done enough to have his eardrums pierced. It was Collins I wanted to be sure of. I didn't want to have to go through this bloody game again.'

452

'Collins? What the bloody hell are you talking about?' Kearns's pebble eyes became almost animated. 'Collins! Jesus, Eoin, you'll be seeing things crawling out of bloody walls next. He's the bloke who started the sodding thing, or have you forgotten? Christ Almighty! You've gotta stop looking under the bloody bed, mate, you've gotta trust someone . . .' He paused and studied McNeela's face closely through narrowed eyes. McNeela was putting on a show. The relaxed air was a sham. Behind his eyes Kearns could make out sadness, and disbelief. 'But why Collins?' he insisted. 'What's he got to do with the leaks?'

'I've just said it, Jack: Collins is another of the fuckers! That's what I meant when I said the bastards are still in amongst us. I thought it was just Fitzpatrick. All I was doing was tossing a bone at Collins to make sure he threw it back. But the bastard picked it up and ran to his fuckin' masters in Whitehall.' The sadness in McNeela's face had run its course and was now replaced by anger. The veins in his temples stood out like bootlaces – he wasn't all that far from a seizure. He'd taken it badly. Collins, his protégé, had pissed on the foundation; he'd let him down, he was one of his failures. It was a hard one for McNeela. He lacked Kearns's practical approach. He stuck people up on pedestals and fell down with them. He'd done the same all those years ago with Stephen Hayes. It was him all over again. But he wasn't finished with Collins yet. 'The bastard goes up the spout, Jack. He can join Fitzpatrick.'

'One at a time, Eoin,' cautioned Kearns. 'Let me have a little talk with Fitzpatrick first. Maybe I can persuade him to open the book on Collins. We've gotta be sure. We can't just go on and on knocking blokes off on assumptions.'

'Too fuckin' late, Jack! Fitzpatrick's already in a hole in a field in Wicklow. I couldn't waste time – the bricks were all falling about my ears.'

'Jesus Christ, Eoin! This isn't right. I should have had a word with him first. Who did it?'

'It doesn't matter. The bastard's paid. And Collins is going too. I'm fuckin' angry, Jack.'

'How can you be sure Collins has gone over?'

'He's the only one who knows about Bettafal.'

Kearns stared coldly at McNeela. 'That's not enough to put a man on the slab, Eoin. Christ! What's to stop the British having a man among the bloody Arabs? Maybe they're trying to get you to kill off the whole Executive by yourself. Who're you going for next – me? Collins wasn't the only one who knew about the Bettafal Oasis.'

'What d'ya mean?'

'I knew.'

'Shit, Jack! Don't be so fuckin' silly. Collins told them all right. He's the only one who could have done. I couldn't, and neither could you. I've no queries on that score, and for that he goes. But it's not all bad – '

'You could have fooled me!'

McNeela shrugged Kearns's interruption aside. 'You nearly smiled there, Jack! No, it's definitely not all that bad. Collins, in his treachery, has done us a favour. He's not only put the bloody cross on his own forehead, he's also buried his bloody mates. The bastards have walked into an ambush. How about that?'

'What bastards are we talking about?'

'Come on, Jack, wake up! The British – those bastards. They're going to walk into a fuckin' trap.'

Kearns studied McNeela's face. 'How?'

McNeela returned the other man's scrutiny. He wasn't quite ready yet – not until he'd worked Collins out of his system. 'That bastard, Collins,' he hissed. He'd forgotten his Guinness, he'd forgotten the trap, he'd forgotten everything. Hatred took him that way. 'The bastard ought to have known, Jack. No one gets a free passage to the top, not in this bloody game. If we don't finish him, the bloody British will.' The thought of Collins's paymasters counting the body bags as they came off the troopship at Southampton calmed him down a bit. The bootlace veins receded and his eyes settled back in their sockets. But nothing came from Kearns, he just sat and stared at his friend.

The silence thudded on and on. It was McNeela who gave in.

'Aren't you curious, Jack?'

Kearns shook his head and picked up his mug, blew over the top of the rim and sipped from it. 'I've already got the picture. Collins has dropped them in the shit. If you don't kill him, they will. I don't need to be curious about the way snouts, theirs or ours, are dropped. The fact that they always are is the only statistic that interests me. But how'd he drop the Brits in the shit?'

McNeela took time off to finish his Guinness. He enjoyed the bottom half much more than he'd enjoyed the top. He wiped the creamy froth from his top lip with the back of his hand and leaned forward across the table to get nearer to Kearns's ear. He lowered his voice to a hoarse whisper, as if there were people with their ears pressed to the outside window. Old habits died hard, even in his own front room.

'I had a visit from Wael al Khaelfa, Mukhabarat's senior liaison officer, this morning. He flew in specially from Tripoli to tell me this because he felt we should take the credit.'

'Credit for what?'

'Getting the British to commit themselves to an away game they can't win. When Jerry Boyle, the Embassy man in London, passed us the whisper he'd picked up from his Westminster friend about the British going in for an unscheduled desert exercise, I had to warn Khaelfa, through his Embassy here, that we'd traced our own leak but hadn't been able to block it before the news of Bettafal had been passed on. Having done that, I sat back and waited to have my arse skinned.'

'I don't want to hurry you, Eoin . . . ' Kearns glanced down pointedly at his watch in a gesture of impatience.

'Listen to this, Jack. By a stroke of luck, the Libyans have got a whole bloody division of their elite troops – armour, heavy artillery, the lot – in the El Ergh and Bettafal Oasis area. They'll be in battle positions in less than twenty-four hours. The bloody Brits, unless they go in heavy and in strength, and Khaelfa reckons they wouldn't have the resources or get the backing from the Ministry of Defence for anything bigger than a lightweight strike force, the bloody Brits will be given the biggest bloody hiding since the battle of Arnhem. Serves the bastards right. The Libyans owe the British a kick in the balls. This one'll really make their eyes water. According to our man in London, his information was that the British task force was already out there, waiting to hit the depot. They must have started moving the minute Collins passed them the word. They've committed themselves; they reckon it's going to be one of those walk-in, destroy, and walk-out things they used to do to the Germans during the war. Tough! Khaelfa promised that not a single Brit pongo'll walk out of this one. The poor fuckers won't know what hit them. It'll be like running into a concrete mountain. No prisoners – it'll be a bloody massacre! Makes you want to fuckin' cry, don't it, Jack?'

'Like you said, Eoin, serves the bastards right.' Kearns picked up his mug and drained it. He stood up to go but stopped at the end of the table. 'Does Collins know this?' he asked.

'Give me credit, Jack. He's already thrown himself out of the bloody tree. Ah, and talking of bloody trees, Khaelfa's made conditions about future cooperation – '

'Fuck 'em!'

'We can't. They hold the strings to that bloody future. I go along with everything they want. It's money, Jack, more than we've ever dreamed possible. We've *gotta* go along with 'em.'

'You have, Eoin. I don't have to. What are these conditions?'

'They want the top cleared out of the Executive. There's no trust at the moment, they want to start a new game. They want you, Jack. They want you at the head of this particular set-up. No one else, Khaelfa's people insist, and by people he means Moamar al Qaddafi himself. It seems the mad bugger likes you. You're the only man in Ireland the bastards trust.'

'No thanks.'

'You've no choice, Jack – you ought to know by now. With Fitzpatrick and Collins in the hole, it's not only the Libyans and the other buggers, but it's us as well, we need you as much as they do to bring some credibility into our share of business. I'm sorry, Jack. You take the high chair – no argument.'

Kearns's face betrayed nothing. He'd have looked the same if McNeela had slipped a noose round his neck and told him he was about to drop. He was still standing and hadn't moved from his position at the end of the table. After a moment he nodded. Whether it was an acceptance of McNeela's invitation or his way of saying goodbye wasn't obvious to McNeela. But there was no ambiguity about his question.

'Who's looking after Collins?'

McNeela looked happier. 'Fleming. He's been given the word. It'll have to be done in Australia, which is no bad thing. He'll either do it himself or get a local to do it for him. It doesn't matter either way. We can have a word dropped in Canberra and let the Brits take the blame for

457

it. I don't think we need worry any more about him; we can trust Fleming to carry that one out. I got the impression he didn't particularly like Collins.'

But Kearns had lost interest in Collins. Collins was a dead man. He moved from the table, stopped at the door, and turned. 'So, to keep the record straight for any more fuck-ups, Eoin, who else among our lot knows the Brits have swallowed shit?'

McNeela's lips parted over dark brown, nicotine-stained teeth. It was the nearest his mouth could manage to a grin of contentment. It wasn't a pretty sight.

'Just me and you, Jack. Just me and you.'

Clive Reason was having one of his rare moments. Shoes off, stretched out on the long sofa, a large glass of gin and tonic – plenty of ice, a nice wedge of lemon – cigarette smoke curling lazily towards the ceiling and the sound turned down on some inanity being performed on the box. Clive Reason was in a state of relaxation. All was right with the world.

Was.

The rattle of the phone broke the spell. The voice at the other end of the line brought him upright, the gin forgotten, the cigarette burning aimlessly between his lips.

'Clive?'

'Jesus! You don't ring me here. I'll come – '.

'Listen, Clive, we've no time for that. It's all right this end, I'm in a public phone box.' The voice was louder but no less hoarse than the whisperings Reason had listened to in the Dublin confessional. But this time there was an urgency, an underlying suggestion of unaccustomed alarm. 'We've been done. McNeela and the Libs have laid this one on. There's a whole fuckin' army sitting around out there waiting for your lads to walk into it.' He stopped for breath. Reason didn't give him time to start up again.

'Jack, hang on a minute. What the bloody hell are you talking about? Start at the beginning.'

Kearns told him of his recent meeting with McNeela. His voice slowed down to its normal hoarse whisper, but it didn't make the news sound any better to Reason.

'It looks as though you're blown, Jack.' Reason removed the cigarette from his lips and dropped it into an ashtray. His brain was going too fast. He tried to slow it down with a large mouthful of gin and tonic. 'If we can't put this one on Fitzpatrick – '

'No go. They've done him,' interrupted Kearns. 'One in the back of the head and into the hole.'

'How about Collins?'

'Same. He'll be up against the wall – probably now. I'm the only one who can warn you of this. You want my advice?'

'Go on.'

'Forget the story, forget the whole bloody game. Get me out of here and I'll go into the woods somewhere. There's nothing else, is there?'

Reason shook his head to himself. Kearns was right. There wasn't anything else. But was it already too late?

Kearns said the same. 'How far are the lads in? Can you get them out without raising a dust storm? They won't stand a chance if a Libyan patrol picks them up – the whole bloody lot'll go up in flames. According to McNeela the Libyans have promised a blood bath, and that's only for the poor fuckers going in. Think what fun Qaddafi'll have afterwards . . . Are you still there, Clive?'

'What?'

'Come on, Clive, talk to me, make a fucking decision!'

Reason stared blankly at the flickering screen in front of him. Talk about what? His mind was numb. *Talk about you, you poor bastard? A sack over your head, no holes in the bloody thing until a nine millimetre cuts its*

*way through and teaches you the error of your ways. Oh,
you poor bugger, it won't be that quick!*

Reason shook his head and tried to dispel the fog.
Time. There wasn't any. 'Jack, keep it all together for the
time being. Don't jump either way. I'll talk to the boss.
Don't make a move. Don't commit yourself until you
hear from me. I don't know what he can do to keep you
intact, but it's got to be his decision. If I don't make contact, sit tight and play it the way you've been playing all
along. OK?'

Kearns had run out of patience. 'Go and see the bastard
– quick. I'll be at the other number in an hour, and I'll
wait for an hour. This is no time for fuckin' around,
Clive. Get those boys out, and then get me out. Don't
waste any more bloody time!'

'We've got two hours to do something for Jack Kearns,'
said Reason when he finished telling General Sanderson
of his conversation with the man in Dublin. 'And a little
bit longer to get Harry and his friends out of the shit
they're about to drop into.'

'Sounds all very dramatic, Clive.' There were no
frowns of concentration on Sanderson's face. His eyes
were clear, unclouded by conscience, but there was no
question about what was happening behind them; he was
thinking and he was several moves ahead of Reason. But
it wasn't to be rushed into. 'Give me one of your cigarettes.' Reason frowned and pursed his lips. This wasn't a
good sign. Richard Sanderson hadn't smoked a cigarette
for two years. When Reason had passed one over the
table and leant forward to light it, Sanderson sat back,
lifted his chin and slowly directed a thin stream of unin-
haled smoke towards the ceiling. 'How reliable is Kearns?
Is it possible he's panicked or misread the situation? Or
worse, has he been turned?'

'Too many questions, Richard.'

'Then start with the last one and work up.'

'There's no time, Richard.'

'I'll decide that.'

'OK. Jack Kearns is reliable. He's proved himself several times over. Half the successes we've had against the people in the North started at his fingertips. Jack Kearns doesn't panic. If he says we've been set up over this Libyan thing, then that's what's happened. He hasn't misread it,' Reason said patiently. 'The thing's blown up in his face – and ours. Apart from McNeela, Jack Kearns is the only one who knows about the ambush, the only one who knows the bloody Libyan Army's camped there waiting. And you want to know if it's possible Jack Kearns has been turned?'

'You turned him, why can't they?'

'Because Jack Kearns is too deeply committed. He couldn't go back. No way.'

'And you're going to tell me why.'

'Sure. Jack Kearns had a son. He was known as Mad Mick. He moved to the North and joined the Provos when they broke away from the Stickies in 1970.'

'Why "Mad Mick"?'

'Because the poor bugger wasn't all there, he was backward. At twenty-five he had a mental age of about twelve. He wasn't evil, just a bloody nutcase. But he became a liability. Started doing things off his own bat – a bit of Proddy murder, a bit of burning, a bit of robbing small banks, all in the name of the PIRA – just a bloody nuisance. Then the C4 boys of the RUC picked him up and the story goes that soon after one or two of the fellows who were keeping themselves to themselves, staying out of the limelight, fell. The coincidence was too much. The Belfast Provo powers-that-be decided that Mick was doing the "business". Their suspicions were confirmed

461

when the RUC turned him loose and helped him out of the Counties and over the border. Funny thing this, though. I made a few enquiries. The poor little bugger had nothing to do with the heads rolling. The RUC had used him as a smoke screen for a real tout who managed to keep his face clean.'

'Does this have a punch line, Clive?'

'You asked about Jack Kearns working for us.'

'I didn't ask for a case history of all his offspring.'

'He only had the one. His wife died in childbirth.'

'Sounds like an old Charlie Chaplin film. Go on, then, let's hear the rest of it. But don't forget, Clive,' he glanced significantly at the carriage clock on the mantelpiece, 'it was you who was worried about the time.'

'I still am,' said Reason. He was on edge, unusually so. 'About twelve years ago I was doing a solitary run in South Armagh and was picked up by a nasty little mob in Newtown-Hamilton and hoicked across the border – '

'I know about that.'

Reason didn't mind the interruption. 'OK, well to cut the story short, one of the blokes watching the performance was this elderly, flat-faced old sod from the South. That was the only time I'd met a real IRA thug. He was one of the oldies, a Stickie, one of the originals before they split the Organization into bastards and awful bastards. The boy who was conducting the interview eventually got bored and finished up doing a bit of target practice on my stomach.' Reason smiled coldly, without humour. 'You know what happened to him.'

Sanderson nodded grimly. 'I presume this old sod you mentioned was our friend Jack Kearns?'

'That was the punch line, Richard. Apparently, after they'd shot me he put a scare into the North team about a Southern army patrol in the area and they all scuttled back across the border and dispersed. Kearns knew I wasn't dead. He bolted in the other direction but came back a short time later. He wrapped me in a potato sack and, on his own, stuck me in the back of a little pick-up and dropped me outside the post office in Cullyhanna.'

'Motive?'

'The obvious one, Richard. He wanted a friend on the other side. And the reason for that was obvious too. About a year later Harry Barlow, who, as you know, was up to all sorts of little party games in Dublin, met Kearns in a backstreet pub and my name was mentioned. Kearns asked to meet me, and Harry, intrigued, and always with an eye to the interesting chance, arranged for us all to get together. Which we did, in Le Havre. Kearns said he wanted to talk to me privately. Harry wasn't too pleased, particularly when Kearns said he found it hard to trust an Englishman, but a guy like me – and I presume he meant a guy with my colour skin – would have the same feelings of mistrust of the English as the Irish have!' Reason smiled again, this time genuinely. 'I always knew that being black was going to be an advantage one day!' The smile vanished almost as quickly as it had come. 'Kearns told me about Cullyhanna post office – there were things about that only he could have known – and he said he was cashing in the favour he reckoned I owed him. He was right – I did owe him.'

'That's all very interesting, Clive, but you haven't told me why Kearns wanted to come and work for us.'

'I was coming to that. It was all to do with Mick. As I told you, Jack Kearns was IRA, not PIRA, so there was nothing to stop him building up a head of steam of hatred and anger over the treatment of his son by the people in the North.'

'What treatment?'

'Oh, didn't I mention? The PIRA godfathers worked up a thousand reasons to prove that Mad Mick had sold out to the Brits. He hadn't, of course, but the rules say you don't do business with the Brits. If you do – and even if you don't but they think you do – there's a formality for getting topped that has to be gone through: the *Green Book*, section 5, Treason. One of the PIRA's hard men travelled down from the North to present the bill. Poor old Mick was given the works. Not content with a night's working-over, drilling his kneecaps with a Black and Decker, and breaking his ankles and arms, the bastard finished him off by hanging him up on a hook in the kitchen and making a call to the *Irish Times* to go and have a look.

'It was at that point that Jack Kearns, Head of the Republic's Official IRA Intelligence and Interrogation Unit, lost his head over the boy's treatment and decided the people from the North weren't very nice people and should be taken off the streets. It's as simple as that, Richard. He wanted revenge and he chose us as the instrument for that revenge. And once you get into the revenge game too deeply, you can't turn the tap off. There's no going back. So Jack Kearns is committed to our cause until the lid slams down on his coffin. He accepts that, I accept that – and so should you. He doesn't particularly love us, but we're all the poor old bugger's got!'

Sanderson's expression didn't change. 'Fascinating,' he murmured. 'But didn't the fact that the boy's father was a senior member of the parent organization carry any weight with these Northern people?'

'Far from it,' said Reason. 'When you stray, you stray, there are no deep feelings about it. You're guilty and that's that. And to make sure no one else gets ideas, the guilty one gets the full menu. As did Mad Mick Kearns.' Reason's eyes locked on to Sanderson's. 'It's the game, Richard, and that's the way it's played – *isn't* it?'

Sanderson made a small movement with his mouth. It didn't amount to a smile. 'You've told me why we should trust Kearns, but you haven't answered my other question. How reliable is he?'

'I've just explained – he goes all the way.'

'No chance of them having read his diary and turned him their way again?'

'I'd have thought that was obvious.' Reason studied Sanderson through narrowed eyes. 'But I don't know what you're getting at, Richard. It's all finished. It doesn't matter now whether Jack Kearns remains sound or not. As soon as the whistle's blown and Harry is told to get out of that place as if his arse was on fire, Kearns becomes surplus to McNeela's requirements. If McNeela gets his hands on Jack after this, Mad Mick's death'll seem like a gentle fairy tickling his balls with a feather compared with what he'll get.'

'You haven't answered the question, Clive. Can Kearns be turned again?'

'Of course he can't. He's in too far with us. One word, one hint – that's all it'd take. He's ours until he dies. He can't go back, Richard, that's why we've got to look after him.'

'Thanks, Clive. That makes the decision for us. I'm not recalling Harry's force.'

Reason looked up sharply. He knew what he'd heard, but he didn't believe it. 'Say that again, please, Richard.'

Sanderson raised his eyebrows and studied Reason. The reply wasn't quick enough in coming.

'I said, say it again, Richard!'

'I'm going to let it go ahead.'

'What!'

'The raid will take place as planned. You've underlined Kearns's credibility. His position as potential head of a new Irish movement must be sustained. His worth is incalculable and he's going to be in there at the heart. More than that, you've already suggested there's going to be a major drug war when the present altercation with us has been concluded, which he's going to be asked to conduct. This is like Rommel being in the pay of the British at Alamein – unlikely, but it's what we've got! You made the case yourself for the raid to go ahead and for Jack Kearns's position to be preserved. And Clive, if you don't mind, there's another thing you've lost sight of: the threat of a possible nuclear-type attack on this country, which he can resolve. Can you equate that with the lives of a couple of dozen men?'

Reason held an unlit cigarette halfway between its packet and his mouth. There was no movement, no attempt to help it to its destination, it looked as though it was going to stay there for ever. Reason's face was frozen solid.

'Is that how generals learn arithmetic?'

Sanderson didn't bridle. 'We're talking about a few dozen SAS reservists whose usefulness as military personnel is basically over. They'll make the attack and they'll be swallowed up. This can be explained away as a sort of voluntary mercenary force, nothing to do with the British Government. The force was raised by a private civilian agency with anonymous funding. Any regular SAS forces and other personnel that we drafted into the unit will remain on the clean side of the start line. If their presence is blown they can be explained away as a joint Anglo-Egyptian covering party for a scientific expedition in the Qattâra Depression area. The Egyptians owe us a favour, they'll back it up. But it won't come to that. The SAS know how to lose themselves in the desert – it's where they began.'

'Did you just work all that out?'

Sanderson glanced at Reason. His eyes remained clear and steady. 'Like learning arithmetic, Clive, generals learn to solve problems on their feet.'

'Is that all you see it as, Richard, a problem?'

'More a reassessment of position. There are times, Clive, when we must sacrifice some of our chips to make a bigger gain on the table later. This is one of those times. The loss of these men will return a dividend, through Jack Kearns, that at this point is impossible to calculate. It's as simple as that.'

Reason stared at Sanderson in disbelief. He shook his head, dropped the crumpled cigarette from his fingers and without taking his eyes off Sanderson fumbled for another one. It was Sanderson who broke the contact. He slowly uncrossed his long, skinny legs and unwound from the low leather armchair. He walked across to the sideboard and placed two glasses side by side, stared at them, then reached for the whisky decanter and grasped its neck. He didn't lift it. He was waiting for something.

It wasn't long coming.

'OK, Richard, so you've tossed away the lives of a handful of good chaps. Let's hope their families agree with you that it was all worthwhile. But isn't it going to look a bit suspicious when Harry hoicks his bergen on to his shoulders and wanders off back to London just before the battle starts?'

Sanderson didn't turn. He made no movement.

'He won't.'

There was a long pause, then Reason forced himself to say it: 'He won't what?'

'He won't leave. He'll go in with them.'

'You mean Harry Barlow goes up the spout too?'

Sanderson clinked the decanter against one of the glasses and half-filled it with whisky. He topped the glass up from a bottle of Malvern water. He made no reply.

'Richard.' Reason's voice became insistent. 'I asked you a question.'

'D'you want water or just ice in your whisky? Or would you prefer your usual gin and tonic?'

'Don't play games with me, Richard.'

'OK, Clive. Accept the fact that we are none of us indispensable. If the party goes up the spout, then Harry goes up the spout with them. He wouldn't want it any other way. Nothing's changed. Harry and his people go in to Bettafal as planned. Harry Barlow's a good man and he's your friend. But this is not a time for sentiment. It's what you said, it's the way the game's played, and this is how this particular game's being played. Jack Kearns as an asset is worth a great deal more than Harry Barlow. Harry's a soldier. He's had a good run. He'd understand the equation, Clive, even if you refuse to. Harry Barlow can be replaced. Kearns can't. That's the equation. Don't try making it any less simple than that – it never works out.'

He paused to allow Reason in, but nothing came. He waited another moment, a sort of requiem to Harry Barlow, then breathed deeply and said, 'I think that's just about covered every aspect of the business. Your game was a success. I can't say any more than that. You achieved exactly what you set out to do. But that's it. Now forget it.' Sanderson gave Reason a prolonged look before turning back to his chore of mixing a couple of drinks. The subject was closed.

Reason sat unmoving. He stared at Sanderson's back, slightly bowed, like a surgeon concentrating on a delicate operation. There was no give in his shoulders and when he turned round with a full glass in each hand to meet what he knew would be Reason's accusing eyes, his face was set normal, there was no apology written across it, and no regret in his voice. He didn't flinch from Reason's grim, set features as he sat down. He had a good idea what was coming. 'Cheers!' he murmured.

'Fuck you, Richard! You're an unmitigated, cold-hearted bastard.'

'Probably,' replied Sanderson. 'But like you keep saying, Clive, this is the way the game's played.'

Epilogue

London, 12 March

Clive Reason heard his phone ringing long before he put the key in the door of his flat. He didn't hurry. If it was important, they'd ring again. Reason's philosophy. But it didn't stop ringing. He closed the door behind him and picked up the phone. There was no impatience in the voice at the other end, no announcement, no name, no hello, no nothing, but he knew who it was.

'There's no packet, Clive. No bomb. It's a bluff. They've got fuck all!' The phone went dead.

Reason placed his finger on the cradle and waited a moment, then lifted it. He dialled a local number.

'You can tell Major to get up off his knees and stop talking to the bastards, Richard. There's no bomb. It was a fucking bluff.'

'Thanks, Clive,' responded Sanderson. 'Come and have a drink.'

'No thanks, Richard, I'm going up to Hereford. They're having a little service for Harry and the others in the chapel tomorrow morning. It's for friends and family.'

'Would you like me to come?'

'I don't think so, Richard.'